I0601564

Guarded Hearts—Book 1

MISTLETOE and MALICE

LORI DEJONG

Copyright © 2025 by Lori DeJong

Published by Scrivenings Press LLC
15 Lucky Lane
Morrilton, Arkansas 72110
https://ScriveningsPress.com

Printed in the United States of America

All rights reserved. No part of this publication may be reproduced, stored in a retrieval system, or transmitted in any form or by any means—for example, electronic, photocopy, or recording— without the prior written permission of the publisher. The only exception is brief quotations in printed reviews.

Paperback ISBN 978-1-64917-535-9

eBook ISBN 978-1-64917-536-6

Editors: Elena Hill and K. Banks

Cover design by Linda Fulkerson - www.bookmarketinggraphics.com

Scripture quotations are taken from the Holy Bible, New Living Translation, copyright © 1996, 2004, 2007 by Tyndale House Foundation. Used by permission of Tyndale House Publishers, Inc., Carol Stream, Illinois 60188. All rights reserved.All characters are fictional, and any resemblance to real people, either factual or historical, is purely coincidental.

NO AI TRAINING: Without in any way limiting the author's [and publisher's] exclusive rights under copyright, any use of this publication to "train" generative artificial intelligence (AI) technologies to generate text is expressly prohibited. The author reserves all rights to license uses of this work for generative AI training and development of machine learning language models.

For Kristi and Wendy, critique partners extraordinaire and much-loved sisters in the Lord.

Prologue

"I met someone, Ri."

Riley grinned at her friend seated across from her at the cozy café, the promise of new love sparkling in Caitlyn's blue eyes. "Explains the dreamy grin you've been wearing since I got here."

Leaning over her garden salad, Caitlyn's smile widened. Her eyes shone brighter than the Christmas lights on the tree standing sentinel in the restaurant's front window. "He's incredible. I've never felt so much so fast for anybody."

Ladling a spoonful of lobster bisque, Riley regarded her across the table. "I'm so happy for you, Cait. Has your dad met this guy?"

Caitlyn's smile dimmed as she sat back in her chair and picked up her fork. "You know my father. Nobody will ever be good enough. And Shane doesn't come with a name. At least, not one that will pass muster with Dad."

Riley cocked her head. "How'd you meet, then?"

"At the club. He was working in the golf shop last month when I went in for a new glove. We talked for a bit, I saw him a few times working around the club, and he finally asked if I'd like to go for coffee. We met up the next morning and talked for hours. Good thing it was Saturday so he wasn't late for work."

"An employee? You're not concerned he's trying to get close to you for the wrong reasons? Like that guy last year who kept asking you out?"

Cait rolled her eyes. "You mean that Jacob guy? He was harmless. I never saw or heard from him after that day you saw him bugging me and told me to report him."

"And did you? Report him?"

"No. I decided if he didn't get the message, I would. Guess he moved on to someone else. But Shane's not an employee. He's an IT contractor hired to overhaul the club's computer system. The day we met, he was installing software on the golf shop computer. He did such good work that they gave him a lifetime membership *gratis*. We've seen each other every day since that first coffee. We work out, play tennis, golf. He loves all that stuff as much as I do."

"He sounds amazing." Riley took a sip of the warm bisque, perfect on this rainy mid-December day. "What does he think about your work as a social media influencer?"

Caitlyn shrugged. "He wasn't sure what to make of it at first, me living my life in front of the world. But then he saw it's only a part of my life I let them see. What products I'm endorsing, where I'm traveling, events I attend. And now, my faith."

After taking a dainty bite of her salad, Caitlyn regarded her again. "When you led me to the Lord six months ago, that didn't sit well with my dad when I shared my decision with my family. Not at all. Now ..." She shook her head. "I bring home this middle-class boyfriend and I'm sure to get another earful about my *poor* choices."

Sighing, she pushed a cherry tomato around leaves of radicchio and kale, her gaze following its path. "I'm dreading it, but I know I need to introduce them soon." She put her fork down and brought her shining eyes back to Riley. "Because I think this guy could be the one. We just click."

Riley's heart went out to her friend. The path before her could be a difficult one if she should choose Shane over her father's wishes. But Caitlyn was one of the bravest women she'd ever met. It wouldn't be the first time she got on the wrong side of her status-focused parents. Thankfully, Riley's own family put more stock in integrity and breadth of character than net worth.

"Makes a good living, but Dad won't be happy with anything less than seven figures a year. I'm praying he'll take all the other things into account, though."

Riley set her spoon on the saucer under her bowl. "Okay, here's the big question. Is he a man of faith? I know you're new to your own, but I hope that's a non-starter if he's not."

"Oh, he is. Definitely." Her smile broadened. "I've been attending his church with him, and he prays with me, Ri. Isn't that amazing?"

It was. And Riley couldn't be happier for her friend. "Just make sure I'm invited to the wedding, if he is indeed *the one.*"

Caitlyn giggled. "Oh, honey, you'll be standing right up there with me."

With his 9 mm Glock resting in its shoulder holster under his suit coat, Colton watched the post-funeral guests milling quietly around the opulent living room of The Honorable Josiah Mulaney and his wife, Priscilla. Their older daughter had married and now lived in her own estate in The Woodlands, according to unsolicited intel provided by his current client.

Their younger daughter had been lowered into the ground that afternoon, under a late April sun, in a box befitting a woman of her means. Rosewood, the officiant had said at the funeral. "A rare and beautiful wood for the rare and beautiful Caitlyn Rose Mulaney."

Colton moved toward the entry hall. He hadn't known the young woman buried today, but his heart still sat heavy in his chest as he'd watched the guests congregated graveside, and now the few chosen attendees partaking of catered *hors d'oeuvres* at the Mulaney estate. He felt like an interloper. A *voyeur* watching grief penetrate this place like a fog. Dense and dark and without remedy. This fog would never go away.

He knew that all too well.

Nodding to his co-worker stationed at the front door, he turned to scan the room. "You ate?"

"Yes, sir. You?"

"Not yet."

"Go get a bite. This place is locked down tighter than the White House. I can keep an eye on the Senator from here and let you know if he wants to leave."

"Not hungry."

"Then at least go get some air. It's been a trying day."

Colton shot a glance at Trevor, a fairly new agent with the private security firm he'd been with for the past four years. Was he that obvious? He'd have to do a better job at not letting his personal life seep into his work.

Still, Trevor had a point. Some fresh air might help him regroup. Senator Congdon was safe enough, ensconced in an armchair, speaking with the judge and two other men Colton recognized as Houston nobility.

"Okay. I'll be back in ten."

"Make it twenty."

He shook his head as he stepped away. The job usually kept his mind and body busy, which he preferred to days like today, when he had too much time on his hands to think. To feel. More than he'd wanted to over the past year, seven months, and four days.

At the graveside, he'd been on alert, watching for anybody who might be a threat to the senator after a high-profile vote last month had garnered more hate mail than normal. Anybody who might know he'd be back in Houston to grieve with his old friend.

Here at the estate, though, there was nothing for Colton, Trevor, and the driver out by their black SUV to do but cool their heels. At least, until the senator was ready to return to his own River Oaks estate, which he kept as well as the tony brownstone he used while working in the nation's capital. Colton's employer had scheduled round-the-clock protection here, along with the detail in D.C. But as head of the team, Colton traveled with the Senator back and forth.

He let himself out a back door, into the waning sunlit afternoon. Dusk would settle in soon, and darkness after that. As it did every day. Day in. Day out. Repeat.

Life went on. Never waiting for grief to loosen its insidious grip.

His gaze raked the area around the large terrace, his focus landing on a woman seated on a stone bench, head bowed and arms crossed over her stomach.

The door shut with a soft click behind him, and her head snapped around.

"I'm sorry." He'd assumed she'd been crying, but there were no tears that he could see. "I didn't mean to disturb you. I'll go back inside."

"No, it's okay." She stood and smoothed her dress over narrow hips. "Just having a little talk with God." She took a few steps his direction. "I don't want to keep all this sunshine to myself."

Praying. She'd been praying. Something he hadn't done in … well, one year, seven months, and four days.

As she moved closer, his brain took the usual notes. Shoulder-length dark hair worn straight and pulled behind her ears. Bangs that brushed her eyebrows. Petite and slender. No doubt another society princess, if the obviously expensive black dress she wore was any clue. Not to mention the ridiculously high-heeled, red-soled shoes, designer sunglasses, the diamond pendant around her neck, matching earrings, and tennis bracelet on her delicate wrist. No wedding ring, but an emerald surrounded by diamonds sparkled from her right hand.

She halted a few feet away and crossed her arms over her middle. "Are you a friend of the Mulaneys?"

"No, ma'am. I'm on the job."

"Oh? What job would that be?"

"Petersen Security. Personal protection detail."

One eyebrow hitched, and she pushed her sunglasses up onto her head, revealing eyes that competed with the emerald ring for most intense color. "And who are you protecting? Personally? From out here?"

He held back a chuckle. This one had spunk. He could hear it in her voice, see it in the set of her shoulders—pulled back, confident. "Senator Congdon. But I'm not needed until we leave the premises."

"I see." When he said nothing further, she offered her hand. "Riley Hudson."

Of course. Daughter of Andrew Hudson, one of the Houston moguls sitting with the grieving judge and the senator inside. A billionaire financier and another of Petersen Security International's high-profile clients. The Hudsons didn't have a protection detail, *per se*, although Petersen installed and manned the high-tech security system at their posh estate. Their driver was also a Petersen security specialist, *aka* bodyguard, as needed.

He gave her hand a quick squeeze and let go. "Ms. Hudson."

Anxious to take his leave, he didn't offer his name. He wasn't there to make friends. And his ten minutes were about to expire.

"I take it the guy with the earpiece by the door is with you?"

"Yes, ma'am."

She nodded, then turned her eyes to the horizon, with the sun settling into its journey to the other side of the globe. Eyes shimmering with the fallout of grief, yet she held a measure of quiet strength about her. Not like she would fall apart any second. Fortunate, because comforting a distraught woman was not among his specific skill set.

He cleared his throat. "I'm sorry about your friend. Everything I've heard today tells me she was special."

"Beyond. She wasn't"—she waved her arm around—"all this. She had depth. Intelligence. People didn't give her enough credit, what with her online presence and all. But everything she did was done with purpose. With thought."

She swallowed and crossed her arms again as her gaze went back to the grounds beyond the terrace. "Only four months ago, she was practically giddy about ... Shane. I can't believe—it doesn't make sense ..." She shook her head and turned back to him. "She shouldn't have died like this. Nobody should die like this."

His chest tightened at the anguish in her eyes. He'd been on the other side of the country when Miss Mulaney had reportedly been found dead by her boyfriend. Stabbed over twenty times in her own kitchen.

That same boyfriend now sat in jail, Caitlyn Mulaney's blood on his hands.

And if there were any justice in the world, Shane Everett would be locked away in a cage for the rest of his life.

Chapter One

Riley flinched as the prison security door clanged shut, the sound echoing through the concrete-floored corridor.

Would she ever get used to it? She'd been at this for five years now, yet it still made her pulse race and blood run cold every time. At least she'd be leaving this place at the end of her meeting and not returning to a ten-by-four cage shared with a roommate of questionable repute.

Like Shane would.

She'd helped others escape a life behind these barbed-wired-topped walls when they should've never been here to begin with. But the jury was still out on Shane.

Well, not exactly. The jury had come back with a resounding *guilty* six weeks ago, after a mere three hours of deliberation, followed by a life sentence. Without a miracle, he wouldn't breathe free air for thirty-five years. And then only if the parole board deemed him worthy.

After news of the verdict reached her in her office that

afternoon, the evidence and arguments she'd seen and heard every day she sat in the courtroom gallery replayed in her mind. The same evidence and arguments the jury heard.

Did she get it wrong? Or did they?

She handed her Texas bar card and driver's license to the man behind the glass partition. He scanned them and typed her info into a computer before returning them.

His unsmiling dark eyes narrowed on her. "You here to spring another of our upstanding guests, huh? Everett already dissatisfied with our accommodations?"

Her stomach roiled. She still wasn't sure why she was here. Why she'd agreed to come. Why she felt compelled to meet with the man twelve people unanimously agreed had slaughtered her friend. Would this prove to be a waste of the three-hour round trip?

Or could she trust her gut?

Pushing her second thoughts aside, she gave the guard a half-smile. "Hard to believe there isn't a line of folks outside itching to take advantage of your five-star amenities. But I don't know yet about Mr. Everett. Just a prelim today."

"Don't let him charm ya. Sometimes these pretty boys are the worst of the vermin we got in here. And what he done to that girl … no forgivin' for that."

Her smile slipped and skin crawled with irritation. He'd have never made that comment to a male attorney. As if she were a frail, docile little thing who could be swayed by a handsome face and a velvet tongue.

Father, forgive my pride, and may I be as gracious with others as You've been to me. The two-second prayer helped her shake off the guard's ill-worded advice. "Don't you worry about me. I've heard it all."

He put his hand under the counter, and an obtrusive buzzer sounded before another metal door clicked open. "Regardless. Watch yourself, Miss Hudson."

Ignoring his warning, she walked through the door, her long ponytail brushing against the back of her navy pantsuit while she followed another guard to her designated meeting room. As with every prison visit, she wore a dark suit with slacks, little makeup, and her hair pulled back. Most of the inmates she met hadn't been alone with a woman even in their distant memory. It was imperative that they see her as a professional with their life in her hands and treat her accordingly.

Minutes later, inside the stark, gray room with a white tile floor and no windows, she laid out her yellow pad, two pens, two pencils, and three different colors of highlighters on the cold metal table. Next to that, she placed the case file she and her assistant had cobbled together over the last couple of weeks since Shane's letter had come.

When the door opened, a guard in a uniform the same color as this depressing room ushered in a man wearing white pants and shirt, with his last name and newly assigned prisoner number stamped on his shoulder.

Shane Everett. Convict. Caitlyn Mulaney's boyfriend.

Murderer?

The man with the slumped shoulders, hooded eyes, and sunken cheeks hardly resembled the one Caitlyn had been so excited to introduce her to little more than two-and-a-half years ago. She'd never seen her friend so smitten, despite her powerful father's objections to the relationship.

Shane wasn't one of *them*. Hadn't been born with a silver spoon in his mouth. Didn't have a trust fund. His parents were nobodies, as far as Judge Mulaney was concerned, and his baby girl deserved so much better. Better than this intelligent, self-made man who only had a club membership because he'd overhauled their computer system.

She stood by the table until the guard left the room, knowing he would remain on the other side of the door with its rectangular window. Otherwise, as this was an attorney visit, they would be alone.

"Shane. Have a seat."

Without a word, he walked to the other side of the table and folded his lanky frame into the hard, metal chair opposite her. He'd been more muscular the last time she'd seen him with Cait, before spending two years in a cell waiting for trial and another month in diagnostic processing after the verdict. He'd been delivered here thirteen days ago, his new place of residence.

He cleared his throat. "I wasn't sure you would come. Considering."

Nodding, she swallowed. She'd changed her mind a few times over the past week, but her conscience wouldn't let her go. She had to at least hear what he had to say, knowing how desperate he had to be to reach out to her, someone who had loved Caitlyn.

"I have to admit, I was a little surprised to get your letter."

His chuckle held no humor. "I'm quite sure. I don't know—there's nobody—my defense team—" He stared up at the ceiling for a long moment before bringing his anguished gaze back to her. "I don't know where else to turn, Miss Hudson."

"Call me Riley. Like you did—" She bit her lip.

Tears flooded his eyes. "Before."

"Yes." She studied him for a moment, the plea in those eyes otherwise devoid of joy. Of peace. "How are you holding up?"

He shook his head. "I don't belong here. I know you hear that a lot, but I don't."

He was right. She heard that a lot. Sometimes it was true, but more often, it was not. Thankfully, she could usually determine within an hour if she was being played.

"My savings are gone," he continued. "And I still owe thousands to my defense team. My parents have depleted their savings, taken out loans, and put a second mortgage on their house to help cover my legal costs. And, to be honest, I wasn't impressed with the way they handled my case to begin with."

Neither was she, but she held her tongue, having learned early on not to burn bridges. She would likely need his former team's assistance in providing her with all they'd done in their efforts to prove him *Not Guilty.*

Which was their first mistake. They didn't argue he was *innocent,* only that the prosecution didn't have enough to overcome reasonable doubt. An argument the jury clearly disagreed with.

"And I don't belong here." The vehemence in his voice matched the intensity in his eyes. "I did not kill Caitlyn. We hadn't been together long, but I was crazy about her. I believe she felt the same."

"So, you didn't send the flowers?"

"I didn't. I don't know where they came from or what the note meant. *Give me a second chance. I can't live without you?* Why would I send a card like that when we weren't having any problems?"

"She hadn't broken it off with you after her dad gave her his ultimatum?" A fact that hadn't surprised Riley when Cait told her about the icy reception Shane received upon being introduced to her father. Caitlyn had stood her ground then. But had she changed her mind as the weeks wore on with no contact from her family?

"No. I told her I didn't want to come between her and her father, but she said she was done with him controlling her life. I told her if God had it in His plan for us to have a permanent future together, I could take care of her. I made a good living with excellent potential for career growth. We would've been fine if we ever got mar—."

His voice broke and tears fell down his cheeks. This man had loved her friend. And he was correct. Cait had been just as crazy about him.

She crossed her arms on the table and leaned in. "Who do you think killed her?"

With a slow shake of the head, he pulled a tissue from the box in the middle of the table and swiped at his eyes and nose. "I have no idea. She was so kind and funny and beautiful. Everybody I knew loved her. I can't think of one person who would be that angry. To do that to her."

Riley couldn't either, but it wasn't a random killing.

Someone had targeted Caitlyn. Someone angry enough to continue plunging that knife into her body long after she was dead.

Contemplating the man on the other side of the table, her mind reeled. Time to reach her own verdict. Was Shane Everett guilty? Or an innocent man doing someone else's time?

Chapter Two

Ah. The perfect day for retail therapy.

Riley raised her face to the mild November sun and smiled as she exited the shoe store in Houston's River Oaks shopping district, clutching another bag.

Her friend Avery hooked her arm through hers. "Those bright pink stilettoes will be perfect with your gown for the New Year's Ball."

"I know, right? I should be all set now."

A little early to be thinking about New Year's, but considering everything else she had going on, it would behoove her to plan sooner rather than later. A lot of work went into the charitable ball her family had hosted for three decades, and which she'd directed the past two years.

The crispness in the air hinted at the holidays fast approaching, with Thanksgiving only a couple of weeks away. After several stressful months on a difficult case, she'd planned to concentrate on her charities more than work to close out the year.

Then Shane's letter had come. And she couldn't ignore it. Not with her conscience picking at her about that verdict.

Meeting with him thirteen days ago had been the final push she needed to right what she perceived to be a colossal wrong.

Caitlyn's killer was still out there.

Avery pulled Riley to a stop in front of a store window displaying designer holiday dresses. "Ooo, let's go in here. I love this store."

"Let's go after lunch." She checked her watch. "We have ten minutes to make our reservation, and Fran will start texting us in eleven if we're not there." And there was no way Avery would be out of this store in less than an hour. "I think I'll run these bags up to the car so they're not taking up space at the table. Wanna go with me?"

Her pretty ginger-haired friend scrunched her pink-tinted lips to the side. "I'll go see if Fran and Barbara are at the cafe."

"Sounds good. I'll be there in a few."

A short stroll to the parking garage, up the elevator to the third level, and she was putting her bags in the trunk of her little BMW sports coupe with five minutes to spare. The trunk closed with a *whump,* and she started back to the elevator.

Twenty-three stab wounds. According to the autopsy in the case file, an early strike to her heart killed Caitlyn within seconds. Likely dead by the time she hit the floor, at least she hadn't been aware of the other wounds inflicted on her body. What kind of madman could—

No. Not today. She wouldn't think about work today, on this beautiful fall Saturday. Even though every minute she spent *not* working on the case meant more minutes Shane spent in that awful—

An arm wrapped around Riley's shoulders, forcing the air from her lungs. Her body slammed against a hard chest. A sharp pain jabbed her in the side.

"Don't scream, Miss Hudson, or I'll end you right here."

The man's tone chilled her.

He pulled her backward. Her pulse hammered in her throat.

The heels of her boots scraped along the concrete, fighting to keep her feet under her. Terror pulsated throughout her body. This couldn't be happening.

Her hands gripped the man's forearm. Her eyes darted from side to side. Where was everybody?

Lord, help me! Please!

He pulled her behind a large car. The trunk sat open. A cold chill ran down her spine.

No. No. No. She had to fight. If he was going to kill her, let him do it now before he took her somewhere he could do whatever he had planned.

Lord, be with me.

She yelled, hoping to draw attention. Twisting, she threw her weight to one side, then the other. His grasp tightened around her neck. She was losing strength. She needed to breathe.

She drew up her knee and kicked backward. The three-inch block heel of her boot made contact. Her attacker's grip loosened.

A guttural expletive blew past her ear as he pitched forward. She pulled her arm in. Rammed her elbow into his face. Twisting again, she broke his hold. Her handbag hit the ground, its contents scattering.

She spun, seeing his face for the first time. Bearded, wisps of dark hair under a baseball cap. Eyes dark and piercing. His left hand swiped blood from his lip. He raised the gun still clutched in his right hand. She kicked again. Her boot collided with his elbow. The gun clattered across the pavement.

She turned to run, but he grabbed her ponytail. Fire shot over her scalp, and she screamed. Clawing at his hand, she dug her nails into his flesh. "Stop!"

"Hey!" A man's voice echoed through the parking garage. "Let her go!"

Her attacker released her hair. She fell to her knees. His

footsteps retreated behind her. Jumping to her feet, she took off toward the man running in her direction. Avery stepped out of an elevator. Her eyes widened and jaw fell slack.

Riley's timely rescuer slowed. "You okay?"

"Yes." Her voice barely squeaked past the fear blocking her throat.

Nodding, he picked up speed again.

"He's got a gun!"

As he neared the car, the engine revved, and the vehicle hurtled backward. He dove out of the way, and the older model Buick sped toward the exit. The still-open trunk lid bounced up and down as the car careened around the corner out of sight, the squeal of tires growing fainter as it neared the bottom.

The man stood and braced his hands on his knees, his breathing harsh.

Riley ran up to him. "Are you all right? Are you hurt?"

He took a few deep breaths and straightened. A brown swath of dirt from the concrete floor stretched from shoulder to hip on one side of his black jacket. "I'm fine. I hoped to get a plate, but it was covered in mud."

Avery finally reached them and grabbed Riley's arm. "What was *that*?"

Riley shook her head. "I was on my way back. He just grabbed me."

Riley's rescuer pulled his cell from his jacket. "I'll call the cops, but let's get you both somewhere safe in case he comes back."

While Avery retrieved Riley's bag and stuffed the contents back inside, he made his call to 911, informing the operator they'd be at the bistro where Riley wished she'd gone instead of bringing her bags up to her car. But then perhaps some other poor girl would be in that trunk and on her way to who knew what brutality. An icy pall cascaded over her skin.

Checking the empty parking spot, she noted no gun. The

assailant must have retrieved it before he got away. If only her blow could have propelled it further afield.

The small crowd that had gathered—where had they been two minutes ago?—parted as Avery and their escort entered the elevator.

Riley peered at the man next to her. "After all of this, I feel like I should know your name."

"Logan. Logan Devers."

"Riley Hudson. And this is Avery. Thank you so much for everything."

"Of course. I'm just glad I got up there when I did."

Divine intervention. Had to be.

Exiting on the bottom floor, Riley walked between them. Her body shook with leftover adrenaline, and she prayed her legs would hold out. "Not everybody would've intervened like you did. I'm so grateful."

"Nothing else entered my mind."

"I can't believe this." Avery held tight to Riley's arm. "Of all places … *here?*"

"And in broad daylight. Low-life predator." At the bistro, Logan gestured at a waiter. "Can you seat the ladies, please?"

"Yes, sir."

He turned back to Riley. "I'll wait for the police. Right now, you need to sit."

A wide-eyed Barbara pushed her glasses up on her nose, her gaze raking over Riley. "What's going on?"

"Riley was almost abducted," Avery answered before Riley's brain had formulated a coherent response. "And if that guy who was just here hadn't shown up, she might be gone without a trace."

Riley shook her head. "I would've fought to the death before letting him put me in that trunk."

Fran's eyes widened. "A *trunk?* My lands." She pulled a chair from the table. "Sit. You look like you're about to fall over." She peered up at the waiter. "Hot tea all around, please. Let's do chamomile. We'll see after that if my friend feels like lunch or not. We may need to get her home."

"Yes, ma'am. Not a problem. And tea's on the house."

"Thank you. We appreciate it."

Frances. Always the collected one of the group. Barbara was the gregarious one, Riley the brainy one, and Avery ... well, Avery was their drama queen.

"Thanks, Fran." Riley sank into the chair and clasped her shaking hands in her lap, letting her gaze roam around the table.

How she loved these women of faith who had seen her through a myriad of ups and downs, hills and valleys in their two-plus-decade association. They'd been there for each other as they navigated their way through adolescence, braces, mean girls, crushes gone bad, college exams, grad school pressures, and the start of their careers. Grief over lost loved ones, joy over new successes or goals realized. Theirs was a friendship forged in iron. Unbreakable. Everlasting.

She couldn't think of anybody she'd rather be with at this minute than these three women.

After the waiter returned with their tea, Logan walked up to their table with one female and one male officer in protective vests and the requisite cop gear strapped to their waists. Her stomach flipped. Now she would have to recount everything that had happened in the parking garage.

So much for her low-stress day.

Chapter Three

"You're off for your golf holiday in a few days, right?"

Colton nodded at the gentleman sitting opposite him in the sleek, custom-outfitted Lear jet. "Tuesday. I have to admit, flying business class to Miami will be a bit of a downer after flying around in this beauty the last six weeks."

The other man chuckled. "I can imagine, although I've never had to fly commercial."

That made sense. Ben Alderon came from *old money*, and Colton doubted that anybody in his family had ever flown, cruised, or driven anywhere in anything other than private transportation.

Ben stared out the window at the deepening shadows. "I'm sure happy to be getting home. Six weeks is a long time away." He leaned his head to the side, his gaze directed to the woman seated farther up, a dark-headed toddler boy asleep in her arms. "I know my wife is especially eager. Sleeping in our own bed, getting back on a normal schedule with our son."

He looked back at Colton. "I don't like working overseas, but it's easier with my family along. Thank you for keeping them safe."

"Our pleasure."

"There'll be a little extra for you in your next paycheck from Petersen. Enough to cover half a dozen golf holidays, if you're so inclined. It's the least I could do. For the others, as well."

"Thank you. That's very generous."

After back-to-back assignments over the past eight months, including this one abroad for the last six weeks with the high-profile CEO and family in London, it would be nice to let down until after the holidays. He planned to take a couple of months off after seeing the Alderons home and couldn't wait to hit the links in Miami for the entire week before Thanksgiving.

The co-pilot emerged from the cockpit and made his way past the other four bodyguards, Ben's wife, and their sleeping son to his boss. "Ninety minutes to landing, sir. But there's a call for Mr. Blankenship."

"Thank you."

With a nod, the co-pilot returned to the cockpit. Ben picked up the wireless handset embedded in the wall of the plane and gave it to Colton.

"Blankenship."

"Colton, we have a situation."

"Mack." He went on instant alert at the tension in his boss's voice. "What do you need?"

"I hate to do this, but I have a new assignment, and I need the best."

"A two-day assignment?" His flight would leave at 7:53 a.m. on Tuesday, and he intended to be on the first course they planned to play by two o'clock Eastern with three of his college frat brothers.

"Undetermined at this time."

Colton closed his eyes. Eight months. Six weeks in London. He needed this break like he needed twelve hours of sleep tonight.

But he couldn't bail on Mack.

Opening his eyes, he turned to the small window as the earth tilted away from the sun. "Okay, yeah. I'll change my plans. Report tomorrow or Monday?"

"Tonight. As soon as you land. I'll have a car there for you. The others can see the Alderons home."

His gut clenched. Something big had happened. Mack hadn't pulled him in for an urgent op in over a year. Meant he'd have to cram to get up to speed. Better load up on the coffee.

"Copy that. See you in a couple of hours."

He disconnected and handed the phone back to Ben.

"No golf holiday, I take it?"

Colton put his head back against the seat. "Undetermined at this time."

At ten minutes to eight, Colton walked into Mack's office at Petersen Security, the only one with any illumination. Aside from the Tech Ops department, where staffers manned computer stations 24/7. The same department where Colton had begun his stint with Petersen over six years ago. A nice, safe job sitting at a computer bank gathering intel and planning operations.

Until it hadn't mattered anymore, and he asked to be put in the field.

Mack gestured him in. "Colton, good to see you. You can put your bags there by the door. This won't take long."

After parking his suitcase and draping his garment bag over it, Colton took a seat in one of the chairs in front of the desk. "What's going on?"

Mack picked up a folder and opened it. "Hudson."

Colton pulled his head back. "As in, Hudson Financial Corporation? Andrew Hudson needs a team?"

"He does. A three-man detail, and they need the best. That's where you come in."

"Thanks for the vote of confidence." Although, at the moment, his jet-lagged self felt far from *the best*. "Did he receive a threat?"

"Not him."

"So, who, exactly, would this detail be for?"

"The daughter. Riley."

An image sprang to his mind. Lovely young woman, black dress, expensive shoes. Eyes the color of emeralds.

"Wait a minute. You're pulling my much-needed vacation to babysit a spoiled heiress? Really, Mack. The last thing I want to do is shop all day and lunch with the girls with some society princess. Can't you use someone else?"

Mack sat up and folded his hands on the desk. "There was a kidnapping attempt made this morning that almost succeeded. A witness intervened, but the guy got away. Now, we don't know exactly what we're looking at here. Could be random. Could be targeted. Regardless, whoever did this is bold. A detective is heading to the estate to interview her tonight."

"Where was she when this took place?"

"Shopping. River Oaks. And on her way to meet friends for lunch."

Colton bit back a word that would've shocked his mother.

"Listen, I know I'm asking a lot." A grimace crossed Mack's tired features. "Expecting you to put your plans on hold. But this girl needs you, Colton. She's scared and bewildered and needs to feel safe again. She doesn't want to be shut inside constantly, and her father is frantic. Called me in a panic this afternoon and insisted I send him my best. That's you. Jamison and Paxton are on stand-by, along with one of the new Navigators. All the bells and whistles. And I think her file might surprise you."

Colton accepted the folder from his boss but didn't open it.

He'd go through it later, when his eyelids didn't feel like sandpaper inside. Couldn't be too much to read up on, anyhow. And tomorrow being Sunday, she'd probably sleep in. Then they could go over whatever her schedule for the week might entail.

"Sounds sloppy, making a move in a public place like that. On a Saturday, no less."

"It does, so it could've been random and there won't be any other threats. And you can start your holiday vacation. You deserve it."

One could hope. "Copy that. Paul Jamison's the best driver we have, and Trevor and I work well together."

Disappointment warred with exhaustion, and all he wanted to do was go home and sleep until he had to leave Tuesday morning. But he'd need to adjust his attitude since this operation clearly weighed heavily on Mack, even if he hadn't been assigned a babysitting op since his first year in the field. He dreaded standing around through shopping trips, spa days, and late-night clubbing. But if Drew Hudson wanted the best for his little girl, he would get nothing less.

Then he'd take a couple of months off to reacquaint himself with his golf clubs. In Hawaii. With his bonus from Alderon.

"When do we report?"

Mack consulted his watch. "Meet at the Hudson estate at ten. I'll text you the address."

"Ten hundred hours tomorrow, you mean."

"I mean twenty-two hundred. Tonight."

He released a heavy sigh. "I was afraid that's what you meant."

Guess that twelve hours of sleep would have to wait, like his golf trip.

He called the guys with his regrets and retrieved his black Jeep Grand Cherokee from the secure parking garage. After grabbing a quick burger and fries, he drove home to the Houston suburb he and Theresa had thought would be the perfect place to grow their family. Another lifetime ago, when dreams still existed. When he still believed God actually listened.

Inside the kitchen, he dropped the file marked *Hudson, Riley C.* on the table. Weary to the bone, he lugged his suitcase up the stairs and dumped the contents on his closet floor so he could repack it. Laundry would have to wait. As would the pleasure of sleeping under this roof for the first time in six weeks. As lead agent on an op like this, he would be on the job 24/7, stationed in the principal's home and on their hip every time they left the premises.

If he were lucky, Miss Hudson would be a lover of daytime soaps or game shows and not want to be out and about until she had an appointment or a little shopping to do. Lunch with friends or a dinner date. Nothing that would require hours of prep work.

To keep from nodding off until he had to report for duty at the Hudsons' River Oaks mansion, he decided on a shower. Maybe the police would resolve her case quickly, and he could finally sleep in his own bed. Alone. As he had the last four years, ever since Theresa … left.

Thank goodness for Petersen Security. Throwing himself into his work had been the perfect remedy, not allowing himself to dwell on the loneliness, the sense of betrayal, the loss of all he'd ever believed in. Home, family, love … faith.

At least the job had never let him down.

Chapter Four

Riley paced in front of the fireplace in her parents' family room, the morning's events rolling through her head like a security tape constantly looping.

Unfortunately, though, the police had discovered there was no actual security footage of the incident. The camera on that floor had been inoperable for the better part of the month. Now maybe they'd get it fixed.

"How're you doing, Ri?" Fran's voice pulled her attention to where she sat in an oversized chair with her legs folded up next to her. "Can I get you anything?"

"I'm fine. Just … restless." She checked her watch. "Nine o'clock. Wish the detective would get here. I feel bad to have kept you guys all day, and not for anything fun."

"I can't believe you stayed for lunch, although you didn't eat more than a couple bites. In fact, you didn't eat much dinner, either. Want me to bring you a plate of Hilda's meatloaf?"

"No, but thank you. And I didn't want to mess up the whole day, so I was fine staying for lunch." If truth be told, she'd been grateful for the extra hour to sit and let her insides right themselves. "And, please, if y'all want to get home, I totally understand. No need for all of us to stay when he only needs to speak to Avery and me."

"Phfft." Fran flipped her hand toward her. "Like we'd make you do this alone. Either of you."

"Yeah," Barbara said. "We're in this together. Besides, we should all hear what the detective has to say."

Riley regarded Avery, who hadn't said more than a few words in the past several hours. Very uncharacteristic for her usually exuberant friend. "You all right, Ave?"

Tears filled Avery's eyes. "You might have disappeared without a trace today, Ri. And it would've been my fault."

Riley's jaw dropped. "How do you figure?"

"If I'd have gone with you, it would've never happened."

Fran hopped up to join Avery on the loveseat and slipped her arm around her. "Oh, honey, it's not your fault."

"Not even close," Barbara said from the couch.

"Completely agree." Riley took a seat on the arm of the loveseat and pulled a tissue from the box on the side table for her friend. "That reminds me. Why did you come up to the garage, after all?"

Avery dabbed at her cheeks. "I decided your idea was a good one and was hoping I'd catch you to put my bags in your car too. I never imagined—" Another tear escaped. "What if Logan hadn't shown up? What if he hadn't wanted to get involved? It makes me shudder to think of it."

Yeah, *what if?* Riley twisted the emerald ring on her right hand around her finger. She'd come face-to-face with evil today, and it would probably be a while before she could walk alone without looking over her shoulder.

She shook off the thought. "All of those what-ifs don't matter. I'm fine. That guy was probably out hunting for someone vulnerable, like Logan said. A low-life predator. He just picked the wrong girl. I have an army of angels around me he couldn't see. Please don't blame yourself. Let's just be grateful we're still all here together."

"You're right. I'm so thankful you're still here with us." Avery's attention moved to the archway from the entry hall, and her eyes widened as a man wearing a suit and tie with a badge clipped to his belt entered behind Riley's mother.

"Riley, honey, the detective is here." Her mother turned to the officer. "Can I get you something, Detective? Coffee? Water?"

"No, but thank you," he answered. "I've had about four cups too many already today."

"I'll leave you be, then." She smiled over at Riley. "Let me know if you girls need anything."

"Thanks, Mom." Riley stood and extended her hand to the officer. "I'm Riley Hudson."

He shook her hand and released it. "Good evening. Detective John Stapleton. Houston PD. I apologize for the late hour, but I was on another call and couldn't get away."

Not a new story. In her line of work, she was well aware the Houston police were overworked and understaffed. A large part of what she would be asserting in Shane's appeal. The police considered the scene, the man standing over the body of his dead girlfriend with her blood soaking his shirt and covering his hands, and made a snap decision. Open and shut.

And wrong.

Riley gestured to the others. "These are my friends, Frances, Barbara, and Avery. Avery saw the guy as he got away."

Her friend finally recovered from her stupor. "Y-yes, Detective. I got a pretty good look at him."

The detective stared at her stunning friend, clearly enthralled, as many before him had been. "And you're Avery …?"

"Avery Sanders."

"Miss Sanders." His dark eyes lingered before he cleared his throat, his pen poised over a small notebook. "You saw what happened?"

"Only after Riley did whatever she did that had him limping away like a dog with his tail between his legs."

Detective Stapleton's eyebrow rose as he regarded Riley. "And that was?"

Riley's face warmed. "Kicked him in the knee with the heel of my boot. An elbow to the nose. Then another kick to his arm so he'd let go of the gun. Oh, and he should have some decent welts on his hand. I think I scratched him up pretty good."

He consulted his notes again. "Right. I see the officers at the scene took scrapings of your nails."

"A little more than that." She held up her hands with their now much shorter, pink-painted nails.

"Yeah, sorry about that."

She folded her arms. "Not worried about it. Hopefully, they'll find something there that will help."

He grimaced. "You should be aware, it can take several weeks to get DNA results back. It's not like it is on TV. And then it's only good if this guy's in the system."

"Oh, trust me, Detective. I'm well aware." Meaning her attacker was free to terrorize other young women for who knew how long. Her empty stomach roiled.

"So, let's start at the beginning. Tell me what you were doing, what time, where you were, and what he did."

Her legs turned once again to spaghetti, so she sat in the chair Fran had vacated to recount the events she hoped wouldn't haunt her dreams tonight. Twisting, twisting, twisting the ring that had belonged to her paternal grandmother. A nervous habit. When she got to the part about Logan running to her rescue, he consulted his notes.

"Logan … Devers. Yes, I have the statement he gave to the officer at the scene this afternoon and plan to interview him tomorrow afternoon."

"After church?" Avery asked.

His gaze went back to her friend. "Pardon?"

"I see you wear a cross lapel pin. May I ask if you're a man of faith, Detective?"

"I am." A furrow creased his forehead. "Why?"

"It means so much more to us to have a praying man working on this for Riley. You will pray about it, right?"

"I certainly will. As I do with all my cases. And, yes. I'll see Mr. Devers after church."

Avery and Detective Stapleton stared at each other before he cleared his throat again. "So, this is where you appeared on the scene? After Miss Hudson used her ... creative self-defense tactics?"

"Yes, sir." Avery's blue-green eyes sparkled with excitement, which Riley would take any day over the shadow of guilt they'd held a few minutes ago.

Content to let her take center stage, Riley let go of the ring, sat back, and clasped her hands in her lap. The officer scribbled in his notebook as Avery gave her rundown of what she witnessed. Perhaps a dramatic embellishment here or there in her Avery way, but otherwise accurate.

"How tall would you say he was?"

"Hmm." Avery's perfectly sculpted brows furrowed. "Maybe a head taller than Riley, and she's five-four—"

"Five-six," Riley said. As the shortest of their quartet, she was territorial about every inch.

"Five-six—five-nine with those heels—and he was lanky. I would say thin but fit."

Riley nodded. "Agreed."

"Anything else, Miss Sanders?"

"You can call me Avery. And, no, nothing I can think of."

He returned to Riley. "Do you have the clothing you were wearing today?"

"The officer by the door bagged it all up."

"Good. Do you have anything to add about the perpetrator?"

"Nothing Avery hasn't already told you. I didn't see him until he let me go, and that wasn't much." She pulled her arms tight across her stomach. "I never expected somebody to grab me in broad daylight."

"It does happen, unfortunately. Do you think this attempt may have been for a ransom?"

"I guess it's possible, but nobody's ever tried anything before."

"Why don't you have protection with you?"

Her eyes widened. "Like a gun?"

"Like a bodyguard."

"A bodyguard? That's a hard no. I had one until I went to college." She gestured at her friends. "We all went to Stanford together. Being half the country away, nobody knew who I was. So, I told Daddy no bodyguards. Ever again. Besides, I always carry my trusty pepper spray."

Though a heap load of good that did today.

"And you're a …" He consulted his book again. "Lawyer?"

"Yes, sir."

"She's a fabulous attorney," Frances said. "Third in her class at law school, and so far, a one-hundred percent win record in court. She could be making a fortune but does it all *pro bono*."

Riley shook her head. "Detective Stapleton doesn't need to know all that."

"Sure, I do," he said. "What kind of law do you practice?"

"Probably your least favorite kind."

"A defense attorney?"

"I head up a group that considers cases of possible wrongful conviction. We investigate, collect new evidence, do DNA tests through private labs, and so on. Once we have enough incontrovertible evidence, we file for new hearings and then try them."

"And how does that work, if you do it all for free?"

"Mostly through grants and investments. Helps that the family business is finance. I also make enough between my trust and investment income that I don't need to pull a salary."

"Wait a sec. Are you the one who just took on the Shane Everett case?"

"Yes."

As he studied her, she could only imagine what he was thinking. "Hmm. Interesting. I'd still put the kidnapping for profit theory at the top of my list."

Weary of the whole thing, all she wanted to do was change into her jammies and curl up in front of a fire in her room with a good book. Maybe *The* Good Book would be the best place to start.

"What happens now?"

"Now we'll need to do a composite and get it out there to see if anybody knows the guy." He turned to Avery. "It would help if you could be here, too, since you got a good look. I can bring our sketch artist to meet you here tomorrow afternoon."

Avery reached over and put her hand on Riley's arm. "I'll be here. I want to get this creep off the street. What if he tries again?"

His eyebrows rose as he regarded Riley. "What if he does? I would highly suggest you not go anywhere alone, and I mean anywhere. Do you live here?"

"About four miles away. Townhouse, but it's a gated community, and I have a gated courtyard entrance."

"Doesn't matter. Until this guy is apprehended, don't go out and get the paper off the driveway or the mail without someone with you. Don't drive, don't shop, don't do anything alone."

Her mind whirled, and she wanted to argue. She'd fought for her independence, not wanting to be accused of living off her name. Resided in a safe neighborhood, had an alarm on her house but drove herself wherever she needed to go, never hesitated to run out for her own groceries or to spend a day with her friends.

Surely today's event was a random act. The guy probably had no idea who she even was. But was getting her back up against the extra precautions worth the risk? Especially when something niggled her at the back of her brain. Something she should remember. Something he said …

She'd replayed it in her mind over and over again, but she couldn't shake the feeling there was something she was missing.

She gave herself a mental shake. "Maybe I'll stay here for a few days. Nobody can get past the gate without approval."

"Not a bad idea. This place is a fortress. And you might reconsider a protection detail. At least until this is over."

"I'll consider it." For about two seconds. No bodyguards if she had anything to say about it.

"Good enough." He reached into his jacket pocket and took out two business cards for her and Avery. "Here's my contact information. Don't hesitate to call if you have anything to add to your statements."

She stood and took the card from him. "Thank you, Detective."

"My pleasure." He tipped his head with another glance at Avery. "Good night, ladies."

He started toward the entry but turned back. "Oh, I forgot to tell you. They found the car. Abandoned and burned. About ten miles from the mall."

"So, no fingerprints, DNA, fibers."

"No, ma'am."

Her heart fell. She'd hoped the car might help identify him. "VIN still legible?"

"Yes. Came back to a resident at a senior living facility who said he wasn't aware it had been stolen. We don't know when it was boosted since the elderly gentleman hadn't driven it for a couple of weeks. We suspect probably last night."

"Makes sense."

"I'll keep you apprised of our progress."

"I appreciate it."

Avery watched him until he was out of sight, her face alight. "After this is over, I'm so gonna ask him out."

Riley shrugged, exhaustion pulling hard at her limbs. "Why wait? Something good should come out of this mess."

Chapter Five

At the light knock on Andrew Hudson's study door, Colton glanced up from his phone, doing a double-take at the young woman he'd last seen over two years ago. He wasn't sure what he'd expected, but not this composed, casually dressed young woman. Not after what she'd experienced today.

Her hair had grown out since he'd seen her last and now hung to the middle of her back. No bangs, her hair instead framing her face like a satin curtain.

"Daddy? You wanted to see me?"

"Yes, honey." Mr. Hudson walked over to his daughter. "I want you to meet some people."

Colton had met the uber-wealthy businessman and his wife ten minutes ago, but was already impressed at the humble way they'd welcomed him and his colleagues into what he could only describe as a modern-day, Texas-sized castle. Rambling two-story mansion on several acres of prime Houston real estate, stone wall perimeter and wrought-iron gate with security cameras, and an intercom system manned by round-the-clock security guards stationed inside the house. A ten-foot-tall front door fashioned from heavy oak at the top of half a dozen stone steps boasted yet another security camera. All that was missing was the moat and a turret. Maybe a suit of armor.

Her gaze skimmed the room, her brows drawn together in question as she took in the four of them in their suits and ties. Their usual work attire, even for a late Saturday night meeting. But when her eyes met his, his pulse jumped.

That was new. And not at all welcome. He hadn't experienced a reaction like that since—

No. Not a chance. He'd put all that away years ago, and he certainly wasn't unpacking it now.

She stepped closer, her eyes narrowed. "We've met, have we not? I feel like I know the face but can't get a bead on context."

"We have. At the Mulaney residence."

"The Mula—" Her face blanched. "After the funeral. You were there with somebody, right? Said you were on the—wait."

Her attention went to Trevor standing beside him. "You were there too."

"I was," he answered.

She regarded his boss standing on his other side. "You're Mack Petersen? Petersen Security?"

The older man nodded. "Yes, ma'am."

She spun on her father. "Bodyguards? Daddy, you know how I feel about bodyguards. I can't stand having somebody on me constantly. I know I'm a people person, but bodyguards aren't people. They're … they're … tactical gear. And just as cumbersome." She glanced over her shoulder. "No offense."

"None taken," Mack answered.

"Tactical gear," Trevor mumbled under his breath. "That was good."

Colton barely suppressed a chuckle. Daddy's little princess wasn't happy. And he'd been called a lot worse than *tactical gear*.

Drew Hudson's face held the kind of panicked plea only a terrified parent could express. "Sweetheart, we can't take lightly what happened to you this morning. I'd prefer a protection detail stay with you until this thing is over."

"What *thing?* I really think you're overreacting. As usual. What happened today was random. I was by myself, nobody else around, and he took a chance. I seriously doubt he'll come hunting me down."

"I still think we should err on the side of caution."

"What if I agree to stay here for more than the next few days? A week or so. Until you see nothing else happens. Can we do that? Bodyguards, Daddy? Please."

Still trying to cover his amusement—he really must be tired—Colton shook his head. He'd seen Riley Hudson in the paper or on the pages of a magazine since their last meeting and had considered her pretty in a high-maintenance kind of way, like he had at the funeral in her designer ensemble.

But tonight, in jeans and a blue sweater she wore with tennis shoes, her dark hair tumbling past her shoulders, and little makeup on her face, she was a knock-out. Even after a trying day which must have put a damper on her usual Saturday night entertainment. She looked young, fresh ... and livid.

Recalling their earlier conversation, he leaned over to Mack as the argument between father and daughter continued. "Scared? Bewildered? She needs me?"

The contrition in Mack's eyes wasn't at all satisfying before he apparently decided to step in to help out his most important client. "Excuse me, Miss Hudson?"

"*What?*" She put her hand to her forehead. "Mr. Petersen, please accept my apology. I didn't mean to snap at you. This isn't your fault." She shot her father a sideways glare.

"No apology necessary. But I'll tell you what. Let my guys stick with you for two weeks. See what happens. These are the best I've got. The best in the business."

"It's all so unnecessary. I'm perfectly capable of taking care of myself."

Colton gestured toward her with his chin. "How?"

"Here we go," Paul muttered from the other side of Trevor.

Ignoring his co-worker, he trudged ahead. "How do you take care of yourself?"

She crossed her arms. "I'm always careful about where I park, where I go. I carry pepper spray with me. And I can run pretty fast."

"Let me see if I understand what happened today. You were out shopping. Meeting friends for lunch. Walking in a parking garage. Were you able to get to your pepper spray? Did you have the opportunity to run? And even if you had, what kind of shoes were you wearing? Low heel? High heel?"

"Well … no, my pepper spray was in my bag, and I was wearing boots."

"Flat boots? High-heeled boots?"

"Three-inch heels. Which actually came in handy, if you'd check the report. It all happened pretty quickly, but I think he'll be limping for a while."

"And if I'd been with you, it wouldn't have happened at all."

One eyebrow shot up. "A little cocky, aren't we?"

"Riley Christine," Mr. Hudson whispered.

Paul and Trevor bowed their heads. To stifle their laughter, if he knew his colleagues.

Maybe he did sound a little arrogant, but would she rather have an insecure bodyguard?

Then again, she didn't want one at all.

"Sorry. Couldn't help it. Mister …"

"Blankenship," he answered. "Colton."

"Mr. Blankenship here seems to think an awful lot of himself."

Trevor nodded. "He is a little cocky." He nudged Paul with his elbow. "Wouldn't you say, Jamison?"

"I'll plead the Fifth on that," Paul answered.

When the corners of her mouth twitched upward, Colton

had to school his features to cover his own amusement. As he'd ascertained two years ago, this girl had spunk and probably wouldn't take kindly to the suspicion he wasn't taking her seriously.

"I just know my job, Miss Hudson. And I do it well."

Trevor jerked a thumb toward him. "That's true too."

She looked back at Mack. "Two weeks?"

"One month," her father countered.

Colton met her head-on when those emerald eyes pinned him again. He'd stared down his share of hostiles over the fourteen years he'd been in security work. He wasn't about to back down from a petulant heiress.

She uncrossed her arms. "Two weeks and not a second longer." She spun on her heel and headed toward the door. "Hope you guys can keep up."

Chapter Six

With a sigh of resignation, Riley sat up in the four-poster bed in her old room and clicked on the bedside lamp. Her gaze roamed the space that was more guest room now than home. The fancy white French Provincial motif wasn't her style, but her mother had redecorated the suite after Riley moved out four years ago.

While she enjoyed spending time here at the estate with Mom and Dad, she missed the home she'd made for herself. Missed her bed in her cozy townhouse. Missed having her stuff, living in her own space. And it hadn't even been one night yet.

Still, there was no denying that as far as safety went, she couldn't be in a better place. While her townhome sat in a gated community, its security paled in comparison to the massive electronic gate and stone wall around the estate. If somebody wanted to get through the gate at her complex, they would only have to follow a car inside, while it would practically take a military strike to get onto the estate.

Deciding a heaping helping of ice cream was in order, she climbed out of bed, donned her robe, and slipped out the door of her suite. Walking on tiptoe, she passed the room where her new security goon slept. Last thing she wanted was for him to think she was making a getaway into the night. Thankful that he made no surprise appearance, she took the main stairs down through the formal living room and into the kitchen.

"Mom?" She stopped at the sight of her mother sitting at the breakfast nook table, a steaming cup of hot chocolate and her Bible open in front of her. "Are you okay?"

"I'm fine, Riley, honey." Her gentle smile couldn't mask the apprehension in the same eyes Riley saw every day in the mirror. "Woke up and couldn't fall back to sleep, so I decided some one-on-one time with God was in order."

"Did a little of that myself before bed." Riley grabbed a half-gallon carton of butter pecan from the freezer and a spoon before joining her mother. "Nothing like a talk with Jesus to get some perspective."

Mom chuckled when Riley plunged her spoon into the carton and dug out a bite. Not at all ladylike. "And ice cream, apparently."

"Definitely." She stuck the entire thing in her mouth.

"Grab me a spoon." Mom closed her Bible and set it aside.

Riley got up to grab another spoon and pushed the carton to the middle of the table so they could enjoy it together. "Why couldn't you sleep?"

"Hmm, let's see. My daughter was nearly abducted at gunpoint today. What could possibly be keeping me awake?"

Her father appeared at the foot of the back stairs and strode into the kitchen in a robe and pajamas. "Probably what's keeping us all awake."

"Hey, Daddy. Come join us."

"I'll do that." He grabbed a spoon from the drawer and sat on the other side of Mom before scooping a bite out of the carton. "Does this mean I'm forgiven?"

"I can't ever stay mad at you for long. You know that."

He threw her a wink. "That's what I was counting on."

Riley studied her parents across the small table. At fifty-nine and fifty-seven, they were a striking pair. Her dad, CEO of the worldwide Hudson Financial Corporation, had a full head of salt and pepper hair, dark eyes, and a fit physique. And her mother, the one-time beauty-queen daughter of a Houston physician and his homemaker wife, was the perfect complement to him, with her creamy complexion, shoulder-length black hair, and still-slender figure.

They'd met at church as teenagers and were married after her father graduated from college, before starting his MBA program at Harvard Business School. He then worked his way up in the company his grandfather had founded almost sixty years ago. Riley's older brothers followed in their father's footsteps, but, although invited to join the legal department after passing the bar, Riley had other ambitions. Different aspirations. And her family had supported her in the decision to open her own practice.

Her family's legacy of ambition, hard work, and philanthropy was born of the belief they owed much because they'd been blessed with much. This foundation of faith they'd built their house upon was the legacy that meant the most to her. That's why it came as no surprise her mother had turned to Scripture when overcome with worry.

"I'm so sorry. I never meant to cause you both so much trouble."

Her father's brow creased. "Trouble? Honey, you're not causing us any trouble. It's this ... person ... out there who's causing the trouble. We have to trust God he'll be found and you'll be safe. But in the meantime, we do want you to stay here."

She rolled her eyes. "Not that I could go home and have that ... man stay there with me."

"You mean Colton? The man who's protecting your life with his own?"

With a sigh, she leveled a mock-glare at her father. "Not fair, Daddy. You've always known my opinion about bodyguards. And that was before one actually stayed around the clock. Seems a bit extreme."

"No such thing when it comes to keeping my baby girl safe."

Against her will, her heart softened, and she took another bite of ice cream, her overly tired brain trying to come up with the words to explain. "It's not that I don't love being here with you. It's just that I want to be—it's important that I forge my own path."

Her mother reached over and covered her hand. "And we couldn't be prouder of the woman you've become, sweetheart. Smart, accomplished, selfless, independent. We don't want to take any of that away from you, but we also need to know you're safe."

Her father nodded in agreement.

She understood they were worried, but she'd gone through high school with a bodyguard after the young daughter of another wealthy American family had been kidnapped and held for ransom. At least she'd been assigned a female agent, but Riley had still hated every minute of it. Not that she'd wanted to get into any mischief, but no teenager wanted their every move scrutinized. No more so than she wanted it now.

"I'll try to keep a good attitude about that ma—Mr. Blankenship. Besides, with God on my side, I already have the best bodyguard there is."

As He'd proved that morning, when He plucked her from the grasp of evil. Evil she prayed she would never have to face again.

Chapter Seven

So far, it was as awful as she'd imagined it would be.

While her parents' driver from Petersen sat at the back of the church, her *shadows,* as she'd taken to calling them in her head, had stationed themselves at various points around the sanctuary. Mr. Jamison—Shadow Number Three—stood at the front entrance, waiting for the closing prayer that would signal him to bring the black Lincoln Navigator with the dark windows to the curb. Mr. Paxton—Shadow Number Two—held sentry at a side door.

And if that weren't embarrassing enough, Mr. Blankenship— her annoying Shadow Number One, so named because he was always *right there*—walked her all the way in, his head swiveling as if someone might spring out of their seat at any second and carry her away.

Finally seated next to Alex, her oldest brother, she bowed her head and put her hand to her forehead. Two weeks. Could she stand this for two weeks? Shadow Number One always walking in front of her to her left, Shadow Number Two a bit behind to her right. Shadow Number Three driving her everywhere.

She understood they were doing their job. She just hated being *the job*.

She opened her eyes and, to her utter mortification, found Mr. Blankenship standing in the aisle between the wall and the pew, his eyes panning back and forth across the congregation.

"Aren't you going to sit?" she asked in a stage whisper, leaning toward him so as not to draw unwanted attention.

Or more accurately, any *more* unwanted attention. The praise team hadn't begun their set yet, so folks mingled while contemporary worship music spilled through overhead speakers. But she hadn't missed the curious glances she'd garnered on her way in with her two lumberjack-sized *guests* flanking her.

He glanced at her and resumed his scan. "Not standard protocol."

"I don't care. You're embarrassing me to death. Sit down."

With a frown, he gave her another glance but continued to stand there, like one of those motionless guards at Buckingham Palace. She smiled a little inside, picturing him with one of those oversized bearskin hats on his head.

"Do you seriously think anybody would try something with you right next to me? Please. Can you sit?"

With a sigh, he finally moved into the pew next to her. A manly scent of sandalwood mingled with leather almost had her leaning toward him to get more of it.

Instead of giving in to the temptation, she pushed her shoulders back and nodded. "Much better. You almost look normal." As normal as he could with the obvious earpiece and his ever-watchful, cold-as-ice glower.

The corner of his mouth hitched upward ever so slightly. Maybe there was some thaw under there, after all.

The band launched into their first number, and the congregation stood. As soon as he was on his feet, though, Shadow Number One again took his place standing guard in the aisle. Riley wanted to sink into a hole. Maybe she should've stayed in and watched the service on live stream. Then she would've been spared this mortifying experience while also getting another hour or so of sleep.

After being ambushed in her father's study last night and reluctantly accepting her fate, she'd tried to sleep. But every time she closed her eyes, flashes of that morning's event would have her wide-eyed and staring up at the dark ceiling. The entire incident happened in less than three minutes yet permeated the rest of her day. And night.

Once seated and the pastor well into the morning's message, she peered at the man next to her out of the corner of her eye. As he had throughout the service thus far, his icy blue gaze raked across the congregation in front of them—back and forth, like a lawn mower. Her attention snapped back to the preacher as her skin erupted in gooseflesh.

Irritation. That's all it was. Colton Blankenship irritated her with his arrogance and the way he'd taken control of her life.

Okay, sure, the man was handsome. And smelled good. When they met after the funeral, she hadn't been in a state of mind to notice one way or the other. But last night, she'd been instantly aware of his quiet power.

Tall, muscular, shoulders pulled back, a face of granite. And those eyes. His presence alone took command of a room. Alert. In control. Capable. But cold as ice inside. Immovable. Not her type in the least. No, *her* man would respect her decisions for her life, never try to impose his will on her.

He leaned in. "Let's go."

"He's praying," she whispered back.

He didn't answer as he took her hand and pulled her up with him. She made a grab for her Bible sitting on her lap and half-jogged to keep up with his long-legged stride up the side aisle to the back of the church. In her straight skirt and four-inch heels, she was more in danger of breaking an ankle than being accosted.

They stepped into the foyer as the pastor said his *Amen,* and the praise band started in on their closing song.

"You have absolutely no clue about church etiquette."

He ignored her comment as he and Shadow Number Two led her out to the waiting SUV. Holding the door open, he scanned the parking lot while she climbed into the back seat. He closed the door and walked around to take his position behind their driver while Mr. Paxton took the front passenger seat.

"I think that was a little over the top, don't you? I'm not the First Lady, for crying out loud. And I like to stay around and talk after church. What's the problem with that?"

"Too many people. No way to secure the area."

"Secure it from *what*? Can we chill a little? I've gone to this church all my life. If this is the way it's going to be everywhere I go, I'll be insane inside a week."

"Even better. A padded room makes our job that much easier."

Her well-educated brain failed to come up with a good retort, so she settled for clasping her arms over her stomach and staring out the window.

"By the way, we'll need to go over what your schedule will be for the next few days sometime this afternoon. If you know it."

She scowled at him. "What's that supposed to mean?"

"I mean, if you could give us some idea of where you might be going, who you might be seeing. Whatever it is you do with your time. So we know what to expect."

Whatever she did with her time? He honestly had no clue who she was.

A smile stretched across her face. "No problem. I'm sure I can come up with something."

Chapter Eight

Stifling a yawn, Colton took a seat in one of the wingback chairs in Miss Hudson's upstairs study. He had to admit, the bed in his guest room was every bit as comfortable as his at home, and he'd slept soundly until his alarm sounded at six. Jet lag still had him by the throat, though, so he hoped she would be headed to bed early tonight. By tomorrow, his internal clock should be recalibrated back to Houston time, and he'd be ready for whatever she had planned for her day.

He watched her for a moment, standing next to her feminine French Provincial desk as the printer on the credenza behind it spat out sheets of paper. "Thank you for including us at lunch."

She grabbed the pages off the printer and walked around the front of the desk. "Of course. Hilda loves cooking for folks, so the more the merrier in her estimation."

"We appreciate it."

He'd been surprised when Candace Hudson invited them to join the family for Sunday dinner. Their wealthier clients usually provided meals for them, but not at the formal dining table with the family. That was a first for him.

Now, however, with a hearty lunch of pork loin, sweet potatoes, balsamic-glazed Brussels sprouts, and homemade yeast rolls on board, he was having an even harder time pushing back the fatigue that still pulled at him after yesterday's transatlantic flight. Especially after only half of the twelve hours' sleep he'd hoped for.

Finding out last night that Miss Hudson planned to attend the nine-thirty service at church hadn't been great news. Not only did that mean she wouldn't be sleeping in, but it meant sitting in a church service for the first time in years. He couldn't even count on keeping his brain occupied with his job, since scanning a crowd of parishioners all focused on the pastor wasn't altogether taxing.

Seeing her riled up in the car afterward had been the best part of the morning. If she knew how cute she was, all annoyed like that, she probably wouldn't work so hard at it.

She handed each of them several of the freshly printed pages. "My schedule, you asked."

He furrowed his brow as he took one. "For the next month?"

"This week." She turned her attention to the copy in her hand. "Okay. Tomorrow, I have a prayer breakfast with the board of Lend a Hand Charities at seven sharp at the Statesman Club. Following that, I have a nine o'clock meeting with my current client's former defense team."

Now wide awake, he looked up at her, over at Trevor staring wide-eyed at the computer-generated, seven-page schedule, then over to Paul, who shook his head back at him.

"I have a lunch date after that, main dining room at the country club. Following that, I'm heading to the office, and at three-thirty, I'm meeting with my investigator to go over our strategy for our current case. I'll need to leave the office by five because I have a dinner party fundraiser at the home of Shawn and Rebecca Cantrell, the sponsors for this year's Save the

Children charity ball coming up in February. *Hors d'oeuvres* are at seven with dinner served at eight, and I'm not leaving without at least seventy-five thousand in pledges, if I have anything to say about it."

Colton dropped his hands and schedule in his lap. "And this is only *tomorrow?*"

"Right." She flipped to the next page. "Now, on to Tuesday. I'm meeting the girls at six-thirty for our weekly Bible study at Holy Grounds Coffee downtown, followed by spin class at the fitness center next door. We work out every Tuesday and Thursday at seven-thirty. I'll be going to the office after that, then I have a three o'clock meeting at—"

"Hold up." He rubbed his forehead, exasperated and not a little irritated at the way this woman had confounded him. "Why didn't you tell us all this last night?"

"You didn't ask until today."

He had to give her that one. He'd never considered her days would be spent doing anything of substance. Guess he should've given that file sitting on the bedside table down the hall a little attention.

"Do you know how much prep we need to do before you can even set foot out the door tomorrow?" He stood to face her, frustrated that he'd broken his number one rule: *Never. Assume.* And now they were playing catch-up because he'd completely misread his client. Church this morning hadn't been a concern since Petersen had previously conducted a security assessment for the elder Hudsons, and their driver was also a certified security specialist. Having a fourth set of eyes and additional expertise on hand made this morning's trek a non-issue.

But this? A whole other can of worms.

She cocked her head. "No. Why?"

"Because we don't know how many others are aware you're expected at the Statesman for breakfast, the country club for lunch, or when you'll be going into the office. I didn't even know you had an office."

Her chin came up in defense. "I'm an attorney specializing in overturning sentences for the wrongfully imprisoned."

"Regardless." But impressive, nonetheless. How had he made such a rookie mistake? "We haven't checked out the building or anybody who might have access to you there. And we don't know if your lunch date told anybody he was meeting you."

"Graham."

"And what about this Graham? We'll have to do a full background on him."

She laughed out loud. "Graham Harding?" Her eyes danced with unconcealed mirth, increasing his irritation. "Of the Fort Worth Hardings?"

"I don't care." His ire rose by the second, although he was more angry with himself than at her. This was her life, the way she lived it. She quite obviously did it well, and he'd drastically underestimated her. "He gets close to you only after we've vetted him. We'll also need to check out the home where the party's being held—entrances, security measures, attendees, everything."

He swung his gaze to Trevor, still seated in his chair, snapping photos of each page of the schedule with his encrypted cell phone. "You sending those over to Mack?"

"Mack and Tech Ops." Trevor's thumbs moved frantically over the phone's screen.

They needed to get people working yesterday on reconnaissance and background checks. Pulling building blueprints and checking for unsecured entrances or other ingress points someone might exploit if they were determined. Contacting the Cantrells' security team, mapping out routes. A good two or three days of work that they now had mere hours to complete.

Granted, he was handed this detail less than twenty-four

hours ago, but he'd still dropped the ball by not getting Tech Ops on it last night. He might've been exhausted, but there was no excuse for such a gross oversight on his part.

"The coffee shop and gym are too public. Let's move the Bible study and workout here. Can you arrange that with your friends?"

She stared at him for a second, and he prepared himself for an argument. Instead, she sighed and crossed her arms. "I think that'll work. Fran's office is about thirty minutes from here, and Barb's about twenty. Avery telecommutes, so she should be fine with it."

Paul held up his phone. "I'll call Transportation. Get them working on routes."

"Thanks, Jamison. Start with various routes from the estate to the office so we can change it up every day."

"On it." He turned toward the door with his phone to his ear. "Dillon, hey, man, I need you to pull everybody in right now." His voice trailed off as he moved down the hall.

She plopped back down in the chair behind the desk. "Mr. Blankenship, really. This is all so unnecessary. You'll be with me in the morning for breakfast. We can even go in a back entrance if it makes you feel better. The office where I'm meeting the defense team has a metal detector at the door, so security is tight there. As for lunch, you practically need security clearance from the Pentagon to get into the club. I'll even let you taste my food if you want. To make sure it's not poisoned."

He glared at her. "Not necessary."

"As for the dinner party, the Cantrells have an entire security staff, the drive is gated, it's invitation-only so if you have no invite, you don't get in. And as for who was invited, I can assure you it's the cream of Houston society. Where do you think we expect to get all that money? They'll probably have their entire detail on duty. Please. Call their head guy. I'm sure he'll put you at ease. In fact, I'll probably be so safe under their roof, you guys can have the night off."

"Not going to happen, Miss Hudson. We go with you. We stay with you."

She shrugged and sat up to fold her arms on top of the desk. "Suit yourself. Got a tux?"

Chapter Nine

Riley threw her jacket, bag, and briefcase into one of the chairs in front of her desk, walked around, and fell into hers on the other side.

Lunch had been a disaster. As soon as she walked into the club dining room with her new brawny entourage, Graham's expression morphed from happy to see her to a thunderous scowl in two seconds flat. After Mr. Blankenship took up his post at the entrance and Mr. Paxton at the other end of the dining room, Graham leaned across the table and glared at her.

"Seriously, Riley? All of this because of that little incident on Saturday? You're fine. Why all the fuss?"

It hurt a little that he considered almost being thrown into a trunk and disappearing without a trace a *little incident*. "Daddy's worried since the guy got away. It's only for a couple of weeks."

"Hopefully, by Saturday, your dad will see it's all for nothing and they'll be gone. Or we should postpone any other dates until after you don't have your chaperones. It's embarrassing."

Embarrassing? To him? The other diners paid the two men who'd come in with her no mind. "Bodyguards aren't exactly a novelty around the club. Nobody even cares they're here."

"I care they're here."

The rest of their lunch hadn't gone much better, often eating in an uncomfortable silence. He didn't even bother walking out with her, taking off as soon as the waitress returned his credit card.

His lack of grace for her detail confused her. It was as if he considered them a threat, rather than the exact opposite. A threat of what, she didn't know. Even if they weren't there as part of their job, it wasn't as if she and Graham were a couple.

In her mind, at least. Over the past few months, though, Graham had started to push for more. She liked him fine, and they'd been friends since high school. But he wasn't husband material. Not for her, anyway. Not when he took his faith so lightly.

Her gaze strayed to the man standing with his back to the window beside her office door, keeping watch in the hall while Mr. Paxton remained in the waiting area and Mr. Jamison in the main floor lobby near the parking garage. The day had been strange, being chauffeured around all morning and ushered into buildings, the two guys flanking her ever watchful of their surroundings.

Yet even as much as she wished they weren't there, her heart had softened as she watched them work. It hadn't been as much fun as she thought it would be, springing her packed calendar on them yesterday after what she perceived was Mr. Blankenship's condescending remark in the car. But all she felt was shame, realizing the amount of work she'd made for them.

She'd given them as much information as she could on every location, the people she would see, the folks in charge they would need to reach out to. But the entire time she'd been with Avery, Detective Stapleton, and the sketch artist later that afternoon, all three men had been on separate laptops and their phones to make sure everywhere she stepped over the next few days would be safe for her.

By the time she'd run out of steam last night and decided to go to bed, she peeked into the study down the hall from her suite, where Mr. Blankenship still sat at the desk at half past ten, phone pressed to his ear, laptop open in front of him. When he swiped his hand down his face, her heart caught. The man was exhausted. Yet there he sat and worked.

For her.

How could she not admire that?

Sitting up with a sigh, she determined to make the best of this situation for the next thirteen days. Certainly, she could last that long.

She picked up a pile of mail and sifted through it. One envelope caught her attention, and she put the others down while she studied it. Red envelope with a card inside, not addressed or stamped. Her name had been scrawled across the front, almost like a child's handwriting, yet in cursive.

With a shrug, she grabbed her letter opener, sliced open the envelope, and extracted a card embellished with a cartoonish figure of a fashionable woman in sunglasses with shopping bags hanging from her arms. With a grin, she opened it.

> *My dear Miss Hudson,*
>
> *I've been watching you, and I'm impressed. You have a reputation for winning, but that might change if you're not careful. Are you sure about your new pet project? This one could be your undoing.*
>
> *Sincerely, Your biggest fan*

Her smile faded as she read from the top again. Her new pet project? Could be her undoing? Did that mean Shane?

Her gaze went back to the man outside her door. While odd, the card was probably nothing she needed to concern him with. She'd received mail in the past from victims' unhappy family members convinced the original jury had been correct. Or from someone finally put behind bars once the true culprit was discovered.

But this one ... was it someone who truly respected what she did? Or a veiled threat?

She picked up the phone on her desk and punched a button.

"Hey, Riley," her assistant Hallie said from the other end. "What can I do for you?"

"This red envelope on my desk, the one with just my name on it. Do you know where it came from?"

"It was delivered up from the lobby security desk. Someone dropped it off for you down there when they couldn't get up here."

"Did the guard say who it was?"

"Some guy. Didn't leave a name. Joe from Security sent it down to the mailroom to have it scanned for hazardous materials before having it brought up here."

There would be video of the front lobby, so maybe she could identify the sender that way. "Can you ask Joe to send me the video footage, please? I'd like to see it."

"You got it."

She eyed the front of the card. Gooseflesh crawled along her skin. A woman with shopping bags.

Coincidence. Had to be.

Chapter Ten

"My, but don't you three look handsome."

Miss Hudson's voice drew Colton's attention to the staircase, and he couldn't pull his eyes from the woman he'd last seen in a conservative business suit. The bright blue, sparkling gown hugged her in all the right places, with short sleeves and a mid-thigh-high slit up one side of the straight skirt. She'd pulled her long black hair up on her head in a simple bun with a ring of diamonds encircling it. Blue teardrop-shaped gems dangled from diamond stud earrings.

What a chameleon she was. From jeans and a sweater Saturday night, to the tasteful red suit she'd donned for work today, and, now, to this stunning gown. Hair up, down, pulled back, or left loose. It didn't matter. She was always striking and comfortable in her skin.

He cleared his throat and held out his hand for her coat. "You look quite nice yourself, Miss Hudson." An understatement, but it would be inappropriate to tell her she was breathtaking. "Your parents just left. We should be about five minutes behind them."

"Thank you." She let him take her overcoat when he reached

for it and turned her back to him. He pulled the coat up to her shoulders, and she faced him again with one of her thousand-watt smiles. "You could be a little less serious, Mr. Blankenship. It is a party we're going to."

"For us, it's work. Shall we go?"

She sighed as her grin disappeared. "Do you ever loosen up?"

"On my own time." They followed the others to the SUV parked in the circular drive, and he opened her door.

"When is that exactly?" she asked as she slid into the back seat.

"When I'm not with you." He closed her door and walked around to the other side, climbing in beside her.

"So, not until this detail is over, is what you're saying."

Clearly, she wasn't going to drop it. "It's the job. That's why it pays so well."

"Does it? Pay well?"

"Well enough. By most people's standards."

Her eyes narrowed. "What does that mean? That I wouldn't understand *well enough*?"

"You do live in a different world than ninety-nine-point-nine percent of us."

"Then you think you know me, based on my socio-economic status. Seems an unfair judgment, Mr. Blankenship."

He glanced away as the SUV made its way down the drive to the gate before regarding her again. "You're right. I pegged you incorrectly based on supposition. I apologize."

"You *supposed* I was a rich, spoiled socialite, and you'd be spending your days following me while I shopped."

He chuckled. "Yeah, maybe."

"Why'd you take this job if you didn't want to do it?"

"Mack asked me to take it. And I never said I didn't want to do it."

"Hmm. Good work ethic. Very commendable. But don't any of you guys have families?"

"I do." Paul checked both directions before turning onto the road. "I'm married with a little boy. Valerie and Landon."

"How old is Landon?"

"Four."

"Don't they miss you?"

"At times like these they do. But I was with the FBI for six years before we got married, and two years after, and was never home. I left a couple of years ago after we had Landon. With Petersen, I get to pick most of my assignments. Sometimes I work a specialized detail, then work in Tech Ops or Transportation for a month or two. Or take off a few weeks after an especially long detail."

"What about you, Trevor?"

He glanced over his shoulder. "Girlfriend. Gemma. We've been together a little more than a year, so she understands the demands."

"Did you work in another capacity prior to Petersen?"

"Military Police, Special Ops. Army."

To Colton's consternation, she brought that dogged focus to him. "Were you in law enforcement before this job?"

"Secret Service. Almost seven years."

"Impressive. Why'd you leave it?"

"Got shot protecting a visiting dignitary." He swallowed the acid taste the memory always brought with it. "Decided it wasn't worth the pay and started looking into other ways I could use my skills."

"Was it bad? Your injury?"

"Bullet nicked my spine. Four months of rehab."

Trevor glanced over his shoulder at him. "Seriously? I didn't know that."

He should've never mentioned it. He didn't share his personal business with people he hardly knew. Riley Hudson must excel at pulling stuff out of witnesses on the stand because he'd opened up like a cracked egg after two simple questions.

"One of the charities I'm involved with is Small Steps," she said instead of pressing for more. Thankfully. "We raise funds for the long-term care of patients with spinal cord injuries. We also fund research. You should consider getting involved on some level. Time, money. However you see fit, since your outcome was so favorable."

"I'll look into it." Their eyes held another moment. "Are you always so straightforward?"

She shrugged. "I'm a firm believer that those of us who are fortunate owe something to those who haven't been. And I don't just mean money. You were blessed with good health after what could have been a devastating injury. So, you owe something because you were delivered from it. See?"

"Sure."

"Besides, I've found it's not only good for those who receive, but for the soul of the person giving. I offer people the opportunity to better their lives by getting involved in charities. It's certainly enriched mine. As if by focusing on someone besides myself, I'm getting out of the way to let God work in my life. It's when I start telling Him how things should go that I get myself into a mess."

"Been there, done that," Trevor threw over his shoulder.

Colton finally pulled his eyes from her to the street view ahead. Another thing he hadn't known about her—her strong faith, which could explain why she appeared to be completely unfazed by Saturday's incident. Why she felt their efforts to keep her safe were a waste of time and resources.

Although Colton was fast coming to the conclusion that not a whole lot scared Miss Riley Hudson.

"So, how'd you end up with Petersen?"

He resisted the urge to sigh. How much longer before they reached their destination? "Mack was the Assistant Director of the Secret Service when I went through FLETC. Oversaw the training of new agents."

Her brow crinkled. "What's … fletsy?"

"Federal Law Enforcement Training Center. Mack heard from a mutual friend I was no longer with the Service and called me a little over six years ago. He'd left a few years before I did and started his own private security operations company. Offered me a job." A gift when he thought he might be washed out of the protection biz for good.

"What about family? Are you from Houston?"

"Isn't this all a little personal?" he countered instead of answering her question. Most of their clients were content to let them do their jobs. They didn't have to be buddies.

"You follow me everywhere, you've checked out all my friends, my co-workers, know what I'm doing every minute. I'm not asking what your deepest thoughts are. Do you have a family? That's pretty tame, isn't it?"

This time, he gave in to the urge and sighed. Nosy woman. "I'm not married, if that's what you mean. My parents live in Spring. Dad's a retired pastor, and I have a sister. Married with three kids."

Her face lit up. "Your dad was a pastor? What church?"

"My folks founded Faith Community Church in our living room thirty-two years ago. I was five and assumed all preachers and their families lived in their churches, until I learned otherwise."

"That's cute."

Cute? He supposed at one time in his life, he might've been considered cute. Maybe as a three-foot-tall mini-human. "My brother-in-law Micah is the head pastor there now."

Her eyes widened. "Your brother-in-law is Micah Thompson?" She snapped her fingers. "And your dad is Fred Blankenship, who retired, what? Two years ago?"

Surprised, he nodded. "You know them?"

"I know *of* them. Hard not to in Houston. That church is huge and does a ton of charitable work. I spoke at a women's ministry breakfast there last year and met Micah's wife, Lisa. She's your sister?"

"She is." This was all a little too close for comfort. She'd met his sister? Had been to an event at the church? The church he'd left without a backward glance? How long before she asked—

"That's where you worship?"

And there it was.

Shrugging, he diverted his gaze to the view out the windshield. "I'm a member there."

When the silence stretched, he turned back and found her studying him with a crease in her brow, as if she could see into his soul. He certainly hoped not. All she'd find was a knotted mass of questions and confusion he'd packed down under layers of ambition and duty.

But, "Raised here in Houston, then," was all she said, even though he suspected she itched to know more. Probably that attorney in her. "Where'd you go to school?"

"Considered Sociology at UT but decided on Criminal Justice at Texas State. Better option for my career track."

He hoped keeping his answers short and to the point would provide her enough to satisfy her.

"Both excellent schools. I applied to the School of Law at UT."

Applied but didn't get in? "Where'd you end up going?"

Turning her attention to the window, she twisted her emerald ring around her finger. It couldn't be that bad. Regardless of where she got her law degree, she was doing a lot with it.

She cleared her throat. "Um, Harvard."

"Harvard Law." So, she wasn't embarrassed that she didn't get into a good school, but humble about attending one of the best in the country. "Nice back-up plan."

She laughed, and his pulse did that twitchy thing again. He'd have to work on that. Or get to a doctor.

"It's okay, I guess."

"You're such an underachiever, Riley," Trevor said with a teasing grin over his shoulder.

She laughed again, and Colton couldn't look away.

What a surprise this Riley Hudson had been, from the first moment he'd set eyes on her Saturday night, to poring over her packed schedule yesterday, then spending the day with her in business mode. Unlike the society princess he'd expected, she'd instead shown herself to be mature, confident, independent, intelligent, and extremely caring of her fellow man.

The only disappointment of the day had been Graham Harding. Nothing like the man he would have imagined she would be with. Too slick, too arrogant. Colton caught himself chuckling from his place when she suppressed a yawn as they'd neared the end of their lunch date. Then the guy all but ditched her afterward without even a kiss on the cheek.

Yes, Miss Hudson could do much better than Graham of the Fort Worth Hardings.

They drove through another decorative iron gate and pulled up to the walk.

Trevor stepped out of the SUV and flashed his agency ID and concealed carry permit at the valet approaching the vehicle. "Personal security for Miss Hudson. We'll handle it."

"Yes, sir," the young man answered before moving to the next car.

While Trevor stood where he could scan the area around the vehicle, Colton walked to the passenger side and opened her door. Tonight, however, instead of taking his usual position, he offered her his arm.

Her surprised smile had his stomach coiling. He hadn't had any reaction to anyone in over four years, and it was completely unacceptable under these circumstances. He really needed that time off.

Paul left to park nearby as he and Trevor, taking his position behind them, walked her into the house. Her hand clutched his arm above the bend of his elbow, as if they were actually on a date. A high-end, completely-out-of-his-league date.

They checked their overcoats at the door and made their way through the receiving line.

She let go of his arm to hug their hostess for the evening. "Rebecca. Senator. This is Mr. Colton Blankenship and Mr. Trevor Paxton."

The elegant woman in a flowing yellow gown smiled warmly as she shook his hand. "Yes, hello, Mr. Blankenship, Mr. Paxton. It's nice to meet the men taking such good care of our Riley. She's a treasure worth guarding, that's certain."

"So I'm told," he replied, returning her smile.

The Senator's wife beamed at the blushing young woman beside him. "I did as you requested, and the caterer was happy to provide two more plates for Mr. Paxton and … Mr. Jamison, was it?"

"Yes," Riley answered. "Paul Jamison."

"They'll both be well-fed tonight." She returned her smile to Colton. "And you will join us at our table, Mr. Blankenship."

"Thank you, Mrs. Cantrell," he responded, surprised by her invitation.

"Now, I know you're on the job, but Riley is safe as the President in this house."

"Yes, ma'am. I spoke to your head of security this morning."

"Then you should enjoy the evening."

"Thank you again."

Colton led Riley away from the Senator and his gregarious wife as Trevor moved into position at the French doors leading to the veranda. "That wasn't necessary." Leaning toward her, he caught a whiff of her subtle fragrance. It reminded him of a garden he'd walked through in Japan a couple of years ago. "We're not here to eat and have a good time."

"But you're here. You may as well enjoy a nice dinner. I hated the idea of you standing around while I partook of some of the best food in Houston."

"Is their security staff eating?"

"They'll eat in shifts in the kitchen. But you are now my plus-one, Mr. Blankenship. I hope you don't mind."

He gave her a reluctant grin. "You've finally given in to your fate, huh? That we're your shadows for the time being?"

"Shadows." She chuckled. "That's funny."

"How's that?"

"Oh. Nothing. Are you ready to mingle? I have a lot of money to raise tonight."

Mingling was the last thing he wanted to do. But as her plus-one, now he had the perfect cover for sticking close.

Chapter Eleven

"Finally, thank you to Senator and Mrs. Cantrell for their gracious hospitality and for welcoming us into their beautiful home."

Riley stood on the stairs in the Cantrells' grand living room, extending her heartfelt appreciation not only to her hosts but to the sixty guests gathered before her. The evening so far had been a smashing success.

Her eyes met her bodyguard's and lingered, surprised to find those baby blues of his watching her with ... respect? Whatever it was, it was a complete departure from yesterday's icy glare during church.

She pulled her attention back to the guests and smiled as her face heated. "Please, enjoy the rest of your evening. And thank you again for your abundant generosity."

The room erupted in applause as she took the three steps down to the floor, where Shadow Num—Mr. Blankenship met her and extended his arm.

"May I escort you to dinner, Miss Hudson?"

She tucked her hand into the crook of his elbow. "It would be an honor, Mr. Blankenship."

Every time he'd held the door of the SUV open for her today, he'd taken her hand to help her out. A gentlemanly gesture.

But this, walking through this opulent home on his arm, felt friendly. Almost … date-like. Saturday, his arrogance had perturbed her. Yesterday, his hard work on her behalf had touched her. Today, his powerful presence had comforted her.

But tonight … tonight his closeness discombobulated her. The man was handsome, no doubt. Confident, good at his job, and—a surprise to her—a man of faith. Being so close to him made her feel safe in a way he wasn't being paid for.

But he wasn't her date. They weren't even friends. He was there to protect her body, not her heart. Yet something inside of her sprang to life the second she'd taken his arm. That had never happened with Graham. With anybody.

Together, they walked with the rest of the guests out to the stately home's veranda and beyond it to a large, elegantly trimmed white tent erected on the lawn. Tables had been set up and tastefully dressed in black, white, and gold for the $500-per-plate dinner.

He led her toward the main table, music from a string quartet wafting through the tent. "You were very impressive. You have a definite gift."

Her gaze snapped to his. Had he actually paid her a compliment? "Thank you."

"What you accomplished over one cocktail hour was astounding. You certainly know how to charm folks into opening up their wallets. I think I counted up to about ninety thousand in pledges by the time all was said and done."

"One hundred five, to be precise. Even I'm surprised by how much we accomplished tonight. Now we can start on the classrooms at the shelter. Educational needs are different for homeless children since their schooling can be so sporadic. It's difficult to integrate them into the public school system unless they're already there and up to speed with their classmates, so if we can accommodate them at the shelter, all the better."

At the table they would share with the Cantrells and three other couples, he held her chair before taking his own. "Your passion for the project is obvious. I can see why they made you chairperson."

"I do have a soft spot in my heart for these kids." She placed her cloth napkin in her lap. "On Thursday's tour through our downtown Lend a Hand shelter, you'll see the new beds and full-service cafeteria. We've incorporated Save the Children with it since many of our homeless are families."

"Yes, the tour." He leaned in. "You're sure keeping our Tech Ops folks hopping," he said in a low voice, so the others wouldn't hear, she assumed. No use everybody knowing he was her bodyguard, not her charming and handsome date. "Doing security checks on all these places and people. Even Mack's gone out on some reconnaissance. I can't remember the last time he did field work."

"Reconnaissance?" Leaning her head close to his, she spoke just as quietly. "You make it sound like a military operation."

"It almost feels like it. You are one busy lady. And we can't wing it. We have to know well ahead of time where we're going, when we'll be there, who will be there once we get there, what the surrounding area's like, whether the building's secure, where all the exits are. You have no idea."

Her eyes widened as he'd counted off his list. "You're right. I had no idea. If it'll help, I'll get you next week's schedule by tomorrow. There might be a few things added later, but it'll at least give your people some notice."

"That'd be great. I appreciate it." With a smile, he sat up and panned his gaze around the room. Out of habit, more than likely. Leaving her wondering if he did the same while off the clock.

They spent the rest of the gourmet, five-course dinner

visiting with the others at the table. After the way he seemed to have judged her, she didn't know how he would relate to them. If he might feel out of place or consider them all society snobs.

She needn't have worried. He was gracious, attentive, asked intelligent questions, and answered queries with confidence and an obvious deep knowledge base. When asked about his profession, he simply stated he worked for an international security operations company. And as she'd known they would be, her tablemates were warm and friendly, funny and smart.

Letting her gaze roam around the table, she smiled with what she could only define as pride, in its most selfless form. Pride in how everyone watched him as he answered a question posed to him by the senator. Pride that they found him engaging and intelligent. Pride as if he truly were her date, and she was showing him off.

Her cheeks heated again. She needed to get her wits about her, having only known the man coming up on forty-eight hours. Nowhere near long enough to entertain such absurd notions.

"Miss Hudson?"

Her head snapped around at his voice near her ear and found him staring at her with a crease in his brow. "I'm sorry. Did you ask me something?"

"Can you pass the butter, please?"

She picked up the butter dish on her other side and passed it to him. "Here you go."

"Thanks."

He doctored up his still hot roll, the aroma of yeast and rich butter wafting toward her. She'd have to remember this caterer for future events. They'd knocked it out of the park with their succulent prime rib dinner.

"You okay?"

She met his eyes again. "Yes. Sure. Fine. Just thinking how much I was enjoying this dinner."

"Amazing dinner. If I keep being fed like I have been the past two days, I'm going to have to up my workout intensity. Or buy new pants."

Doubtful he'd have to worry about that. "Feel free to use the gym at the estate any time. In fact, you can join the girls and me tomorrow morning, if you'd like."

He chuckled and picked up a forkful of baked potato. "I used it yesterday before church, but I'll leave it to you ladies tomorrow, since you all were so agreeable to moving your workout to the house."

"Afraid we'll show you up?"

"That's it exactly."

Laughing, she cut off a piece of the juicy beef. Who knew he'd be such a charming pseudo-date?

Following the dessert course, several couples took to the dance floor in the middle of the tent, including her parents and oldest brother, Alex, and his wife, Delia. Her other brother, Kevin, and his wife, Sadie, remained at their table, immersed in conversation.

She located her friends at another table—Frances with her fiancé, Barbara with her brother, and Avery with a friend they'd gone to high school with. She'd join them, but didn't want Mr. Blankenship standing at her chair keeping watch. Much too distracting.

Besides, she had a better idea.

Grinning, she leaned toward the man next to her and put her hand on his arm. "Mr. Blankenship, if you're going to be guarding this body, then you'll have to join me on the dance floor. And if you won't dance with me, I'm sure I can find somebody who will."

His eyes traveled from her smiling face to where her hand rested against his arm and back again. "When duty calls, as they say."

Butterflies took flight in her stomach as he stood and held

his hand out to her. He led her through the tables and stopped at the edge of the floor, where he watched the other couples with widened eyes.

"Uh, Miss Hudson. I'm not extremely well-versed in ballroom dancing."

"No problem. I'll follow you."

"Then we probably won't be moving around much."

She giggled as they walked onto the floor, and she stepped into his arms. "Works for me. This dress isn't exactly made for ballroom dancing."

They swayed with the music. "Then why'd you want to get out here?"

"I love to dance. And, to be honest, I couldn't resist testing you, Mr. Blankenship. To see how far you'll go to do your job."

His smile changed his entire demeanor. The man should do it more often. "Bring it on, Miss Hudson. I've faced worse things than ballroom dancing."

She threw her head back and laughed, the first of several bouts of laughter they shared as they glided around the floor, dodging other couples with more expertise than they.

"You're not bad, Mr. Blankenship. You underestimate your abilities."

"That's a first," he said with a chuckle. "By the way, I couldn't help noticing you address Paul and Trevor by their first names. Why so formal with me?"

"Oh. They asked me to, while you were on the phone earlier today."

"Then call me Colton. Mr. Blankenship is a mouthful, and I keep looking around for my dad."

"Colton, then. And, please. Call me Riley."

"Riley. Your mother's maiden name, correct?"

"Yes. Alex is named for my paternal grandfather, and Kevin for Mom's dad. Grandpa Alex passed away three years ago, about two years after my grandmother Christine." She pulled her hand from his shoulder and stared at her ring. "This was hers. My grandfather gave it to her for their twenty-fifth anniversary, then to me after she passed."

"It's beautiful." His eyes met hers again. "Christine? So, you're named for both sides of your family."

"I am." Her hand moved to the collar of his tuxedo jacket, where her fingers played with the lapel. "After Grandpa turned the reins of the company over to my dad nine years ago, he and my grandmother spent three years doing short-term mission work. Until Grandma got sick and passed soon after they returned. Grandpa died from heart failure in his sleep a few months later, but I think he was simply in a hurry to get home, to be with her."

His arm around her waist tightened. "They sound remarkable."

She smoothed his lapel and splayed her hand against his shoulder. "We were blessed with two sets of extraordinary grandparents. You met Grandpa Kevin yesterday at dinner."

"He lives out in the guesthouse."

"Right. And comes to the main house usually for meals. He was an orthopedic surgeon, retired about ten or so years now, I guess. My grandmother Eleanor was a strong woman of faith, like my mother. When she passed a couple of years ago, Mom insisted Grandpa move to the estate so she could be closer to him."

"That's nice."

"Grandma Eleanor was wonderful. Loved doing the Thanksgiving dinner down at the shelter." She tilted her head. "You guys will be off on Thanksgiving next week, won't you?"

"Not unless you're at the estate all day, with no outside guests. You go out of the house, we go with you. Or if you have several outside guests in, we stay."

Her heart fell. "I didn't think about that. You ought to be with your own families on Thanksgiving."

"Don't worry about it, Mi … Riley. We know what the job is. It's fine."

"Maybe I won't work the charity dinner this year. I'll be safe as a bug in a rug if I stay in with my family all day."

"Please don't do that. Not on our behalf. I know how important your charity work is to you. We'd never ask you to give up doing what you want to do to give us the day off. *You're our job right now.* We're okay with that. You should be too."

She hadn't been. Okay with that. She'd actually been resentful of it. But every day she learned more about what these guys did, and although she still didn't like being chauffeured and escorted everywhere, she couldn't help but respect them and the work they did to protect perfect strangers.

"If you say so. But I wish there was something I could do."

"Stay safe. It's called job security for us."

She looked at her fingers fiddling again with his lapel. "I'll do whatever you say."

"Riley, hey." He waited until her eyes met his again. "It's okay. The shelter dinner will be a great way to spend Thanksgiving. Please don't worry about it."

She nodded but remained unconvinced. Glancing up, she caught the side-eye look that passed between Paul and Trevor at either side of the tent entry, neither of them smiling. Once again, she'd forgotten Colton's role there. He was her bodyguard, not her *plus-one.*

No matter how much she wished otherwise.

Chapter Twelve

"Think you'll dance with your hunky bodyguard again tonight?"

Barbara grinned at Riley's reflection in the ladies' room mirror Friday night. Riley, Avery, and Frances had pulled off a minor miracle to surprise her for her thirtieth—the last of their foursome to hit the milestone birthday— along with fifty or so other guests at a popular new upscale downtown Houston restaurant they'd bought out for the evening.

Riley threw her friend a side-eye in the mirror. "Hard no. *Not standard protocol.*"

Frances chuckled. "Didn't appear he was too worried about protocol Monday night at the fundraiser. You two were downright cozy on the dance floor."

"He only accepted my invitation because it was a private residence with its own security team. This might be a private party, but I'm sure he'll stick to his post tonight. Not when there was no way to vet everybody here."

Riley studied her reflection. Rethinking her decision to wear a black blouse with her black jeans and boots, she cocked her head and scrunched her lips to one side. This was a party, after all, not a wake.

Her eyes met Fran's in the mirror. "Frannie, trade tops with me. I look goth in all this black."

"You look amazing in all that black," Frances replied, while at the same time lifting her red sweater over her head. "But you look amazing in red too. Here you go."

Barbara pulled her hands through her shoulder-length brown hair while Riley and Frances traded clothes. "Is he a believer?"

"I think so. His family founded Faith Community Church, but I don't think he's very active. Probably because of his work, but I couldn't shake the feeling there was something … painful there."

Avery blotted powder onto her face with a small pouf. "If he's struggling with his faith, hanging with you can only be a good thing."

Riley pulled the red sweater over her head. "For another week and two days."

Then she'd probably never see him again. It surprised her how that didn't thrill her like it would've a few days ago.

Grinning, Barbara's brown eyes sparkled behind her fashionable cat-eye glasses. "I don't think I'd mind having that Colton around so much if it were me. Is he dating anyone?"

Riley shrugged, her belly squirming at the image of Barbara and Colton … dating. "No idea. Want me to ask him for you?"

Barbara's mouth dropped open. "No. Not for me. For *you*."

Oh. "Yeah, no. Not gonna happen." She pulled her hair out of the sweater and let it fall over her shoulders. "This is so much better, Fran. Thanks."

Avery finished applying a coat of lipstick. "I wouldn't be in a hurry to lose your detail if I were you, Riley. John said they're no closer to finding the guy than they were at the beginning. You should think about keeping them around until they do."

"We'll see." She smiled at her red-haired friend. "I noticed you and Detective John seemed awfully smitten. Did he ask you out, or did you ask him?"

"Both, actually. I asked if he'd like to grab a coffee after we did the composite sketch on Sunday, and when he walked me to my car after, he asked if I wanted to have dinner with him Wednesday. Then I invited him to Babs' birthday party tonight."

"You've seen each other two other times this week, and we're just now hearing about it?"

Avery's eyes glinted with her girlish giggle. "I didn't want you guys thinking I was crazy. But he's amazing." Her smile beamed as she turned from the mirror. "I mean it. A man of faith, strong values, close to his family. Even Mom likes him, and you know how picky she is about the guys I date."

"I'm happy for you." She picked up her small black bag. "Let's go back to the party. I want to dance, but I don't want to keep these guys out too late. They've already put in a hectic week with me."

Avery pulled her arm through Riley's on their way out to join the other guests. "What does Graham think about your tall, blond, and gorgeous knight in shining armor?"

Riley winced. "He wasn't thrilled to be watched at lunch on Monday. But I haven't talked to him since then, so I don't know."

Fran shook her head. "Riley, you have to cut him loose. This is not a love match. You're much too good for him."

"Oh, I don't think it's that I'm too good for him. I just never intended for it to go anywhere beyond friendship, and it's becoming more and more clear he has different ideas. I definitely need to rein it in, but I know he'll be hurt."

"Do it soon, sister," Avery said over a heavy bass line thumping through speakers hanging overhead. "It'll get harder the longer you wait. And, besides, you have a much bigger fish to reel in."

Riley rolled her eyes. "Oh, please. Trust me. Colton in no way finds me attractive."

"I'm not so sure about that," Barbara said with a coy smile, staring across the dance floor. "Isn't he supposed to be watching the room, not just you?"

Following her friend's line of sight, Riley's gaze snagged onto Colton's across the expanse of the dance floor. And for a split second, she thought there might have been a spark of something in those amazing baby blues. Until he looked away.

Annoyance. More than likely all it was. Probably for being out of sight for too long.

Frances grinned. "Yeah, switching tops was smart. That red is definitely eye-catching."

Chapter Thirteen

Thunder cracked and lightning split the sky as Riley shrugged into her jacket on the way out the door of the club. With the deluge coming down, she was glad, for a change, to have the SUV brought to her. Perspective was a powerful thing.

Ducking under Colton's arm, she scrambled into the back seat. "Get in on this side," she called back over her shoulder as she slid across the seat behind Paul.

"Good idea." He climbed in next to her and shut the door against the onslaught, both of them brushing raindrops off the shoulders of their jackets.

"Brrr." She shuddered as they pulled away from the curb and rubbed her hands up and down her arms.

Colton leaned forward to remove his brown leather jacket, revealing the shoulder holster and gun she usually found easy to ignore since the guys always wore coats. Except dancing close to him on Monday. She'd been aware of it then, even under his tuxedo jacket.

"Here." He draped the coat around her shoulders. "That should help."

"Thanks. But aren't you cold?"

"I'm fine." The rain beating against the window drew his focus. "It's getting bad. I got a flash flood notification about an hour ago, but I didn't expect the cold. Mid-November is early for such a strong front."

"I hope you guys get home all right." She curled her arms up under the jacket and tucked it close, the warmth from it being on Colton's body all evening seeping through her layers to her skin. "You could stay at the estate tonight, although clothes might be a problem."

Trevor shook his head. "We never know what the dress code might be, so we always have extra duds with us. And toothbrushes. But we'll be fine getting home. No worries."

"I shouldn't have kept you guys out this late, but I wanted to be with Barbara for her birthday. And after the week I've had, I needed to blow off some steam. Thank you so much for your indulgence."

"Are you kidding?" Paul said. "Val and I have been dying to get to this place for months, but it can take a week to get a table. We'll have to make plans to come back here when I can plan something farther out than a few hours."

"After you're through babysitting me, that is." Guilt squeezed her chest. Her guys couldn't even make dinner plans in advance with their loved ones due to her schedule.

"We keep telling you not to worry about it, Riley." Paul gave her another glance in the rearview mirror. "Most principals don't give us a second thought. We know it's the job. You should relax."

She shrugged. "I can't help it. I worry about you guys."

"Because you want to take care of everybody," Colton said.

She narrowed her eyes. "Pardon?"

"You want to take care of people." He turned to her. "For some reason, you need to make sure everybody's happy, everybody's taken care of. It's like an obsession."

And that was a bad thing? She stared at him in the darkened confines of the vehicle. He probably hadn't meant for the comment to have a bite. He'd simply stated the facts, as she'd learned over the past six days he was prone to do. But he'd inadvertently struck a nerve. She did have a need to help people. She always had.

Because, for some reason, God had seen fit to bless her immeasurably more than she deserved. Born with the proverbial silver spoon in her mouth. Grew up in a mansion with a cook, maids, drivers, gardeners, a maintenance crew, and a private security team, not including her current detail. She'd gone to elite schools and had traveled the world. She spoke three languages and drove a new car every year or so.

And she loved clothes. Designer clothes. They were her one weakness, but she'd found a way to make that work for others as well. Whatever she spent shopping, the same amount would make its way to some lucky charity the next day. Every time she cleaned out her closet, all her business clothes went to help welfare mothers dress for success as they applied for and started new jobs, while her gowns went to a program that provided girls in low-income areas with dresses for prom or their *quinceañera*. Most of them probably had no idea the gown in their prom pictures cost thousands and had been worn only once.

Charity work had been her life's passion since she was a teenager. She'd worked in soup kitchens, spearheaded clothing and toy drives, took part in walk-a-thons, phone-a-thons, and still manned a booth every year at the county fair to educate the public about the plight of the homeless in America.

She had a heart for people. And with her bankroll and education, her contacts and family name, there was much she could accomplish. She'd only scratched the surface.

Sinking into her seat, she pulled the coat up to her chin and closed her eyes, the *swish-swish-swish* of the wipers and earthy man-scent mixed with leather from Colton's jacket pulling the tension from her body.

"Riley." Colton's voice sounded far away until she opened her eyes. "You're home."

"Oh." She lifted her head and pulled her hair back with her hand. "I'm sorry. I didn't mean to fall asleep."

"No problem. How you keep going on your schedule is beyond me."

She handed him his coat. "I plan on sleeping in tomorrow, so you guys should too. I have no plans to be anywhere until dinner." If she didn't cancel it. Sharing another meal with Graham sulking wasn't what she'd call a good time.

Except they did need to have a heart-to-heart about their relationship. A conversation she dreaded as much as she knew it had to happen.

Colton laid his jacket across his lap. "You promise you won't leave the house?"

"Cross my heart." She drew an imaginary *X* across her chest with her finger. "I have a million calls to make and tons of work to do. Correspondence, flyers for the Christmas toy drive, some last-minute things for the shelter Thanksgiving dinner next Thursday, that sort of thing. I'll be busy all day. Please. Take some time off."

He addressed his cohorts. "Okay, then. I'll see you both tomorrow, say, four o'clock?"

"Copy that," Paul said. "My kid will love having me home for a while."

"Enjoy your time."

Colton opened the door and stepped onto the stone pavers in front of the steps, offering his hand to help her out. Riley took it as she'd been doing all week, but the spark of awareness hadn't lessened from the first time. She let him go and hunkered down into her scarf as they hurried up the steps to the front door.

Once inside, he helped her off with her coat.

"Thank you." She unfurled her scarf from around her neck and handed it to him to hang with the jacket in the foyer closet. "You're quite the gentleman."

He closed the closet door and walked back over to her. "But I offended you. I'm sorry about that."

"I don't know what you're talking about." Avoiding his eyes, she brushed an imaginary piece of lint off her borrowed red sweater.

"Come on, Riley. I'm trying to apologize here."

She let out a breath. "So, I'm a little sensitive. Don't apologize for telling the truth. I am a little obsessive about taking care of people. I probably should have been a nurse or doctor or something."

"I'd say you're doing plenty with a law degree. I'm sorry if I hurt your feelings."

"Not your fault. Now, since I'm staying put, you should go home and spend the night in your own bed. Before the weather gets worse."

"Maybe I will. I need to get some more clothes, anyway. I asked your house manager if I could do some laundry, but she told me to bring it here and she would take care of it. I hate to make work for somebody else, though."

"Yeah, good luck getting Irene to let you do any of your own laundry. Any of your own anything. That's her domain. And, to be honest, she loves serving people. She and Hilda are cut from the same cloth. They've both been with us since I was little, and I adore them like family."

"Okay," he said with a shrug. "Then I'll grab it too. I could get spoiled staying here much longer." He looked down at her outfit and back up again. "Do you and your friends make it a habit to switch clothing mid-evening?"

Riley laughed while at the same time her heart skipped a beat. "Noticed that, did ya?"

Averting his eyes, he cleared his throat. "Being observant is part of the job."

Of course. The job. She was *the job*. It would do her good to remember that.

"Yes, to answer your question. We're constantly wearing each other's clothes. We shared a house while we were all at Stanford, and when we were packing to move back here, it was impossible to remember what belonged to whom. I think I got to Boston for law school with clothes from each of them."

"You're fortunate to have such great friends."

"I am. They're amazing."

He nodded, his expression thoughtful, before he straightened. "I'd better hit the road. Sleep well, Riley."

"I intend to," she answered over her shoulder as she started up the curving staircase to her suite of rooms. At least, she hoped she'd tired herself out enough to get more than the snatches of sleep she'd had the past week. "Please be careful going home, Colton."

"No sweat."

On the way through her study to her bedroom, her gaze landed on the cards she'd received. The first on Monday, another Wednesday, and yet another this morning. The video footage showed a different man each time. Tall, skinny, with long hair and a mustache on Monday, a heftier man with curly black hair and dark sunglasses on Wednesday, and today a bespectacled man in a business suit carrying a briefcase.

The handwriting on the cards themselves hadn't changed, while the deliveryman had. Yet, somehow, they all seemed familiar.

She picked up the card she received that afternoon but didn't open it. After reading it three times at the office that morning, every word had etched itself into her brain.

My dear Miss Hudson,
There's a price to be paid for misplaced pride. Your
stubbornness will leave you with nothing. You've been warned.

And then there was the phone call.

A cold chill ran the length of her spine, and it had nothing to do with the hail pelting the windows outside.

Maybe it was time to tell Colton.

Chapter Fourteen

"Good work, Blankenship."

Colton berated himself after Riley disappeared at the top of the stairs. He hadn't meant to offend her with his comment. In fact, he found her compulsion to take care of others admirable. But his tendency to speak the truth bluntly had inadvertently struck a nerve. Probably why the Bible had a lot to say about taming the tongue, although he hadn't consulted the Good Book much in the past few years. Not since—

His phone went off, and he pulled it from his back pocket. "Blankenship."

"Hey, Colton. Dillon with Tech Ops. Something you should see came up on the social media scan I just ran."

"Send me the link." He took the stairs three at a time to the upstairs study they'd been using for daily briefings, where his laptop sat on the desk. So much for sleeping in his bed tonight. By the sound of the hail hitting the windows, he wouldn't be going anywhere.

He put Dillon on speaker as he took a seat and opened his laptop, clicking the link when the instant message from Tech Opps popped up.

A social media page opened with a smiling Riley in the profile picture and her name at the top. He scrolled through the posts from the past two days, his pulse quickening. "This can't be her page."

"It's a fake. Somebody's posting as Riley."

"Where'd they get these images?"

The latest post had come in twenty minutes earlier. Riley in a club dancing up close and personal with an unknown male who resembled him from behind. Not from tonight because her outfit was different, and he didn't dance with Riley at the party.

And if he ever had another chance to be with her on a dance floor, he certainly would never hold her like *that*. Riley was a woman a man treated with respect. Not like she was a piece of meat for his gratification.

"From what we've been able to ascertain, they're altered. We're pretty sure that's not Riley, but her face has been switched in. And we know for sure that's not you."

The caption below the image made his stomach turn. *Bodyguards have all the best moves!*

If Riley saw that, she'd be mortified. And livid.

Scrolling to the next image, he shook his head. Riley in a bikini, holding a drink in a martini glass, draped over a man much too old for her. The explicit post about mature men and experience had his gut churning. He had no doubt she was every bit as fit as whoever this was in the photo, but he couldn't reconcile modest Riley with the woman on the page showing off all her assets. And not once had he witnessed her drink anything with alcohol. Even tonight, while her other friends enjoyed a glass of wine, she opted for ginger ale.

"Do we know who's in the second post?"

"With the older guy?"

"Yes."

"We don't know who the girl is. Again, Riley's face has been overlaid on it. But the male is a former executive with Hudson Financial. Former, as in fired a year ago."

"So, this photo would insinuate he was fired because he was mixed up with the boss's daughter."

"That would be my guess."

But it was the next image that had him stumped. He leaned in to peer more closely at the photo. "Is that the guy convicted of killing Caitlyn Mulaney?"

"Affirmative." Dillon tapped keys on his end. "Riley's current case."

His head popped back. "Wait. What?"

"You didn't know? She's repping Shane Everett to get him a new trial."

That couldn't be right. Caitlyn and Riley had been friends. Good friends. He'd witnessed himself the depth of grief in those green eyes the day of the funeral.

It didn't fit with the Riley he'd come to know over the past few days. A woman of faith. Loyal to her friends. A champion of the underdog.

There was no greater underdog than a woman murdered by the one who professed to love her.

"How did you get that intel?"

"News. She had a press conference a couple of weeks ago about it."

While Colton had been out of the country. If Jamison or Paxton were aware, they hadn't mentioned it. But, then, there had been no reason to. It had no bearing on their assignment.

"Is this one doctored too?"

"Looks to be. Still working on it."

More key-tapping on the other end of the line while he studied the photo of Shane Everett and Riley in a clinch. Or someone who appeared to be Riley. He couldn't imagine she'd stepped out with her friend's boyfriend.

This guy is innocent, read the caption under the image. *Trust me. I know. Just don't ask me how.* Followed by *#freeshanenow.*

"Wait. That's not right."

"What?"

"I saw Riley two and a half years ago. She had shoulder-length hair and bangs. If this is supposed to be around the time of the murder, that's not how she appeared back then. This is much more recent."

"So, somebody again photoshopped her face onto another girl."

Probably Caitlyn, which was even worse. "That's a viable assumption. Caitlyn Mulaney was a social media influencer. See if you can back-check her old account. Maybe this photo was originally posted there."

"That's some kind of twisted, if this girl is indeed Miss Mulaney."

"You might also see if you can find that image of the Hudson exec. See who's really in that photo."

"Copy. We'll keep working it and see if we can get anything on whoever set up this account in her name. We'll also get it taken down."

"Good work. Thanks."

He disconnected and clicked over to Riley's actual page. Scrolling through, he found images of nature overlaid with Scripture verses, photos of her with her friends on various trips or working at a charity function. In fact, the majority of her posts centered on her charities—their objective, how to get involved, how to give.

Not one thing about any of her cases, although others had posted either congrats for another win or their opposing opinion. If anybody compared the two accounts, they would see the cloned one couldn't be hers.

Unless she was living a double life, and he knew that wasn't the case. No way could she fit another life into her already packed schedule.

No, the Riley he'd come to know was the authentic Riley Hudson. He'd bet a year's salary on it.

Did this attempt to discredit her go back to last week's attack?

Or were they missing an even bigger picture?

Chapter Fifteen

Riley bounded down the back stairs in gray sweatpants, crimson Harvard sweatshirt, and thick, white socks, her defense against the cold from the storm that still howled outside. She'd slept later than usual, jumping out of bed at a quarter past nine. Leaving her face clean, she'd pulled her hair into a ponytail and called it good. No need to get prettied up to work from home all day.

"Good morning, Hilda." She kissed the cheek of the cook she'd known since she was nine years old.

"Hi, sweetie." Hilda scooped pancakes from a griddle onto a plate with eggs, bacon, and hash browns. "Sleep well?"

"Yes, ma'am." Except for the nightmare. The same one she'd had too many times over the past week. That voice. So near her ear. The arm pressed against her neck. Something he said …

She gave herself a mental shake. "Too late, probably."

"Nonsense. It's Saturday. Get all the rest you need."

She took the plate Hilda held out to her. "You're the best. This looks fantastic."

"Eat up."

"I plan to," she answered with a wink as she poured herself a glass of orange juice.

"The others are in the dining room, dear. Everybody got a later start today."

"Thanks."

She backed through the swinging door, turned, and stopped. "Colton? What are you doing here? You had strict orders to go home and not report back until four."

He grinned at her. "You think you're giving the orders, huh?"

"But of course." She set her plate down. "Good morning, Mom. Daddy." Before she took her seat, she walked to the end of the long, cherry wood table and hugged her grandfather from behind. "Good morning, Gramps."

"Good morning, sugar. Glad you could join us."

Riley took the seat next to Colton, across from her parents, and picked up the syrup to douse her pancakes. "Why are you here so early?"

"I, uh … I never left."

"Never left?" She cut a three-layer bite and picked it up with her fork, syrup dripping onto her plate and the scent of maple mixed with vanilla making her stomach growl. "Why? Roads bad?"

He peered down at his half-eaten stack. "We can talk about it later."

"Arrout rhat?" she inquired around the huge bite of fluffy pancakes.

Her mother shook her head. "Riley, I swear, you eat like a linebacker."

She swallowed and followed it with a gulp of orange juice. "Only when it's us, Mom, I promise. I'm the very picture of manners in public. Ask Colton. He was right next to me at the Cantrells, and I didn't put my elbows on the table or anything."

Colton turned to her mother. "Yes, ma'am. I can attest to the fact she was on her best behavior."

"Glad to hear it," Mom replied with a wink.

"So, talk about what later?" Her gaze roamed from Colton to her father's furrowed brow and returned. "Something happened. With the creep? Or something else?"

The two men exchanged a glance.

"Hey. Right here." She pointed two fingers at her eyes, to Colton, and back. "I'm a big girl. Tell me already."

Her dad looked at the man next to her. "Go ahead. Or she'll badger you senseless until you do."

She inclined her head toward her father. "What he said." She forked another bite of pancake into her mouth. All that dancing last night must have burned a ton of calories, because she was famished.

With a sigh, Colton put down his fork and finally gave her his full attention. "I got a call from Tech Ops last night after you went up to bed. They found something in a social media scan."

"Is that as serious as your face is saying right now?"

"Somebody cloned your social media account and has been posting as you since Thursday. Some pretty questionable stuff. Designed, we surmise, to tarnish your reputation or credibility. Petersen got it taken down, but we don't know what damage might've already been done."

She stared at him for a pregnant second. "I see."

His eyes narrowed as he studied her. "Except you don't appear all that surprised."

Nodding, she wrapped her cloth napkin around her hands in her lap. "I guess I should've seen something like this coming."

He twisted in his seat to face her. "Now I'm getting the feeling there's something *you're* not telling *me*."

"In my defense, I didn't know if there was actually anything *to* tell you."

"Until ..."

"Last night."

His eyes widened. "Last night. After we got back?"

"Yes, but I thought you'd left. Figured I'd tell you today."

"Tell me what, exactly?"

The icy glare was back. Perhaps she should have clued him in after the first card arrived. What was that thing about hindsight?

"I got a card." She moved her head from side to side. "Actually, three cards. One Monday, one Wednesday, and the last one yesterday. Delivered to the lobby security desk."

"Like greeting cards?"

"Yes. Unsigned. The first one was ambivalent. Couldn't tell if it was good or bad. Said they were *a fan*, but I should be sure my current *pet project* wasn't my *undoing.* The second one said he hoped I would *see the light* before the *train* hit me. That nobody could survive a hit like that. I assumed he meant my career taking a hit—maybe my reputation—if I lost my current case."

"You believe they pertain to the Everett case?"

"That was my first guess, of course, since I don't have any others right now."

"Why did you take that case? I thought Caitlyn Mulaney was your friend."

She glanced at her father, then her mother sitting with her head down. She understood why that would be hard to comprehend and was all too aware of the problems her decision had already caused her family.

The Mulaneys had been long-time friends, but the judge wasted no time letting her father know his opinion on the matter. A day later, Priscilla Mulaney uninvited Mom to a Christmas tea at their home the week after Thanksgiving—a tea her mother had been attending for over a decade. And Caitlyn's sister hadn't spoken to Alex's wife Delia since the news conference about Riley taking over Shane's case almost two weeks ago.

All three situations were painful and disconcerting, but her family, to a person, had encouraged her to be true to her convictions.

Her gaze went back to Colton. "I was never convinced the cops got it right. And that was before I sat through every day of the trial. There were ... a lot of holes. Yes, Caitlyn was my friend. That's why I want to be sure the right person pays for what he did. I don't believe that person is Shane Everett."

Those cool blue eyes considered her for a long, silent moment. "Were you ever involved with Everett?"

She pulled her head back. "What? No. Of course not. I didn't meet him until after he and Caitlyn started dating. About three months before her death. And was never alone with him until I interviewed him at the prison last month. Why would you ask that?"

"One of the phantom posts was a photo of the two of you. Let's just say it was a little more than friendly."

Her face heated. "Show me."

With a wince, he pulled his phone from the back pocket of his jeans and brought up a screenshot of the post from the now-deleted page.

Her skin crawled as she scrutinized it. "That's Cait. It looks like me, but that's definitely Cait." She put her hand on her stomach, where the breakfast she'd been so enjoying now stirred violently. "That's really sick."

"Agreed."

"What else was posted on there that I may have to answer for?"

Her father sat back and crossed his arms across his stomach, drawing her attention.

"What? Was it about you? The family?"

He shook his head. "Remember when we let Arman Fletcher go a year or so ago?"

"Of course. Major stink."

"Somehow, this ... person pulled up that old photo of Arman

with one of our interns. The one that broke the camel's back after she posted it."

"Don't tell me. He doctored it to look like me."

Mom's eyes widened. "That sounds very tech-savvy. To clone someone's page and doctor images?"

Colton nodded. "It does take some tech know-how. I don't think your average user could make images that credible to the general public. Our techs know what to look for to determine authenticity, but most people would take it at face value, unfortunately."

Dad sat up and folded his arms on the table. "Hopefully, anybody who might've seen it will remember he was fired due to his indiscretions with that intern. That it had nothing to do with you."

Yesterday's phone call made sense now. She hadn't recognized the voice—obviously altered—but the message appeared a bit more focused.

"*I told you,*" the man had hissed on the other end of the line. "*Your confidence is actually your weakness, Miss Hudson, misplaced as it is. I'm trying to keep you from making a big mistake. One there's no coming back from. How much is your reputation worth to you?*"

He'd hung up before she could come up with any words, but it had left her stunned and confused.

A mistake there was no coming back from? Did he mean the loss of her career? The loss of her credibility?

Or something even worse?

"I want to see those cards." Colton studied her with that furrow in his forehead that told her he saw more than she wanted him to. "Is there anything else I should know?"

She swallowed hard. "Um, well, he … he called. Yesterday at the office."

Gramps' mouth gaped open. "You actually spoke to this person?"

"Not exactly. He hung up before I could say anything."

Colton turned fully in his chair to face her. His dismay quickly morphed into anger. "Yesterday? And you opened three notes from this person in your office over the past week? With me standing right outside your door? Riley, I have to know these things. When are you going to get that?"

"Sorry." His sharp tone took her aback. "I wasn't sure it had anything to do with what happened last week or not. And I didn't want to worry my family any more than I already have."

He released an impatient sigh. "Riley, listen to me. You cannot keep these things from me. Nothing. I want to know about every questionable phone call, e-mail, letter, or even if you notice somebody looking at you the wrong way. Understand? This is not a game. It's not a joke. You have to level with me, or I'm useless to you. Got it?"

"I got it, Colton. Chill."

"I don't have the luxury to *chill*. It seems clear your life could be on the line here. If this is the same guy who attempted that grab last week, he's not just pulling your chain. He means business. Do you not get that? Do you not understand how serious this is? *He wants to destroy you.* One way or the other. And it's the *other* that has me concerned."

If this is the same guy ...

Her chest constricted her lungs as that morning exactly one week ago rushed back to her.

Don't scream ...

That voice. Over her shoulder. Hot breath brushing her ear.

Colton's face swam in front of her as those harrowing moments replayed in her mind. Panicked. Confused. Why her? Where was everybody? Her frantic prayer.

Don't scream ... Miss Hudson.

Her hand flew to her mouth. It couldn't be. It was random. A crime of opportunity.

Don't scream, Miss Hudson, or I'll end you right here.

Colton's eyes narrowed. "What?"

She shook her head. To say the words would make it true. And it couldn't be true.

Her stomach heaved. She jumped up and ran toward the downstairs bath.

"Riley …"

Ignoring him, she made it there in time to lose what little of her breakfast she'd had time to eat.

Sitting with her back against the wall, she braced her elbows on her bent knees and covered her face with her hands. Her eyes stung, her throat burned, every inch of her trembled.

A knock sounded at the door. "Riley, honey." The worry in her mother's voice again had her fighting tears. She hated what this was doing to her family. "Are you okay?"

She took a deep breath and cleared her throat. "I'm fine, Mom."

"Let me know if you need anything."

"I will."

Another moment passed before Mom's footsteps faded, heading back toward the dining room.

When the shaking eased enough to allow her to get her feet under her, Riley stood and made her way to the vanity. She rinsed her mouth, then studied her reflection in the mirror. Fear had sucked all the light from her eyes, the color from her face.

It couldn't be true.

Chapter Sixteen

He'd done it again. Let his mouth get ahead of his brain.

Colton winced at the stricken look on Mrs. Hudson's face when she returned to the table. "I'm so sorry. I shouldn't have been that hard on her."

She dabbed at her cheeks with her cloth napkin. "No, please. Don't apologize. I agree with you. She needs to tell you everything. Tell all of us everything."

Riley's grandfather regarded him with eyes creased with concern. "I had no idea it had come to this. Please do whatever you have to do to keep our girl safe."

"Yes. Please, take care of my daughter."

"That's exactly my plan, Mrs. Hudson."

"Please, call me Candace." She pushed her plate away. It appeared Hilda's stellar breakfast would go unfinished.

"Candace. I'll take care of her."

Mr. Hudson shook his head. "Why is this happening? When she's done nothing but help people her entire life? Is it because of me? Our money? Is it because of some business deal I was a part of that somebody wasn't happy with? Why is this happening?"

"I wish I could tell you, Mr. Hudson."

"You can call me Drew. I think it's appropriate we're on a first-name basis since it appears you may be living under my roof indefinitely."

It certainly did. From his first day on this gig, Colton had hoped nothing else would happen, proving the attack had been isolated, and he could salvage some of his holiday vacation time. With this new information, the stakes had been raised. Everything in him said her life was on the line.

"Drew. I wish I could tell you why this was happening. If we had the motive, we'd be closer to nailing this guy."

"You think it's one person and not more?"

"With the threatening notes—and, if it's the same person, the guy trying to grab her—it reads like a stalker. One guy. But is it someone who simply saw her and became infatuated? Is it someone she went up against in court? Is it because she's a Hudson? We need to know more."

"And, of course, convincing my daughter to stay in is a futile effort."

Colton knew that all too well. Tech Ops had been working on next week's schedule since Thursday.

The bathroom door opening pulled his attention to the arched entry from the dining room to the living area. But Riley never appeared. "I should check on her to apologize. If you'll excuse me."

Candace nodded. "Of course. Although you owe no apology for being honest."

He put his napkin next to his plate and stood. An apology was definitely in order, but he needed to know what happened in those green eyes after his not-so-gentle reprimand. She'd gone somewhere. In her mind. Somewhere that scared her.

He needed to know where. What she saw or heard. What had literally made her sick.

After taking his plate and glass to the kitchen, he grabbed a bottle of water from the fridge and headed back through the formal living room to the main staircase. He'd taken three steps up when, out of the corner of his eye, he spotted her sitting in the family room, her legs curled up under her and a pillow clutched to her stomach as she stared into the fireplace.

Not wanting to startle her or interrupt her thoughts, wherever they may be, he walked to the mantel and stood in silence. Her focus never left the tall flames, as if she wasn't even aware of his presence. The heat from the fire warmed his jeans-clad legs, and his sweatshirt bearing the Petersen logo would probably carry the smoky aroma of burning logs the rest of the day.

"Riley, I apologize if I—"

"He knew me."

He inclined his head. "What?"

"He knew my name. Called me *Miss Hudson*. He knew me."

Confused, he regarded her for a moment. "You're not talking about the phone call or the cards."

"No. The creep. Last week. It all just came back to me, but I can hear it in my head, plain as day. He knew exactly who I was."

A chill traveled over his skin, despite the flames behind him. "That's where you went. A few minutes ago. You'd blocked it out before, but now you remember."

Her eyes traveled to his. "I'm sorry, Colton. I never meant to mislead anyone. I honestly didn't remember until five minutes ago."

The stark fear painted in the lines of her face pulled at his gut. His natural protective instinct wanted to do everything in his power to make her feel safe again. But the temptation to take her in his arms disconcerted him. Certainly not standard protocol, yet in this moment, his entire body longed to do just that.

He swallowed and moved closer to kneel in front of her,

handing her the bottle of water after loosening the cap. "That's not uncommon. A traumatic event can block a memory for days, weeks, even months. And as much as you want to pretend you're okay, your mind is still processing it. It's okay you didn't remember until now. It's okay to not be okay."

She took a deep breath in. "I was so ... scared. When he grabbed me. Just ... panic. It all happened so fast. Afterward, I was convinced it was random. That he was waiting for a vulnerable woman to cross his path. Until you said something about all of this possibly being the same guy. That he wanted to destroy me. And I could hear him. His voice. That he used my name."

"Did you recognize him from anywhere? A past case? Anything?"

"Not at all."

"So, you don't know of a reason why he might have wanted to hurt you."

She took a swallow of water. "Only because of who I am. But he wouldn't put me on alert by sending me notes or calling me if he planned to try again for a ransom grab. He wouldn't be trying to impugn my character on social media with no threat of extortion. If he's not after money, what's it all about?"

The same thought crossed his mind. If the guy was after a big payday, the smart move would be to chalk his failure up to a learning experience and move on to another target. One who hadn't already involved the authorities.

But this guy ... No, this guy was all about Riley. He couldn't take her last week, so what was his new endgame? Take her integrity? Her reputation?

Her credibility?

But why?

And was it tied to the Shane Everett case? The notes warning her off her new *project* and the photo insinuating they'd been involved before Caitlyn was killed strengthened that possibility.

He stood and sat next to her on the edge of the sofa, turning toward her with his hands clasped between his knees. "We need to call Stapleton. This changes things for them. They need to start looking more closely into who might want to hurt you personally, rather than a guy out there targeting vulnerable women. Do you have the cards here?"

"In my room."

"I'll bag them up to turn over to the police."

"And I have video."

His brows rose. "You what?"

"I requested video of the drop-offs from Security, so I've seen the guys who left them."

"Wait. *Guys?* As in, more than one?" That wasn't what he'd expected. He'd told her father he believed it was one person. A stalker or someone wanting to upend her life for reasons only they knew. But *guys?*

"Three different people. But the handwriting didn't change, so I don't know which one would be the author of the notes, or if any of them are and not just dupes he used to deliver them."

"That could be." And made much more sense than three different people being involved here. But they couldn't assume, either. Everything was on the table now that they were aware she'd been specifically targeted.

"You have the links?"

"Yes."

"That was good thinking, getting the video. Shoot me the links. I want to see the footage, and I'll get it over to Detective Stapleton."

She nodded, her haunted eyes staring into his as if she were searching for something, anything, to tell her all would be well, and soon. If only he could make such a promise. But the truth was, even though this new information would steer the investigation in a different direction, they were no closer to identifying the person—or persons—responsible.

"I don't know what to do."

His thoughts stilled at her quiet voice. "You trust me, Riley. Trust that I know best. Trust that I can take care of you. That I won't let anything happen to you."

"I do trust you."

"Then you need to talk to me. Tell me everything. As it's happening, not after the fact. Any weird letters, I see them immediately. Any phone calls, you give me a signal. I'm never more than a second away from you, even in your office. I'm always right outside the door."

"I'll tell you. I promise."

She held his gaze, and he was powerless to look away. She didn't have a lick of makeup on, as she had every other time he'd been with her. But she was no less stunning. Completely natural. Her skin flawless, her eyes large and green, and at the moment, so filled with uncertainty, he would do anything in his power to bring back their usual sparkle.

"I'm scared, Colton." Her whispered confession squeezed his heart. "And I don't want to be. I don't like to be afraid. I don't like feeling out of control of my own life."

"I understand. I do. But it's probably good you're finally scared. Fear puts you on alert if used effectively. Don't let it paralyze you. Let it galvanize you. Be ultra-aware of your surroundings, the people around you. You can be your own best weapon in keeping yourself alive. I'd almost rather have you a bit scared than indifferent."

"I'm not used to that. Being afraid. I always trust God is in control. That He's on top of things, so I don't need to worry. But this …" She swallowed hard. "Thinking somebody may want me dead? That's a lot to take in. And my faith suddenly feels very small."

He didn't know what to say to that. Who was he to judge

another's faith after his own had shattered in the face of tragedy?

Yet from what he'd witnessed in the week he'd been with Riley, her faith was not small or weak. Not in the slightest. Watching her lead the prayer breakfast Monday morning, then at Tuesday Bible study with her friends, the way they pored over their Bibles in the family room, then sat holding hands with heads bowed close together. The many times over the past week he'd glanced across the backseat of the SUV to find Riley consulting the Bible app on her phone. God clearly played a big role in her everyday life.

But she was being tested now, in a way few people ever were. Would God act?

Or would He stand back and let another young woman die?

Chapter Seventeen

Words. So many words. Right there on her laptop screen. And Riley couldn't focus on any of them.

Not when her head kept going back to the family room and her conversation with Colton. Again, it wasn't so much about the words but the … connection. A current running between them.

Even with everything going on in her head—the fear, the memories assailing her senses—she'd experienced a closeness to him she hadn't expected.

Had he felt it too?

"Riley?"

She jumped, and her head snapped around to her doorway.

Colton grinned, which did nothing to slow her racing pulse. Or cool her overheated cheeks. "Sorry. Didn't mean to startle you."

"No worries. Did you need something?"

"Is your date still scheduled for seven tonight?"

Okay, so maybe she'd imagined the whole thing, after all. He certainly didn't appear the least bit bothered about her being with someone else for the evening. On a *date.*

"Oh, uh, no. I've canceled my plans for the evening. With my friend."

His brow furrowed, and she wanted to sink into the floor. *With my friend? Really?*

"You're in for the duration, then?"

"Yes. So y'all can have the whole day off."

"I'll call the guys. They'll be happy for the downtime, especially with this storm parked over us."

"What about your downtime? Do you have downtime?"

He stepped into her study, leaned back against the wall by the door with his arms crossed over his chest and one ankle over the other. "Sure. Like the other guys, I'll work an assignment for a few weeks or even months, take some time off, then take another op. During my time off, I travel, golf, catch up with friends, my family."

"Daddy's driver and the house security change shifts. Why is it I have the same three guys and one who stays around the clock?"

"Because this is a special assignment. Temporary. Once this guy is caught and you're safe, then we're done."

"Oh." A week ago, she'd given them an expiration date. But today, his matter-of-fact explanation had her oddly disappointed at the prospect of losing hi—them. "Then, let's hope the police catch this guy quickly. It would be nice if you had the holidays off."

He stepped away from the wall and turned, his gaze panning across the pictures she'd left here of her and her friends in high school and college that Mom kept in place when she redecorated. Some from their travels as young twenty-somethings discovering the world. Mission trips to Africa, Mexico, and Peru. Graduations, holidays, and birthday celebrations.

"Tell me about Graham."

Out of all the questions he might've asked her, she hadn't expected that one. "Graham? What about him?"

"I've been with you for a week now, and as far as I've seen, you've only been together once. Under the circumstances, I'd think he'd stick a little closer."

"Why's that?"

"If it were my lady's life being threatened, I sure would. I wouldn't leave her to deal with it alone. It doesn't seem like a hot and heavy romance to me."

His lady? But of course he had a lady. A man like Colton could probably have his pick.

"Because it's not. Not even close."

He faced her again. "But you're dating?"

She shrugged. "That's what he calls it."

"What do you call it?"

She rose from her desk chair and plopped down on the couch. Tucking one leg under her, she grabbed a throw pillow and held it across her stomach. "We're friends. We've never talked about being exclusive and, to be honest, I never saw us going that direction."

He took a seat at the other end of the sofa, the pink and periwinkle blue floral fabric a complete juxtaposition to the raw masculinity of the man. "Maybe you should make him aware of that."

"I know. I've never treated him as more than a friend, so I'm not sure why ..." She shook her head.

"He wants more? That's easy to see. He could do a lot worse."

She threw him a sardonic grin. "You say the most charming things, Mr. Blankenship."

He shrugged. "I'm a charming guy. Can't help it."

"You might want to try." She laughed, and her pulse skipped when he joined her. He really should laugh more. His entire countenance softened from that granite visage whenever he laughed. "Graham and I met the summer between our junior and senior years of high school. A month-long student trip through Europe. I had a boyfriend on that trip, but Graham kept after me and after me. He and my boyfriend actually came to blows one night in Vienna. He kind of cooled it after that but kept writing to me throughout the next year."

"Kind of a rush, wasn't it? Two boys fighting over you?"

"I was mortified. About capped them both right there. Didn't speak to either of them for two days. Graham and I kept in touch throughout college and both ended up in Boston for grad school—me at Harvard, he at BC—then came to work here in Houston. He's a lawyer, too, but he's in international corporate law. Big money. And he travels a lot. He was engaged to be married, but it fell apart about a year ago. He called, we started spending time together, he cried on my shoulder a lot, and I guess he got so used to being around that now he considers it a relationship, of sorts."

"Of sorts."

"I don't think of him like that, like someone I could have a future with. I've been trying to find a way to tell him we need to step back, but there hasn't been a good opportunity. And now with the holidays and all, well, I really don't want to hurt him."

"Keeping him hanging will be worse. Take my word for it."

She cocked her head. "Sounds like you have experience with this sort of thing."

"Once. I wasn't involved in a serious relationship and had a friend in the same boat. I guess this was a year ago now. She was a co-worker, someone I could talk to, someone I could go to events with and not feel out of place with all the other couples. She eventually expressed she wanted more out of the relationship, and I had to tell her I didn't feel the same. And that was the end of the friendship. I see her in the office from time to time, but it's awkward."

"Yeah. I'd hate to lose Graham's friendship. Although, I can see how our lives are heading in different directions. He's very into the Houston society scene, and I'm not. I'm comfortable there because that's what I grew up in, but my parents also instilled in us a great appreciation for people who don't live in this world. We all worked in the company in high school and during summers in college. Starting with the mailroom, answering phones, or manning the copy machine."

"So, that's where your work ethic comes from. In the week I've been with you, I've seen how hard you work. And you're always on *my* case about downtime."

He threw her a wink, and her insides tumbled all over themselves. She was thirty years old, for crying out loud. Shouldn't she have grown out of this twittery stuff by now?

Smiling, she shrugged. "I have my downtime too. And my friends. Especially my girls. We went to the same private school, but Frances and Barbara were scholarship students. From the first day Barbara showed up in fifth grade, we were inseparable. Our different backgrounds never mattered to us."

"I have to admit, I used to think high society people were snobs. No offense. I've worked for a few who definitely fit that bill. But after sitting with you and the others at the table on Monday, it dawned on me I had always considered *myself* as better because I could get by without all that money. Which makes *me* the snob. In a weird way."

"I think there are snobs in every social tier. I've run into people at the shelter who are snobs. They have nothing, and they're almost hostile to those of us trying to help them. But it's their way of holding on to their dignity. Their way of saying 'I don't need to be taken care of. I'm capable.' And we do our best to convince them that's true. They are capable. We're just trying to give them one less thing to worry about so they can go on to better things."

He smiled at her. "You should have been a psychologist. You have an uncanny ability to understand people."

"I actually have a double major. Criminal justice and psychology."

"And your law degree? Boy, Trevor was right. You really should step it up. Slacker."

"Stop." She threw the pillow at him, and he grabbed it with one hand. "I always loved school, so it was okay with me to put in a little extra effort. And my psych degree has helped a great deal with my work, at the office and the shelter."

"I enjoyed the tour of the shelter on Thursday and wanted to talk to you about some of the opportunities down there. Ways I might be able to help, besides giving them my money."

She couldn't help the huge smile that came over her face. "You want to get involved at the shelter? Honestly? You're not just saying that?"

He chuckled. "No, I'm not just saying that. It got to me, seeing all those people who would be on the streets if not for the shelter. But those kids. Man. No kid should have to deal with the harsh realities of life like that. I lost a lot of sleep that night thinking about it."

"That's why I conduct the tours, so people will understand there's a whole other world out there, and it's up to us to make it go away. Those of us who have so much need to make sure no child goes without a meal or an education. No family should have to be on the streets."

He nodded, his expression sober. "I'm looking forward to being down there on Thanksgiving with you. I'll be on the job, but since I have to stick so close, there's no reason why I can't put on an apron and help out."

She sprang forward without thinking and enveloped him in a tight hug around the neck. "Thank you! Thank you so much!" She planted a kiss on his cheek and pulled back, her hands splayed on his shoulders. "You don't know how much that means to me."

"Yeah. I think I do."

Realizing what she'd done, she let him go and sat back in her place on the sofa. "Oh, wow, I'm sorry. I get so excited. Our relationship is a business one, and that was over the line."

"For business, maybe."

Her heart sank, but she understood it. Understood he was there for a job, not to be her buddy.

"When I'm on the clock." The corners of his mouth tipped up. "But for next-door neighbors, not so much."

She couldn't hold back her laugh. "Neighbors. I'm glad you're my neighbor, Colton Blankenship. Even if that means just down the hall."

For now. Until she was deemed safe, and he would leave.

"Back atcha. Now, I'd love to sit here and talk, but I need to get home to do some packing."

She inclined her head toward her study windows. "Sounds like it might be dying down a bit. I was going to ask if we could go by my place sometime so I can get some things, as well. If you're going out anyway, maybe we can do it now."

"Not without the other guys."

"Daddy only has his driver whenever he's out. Granted, he's also a Petersen bodyguard, but what's the difference? I'd be with you, and as long as we're in another vehicle, nobody would expect it to be me, since every time I've left in the past week it's been in the Navigator. And as twisted as this guy is, I still doubt he's waiting around in the freezing rain on the off-chance I might go somewhere without my detail."

He studied her for a moment. "We might be able to do that. I'd have to run it by Mack first, but if he gives us the go-ahead, I wouldn't want to take my Jeep. And your car's out of the question."

"We could take one of Dad's."

He pondered it for another moment, then stood. "All right. I'll check with Mack. If he gives the green light, I'll see about getting a car from your dad's driver. But at the first sign of anything, and I mean *anything*, that looks hinky, you do exactly as I say."

Popping up to her feet, she pulled her shoulders back and gave him her best salute. "Aye, aye, sir."

Chuckling, he shook his head and started for the door. "I'm regretting this decision already."

Chapter Eighteen

The garage door closed behind the Range Rover borrowed from Drew Hudson, and Colton's shoulders relaxed for the first time since leaving the estate.

Seeing Riley reach for her door handle, he put his hand on her arm. "I got it."

Her grin matched the teasing glint in her eyes. "Is this Colton the bodyguard talking or the gentleman in you?"

He shrugged as he stepped out of the car. "Both?"

The sound of her laughter faded behind the closed door, and he walked around the front of the vehicle to her side.

"Thank you," she said as she took his hand and stood. "To both of you."

He dropped her hand, returning her smile. "You're welcome. From both of us."

He led her into the house, through the immaculate kitchen, and into the family room. "I'll be right back." He scanned his orderly home, kept the way he liked it, even if he hadn't spent more than an hour there in the last two months. "Make yourself at home."

As she gazed around the room, furnished in leather and

warm wood tones, her smile brought a warmth to his chest. Did she like what she saw? After being raised in such opulence?

Leaving her there, he hurried upstairs to the master suite, where he threw a few sweatshirts, tees, two pairs of jeans, and socks into an extra suitcase, then pulled out a couple of suits to place in a hanging bag. He considered the laundry piled in the closet for a few seconds before stuffing it all into a duffel bag. He'd go through it later to determine what he needed and what could wait. He didn't want to keep Riley out any longer than necessary.

He appreciated Mack's faith in him, but with Riley waiting for him downstairs, the second-guessing had begun. Not that he couldn't keep her safe. Of that he had no doubt. His head had been on a swivel, focus constantly moving from the road to his mirrors and back again the entire drive over.

But having her here, in his home, this place he retreated to when he needed to refuel, felt a little too familiar. Friendly. He'd never once let himself get close enough to a principal to call them *friend*. Yet here he was, with Riley. In his house.

After a last perusal around the bedroom, he toted the duffel-turned-laundry-bag, his garment bag, and suitcase down the stairs to his family room. Bless Irene. She wasn't having it when he'd asked if he could use their laundry facilities. Insisted he bring back to the estate whatever he needed done and the housekeeping staff would take care of it.

The Hudsons had certainly surrounded themselves with loyal employees. It said a lot about the family that most of their staff had been with them for a decade or more.

At the foot of the stairs, he set his bags on the wood floor and ambled over to Riley, standing in front of the built-in bookshelf beside the limestone fireplace.

"Your family?" She pointed to a framed photograph. "I recognize Lisa."

He drew his focus to the photo of the people smiling—no,

laughing—into the camera with the familiar landscape of Disney World behind them. "Vacation. Summer before last." He pointed to the older couple. "My parents, Fred and Evelyn. Lisa, her husband Micah with their three—my nieces Autumn and Quinn, and nephew little C.J. Best kids ever."

And probably the only children he'd ever have in his life, as he'd never have his own. The old pain threatened to rear its ugly head again before he tamped it down. No use wallowing in old mud.

"C.J. For …?"

"Colton James." His face warmed. "Named for me with Micah's middle name."

"What's your middle name?"

"Brooks. My mother's maiden name."

"I like that. Sounds distinguished."

"Yeah, I was misnamed."

Her laugh brought a smile to his face, as it always did. Seemed he'd been doing more of that lately.

"How nice that you have a little namesake." She glanced over her shoulder at him. "You and your sister must be close."

"Since we were kids. She's five years younger than me and, of course, I always thought I had to watch out for her."

Turning away from the shelf, she scanned a grouping of pictures on the wall, her eyes coming to rest on an eight-by-ten of him and a striking blonde, their cheeks pressed together as they smiled into the camera. His heart squeezed as she stared at it for a moment before moving on. Seemed very un-Riley-like of her not to ask, but he welcomed her restraint. He never relished dredging up those memories.

"You know, we're not altogether different, you and I." She spoke while still perusing the photographs, mostly of his family, some of trips he'd taken with friends. Many with their golf bags standing next to them.

"How's that?"

"We both care about people … enjoy taking care of people. Our lives revolve around it, and we'd never even consider doing anything else. It's what we do. Who we are."

"Hmm. I guess you're right. And speaking of helping people, we need to get to your place, then back to the estate, where you're the safest."

"Okay." She followed him back through the kitchen to the garage. "I like your house, by the way. Did you do the decorating?"

"Sort of."

"Sort of? Did somebody else do it and you just paid for it?"

"Yeah." He avoided her eyes as he walked around to the passenger side of the Range Rover. "Pretty much."

"It's nice. But isn't this place a little big for you? What is it, four bedrooms, three baths?"

"Three-and-a-half baths."

"And your kitchen is to die for. Do you use all that space?"

He threw his bags in the back, then opened her door. "Secret?"

"Oh, yes, please." She rubbed her hands together like a cartoon villain. "I love secrets."

He chuckled. "I enjoy cooking."

"You do?" The delight on her face made his pulse skip. So, it was definitely her and not something medical he could fix. Not good.

"Picked it up in college. I got so sick of fast food that I finally broke down, got some cookbooks, some pots, pans, and started cooking. Found I really liked it."

"I'm not great at it, to be honest. Mom cooks with Hilda quite a bit and handles the cooking whenever Hilda's off. And although I've hung with them a few times in the kitchen, I've never really caught on. I'd make someone a horrible wife, I'm sure."

"More to being a wife than being a great cook, Riley." And

any guy fortunate enough to be with her the rest of his life probably wouldn't miss the cooking.

He closed her door and walked around to his side to climb behind the wheel. A quick click of the garage remote brought the door up, and he backed out slowly, searching for any out-of-place vehicles or people. No people that he could see on this frigid, cold day, and the only cars still on the street or in driveways had been there when they arrived.

On the way out of the neighborhood, he again kept a watch on the rearview mirrors and traffic around them to determine if they were being followed. While Paul was without a doubt the best driver at Petersen, Colton's thorough Secret Service training had included high-speed maneuvering and braking techniques, attack recognition, and defensive positioning. Mack also made sure his operatives went through their paces behind the wheel every two years to keep their skills sharp.

Hopefully, they wouldn't need to take advantage of it today.

"Beautiful." Riley gazed out the side window as the car meandered through the tree-lined subdivision. "Like something from one of those TV shows, where everybody on the block knows one another, and you can run to a neighbor's house to borrow eggs or sugar. Or let your littles play while dishing with the other moms over a cup of coffee."

Smiling, he glanced over at her. "It's a friendly neighborhood. I've enjoyed living here. My next-door neighbors take care of my house when I'm on an op where I can't be home for a while."

"How long have you been here?"

"About six years."

"It's lovely."

She watched the rows of upper-middle-class homes go by, wisps of smoke rising from almost every chimney. Why was she so mesmerized by this humble neighborhood? Had she grown up in that vast house longing for the simple pleasures of American suburbia?

Could she really be happy living in a place like this?

Not that it mattered if she would be or not. He'd certainly never find out.

He cleared his throat. "Where to?"

"Head back toward River Oaks. I'm a little west of my parents." She gave him directions to her house, and they spent the forty-minute drive talking about his work, her work, current affairs. The detours around flooded roads and the drizzle of sleet still coming down made for slower going than usual.

She pointed to an entrance leading to curving rows of private luxury townhomes on the other side of a decorative wrought-iron gate. "Five, two, seven, nine."

Once he'd punched in the numbers, they made their way inside, meandering along the curved lane until she gestured to a two-story, white, Mediterranean-style home on their right. He parked next to the curb and came around to let her out, both hunkering down into their heavy coats.

They hurried up the walkway, passing through another gate that led to a courtyard on the way to her front door. "This is nice."

"Thanks. I love living here. It might sound prideful, but it's the first home I've called my own." She pulled a set of keys from her jacket pocket. "It was a blast dec—"

He grabbed her by the arm, pushed her up against the wall. Shielding her body with his, he stared at the door.

Her brow creased. "What's—"

"Shh."

"But—"

"Hush, Riley." He reached under his jacket for his gun and held it up against his shoulder.

"Colton …" she said on a breath.

He peered down at her upturned face mere inches from his. "Don't. Move."

Her eyes wide and frightened, she nodded. He drew his focus back to the entry. The decorative beveled glass had been shattered and door left ajar. Moving slowly until he reached it, he strained to hear any movement from inside. Cautiously, he looked into the house between the shards of glass, giving him a full view into the foyer and what appeared to be a formal living room.

At least, it used to be formal. The sofa and chairs had been ripped apart and their stuffing thrown about the room. A curio cabinet had been toppled, and the probably very expensive figurines once displayed there were scattered in fragments on the floor. Pictures lay strewn about in broken frames, the tables upended, and books, magazines, and other items had been left in disarray.

He took her by the arm, steering her through the gate and down the walk to get her back in the car. He holstered his gun as he hurried around to climb behind the wheel, started the vehicle, and drove away. Grabbing his cell phone out of his pocket, he instructed it to call John Stapleton, put it on speaker, and set it in the cup holder.

"What's happening?" Her voice shook as they sped out of the complex and pulled into traffic.

The call picked up after two rings. "Stapleton."

"John. Colton Blankenship."

"Hey, Colton. I'm here working on Riley's case after the new intel you provided earlier."

"Great. But, listen, we have another problem. We were just at Riley's townhouse. It's been tossed. You'll need to get a team out there. Seventeen-five-three-two Saddle Creek Ln. Gate code five-two-seven-nine."

Finger snapping sounded in the background. "I need units

rolling right now. Lights and siren." John spouted off the address and passed on the gate code.

"On it," a voice answered from a distance.

"Sending units now, Blankenship, and I'll get forensics out there in the next hour. You still there?"

"No. I need to get Riley back to the estate." He grimaced at the pallor of fear on her face as she stared straight ahead at the road.

"She's going to need to tell us if anything's missing. And what information the perpetrator might have found. Once we clear the house, can she be there? Is she up to it?"

"I'll go," she answered in a tight voice.

He reached over the console and took her hand. "We're going to grab a cup of coffee and will meet you there. I'll call in the other guys since we don't know for sure the perpetrator isn't in the area."

"I'll see you there."

Colton disconnected and told his phone to call Mack.

"Blankenship. What's up?"

Stopped at a red light and keeping his eyes on traffic around them, he repeated the bullet points of what had occurred. "I'm calling Jamison and Paxton to meet us at her place."

"I'll take care of that. And I'll also call Drew Hudson to keep him in the loop."

"Appreciated." He accelerated hard through the green light, darting from the left lane to the right and taking a quick turn without signaling to see if anybody followed. Thankfully, all the maneuver garnered was an angry honk from a girl in a red Beetle.

"No sign of anybody still there, right?"

"Not that I could determine, but I didn't go in. All appeared quiet, though."

"Okay. Good work getting her off the property right away. She's your first priority."

"Copy. Talk to you later."

He disconnected again and glanced at the woman next to him. "I'm sorry, Riley."

"Everything's destroyed?" Her voice trembled as she clutched his hand.

"It looks that way. The living room, at least. I didn't want to go in and mess up any evidence."

"Why didn't my alarm go off? I would've received an alert, and it goes directly to the police department."

"You sure you set it last time you were here?"

Her forehead scrunched. "That would've been last Saturday, after … well, after. I picked up some clothes to get me through a few days, toiletries, laptop, work stuff." She took a deep breath and let it out. "Avery and I had gone shopping together in my car—she lives around the corner—but I was still pretty shaken up when we left the restaurant, so she drove us back here, then out to the estate. I guess … maybe I forgot to set it on my way out. Which is really stupid considering what had just happened."

"You had a lot on your mind that day."

"I wonder if they found my safe. In my office. Third floor."

"Built-in or able to be carried?"

"Not built-in, but it has to weigh over two hundred pounds. No one person could carry it out, especially down two flights of stairs."

"Please tell me you kept all your essential papers in the safe."

She cleared her throat. "It's where I kept all my valuables. Jewelry, some collectible heirlooms. I kept a copy of my will in there, my passport, birth certificate, and some other personal papers. But papers with my social security number and other pertinent information were in my files. They were locked, but those filing cabinets aren't like a safe. There are ways to get in."

She swallowed hard. He expected her to cry, to see tears. But as usual, she refused to give in to them. How could somebody so tiny have such an iron will?

"Why? Why would somebody do that? Destroy my home? Why?"

The imploring in her eyes tugged at his heart and fueled his ire. Life was too cruel sometimes to the people who least deserved it.

"If it's the same guy—and that's my bet—he's playing with you. I don't know why he's picked you. I wish I did, because we'd be that much closer to finding him." Assured they hadn't been followed, he pulled into an empty coffee shop drive-through. "But we will. We will find him. I promise you."

"Before he finds me?"

"I won't let him hurt you, Riley." He leaned in, making eye contact. "You have my word."

Chapter Nineteen

"*It's only stuff.*"

That's what Riley had told Colton as they stood in the middle of the debris that used to be her haven of rest and security. A place she wasn't sure she could ever go back to. Ever again sleep in the master suite she considered her retreat from the world, read in front of the fireplace at the end of a stressful day, or enjoy quiet time with her Bible and a cup of coffee on her flower-bedecked back patio.

Even though she'd lost some precious keepsakes—gifts from loved ones, treasures from her travels—the deepest loss was the sense of *home*. Her little piece of the world she'd bought and put together as an expression of who she was and what she held dear.

No, it wasn't about the *things*. It was about the violation. The knowledge that this stranger had been in her personal space, going through her things, destroying what he believed valuable to her.

Thankfully, she'd had plenty to do to keep herself busy after they'd been stuck at her mess of a house for hours, going through each of the rooms to determine what was missing as opposed to what simply lay in ruins. Once back at the estate, she'd come straight to her suite and jumped into her myriad tasks, anything to keep her mind occupied. Hilda brought her a tray with dinner a little after seven, but she hadn't seen anybody since Colton popped in to check on her around ten.

She hit the Print button and picked up her cup from next to her laptop. Her hot cocoa had long ago grown cool, but since sleep probably wouldn't be coming any time soon, another wouldn't hurt.

Not wanting to alert Colton, she moved carefully past his door. In the kitchen, she rinsed out her cup while milk heated in the microwave. She turned and gasped at the sight of a man on the back stairs.

"Colton! You scared me to death."

"Sorry." His boyish grin was at odds with the midnight stubble on his face. "I didn't expect you to be skulking around down here at midnight."

"I wasn't skulking."

"My mistake." His sock-clad feet made no noise as he walked to the fridge and pulled open the door.

She poured hot milk over the cocoa mix and stirred it together. Stealing a glance in his direction as he stared into the refrigerator, she was grateful she'd donned a set of warm, modest pajama bottoms with a loose-fitting long-sleeved sweatshirt, since she hadn't thought to grab a robe. He, too, wore a pair of plaid pajama pants, and his gray T-shirt outlined an impressive six-pack and hugged his muscular arms. He'd apparently been in bed at some point. His hair had that mussed look of someone tumbling around trying to get comfortable.

She rinsed the spoon in the sink and cleared her throat. "What's your excuse for *skulking* around in the wee hours?"

He pulled a platter from the refrigerator and shut the door. "I got a hankering for some of Hilda's roast beef. Thought I'd make myself a sandwich."

"Sounds good."

"You want one?"

She shook her head. "Not hungry. You enjoy, though. Make yourself at home."

"Your mom's been telling me the same all week, which is why I'm down here raiding the kitchen like I own the place. Boy, that cook of yours makes one great roast."

"Maybe you and she can compare notes."

"I'm sure I could learn a thing or two." He pulled out two thick slices of homemade bread and set them on a plate on the kitchen island, generously slathering them with mayonnaise before turning his attention to her. "You okay?"

"Sure."

His stare didn't waver.

"I couldn't sleep." Not that she'd tried, but it would've been a losing battle. "Figured I'd get some work done."

"You worked all evening. Even missed dinner."

"Yeah, lost track of the time." She blew across the top of her steaming cup. "The holidays are busy times for charity work, but it's the most lucrative time of the year, so it's worth the extra effort. Not to mention Shane's case. I hadn't expected to take another client until after the holidays, but I couldn't put him off. The man needs some hope."

He nodded but kept piling roast beef onto the bread. She got the impression that morning at breakfast he felt she was being disloyal to her friend. Hopefully, he'd eventually see nothing could be further from the truth, since that's exactly what she sought—the truth about who killed Caitlyn.

"What about you?" she asked. "Couldn't you sleep?"

"I did for a couple of hours. A lot on my mind, I guess."

"Work stuff?"

He sat at the table. "Some."

"Would you like something to drink? Milk? Water?"

"Milk sounds good."

She took the milk back out of the fridge and poured him a glass, then carried it with her hot chocolate to the table.

"Thanks."

"Care for some company?"

"Have a seat."

She took the chair across from him. "So, what else?"

He cut his sandwich in two. "What else what?"

"You said *some*. What else is keeping you awake?"

He plucked a napkin from the holder in the middle of the table, put one half of his sandwich on it, and slid it over to her. "Eat that."

"Okay. Thanks."

"No problem."

"So, what else?"

"You're very nosy."

"I am." She took a bite of the sandwich. Maybe she was being nosy. But her curiosity had its limits, and she was dying to know who was with him, looking oh-so-cozy in the picture on his wall. "A woman?"

Taking his own hefty bite, he lifted his head and chewed for a moment, watching her with a thoughtful expression until he swallowed. "Maybe."

"The blonde?"

His brow crinkled. "What blonde?"

Okay, that was interesting. "The one from your house. In the picture on your wall."

His face blanched, and he dipped his head. "The blonde."

"She's lovely." She hoped she hadn't stepped too far into his personal business. He always seemed to shut down if she got too close. "Is she … special?"

"Yes."

"Serious?" She took another bite and wished she didn't care. Was she a girlfriend? Current? Former? And why did that idea make her pulse catch?

Several ticks of the clock above the table went by in silence before he cleared his throat. "My wife."

That last bite of sandwich went down hard. "I thought you said you weren't married."

"Theresa passed away four years ago. Leukemia."

Her heart constricted. "Oh, I'm so sorry."

"So am I. She was a spectacular person. We were childhood pals, started dating in college, and got married a week after we graduated."

"Then you were married a while before she … well, you were married a while."

"Ten years."

"And you had no children?"

"We wanted them. But after years of trying and a lot of tests, we found out she couldn't. We were on the list to adopt, but then she got sick, and for two years, our lives revolved around getting her well. We thought we'd licked it when she went into remission. But less than a year later, it came back. She died waiting for a marrow transplant."

Her heart ached for the tragedy he'd endured. "I'm so terribly sorry for your loss. It was obvious from that picture you were happy."

"We were."

"Is that when you decided to get lost in work? After she died?"

His gaze turned wary. "Why do you say that?"

"I asked Paul if you'd always done special assignments. That it didn't seem right for such a young man to give himself so wholly to his work. He said you used to work in Tech Ops before moving into the field a few years ago."

"After I got shot, Theresa wasn't thrilled that I went back into protection services. So, instead of working on a detail, I took a position in Tech Ops. Once she was … gone, I needed to get out of the office, do something more active."

"Did you give yourself time to grieve?"

"I thought I had. Then, on the first anniversary of her death, I completely fell apart. It hit me like a ton of bricks. Had to take some time off because I could hardly function."

"That's completely normal. I'm glad you finally gave yourself that time. Being busy is all well and good, but it only medicates you. You eventually have to let yourself get through it or you get stuck there."

"Yeah, I was basically on autopilot for the year after she passed, going through the motions. As long as I was working, I could be alert, involved in life around me. But as soon as I hit the front door, I shut down. It was either that or let the anger eat me up."

"Anger?"

He gave his head a shake. "I know you have a strong faith, Riley, and at one time, I did too. Or so I believed. But Theresa suffering like she did … dying like she did. So young and way too soon. Praying for a miracle that never came … well, I guess I blamed God. I know our relationship hasn't ever been the same. It's just hard to talk to Him anymore." He took the last bite of his sandwich and walked his plate over to the sink.

"Do you try?" she asked quietly, not wanting to offend him while at the same time knowing what he needed most was the one thing he'd pushed away. He needed his faith, his God … the hope only Jesus could bring. A lasting hope.

Taking his seat again, he moved his head from side to side. "Sometimes. But I never get very far. And to be honest, I'm not all that angry anymore. I guess I've moved through the stages and now accept it. I think I've walked so far away from God, though … put so much time and space between us, I can't seem to find my way back."

"But He hasn't moved. He's still right there, right where you left Him. Waiting for you to reach out. He won't push His will on you, but He is there for you."

He studied her but said nothing.

"Was Theresa a believer?"

"Yes. Had a strong faith. All the way to the end."

"So, she's with her Lord now."

"Most definitely." He chuckled. "Probably telling Him to give me a swift kick to the backside."

She gave him a half-smile, wishing she could help him come back. Help him bridge the abyss he felt existed between himself and the God he once knew. "Why do you still work such obscene hours if you've accepted her death? You don't have much opportunity to form new relationships with your schedule."

"Because it works for me. I like the intensity of an assignment like this. I'm good at it. And I have no intention of ever getting involved with anyone again, so why date?"

No intention of getting involved with anyone? Ever?

She stared at the quarter sandwich still in front of her, letting his words penetrate. "Why don't you think you'll ever be involved with anyone again?"

"Don't want to be. I had a great wife. A great marriage. I can't imagine being with someone like that again."

"You had one successful marriage. There's no reason to believe you couldn't have another. The odds are in your favor."

"I've never found myself even remotely curious to find out if I could again."

She swallowed hard against the lump in her throat. "I hope you find someone someday. I really do. You're a great guy. And you were obviously a good husband. You should get married, have those children you wanted, and live a wonderful life. I'm sure Theresa would want that for you."

His lips pressed together, and he turned his face away. The fingers of his right hand grasped the base of his left ring finger, as if searching for what was no longer there. How long had it been since he quit wearing his band?

"She told me to find someone." He cleared his throat. "To have kids. Said she always believed I'd be a great dad. I don't know about that, but it was nice she thought so."

Riley picked up her sandwich and took another bite, looking down into her cocoa as her mind spun. Colton had been married. Very happily married. But he'd lost her. All because she couldn't find a match in time.

How many others lay in hospital beds or at home, praying for a miracle?

She stuffed the rest of her sandwich in her mouth and picked up her cup. "That was good." She wadded up her napkin and rose from the table. "Thanks for sharing your sandwich with me."

"Thanks for listening."

"Anytime. I mean it."

"Back atcha." He joined her at the counter, concern written in those azure eyes. "I know what happened at your house had to have rattled you, but hiding away isn't going to help you get past it. If you need to talk, come find me."

"Thank you. I appreciate it. And since you already know I don't like beating around the bush, let me encourage you to listen to your own advice. You may not be hiding out physically, but you are emotionally, spiritually. And that's not healthy either."

She put her hand on his arm. "God loves you so much, Colton. I know you don't understand why things happened as they did, but the world is a broken place. These earthly bodies are temporary, and this world is not our home."

Dropping her hand, she crossed her arms over her middle. "Theresa's living every day whole and healthy with the God she loves. Growing up the son of a pastor, you probably know a lot of stuff in your head. But God is all about the heart. And He wants to hear from you. Just simple words. Tell Him exactly how you feel. He already knows, but He's waiting for you to give it over so He can heal it."

His gaze never wavered. *Lord, open his heart to You. Help him find his way back. Use me any way You see fit to help this amazing man.*

"I'm going to head back up. There's some of Hilda's cherry pie left over in the fridge and ice cream in the freezer. Help yourself to anything."

"Yeah, that sounds good." His usually confident voice was little more than a husky whisper. "Thanks, Riley." He took her hand and gave it a quick squeeze. "For everything."

"Any time. You know where I live."

He chuckled. "That I do. Good night."

"'Night."

She walked back through the house, her pace quickening as she neared the stairs. In her study, she sat down at her laptop.

How many others?

Chapter Twenty

Colton gave Riley another nudge with his elbow, and her eyes snapped open. She threw him an embarrassed grin and turned her attention back to the preacher. Apparently, she'd had as little sleep as he had after their chat into the wee hours. The scene at her house that afternoon had probably kept her awake, but he'd lain in the dark thinking about what she said.

Theresa's living every day whole and healthy with the God she loves.

Lying in bed, picturing Theresa healthy—her lush hair falling around her shoulders, the brightness in her blue eyes, her full-throated laughter—had brought peace to that place in his heart where she still remained. That place he'd held closed and protected these last four years, where the hurt festered and burned.

Before Riley painted a new image for him. An image of Theresa returned to the joyful soul she'd always been.

He'd blamed God for taking her, but she'd been in such pain, so sick. A mere shell of the woman she'd once been by the time she went … home. Maybe in the grip of his grief, he'd perceived it all wrong. Maybe God had been acting out of mercy and grace, not cruelty or to punish him for some unknown wrong he'd committed. He'd been gifted with ten years of marriage to her, and, even with all the ups and downs, he wouldn't trade that time for anything. Even knowing how it ended.

Unlike last Sunday, sitting here in this pew with Riley and her family, this week he'd tuned into the pastor's message while keeping watch over the crowd. And something inside of him, deep down, stirred as if waking from a deep sleep. Riley must have noticed him glancing at her Bible because she slipped it over to rest partially on his leg. As he followed along with the reading, the words jumped off the page.

I will never forget this awful time, as I grieve over my loss. Yet I still dare to hope when I remember this: The faithful love of the Lord never ends! His mercies never cease. Great is His faithfulness; His mercies begin afresh each morning.

His father had read this passage from Lamentations at the funeral. But Colton had been closed off, so angry, and in so much pain, he hadn't heard, hadn't comprehended, what his father had tried to convey. That God was still there. That God wasn't punishing him. That God had shown His mercy by healing Theresa on the other side of this life.

Was he ready now to let go? To let God back in? Could he trust without question?

As Pastor Troy began his ending prayer, Riley pulled the Bible back and closed it before reaching for her handbag. Their eyes met, and he took her hand to lead her out of the sanctuary to the waiting SUV.

"Thanks for keeping me awake in church." She stifled a yawn as she buckled her seatbelt. "Three hours of sleep doesn't cut it."

"Three hours? Did you work all night?"

She shrugged. "Most of it, I guess."

"Because of what happened at your house?"

"No. Maybe." She sighed. "I don't know. Just a lot to do. A lot on my mind."

"If you need anything—"

"I know. And I appreciate it. I need to work some stuff out on my own, but I'll let you know if there's anything."

He nodded and faced front again, catching Paul's concerned glance in the rearview mirror. His co-workers didn't need to know about their middle-of-the-night chat. That he'd shared things with her, confided in her, in ways he hadn't with anybody since Theresa.

He'd crossed a line and wasn't sure how to get back. Or if he even wanted to. He enjoyed this newfound friendship with Riley, while at the same time warned himself not to get so close he couldn't be of the best use to her.

After Sunday lunch with the Hudson family, she let them go, assuring them she would be home for the duration, and then retreated to her rooms upstairs. He took advantage of the quiet afternoon to call his parents before giving in to a much-needed nap, followed by laps in the indoor pool and a long, hot shower. Living for the time being at the Hudson estate was akin to a vacation at a luxury resort.

He'd just put six strips of bacon in a skillet for a triple-decker club sandwich when she ambled into the kitchen.

"Bacon." Her tired eyes lit up. "You're making bacon?"

"I am. Want some?"

"Yes, please. I never pass up bacon."

He pulled six more slices from the package. "What do you want? Breakfast for dinner, BLT?"

She pulled herself up on a stool in front of the island and yawned before bracing her elbow on the counter and sticking her chin in her hand. "What're you having?"

"Club sandwich."

"Can I have one of those?"

"You got it."

"Need any help?"

"Nope. Sit there and take a power nap."

"I can't sleep sitting up."

He glanced at her perched on the stool with her eyes closed, her hair up in a haphazard bun, dressed again in sweats and white socks. "Could've fooled me."

Her eyes popped open. "I'm not sleeping."

He guessed there was more truth there than she meant to confide.

Bacon sizzled in the skillet while he went to work cutting up lettuce, tomato, and onion, and plopped six pieces of sourdough bread into the toaster. "Get a lot done? It's after eight, and you haven't been down since lunch."

"I did. Still more to do, but isn't there always?"

After pulling the bacon from the pan, he let it sit on a paper towel while he assembled the first layer—ham, turkey, cheese, lettuce, tomato, and red onion on sourdough toast slathered with mayonnaise. He stuck three pieces of bacon on top of each stack, set another slice of sourdough on top, and repeated the layers, topping it all off with the last piece of toast.

He cut each sandwich into quarters, shook potato chips out of a bag onto each plate, and slid one toward her. "Your sandwich, madam."

Sitting up, she stared down at her plate. "Sandwich? More like a work of art."

After grabbing two bottles of water from the fridge, he joined her at the island, sitting at an angle to her.

"Mmm. So good."

That was all the compliment he needed, and he grinned at the dollop of mayonnaise at the corner of her mouth.

"What? Got it on me, didn't I?"

"A little." He pointed to the corner of his mouth. "Right here."

She licked it away and went in for another bite. "Red onion. I've never had onion on a club sandwich before. You've spoiled me for all other club sandwiches on the planet."

"Wow. High praise." He took a bite of his own and had to admit it hit the spot.

He finished half of his before gulping down some water. "Tell me how you got into the criminal defense biz."

She chewed and swallowed. "Wasn't the original plan. At Harvard, I'd planned to go into corporate law. Not necessarily to work at the company, but because it interested me. The setting up of corporations and so on."

"What made you change course?"

She finished the first quarter of her sandwich and picked up another. "Do you remember the man with Barbara at the Cantrells'?"

His brain scanned back through the evening at the Senator's home. "Tall, dark hair, glasses?"

She nodded. "Her brother, Tommy. About six years older than we are. While we were in college, his wife was murdered, and he was subsequently arrested and convicted for it. Barbara was a mess through that whole thing. Not only had she lost someone she loved, and violently, but she steadfastly believed his claims of innocence. But you know they always suspect the significant other first, and, unfortunately, if they can get the pieces to fit, many times they quit looking."

"Like you believe happened with Shane Everett." He picked up some chips and popped them in his mouth.

"Exactly. By the time I got to law school, Tommy had been inside for a year, still adamant he didn't do it. I took a criminal defense class my second year, and when we got to the appeals process, I was hooked. I thought about all of Tommy's appeals and was astonished he couldn't get somebody to champion him. And my career was born. I knew before I ever graduated he'd be my first *pro bono* case."

"Successful, apparently, since he's out."

"It was. But I was so scared that if I couldn't help him, nobody ever would. The stress and exhaustion from that case put me in the hospital for two days. A rough way to learn to manage my time better. It's hard, because when I believe someone is sitting behind bars and shouldn't be, I want to get them out as fast as I can.

"But Tommy almost paid the price for me overworking myself, since I literally collapsed two weeks before our appeals court appearance. Now I make sure to take some time on weekends or evenings, work with my charities, or spend time with my friends or family. It's better for my clients, too, because I'm able to give the best of myself to their case."

"Did you find who did it?"

"Their neighbor. He was obsessed with her, had made several unwanted advances, would leave her gifts. He testified at the trial they'd been having an affair and Tommy killed her in a jealous rage. Everybody who knew them thought that was crazy. Tommy was the nicest guy, and she was wild about him. Very strong Christians. During a search of the house, the police discovered an application for a restraining order Tommy's wife had filled out against the neighbor, and we found it buried in the file from the DA's office. Evidence never provided to the defense, which got us a ruling of prosecutorial misconduct and Tommy a new trial."

"Prosecutorial misconduct is serious."

"I definitely got crosswise with the District Attorney who was in office at the time. Defense attorneys aren't their favorite people, anyway, especially doing what I do. But proving something that brought sanctions didn't bode well for my relationship with the DA's office."

"I can imagine."

"Anyway, to prepare for trial, I hired a pathology expert, and she noticed a strange wound in the autopsy photos. We exhumed the body, and she found a bite mark the coroner had passed off as a bruise. We took a set of impressions from Tommy and requested a court order for a set from the neighbor.

Even the State's expert agreed there was no doubt who it belonged to. The fact that it could have only been administered at the time of death was the clincher."

"Wow. What's Tommy doing now?"

"Went back to prison. He's actually the chaplain where Shane is. I gave him Shane's info, and he's been able to spend some time with him. Shane's also been going to the Sunday service. Anything to give him hope until I can get him out of there."

"You sound confident."

"I have to be. The idea of somebody rotting away for someone else's crime is almost more than I can bear."

He rubbed his fingers along the stubble on his chin, still not as certain as she seemed to be. But her earnest conviction was hard to discount. "Petersen has an investigative arm that works jointly with law enforcement and attorneys. We've worked with both defense and prosecution and provided expert testimony at trial. If we can help you with anything, let me know."

"Seriously?

"Seriously. If Everett truly is innocent, he needs to be free. Sounds like the best way to prove that is to find the true killer."

She nodded, but her eyes clouded. "I can't help but wonder if we've already seen him."

Chapter Twenty-One

"Colton."

He peered over his shoulder at the sound of Riley's voice from her office door. "What's up?"

She motioned him in. "I got another one."

"Another message?" He followed her to her desk, where a greeting card lay unopened on top of a stack of files.

"I recognized the writing, so I left it alone."

"Good thinking." He tapped his earpiece. "Trevor, ask Security to send us the video of whoever dropped a card off for Riley this morning. We need it ten minutes ago."

"On it," came the voice in his ear. "You want me to call Stapleton?"

"Affirmative. John will want to send a uniform to pick this up."

"Copy."

Riley looked up from the envelope. "I want to know what it says."

He hitched a brow. "Do you?"

"It can't be worse than what he did to my house."

"We'll have to wait for Stapleton to get it processed before it's opened." He consulted his watch. "Your meeting is in an hour, so if you have time, let's run through the previous three videos and compare them to the one Security's sending."

She picked up the phone from her desk. "Hallie, can you bring your laptop in here, please? And see if you can get two more."

"Will do."

He grinned down at her. "You should've been an investigator."

"I've done this kind of thing with our investigator many times. Easier to see them together side by side than to keep changing screens."

"Exactly. I'll have to take you on a tour of Tech Ops at Petersen sometime. Each station has a minimum of four monitors, and one entire wall is nothing but screens. Most of it's security footage from various locations, but also if we need several eyes on the same images."

Her face brightened. "I'd love that."

Hallie walked in carrying three laptops at the same time the email from Security popped into Riley's inbox. "Got it, Trevor. I'll be in Riley's office, but stand your post."

"Copy that."

Hallie set up the three laptops next to Riley's on the conference table, and after some forwarding of links, the four videos looped on separate screens.

"Need anything else?"

Riley shook her head. "Not for now, Hal. Thanks."

Hallie returned to her office as he and Riley leaned over her laptop. The man today had appeared as a courier, complete with satchel, skin-tight leggings, polarized wrap sunglasses, and a bike helmet over long, curly red hair.

Riley sat in a chair and studied the first image, then the second. "I wish we could zoom in. There's something on his right hand in each of these."

Colton bent over her and peered at the screen. Her signature oriental garden fragrance floated in the air around her, and he almost leaned closer to get more of it.

Focus. He needed to focus. The right hand. "I see it." He straightened and pulled out his phone. "I sent these to Tech Ops on Saturday." A voice answered at the other end. "Hey, Dillon, you still have the footage handy I shot you this weekend?"

"Of the ever-changing deliveryman?" Dillon tapped keys on his end. "Got it. What do you need?"

"Can you zero in on his right hand from last Monday, then from last Wednesday?"

More tapping ensued before it quieted again, as Dillon no doubt used his mouse to sharpen the image. "Got it. A bit blurry, but maybe a bandage of some sort. Wrapped all the way around."

Colton looked at Riley. "A bandage, he thinks. So same guy."

Standing, she jerked her head toward the third laptop with Friday's deliveryman. "But not on Friday. Can we get a closer look at the top of his hand?"

"Dill—"

"I heard her. Working on it now." Dillon hummed some unidentifiable tune while his fingers worked away. "Oh, wow. This guy's all scratched up. Like a cat got to him."

Colton's eyes caught on Riley's. "Or fingernails?"

"Yes. Could definitely be from fingernails. Appears scabbed over, which is probably why he didn't bandage it."

"Thanks, man. We know it's the same guy every day, then."

Riley sank back into the chair and stared at the first screen, her elbow on the table, hand covering her mouth.

"I'm sending you another video from this morning. Take a look and get back to me with anything you see that could be the real face or form of this guy. He's disguising himself, but let's see what's common in each of them. And send me some stills of the face, as close as you can get."

"Shoot it to me, and I'll get right on it."

Colton disconnected, then sent the link through his encrypted phone.

As Riley studied the image, now motionless on the screen, he took the chair next to her. She turned and their gazes locked.

"It's the creep," they said at the same time.

"But you left your mark on him. This is a big get, Ri. At least we know the person sending these notes is connected to your attack. And it's highly likely the notes are connected to the social media smear. All one guy."

"I'm so thankful y'all were checking social media. I know some people saw it and made comments, but hopefully nothing that will harm Shane's case."

Just like Riley. More worried about how any mark against her could affect someone else.

Her face tightened. "The call from Cait's sister was a surprise, though. That she would believe I ever had a thing going with Shane. I think her grief blinded her to the fact the girl in the photo was too tall to be me. Cait was a good four inches taller than me, and over six foot with heels. Shane is six-three. But I couldn't bring myself to tell her it was Cait's body in that image. It was better to let her vent. I can't even begin to understand the pain that family is in. And I'm contributing to it."

He reached for her hand and curled his fingers around hers. "Find the truth, and you'll be helping them. They just can't see that now."

"Still makes me angry that someone could use her image like that. How heartless do you have to be to put something like that out there?"

"I think it's clear we're not dealing with a stable person here. I'll ask John to put a man on the lobby in case another card comes this week. Or next, if we need to, since you're out of the office Thursday and Friday. Plainclothes. The guard at the desk can give him a signal, and then we've got him. This could be over by next week."

She regarded him for a long moment. "Next week."

He nodded. Then he'd leave her. Back to her life. And he'd go back to his.

In the house that would feel more empty than ever.

Chapter Twenty-Two

"That should wrap it up for tonight." Colton addressed his colleagues seated across the desk in the upstairs office Riley's father had invited them to use.

Trevor chuckled. "With as much as she's been working the past two days, this week's been a breeze compared to last."

That much was true. Other than going into the office yesterday and finding the fourth message, the rest of her time had been spent upstairs. Same thing today, except for her usual Tuesday Bible study and workout with the girls at the estate that morning.

"I guess we can be grateful we're not having to do any more last-minute prep."

A light knock sounded before the door opened and Riley poked her head inside. "Hey, you guys have a few minutes?"

Colton stood and waved her in. "Sure thing. We're done here."

She walked over to the desk. "I need to give you a revision to my schedule this week. Then, as far as I'm concerned, you can take off for the night. I'm not going anywhere."

Spoke too soon and jinxed it. Colton held back his sigh as he took his seat again in the buttery soft leather office chair. Hopefully, this change wouldn't constitute another late night of prep for a spur-of-the-moment outing.

"What's this revision?"

Her smile turned shy, uncertain, which piqued his interest even more. "I need to add an event on Friday."

"Please tell me we're not going Black Friday shopping."

She giggled, and he couldn't help grinning back. "No, I would never torture you guys like that. This is something I've spent the last few days setting up. I wanted to do it before Christmas, but the last piece didn't fall into place until about a half-hour ago."

"No problem," Paul said. "I'll take anything over Black Friday shopping."

"I've been doing some research and making a bunch of calls, and I've started a new non-profit."

"Another one?" Colton sat up in disbelief. "How many jobs do you need?"

"I'm actually hoping somebody else will chair the board instead of me. It needs to be someone who will give it direction, instill a sense of purpose in it, otherwise it will fail. And I think it's too important to let it go by the wayside."

"So, what are we doing Friday?" Colton's brain was already going over what details they needed to start working on.

"Spending the day at Houston Med. To test for potential bone marrow donors."

Colton caught the quick glances of his coworkers in his periphery, but he couldn't quit staring at Riley. "Bone marrow? This is your new charity?"

"A new non-profit. I spent a lot of time online Saturday night, or I guess I should say Sunday morning, and found there are thousands of patients waiting for bone marrow transplants. Most of the time, the donor comes from one's own family, but that's not always possible. And from what I found in my research and speaking to some experts in the field, it's alarming how many people are waiting for a donor. Unlike most other transplants, the donor doesn't have to die to donate. Nobody should die waiting for a transplant."

Colton sat for a moment, his blood roaring in his ears. "And why in such a hurry?"

"It can take a few weeks for the test to be processed, then the donor has to undergo more testing, and then a five-day regimen of injections to increase stem cells in their blood. I thought if we could at least do the cheek swab tests now, someone might get the gift of hope for Christmas. Hope that their new life can start after the New Year."

Colton stood and walked over to the mantel, staring into the cold fireplace, silence filling the room. "You did this for Theresa. Because of Theresa."

"I did this for the living. As a tribute to Theresa."

He turned back to her. "Why? Why'd you do that?"

She stepped closer to him as Paul and Trevor stood and left the room. "I was so moved by your story. It's heartbreaking to think of someone so young and vibrant losing her life waiting for a donor. There are probably half a dozen people walking around who would have been a perfect match for her, but they didn't know it. Because they weren't tested. Because they didn't know somebody was in dire need of what they possess. I've never thought twice about my marrow. I've never even thought once about it. But what if there's somebody out there dying and my marrow is a match? How can I not give it to them?"

He stared at her, lost in those green eyes imploring him to understand.

"Please don't be upset with me."

"Upset? Riley, I'm not upset. I'm flabbergasted. You did in three days what I haven't done in four years. I never made the effort to ensure that what happened to her didn't happen to anybody else. I tell you about it, and within minutes, you're trying to fix it."

She shook her head. "It's not about me. It's about meeting a need because we can. Because we're able. I've established a lot of connections through my other organizations, so I started by reaching out and asking questions. I prayed hard about it after I went back up to bed that night we talked, and God started opening doors. I was even surprised at how fast it all came about."

"Fast is an understatement. Five days from our talk to actually running a donation drive? That's … astounding."

"Like I said. I have an incredible network. It wasn't all me, not by a long shot. Lend a Hand will sponsor the foundation until we get non-profit status, then I want to call it the Theresa Blankenship Foundation for Bone Marrow Matching. But I wanted to get your permission first. And I'd like for you to serve as board chairman. It needs someone who has a passion for it. I think that's you."

A lump took form in his throat. "I'd be proud to serve if you'll guide me until I get the hang of it. And Theresa would be honored to have her name on something created to make a difference. Something that might have saved her life if only somebody like you had come into it."

"She had you. I'm sure that was enough."

Before he'd given a thought to his actions, he reached out and wrapped her in his arms, holding her close and putting his lips close to her ear. "Thank you." He somehow pushed the words past the thickness in his throat.

"Thank you for letting me do this."

He held her in silence for a moment, closing his eyes against the onslaught of unfamiliar emotion that tightened his chest. He hadn't cried in three years. Not since the first anniversary of Theresa's death. Once he got himself put back together after several long, hard weeks, he'd held himself in check ever since.

Now he wasn't sure he had it in him to push back. Not with Riley holding him so tight, her arms clutched around him with her hands gliding up his back.

What was happening? His heart beat hard against his sternum, and a coil of warmth from the pit of his stomach circled outward. He'd only experienced this once before, many years ago, as a sophomore in college who suddenly realized his boyhood chum wasn't one of the guys but a beautiful woman. He'd been falling in love and suffered from all the requisite symptoms of that particular malady.

But he certainly wasn't now.

No. Impossible. This was simply a man who hadn't been near a woman in far too long, holding one who was lovely, inside and out. Its name was loneliness. Gratitude. Maybe a little attraction. But certainly not love.

Someone cleared their throat from the doorway, and he let her go, swiping at his face before turning. "Yeah, Paul?"

"Sorry to interrupt. Riley, Avery's here. In your suite."

"Thanks." She glanced at Colton again before stepping out of the room.

He sank slowly into the leather loveseat in front of the fireplace. "Can you believe that?"

"She's a pistol." Paul took a seat in the armchair adjacent to the loveseat. "But if I can ask, how did she know about Theresa?"

"I told her. Saturday night. We split a sandwich the other night when neither of us could sleep, and she asked about the blonde in the picture on my wall."

A crease appeared in Paul's forehead. "Wait a minute. She was at your place?"

Colton winced. Hadn't meant to let that slip. "Saturday afternoon. Before we found the mess at her house. I needed to pack up some clothes, so we stopped there first. Mack was aware."

"Mack was? Huh. I would have never expected that from you, taking a principal to your home."

"Probably wasn't one of my brighter ideas." Except would there be a foundation in Theresa's name now, all because Riley saw that picture? Could this all be of some divine direction?

"Which is exactly what worries me about this thing."

Colton popped his head back. "What thing?"

"This … thing," he answered, waving his hand between Colton and the door. "Between you and Riley." He leaned forward, bracing his elbows on his knees with his hands folded between them. "Riley's a beautiful, smart, articulate woman with a great sense of compassion for her fellow man. I know she was a surprise to you. She was to all of us, and we've all come to respect her. Very much."

"Cut to the chase, Paul."

He took a deep breath and let it out. "Maybe you've crossed the line here. Maybe you're too close."

"We've all been on assignments where we were positioned inside the principal's home."

"I don't mean in proximity alone."

He stared at his long-time friend and co-worker. "You think I'm falling for her."

"I think you might be on your way. It's certain she has for you."

"In little more than a week?" That couldn't be. None of it. "I don't think so."

"A week of spending practically every waking minute together. Even in the middle of the night, apparently."

"Nothing to see here, Jamison. Riley has a need to fix what's wrong. This thing with the bone marrow is simply because she can't stand the thought of anybody else dying waiting for a transplant." He swallowed and turned his attention to the fireplace. "And you know my opinion about getting involved with a principal. You're way off base, my friend."

Paul shrugged and stood again. "Okay. You know I would never question your professionalism, unless I believed it endangered our client."

"Duly noted."

While he didn't agree with it, he appreciated his co-worker's candor. Because if anything happened to another woman on his watch, he'd never be able to live with the guilt.

Not again.

Chapter Twenty-Three

"I guess we should get down to business." Sitting in the chair next to Riley's desk, Avery fairly glowed.

Riley returned her beaming smile. "Guess we should. But I'm happy for you, Ave. I truly am. John's terrific."

Riley had spent the last five minutes listening to her friend gush about her first kiss from her new beau and how wonderful it was to find such a fine man of God after praying for one for so long. It gave Riley hope that one day, she too might find her soulmate.

"That's an understatement. But you'd better not get me started again, or we'll never get this publicity blitz planned for your new project. Okay. Media. I assume you want print ads …"

"Check."

"Radio spots …"

"Check."

"Flyers until we get the brochures done?"

"Check."

"What about television?"

"You tell me. You're the marketing expert. Do we have time?"

"This already being Tuesday, it could be a challenge. But I'll do a press release, and we might be able to get you on one or two of the local newscasts. Maybe a morning show or two."

"That would be terrific."

"I'll fax the release out first thing in the a.m."

"It's almost eight, Avery, and you're still going to work on this tonight?"

"Absolutely. We all are. What you're doing here is phenomenal. Babs should have your papers together to file tomorrow for your non-profit status, and Fran said she'd have the logo to me tonight, along with the graphic design for the brochures I'm sending out."

"You guys are the best. What on earth would I do without you?"

She prayed she'd never have to find out. All three of her friends had known since Sunday afternoon what she'd been working on and jumped on board from the first minute. During a conference call right before she went down to talk to the guys, they'd wrapped up the final pieces. Avery said she'd come over since she was out already, anyway. At dinner. With her dreamy detective.

So, while Avery still appeared every inch the put-together professional, Riley had wasted no time in changing into an oversized sweatshirt and jeans after work.

"We're a team. Always have been, always will be." Avery put her notebook into her large handbag. "Anything else we haven't covered?"

Riley scanned over the spreadsheet on her laptop. "I think we've got it." She turned back to her friend. "And thanks for sharing your good news with me. If I can't have a sizzling love life myself, I at least get to live it vicariously through you and Frances."

Avery harrumphed. "You absolutely need to let Graham

know what's what, friend of mine. Please. You are way too much woman for that … man."

"Good girl." Riley chuckled. "I was worried about what you were going to say there."

"Just sayin'. The longer you wait, the more he's going to think of you as a couple. And you can't move on to the bigger, better thing you have waiting until you do."

"What thing?"

Avery gave her a sardonic look. "You know, Ri, you don't play dumb very well. I mean that hunk of a bodyguard of yours."

Riley glanced up at her door, grateful she'd remembered to close it. "Please, Avery, not this again."

"Tell me you don't feel anything for him. Going to all this trouble because of the pain he suffered losing someone who didn't get a transplant in time. This has *lovestruck* written all over it."

Riley's stomach knotted, and she prayed Colton wasn't of the same opinion. That could get … awkward. "I am not *lovestruck*. It made me sad listening to what happened to his … to Theresa. And when I did some checking, it seemed to me I could do something."

"You can't even say it."

"Say what?"

"His *wife*."

"Okay. His wife. It's sad his wife died so young when she didn't need to. I want to help others not to suffer the same fate."

"Is he going to chair the board?"

"He said he'd be proud to."

"Of course he would be. It's a huge compliment you asked him. That you did all of this for him."

"Avery." She shook her head. "I didn't do this for Colton."

"Okay, okay. I'll drop it. And I'd better go so I can get started on all this." Avery closed her laptop, slipped it into her bag, and stood. "I'll talk to you tomorrow to bring you up to speed and let you know about news and radio spots."

"Thanks, Avery." Riley stood to walk her friend downstairs. "I know doing this all so quickly is a huge ordeal, but I wanted to get some donors tested before the holidays. How cool would it be to get a bone marrow transplant for Christmas? It would be like getting a new life."

"It certainly would be."

They reached the top of the stairs, and Colton came out of the study. "Hey, Avery, you taking off?"

"Yep. A lot to do to get this off the ground. But I'm excited to be involved, and we appreciate you being willing to chair the board."

"It's an honor. I'll walk you out."

Avery threw a questioning glance at Riley.

"I'm not allowed to go to the door," she explained with a roll of her eyes.

"Ah. I see. Then, I'll talk to you tomorrow."

Riley returned her friend's hug. "Tomorrow."

She waited until Colton and Avery had gone, then made her way back to her suite. Sitting at her desk, she stared at the screen on her laptop. She needed to get started on the work she'd brought home from the office—go over the interviews her investigator had gathered from the defense witnesses, read over the depositions of the responding officers who found Shane, shocked and despondent, with Caitlyn's blood all over him.

Instead, she found her mind wandering back to the upstairs study—back in Colton's arms. The way he'd held her—so tight yet tender against him, his chin resting on her head. She'd never been so aware of a man before. His scent, a combination of musk and that earthiness one carried after going about business for the day. The fabric of his dress shirt against her cheek, softness covering the hardness of his chest.

He'd been touched by what she'd done. Surprised, a little

unnerved, maybe. Emotional. She tried not to get lost in his embrace but had conceded defeat the second her cheek laid against him. It had been a thank you, a gesture of appreciation, gratitude. Nothing more.

If only she could convince her runaway imagination.

Chapter Twenty-Four

This could be over next week.

Riley gave her head a shake to chase Colton's words from her mind, where they'd ricocheted around the last three days. Focusing instead on the older woman on the other side of the glass, she smiled as she handed her a plate. "Happy Thanksgiving."

The woman wouldn't meet her eyes. Riley's heart squeezed. Nobody should spend their later years like this. Nobody should spend *any* of their years like this. No place to call their own. Wearing the same clothes for days on end. Not knowing if they'll eat that day. Or the next.

She took the plate Colton passed her, put a hot roll on top of the turkey slices, and handed it to the man next in line. "Happy Thanksgiving."

"This sure looks good," he said with a gap-toothed grin. "Thank you kindly."

As he walked away, she shifted her weight from one foot to the other and peered out over the room. She'd worn tennis shoes since she would be on her feet most of the day, but exhaustion pulled on her limbs. Everything ached. Probably from tossing and turning so much the last twelve days.

The volume had increased as more showed up for their free meal, the comforting aromas of baked turkey, fresh bread, stuffing, and mashed potatoes with gravy diluting the odor of so many bodies in one place. The shelter had offered the use of their shower facilities to everybody who showed up for a meal today. Someday, maybe they'd even have enough beds for them all.

She grinned at a little girl clutching a doll with a smudged face and held out the child-sized plate Colton handed her. "Here you go, sweetie. Let me know if you want seconds. There's plenty." Her wink at least brought a hint of a smile, but her heart ached for the child now walking under the protective arm of her father to a table. A family of four. Mother, father, the little girl, and an older boy. All without a home.

So incongruous to the place she'd return to today to celebrate the holiday with family and friends. If only there were more she could do.

This could be over next week.

The possibility brought a puzzling mixture of hope and dread. In a matter of days, this could all be behind her. The townhome would have to be sold. She might need sleep, but she would never again lay her head down under that roof. A real estate agent had already been contacted and would list it after the holidays. She'd move anything salvageable to storage and stay at the estate until she could find a new place.

She'd love to get back behind the wheel of her little BMW sports coupe, but she would miss the banter with the guys during their time in the SUV. And while she'd like to go about her business without wondering if another note might come, or another call with that blood-curdling altered voice, she took comfort whenever she looked up from her work and found

Colton standing outside her office or walking up and down the hall.

A nudge to her arm brought her gaze snapping up to the man beside her. "You're holding up the line, Hudson."

She chuckled at his teasing wink. "Sorry." She took the next plate, served the roll, and passed it on with her usual "Happy Thanksgiving."

"Take a break if you need it. They have folks to cover for us."

"I'm fine."

Sort of. Along with Colton's confident statement of how soon she would no longer need them, need *him*, she couldn't stop thinking about the last note. John had sent Colton a picture of the open card after the envelope had been processed. A picture she'd badgered him into sharing with her.

> *My dear Miss Hudson,*
> *Your confidence is going to be the death of you. Don't get too comfortable with your goons. They're only human, after all. Dispensable. You'd be surprised how easily.*
> *See you soon. Very soon.*

Colton hadn't appeared the least bit concerned by the not-so-veiled threat. *Dispensable?* What did that mean? That the creep could do something to her guys? Harm them in some way? Or worse, take them out? She couldn't live with herself if something happened to any of them on her behalf.

Colton gestured for the kitchen manager. "Can we give Miss Hudson a quick break?"

Riley grabbed his arm. "No, I'm fine."

He glanced over his shoulder. "No. You're not. Fifteen minutes and you can come back."

The woman nodded. "Yes, take some time. You haven't stopped since you got here."

She waved at two men seated at a table nearby, and they

made their way to the kitchen door, manned by one of the additional Petersen security operatives provided for the event, since it would've been impossible to vet everybody. Paul and Trevor had both been posted at the entrance since they got there, checking coats and bags for weapons, as well as comparing each face to the close-up images from the security videos for anything familiar.

Riley, too, had been studying all the men around his height who came through the line, her focus going to their hands before their faces. So far, nothing. No scratches or bandages.

Her nerves hummed like live wires. Maybe Colton was right. A break might be good.

Aproned up now, their two subs took their place, and she followed Colton to a room behind the kitchen designated as a break room for the volunteers.

He led her by the elbow to a rectangular metal collapsible table. "Sit. I'll grab us some coffee."

Giving in instead of arguing seemed like the better bet. "Thanks."

At the counter, he poured coffee into two Styrofoam cups, doctored his with sugar, and brought them back with two creamers and a packet of sweetener for her. "Not exactly your preferred Americano, but hopefully it'll perk you up."

"I'm sorry I kept drifting off. I don't usually have such a hard time focusing. I love this event."

He pulled up a chair next to her. "You're exhausted, Riley. In every way."

Thankful they were alone in the small room with the wall heater puffing out air full blast, she poured one creamer and the sweetener into her cup. "How do you do it?" She took a sip and let the bitter liquid slide down her throat.

After taking a hearty swallow of coffee, he winced and set the cup down on the table. "That stuff is terrible."

"The worst. But I'll take it."

"So, how do I do what?"

"Work with so little sleep."

He shrugged. "I have to admit, the first couple of days on your detail were a bit brutal. But I'd just flown in on Saturday evening from London, so I had a bad case of jet lag."

"What?" Her jaw dropped. "Why did Mack put you on my detail so fast, then? You should've taken a break."

"I guess he had faith I could handle it."

"Handle it." Her gaze narrowed. "The night we met in Dad's study, he said you guys were the best he had. Is that why you got stuck with me? Because you're the best?"

"Riley." The look he gave her was the same one she remembered from her childhood, when her mother would shake her head and press her lips together at some new mischief Riley had delved into. "We're not *stuck* with you. In fact, I was under the impression you felt it was the other way around." He brought the cup back to his mouth. "That's how I remember it, anyhow." After taking another swallow, he grimaced. "This is worse than the sludge Mack keeps in his office."

She laughed and passed him the extra creamer he'd brought to the table.

He shook his head. "This is beyond help. How can you keep drinking it?"

"I guess I'm desperate for the caffeine infusion." She took a swallow and forced it down. It really was awful. Had probably been sitting in the pot for hours. "I'm sorry you had to come onto my detail without getting some rest first. And especially for not letting you guys know my schedule earlier and throwing all that work on you."

"That was my fault. Not yours. I had your file in my hands Saturday before I ever set foot at the estate. I just didn't look at it."

Somehow, that pricked at her a little. He really had judged her as shallow and entitled. Not even worth a look at her file.

His expression turned contrite. "Sorry. That sounded bad."

"Sounded truthful. I like that about you. You're always honest with me."

"But not always in the most polite way. I was wrong about you from the first moment. I apologize for being so short-sighted."

"Forgiven. And I'm sorry I called you cocky. And tactical gear."

"Both descriptions I wear proudly."

She giggled and finished off her coffee. "Okay, I'm ready to get back to work."

Standing, she pulled at the vest she'd been instructed to wear under her sweater for the day. *Soft body armor,* Colton had called it. The same thing they wore under their shirts with their suits whenever they were out. She hadn't even known they were wearing body armor until he told her a couple of days into her detail. He sure hadn't been wearing one at the Cantrells'. As close as she'd been to him on the dance floor, she would've been aware of it. Apparently, they'd been satisfied with all the extra security that night and left the body armor behind.

"How do you guys wear these every day? It's like a corset."

"You get used to it. I'm not even aware of mine anymore. Not that I know what a corset feels like."

"Me, either, but I would imagine something like this."

He stood and reached for her cup. "Only a couple more hours until you're home and can take it off. But I want you in it every time we're going to be in public. No arguments."

"Yes, sir." She threw him her best stink-eye, but it bounced off him like a bullet to his *soft body armor.*

"Maybe after your family dinner, you can kick back and relax."

"Definitely the plan."

The door opened and Trevor peered in. "There you are. We have someone out here who might be our guy."

Her pulse skipped. "Really? Here right now?"

"Going through the line as we speak. Scratched-up hand. You up to take a look and see what you think?"

"Absolutely." Either the caffeine kicked in or her adrenaline spiked. This could be it. Could be the moment she would come face to face with the man in her nightmares. Either way, her heart raced like a bomb ticking down the last few seconds before detonation.

Colton's expression hardened back into protector mode as he preceded her and Trevor out to the kitchen. "Which one?"

Trevor turned his back to the line. "Red beard, stringy hair, black coat, too-big glasses. You see him?"

Riley eyed the man Trevor had described, her breath catching when he looked up and caught her staring. Her gaze snapped back to Trevor as her heart fell. "Not him."

"You're sure?"

She nodded. "The eyes are wrong."

"How can you know?"

"Because I looked straight into those eyes that day, and I'll never forget them. Besides, that's a fairly new injury. Not scratches almost two weeks old. He's not the guy."

Colton put his hands on his hips. "She's right. Back to posts. We keep looking."

Looking for the hunter before the hunter found her.

Chapter Twenty-Five

"That was intense." Colton climbed into the SUV and snapped his seatbelt, relieved to be getting Riley back to the safety of the Hudson estate. Then it was off to his parents' for Thanksgiving leftovers and football.

Paul pulled onto the freeway. "Sure kept us on our toes. I was watching hands like crazy."

"It'll be nice to let down a little. Hope the folks saved me a huge plate, because I'm starving." He looked at Riley. "You promise you won't be leaving again today?"

A grin crossed her face. "Oh, absolutely. I want you guys to enjoy some time with your families, so don't worry about me."

As if he could help it. Still, he couldn't wait to spend some downtime with the family. And as long as Riley was safely tucked away at the estate, she would be fine.

"Okay, but I'll be back later tonight."

"I'm not worried."

She pulled out her phone and typed out a text. A week ago, her *I've-got-a-secret* grin would've put him on alert. But now she was much too aware of the danger that lurked outside the Hudson gate.

As the SUV continued down the interstate, Paul taking one exit, driving along the feeder road, then taking the next freeway entrance to determine if they were being followed, Colton put his head back and closed his eyes. The tension of the day slowly ebbed from his shoulders as he relaxed into the leather interior.

"Wow!" Trevor's exclamation jolted him upright as they pulled through the gate and made their way toward the house. "I don't think I've seen so many limos in one place since the Oscars."

"You got to cover the Oscars?" Paul asked.

"Last year. Blankenship and I were hired for an actor who lives here in Houston. He wasn't a nominee, but we got to walk the red carpet. That was kind of cool."

Colton threw Riley a glance. "I didn't know you were expecting guests today."

"Trust me." There was that grin again. Like a little girl with something she was dying to tell. "I'm perfectly safe with these guests. But I'm sure you'll all want to come inside to check it out."

"Absolutely." And he'd probably have to let his family know he wouldn't be there, after all. With this many people at the estate, how could they know for sure their man of many disguises hadn't found a way in?

Paul pulled up to the steps leading to the front door to drop them off before he took the SUV to the garage. Colton came around to open her door, taking her hand to help her out as he'd always done. But when she smiled up at him, his irritation at not being alerted to today's festivities dissipated into the brisk November air.

If he had to miss Thanksgiving with his family, he couldn't think of another he'd rather be with for the holiday. Maybe he'd let himself get drawn in a little more than he usually did, but it was impossible to spend the amount of time they'd spent with Riley and not be her friend. It was as if she wouldn't stand for it.

If she was going to be anywhere near you for any length of time, she was going to get inside.

And she had. More than anybody before her, besides the woman he'd married.

In the house, the din of dozens of voices talking all at once and music emanating from speakers in the family room mingled with the enticing aroma of whatever five-star-quality dishes Hilda had prepared. After taking Riley's coat and hanging it with his in the closet, they walked through an arched entryway to the family room.

Colton stopped short. "What on earth?"

Riley turned and smiled up at them. "Happy Thanksgiving, you guys. Trevor, Gemma and the rest of your family should be here somewhere. Colton, yours—"

"Colton, my boy!" The booming voice from the middle of the room could belong to only one person.

"—are here too." She finished with a chuckle.

Sure enough, his still distinguished, gray-haired father appeared from the milling guests and walked toward them with Colton's striking ash blonde mother.

"What are you doing here?" he asked his parents.

His dad stood smiling at Riley while his mother gave him a hug. "You must be Miss Hudson."

"Yes, sir. Call me Riley."

"Fred Blankenship. And this beautiful woman here is my wife, Evelyn. Lisa and the kids are out in the gym, and Micah's planted in front of the football games. You have a beautiful home here."

Colton couldn't seem to engage but instead stood there and stared like he'd never set eyes on any of them before. But then, his professional life had never collided head-on with his personal one before, and he was still reeling from the impact.

"Actually, I don't live here." Riley apparently had no problem finding her words. "Only until I find a new place. I don't plan to go back to mine longer than it takes to pack it up."

"Oh?"

"Long story, Dad." Colton's brain finally caught up to what his eyes were seeing. "But, again, what are you doing here? I thought you were just going to keep a plate for me."

"Your Riley here gave us a call last week and asked if we'd be interested in having our family dinner with hers, so you could have Thanksgiving with your own. Took us about half a second to accept. Private car picked us up and the whole nine yards."

"That's so … nice."

And so Riley.

Her laughter did that thing to his pulse that had him thinking a check-up might be in order. "We had to use two different car services to have enough vehicles to get everybody here. Wanted to make y'all feel special."

His father gave her a wink. "It worked. We felt like celebrities."

"As you should. I hope you're all being well taken care of. I apologize we were longer at the shelter than we intended. We've planned our family Thanksgiving for the evening since we started serving down there several years ago."

"Early, late. Doesn't matter. And your family has been taking extremely good care of us."

"Riley, honey." Candace strolled up to them, her usual smile in place.

"Hi, Mom. Thanks for welcoming all my guests."

"Of course. Where's Paul?"

"Right here." Paul appeared at her side, his bewildered gaze raking the bustling room.

"Paul, your lovely wife and little boy are with Alex and Delia upstairs. They should be down momentarily. Your mother is out in the greenhouse—my dad loves showing off his flowers and found a kindred spirit in your mom—and I believe your father is upstairs in the media room."

"They're here?"

"Riley arranged it. She wanted you boys to share the holiday with your families. And we were only too happy to comply."

"Wow. That was really thoughtful."

Riley blushed again and glanced over at Colton. He must look like an idiot, but he couldn't stop staring at this woman who apparently knew no limits.

"I hated the idea of you guys being stuck with me on a holiday. So, the day after the fundraiser at the Cantrells', I called Mack to tell him what I wanted to do. I was delighted he finally relented and gave me all the phone numbers. I simply told him I doubted you would sue him for allowing me to arrange for your families to have a gourmet Thanksgiving dinner. Then, of course, extending him an invitation as well."

Candace craned her neck. "Yes, Mack and his family are here somewhere too. Now, you all have strict instructions to enjoy the rest of the day. Riley's perfectly safe here, so you guys are officially off-duty. No weapons allowed at the table."

Trevor chuckled. "Maybe we should ask Mack about that."

"Mack's on board. You can secure them in the study, out of the way of children. The gate is closed, and our regular detail is covering the cameras in shifts so they can eat. Nobody's getting onto the estate who shouldn't be here."

Colton inclined his head toward her. "Yes, ma'am. We'll take care of it."

Once they'd left their firearms in the locked study, Colton returned to the family room. A buffet of appetizers and drinks had been set out on the heated veranda, children of various ages and sizes ran throughout the rooms, and people stood in groups he'd have never expected, visiting like old friends.

He caught sight of his sister and her kids walking in the door from the veranda laughing with Sadie, Riley's sister-in-law, and her daughter. His mother and Candace stood chatting like they'd known each other for years, and Trevor's mother sat with a woman he remembered from Barbara's birthday party the previous week. Avery's socialite mom?

And then there was Detective John Stapleton and Riley's brother Kevin moving quickly down from the screening room to the buffet table and back up again.

He located Riley, now with her friends on the other side of the room. She peered over her shoulder, her eyes meeting his across the expanse as she sent him one of those smiles that warmed his insides.

A hand clapped him on the shoulder from behind. "A little thunderstruck, son?"

He pulled his attention from the petite dynamo across the room to his father beside him. "I am a little, I guess. Riley definitely does not operate between the lines."

His dad gave him a little shake. "Come on. Let's get some appetizers and head upstairs to catch some football."

Colton glanced at Riley and back to his dad. "Sure. I guess she's all right."

After grabbing some finger foods and a soda from the buffet, he and his dad made their way to the media room upstairs, where three football games played at once on separate screens. The one in the middle had the sound turned up, the two on either side muted. Several men, and even a couple of ladies, sat comfortably in rows of fat, cushioned recliners with beverage holders built into the arms, while others stood in the back.

Although living in such extravagance was foreign to him, he could definitely get used to having a room outfitted with multiple large-screen televisions and seating for all his buddies. He wasn't sure sitting on the sofa in front of his flat screen at home, clicking between channels to check various scores, would suffice after this.

Riley's oldest brother walked up to him. "Colton."

"Alex. Quite the day."

"It always is, with the shelter dinner, then ours. Although my sister has outdone herself this year." Alex's laughter matched his eyes. Brown, like Drew and Kevin, as opposed to deep emerald like his sister and mother. "We saw y'all at the shelter dinner, but you looked pretty busy, so we thought it best to stay out of your way."

"Busy's an understatement. Having an extra detail along with us was huge. Too many things to watch at the same time."

Alex's expression sobered. "I can't believe it's come to this. That we'd have to be concerned about somebody hurting Riley. *Riley.* Of all people. The woman who would give the coat off her back in the middle of a blizzard if she thought someone needed it more." He shook his head. "I don't get it."

"I don't either. Only thing I can figure is it's either her station or her work."

Alex's brow furrowed. "Her social station, I understand. But her work?"

"She gets people off who were convicted of horrible crimes. I'm sure, even with all of that evidence, there are folks who refuse to see the truth. She said she gets letters sometimes from family members or loved ones of victims who think she's on the wrong side. Could be somebody out for revenge."

"Threatening letters?"

"She didn't indicate they were, but who knows? Then again, it could be straight-up stalker."

Kevin's wife Sadie walked in to announce dinner was ready to be served.

Alex put his hand on Colton's shoulder. "We'd better head down, but I wanted to say thanks for all you and your guys are doing for my sister. If there's anything we can do for you, for any of you, please let us know."

"Thanks. It's an honor to do everything we can for Riley. She's ... special."

Alex grinned as they sauntered down the hall with a dozen other guys, including Drew and Dad still discussing the Houston Texans last touchdown. "She is that. Now she just needs to set ol' Harding straight."

Colton chuckled. "An odd pairing if I've seen one."

"She felt sorry for him after a failed relationship and didn't realize until it was too late he'd decided theirs was the real deal. Now she doesn't know how to get out of it without hurting him again. That's all according to Delia. Girl talk and all that."

They rounded the bottom of the stairs and moved into the living room, where several tables dressed in fall finery had been set up for the day's feast. "I've only seen the man once, but when we vetted him, there wasn't a whole lot on his background aside from his financial history. Not a lot of substance."

"She'll come to her senses." Alex stopped at the table designated for the Blankenship family. "And hopefully find someone more deserving of her." He held out his hand, and Colton took it in a firm shake. "Glad your family could be here with us today. Enjoy your dinner."

"Yes. You too."

As Alex walked away, Colton panned the room and the guests taking their places behind their chairs to wait for grace to be said and the line to start through the mile-long buffet. His eyes met Riley's across the room, and everything else faded into the background. The conversations taking place around him, children's laughter … all drowned out by the beating of his heart.

Kevin said something to her, and she pulled her focus away, shattering the spell. Giving his head a shake, Colton turned back to the table and stared down at the china plate waiting to be filled.

He was in uncharted territory here. He'd been immune to the charms of other women who had tried to get his attention for four years now. On purpose. Yet in mere days, this woman—

this one small, silken-haired, doe-eyed beauty—had managed to get under his skin like nobody had in … well, that nobody ever had.

Being with Theresa had been simple. They'd been friends forever before settling into marriage. No skyrockets or fireworks. It was comfortable … uncomplicated.

Until it wasn't. A gunshot wound and arduous, four-month-long recovery, followed by infertility, and then cancer had tried them to their very souls. But they'd been in it together to the tragic end. After which he'd told himself never again. He'd never again bind himself to someone so closely that life could be that painful. That he could be left so bereft at the end of it.

So, how, in less than two weeks, had Riley Hudson managed to penetrate his steel-plated heart? To get inside him, get him to open up, confess things to her, make him feel things he'd never wanted to again?

It didn't matter that she was a beautiful, fun-loving, smart, caring woman any man would be blessed to be with. She had no place in his life. In his heart. None. He had to get that straight. Or he was of no use to her in the one way, the only way, he could be.

He needed to protect her. Take care of her. Keep her alive.

And then leave her.

Chapter Twenty-Six

With a sigh, Riley sank into the wine-colored sofa in the family room after the last of their guests had made their way out to the black cars waiting in the drive. "What a wonderful day."

Her mother smiled and took a seat on the other end of the couch. "It most certainly was. You did a good thing here today, sweetie. Just like always."

"It was the only thing to do. When I found out my guys had to be with me all day and go home to leftovers, how could I not bring their families to them?"

"Most people wouldn't have done that. You're a very special lady, daughter of mine."

"If I am, I come by it naturally. You're the one who taught me how important it is to give back. To never take what we have for granted, but to use it to better the world we live in. I got that from you."

Mom stared at her for a moment. "How are you, honey? Holding up all right?"

Shrugging, she stared down at her hands crossed over her stomach as she sat slouched down into the cushions, the fingers of her left hand again twisting her ring. Around and around. Like the images in her brain. "If I don't think about it, I do great. But the nights are the worst. I can't sleep, and when I do, it's only until the nightmare wakes me up again."

"Oh, honey, I'm so sorry you haven't been sleeping. I'm sure you're praying about it?"

"All the time. And while my heart knows God's in control, my head keeps reminding me there's somebody out there watching me. Somebody who wants me *dead*. I don't understand that. What could I have done that someone doesn't even want me on this earth?"

Looking away, she shook her head. "Truth is, I didn't even know that until Colton made me realize what was going on. That morning at the table was the first time I truly understood. When I remembered that the attack wasn't random but targeted. Now, every time I'm away from here, I'm watching like crazy. Today was the first time I couldn't let down and enjoy the shelter dinner as much as I have in the past. I was jumpy and distracted. Colton even made me take a break because my mind kept drifting."

"Colton's a good man. I know he didn't mean to scare you. He just wanted you to see what was happening. To not hold anything back from him."

"I know. And he is a good man. A very good man."

Mom's gaze went to the stairs and back. "Where is he right now? I haven't seen him since his family left."

"He took his parents home instead of them going back in the hired car. I think he misses them."

"That's understandable, doing what he does. Probably takes him away quite a bit."

Riley pulled off her tennis shoes and curled her legs up onto the sofa. "He told me today he'd just flown in from London the same night he started on my detail. How crazy is that? He's like a machine."

Mom laughed, kicking off her shoes to put her feet up on the coffee table. "I don't know about that. He has too much heart to be anything but human."

"Very true."

He'd proved it in the way he'd taken care of her Saturday morning after her memory had literally made her sick. In the way he'd protected her after they found her house wrecked. In the way he'd treated the folks at the shelter today, and in the care he'd shown her when she couldn't keep her focus on the task at hand.

She sighed. "What a neat family. I'm glad we got to meet them."

"They're very special. Easy to see why Colton's the man he is." Mom regarded her for a moment. "What do you think of Colton, Riley?"

Her pulse raced. "I just told you. I think he's a good man. And great at his job."

"I see. That's all?"

Laughing, Riley sat up, leaning forward with her elbows on her knees. "I think he's a major hunk, if that's what you're getting at. And those eyes. He has the most intensely blue eyes I've ever seen. But other than having a whopper of a crush on the guy, he's my bodyguard. That's all I can think of him. He's very much out of my league."

Mom tilted her head, her brow furrowed. "In what way?"

"Every way. He's very serious and probably thinks I'm too laid back. He's worked hard for the things he has and the things he's accomplished, and I know he feels I've been handed everything on a silver platter. And he prefers blondes. I don't think I'd look so great as a blonde."

"Don't change a thing about yourself. Not for anyone."

"I wouldn't. Not even for a very cute bodyguard-type person. Besides, he isn't looking. Doesn't have any intention of ever being involved with anyone again. Not after losing his wife."

"I don't know, honey. Everybody can have a change of heart. Maybe he just hasn't met the one who can make him want to change his."

Riley looked down at her hands in her lap. "Precisely."

"Or maybe he just doesn't know it yet." Mom rose and walked over to kiss her cheek. "Good night, sweetheart."

"Good night, Mom. Love you."

"Love you more," Mom replied as she started up the stairs.

Maybe he just doesn't know it yet.

Could that be true? Was there any reason to hope he might one day see her as something other than a job? A body to be guarded?

Sighing, she sat back into the cushions, hands clasped over her stomach as she gazed up at the beamed ceiling. No. It was doubtful she had what it took to turn his head. To change his mind about his resolve. It would have to be someone truly special.

As special as Theresa.

Chapter Twenty-Seven

By all appearances, some would definitely receive the gift of hope for Christmas.

Colton did another pass down the line of folks waiting in the hospital corridor to register for the bone marrow donor drive. Once they'd completed the necessary paperwork and signed the authorizations, they would have their cheek swabbed.

Then wait. Like he'd been doing the past four years.

Back in the room where two lab techs administered the test, he found Riley having her cheek swabbed.

She smiled at the tech labeling her packet. "That was easy. Thanks."

The young woman reached out to hug her. "Thank *you*. I was a match for my brother two years ago, but there are so many who don't have a good familial match. This event is going to change lives."

With a nod, Riley moved away to let the next person take her spot. Since Tuesday, the girls had launched a major media blitz —radio ads, newspaper ads and articles, broadcast emails, interviews on two separate television stations, and every social media platform there was. Apparently, many had been listening, reading, or watching.

He followed her back to the post she'd held all morning, handing out cookies and expressing her appreciation as folks left. She relieved Hallie of the platter and her assistant made herself available to the techs to label kits.

His gaze locked on a young man being tested who'd been staring at Riley almost from the moment he walked into the room. Not the creep, he ascertained after checking for any healing scratches on his hand. Just a guy staring down a pretty girl.

With his back to Riley, he stepped into the man's line of sight and pinned him with a glare. The man's eyes widened before he thanked the lab tech and left through the other door.

Riley's brow crinkled. "That was weird. Nobody's left without a cookie."

"Probably avoiding sugar." He stepped back next to her.

"Huh. Maybe." She held the platter out to a woman exiting the room. "Thank you for coming today." The woman made her choice, and Riley turned the platter toward him. "Here. You're not avoiding sugar, are you?"

"Never." He grabbed a chocolate chip cookie from the tray. "Thanks."

"'Welcome." She offered another to a woman with a thank you. "Did you get tested for Theresa?"

"Absolutely. I've never been matched, but I hope I get the call someday."

Hopefully, God would answer that prayer as He had his request that Riley's event be blessed with good attendance. The numbers so far had surpassed their goal, and extra testing kits had already been brought in.

Riley's friends had come early, carrying platters upon more platters of cookies, and now sat at the registration table. Her entire office staff and her family had been there. Colton's family made an appearance—for moral support as they were also still in the bone marrow registry—Gemma and even Valerie with little Landon in tow.

When Theresa's parents, her brother, and his wife arrived first thing that morning in support of the donation drive with Theresa's name on it, he took a few minutes to catch up with them before taking his post near Riley as potential donors began to arrive. Trevor and Paul were both tested before taking point on either side of the registration table, since nobody could get past without filling out the formal paperwork to be tested.

Colton had also prayed their guy would show up and fill out the paperwork. Name and address would be a great help.

A commotion in the hall had him rushing out the door. A man stood at the registration table, blocked by a six-foot-three wall named Trevor.

If Graham Harding's glower could be considered a weapon, it was a good thing Trevor wore a protective vest under his shirt. "You can't keep me from seeing Riley. She's not the queen, for crying out loud. You're all being ridiculous."

His rant drew some barbed stares from the waiting patrons, and Colton himself had trouble keeping his disdain from showing on his face. What was with this guy? Did he not care at all that somebody out there was hunting Riley? A woman he professed to care about?

Colton approached the table, drawing Graham's heated glare. "Paxton, let him through. I'll walk him back."

Trevor stepped aside, and Graham barreled his way past the table. Without a word to the other man, Colton turned and led him down the hall to the room where Riley still handed out cookies.

"Graham." Her eyes widened. "I didn't know you'd planned to come today."

"I didn't. But I apparently have to chase you down if I want to see you."

Colton bristled at the man's tone of disrespect and fought the urge to take him by the collar and throw him out. Riley deserved so much better.

Her face reddened as she turned to him. "Colton, can you give us a minute, please? I promise not to leave your sight."

He scanned the large room and pointed to a far corner. "Over there. No windows."

Harding rolled his eyes. "As if there's a sniper set up on the roof across the street."

Ignoring him, Colton held out his hands for the platter. "I'll handle cookie duty."

"Thanks." She handed him the platter, and Graham grabbed her hand. *Sorry,* she mouthed over her shoulder as her so-called friend pulled her away.

The unhappy couple stood in the designated corner conducting a quiet but apparently intense discussion. Graham left soon after, and Riley returned to her cookie post.

Colton handed her back the half-full platter. "He's not here to donate?"

"Uh, no. He was wondering if I was free for dinner tonight."

"Riley, we need—"

"I know, I know. You need forty-eight hours' notice if I'm going off the estate. I invited him to the house instead, but he declined."

"He looked upset."

"He was a little, I guess."

"Did he have reason to be?"

She offered cookies to two more people exiting the room. "He thinks he can't see me with you guys around all the time, especially with you staying at the house."

"Does he understand there's somebody out there after you?"

"He thinks it's somebody playing a joke, a hoax, and we're taking it too seriously."

Looking away, he shook his head in disgust. "I don't get that guy. He says he cares about you, wants to be in a relationship with you, but he takes threats against your life as a joke."

"Yeah." She sighed. "I need to let him know there's no future for us. But I know he'll think it's because of ..."

He waited for her to finish. "Because of what?"

"Nothing. I just don't think he'll understand. But I need to do it. And I will."

"Good luck."

"I'm going to need it. I'm not good at things like this."

"Because you're too nice."

"Oh, you think so?" she replied with a chuckle before swiping a cookie from the tray.

"When you're not in court, that is. Hallie showed me a video the other day of you going after a guy on the stand during your last trial."

"Well, he lied. Straight out. At the first trial." She took a bite of her sugar cookie. "Fingered our guy and the so-called witness wasn't even in town that day. If it hadn't been for his testimony, our client wouldn't have spent a day in jail, much less six years."

"Forty minutes of jury deliberations. Unbelievable."

"A new record for me." She smiled and held out the platter to a man in a business suit leaving the room. "Thank you so much for coming."

The man took a cookie from the tray with a nod.

"I'm hoping for as good an outcome for Shane. His defense team pretty much phoned it in. Makes me nuts when I see lazy representation. Now I've got a guy sitting in prison for a murder he didn't commit. If we only had an inkling who it might've been."

His gaze took another pass around the room as two more donors walked in. "You feel pretty strongly about him. His innocence, I mean."

"I do. I know I shouldn't gamble so much on my gut, but I never felt certain he did it. Even that day you and I met, the day of the funeral. Everybody was talking about him, but I couldn't reconcile it. Of course, her father being on the bench himself didn't help. Probably another reason the defense was so pathetic. Nobody wants to get on the wrong side of Judge Mulaney."

"Except you, apparently."

She winced but recovered quickly with a smile for the couple leaving. "You have to speak up for the truth, or why bother? I'm not in this for me, and there's no reason this really nice guy who had a great life mapped out in front of him should do somebody else's time. I'll take whatever heat comes with it, but you have to stand for something or get out of the way."

He smiled down at her. She was beautiful even all fired up. It had been fun, not to mention eye-opening, watching her in lawyer mode on that video. She might be tiny, but she had a fierce will. "You're good at what you do. Everything you do."

"So are you."

Trevor appeared in the doorway. "Hey, guys. No more line at registration. Ri, do you want the ladies out here to wait for any latecomers or pack it up?"

She checked her watch. "Oh, my. We're an hour over already. I didn't realize that. Let's go ahead and call it." She offered Trevor the cookie tray. "Take this up for you, Paul, and the girls. Thanks for all your help today."

"A pleasure." He took the tray. "I'll let the ladies know we're shutting it down."

Back at the estate that afternoon, Colton dismissed the other two after discussing the next day's schedule. He walked upstairs and peered into Riley's suite, where she stood with her back to him, leafing through a stack of mail forwarded from her home address.

Leaning against the doorway, he watched her for a moment. It pulled at his heart she would never return to that stunning home she'd made for herself. A sanctuary, she'd called it, now scarred forever with the memory of its decimation.

How he wished he could offer her more than the protection dictated by the parameters of his job. She deserved everything she seemed to believe she hadn't earned. Is that why she worked so hard? To prove her worth beyond simply being a Hudson?

If so, she'd done that in spades, and then some.

"You did a good thing today, Riley."

"No. All of those people who showed up did a good thing today." She glanced over her shoulder at him. "I just gave them the opportunity to do what was already in their hearts. That's what charity work is about. Giving those who have a chance to give to those who don't. I don't care what it is."

"You'll be happy to know I've put together my board. My sister, Theresa's brother, and her best friend. Barbara also expressed an interest, so I asked her. And a couple of others you don't know. Friends of mine who went through all of that with me. They were all there today, but I didn't get a chance to introduce you."

"That's fantastic. I'm excited to hear that."

"I need to set up a time to meet, once I'm done here, but I'd appreciate it if you could give me some pointers on how to get started. I know you're busy and we can work—"

"You name it, Cole, and I'll be there. Any time."

Taken aback by her use of the nickname, he stared at her. Only one person had ever called him Cole, and he hadn't heard it for over four years. But somehow it sounded … right.

He cleared his throat. "Maybe when you don't already have so many irons in the fire."

She studied her tidy desk before turning to him. "We can do it now, or we can get together tomorrow after we get back from the boat christening. Whatever you'd like to do."

"You have time now?"

"I have it."

"Super. I'll grab my notes. Meet you back here?"

"Sure thing."

He started to leave but turned back. "Tell me. About that christening. Why are they christening a boat in November? Don't they usually do these things when it's actually warm?"

She giggled and put her mail down on her desk. "The Daytons got married three weeks ago and are taking a six-month honeymoon. They leave Sunday to sail down to the Caribbean. They'll anchor there and island-hop a while before coming back here in May."

"Ah. I see. A six-month honeymoon. I should have guessed. Doesn't everybody take a six-month honeymoon?"

She giggled again. "Oh, I don't know. A six-month honeymoon sounds pretty good."

He gave her a nod before heading down the hall to his guest room. Yeah, it did, come to think of it. If one were fortunate enough to find that special someone to spend life with, why not?

If one were fortunate enough.

Chapter Twenty-Eight

Riley flung her briefcase into a chair, her handbag and coat following. Taking a seat behind the desk, she sighed at the stack of mail and sundry other documents left for her.

She'd enjoyed the four-day weekend. The blood drive had been an enormous success, the boat christening a fun day with friends, and church yesterday had been a balm to her soul. Now it was time to get back to work. Shane should be as free as she was to enjoy his days with friends and family.

A hearty swallow of her Americano coffee and she was ready to dive in on this thankfully warmer Monday morning. Her phone buzzed as she reached for a stack of documents needing her signature. Appeared she would be hitting the ground running this morning.

"Yes, Hallie?"

"A Mr. Laraby on the line. Said he's a lawyer calling about a potential case, but it's apparently time-sensitive."

Time-sensitive? Maybe a death penalty case? Her docket was full, so taking on another case wasn't possible. But maybe she could provide a little guidance or refer him to an associate.

"Okay, put him through."

She inventoried the documents on her desk while she waited. So much work. Hopefully, it would be a short call.

The phone buzzed again, and she picked it up. "Riley Hudson."

Silence for a moment, then that chuckle that sent chills up her spine. "Miss me, Riley Hudson? It's been a while since we've talked."

Her heart racing, she sprang out of her chair, picked up a pen, and threw it at the window next to her office door. When it hit, Colton turned and looked in at her, his eyes narrowing as she motioned for him to come in.

She cleared her throat of the fear almost choking her. "Um … and you would be …?"

That snicker again. "Nice try, Miss Hudson."

"Is it him?" Colton whispered, closing the door behind him.

She nodded, and he grabbed his cell phone, making a circling gesture with his hand as he put it to his ear. Keep him on the line. She needed to somehow keep this creep on the line, as if it wasn't bad enough she already heard his voice in her nightmares.

"I need a trace on Riley Hudson's office line right now," he said to somebody on the other end.

She hit the speaker button on the phone base so Colton could hear both sides of the conversation and quietly hung up the handset. "I just like to know who I'm dealing with. Seems you have the unfair advantage, knowing me but me not knowing you."

"I've greatly enjoyed getting to know you."

Unable to stand on her quaking legs any longer, she sat back down in her chair. "You know, it's never too late to turn to God. Whatever you've done, He—"

"Spare me the sermon. I've heard it all before. And since I'm clearly on speaker now, I assume your hired thug is standing there with you. Like he was at the shelter. You sure know how to work a white apron, Riley Hudson."

Startled, her gaze shot up to Colton's. A muscle worked in his jaw as he kept the cell phone to his ear. This guy had been right there, despite all their precautions.

"I … um … I hope you were able to enjoy some Thanksgiving dinner. That's why we were there, to feed folks."

"The turkey was a little dry, but all in all, it wasn't bad. Oh, and by the way, I sent you a little something. *Ciao* for now, Miss Hudson."

"Wait!" The line went silent. "Hello?"

Colton frowned. "Okay, thanks." He disconnected and put his phone on her desk. "Close but no go. Needed about thirty more seconds."

"I'm so sorry."

"Don't be. You did fantastic. Honestly. Although, seeing how composed you are in court, I'm not surprised." His gaze traveled to her stack of mail. "Check that real quick."

Her hands shook as she leafed through her mail until she came across a padded manila envelope with her name and office address hand-scrawled on the front.

"Don't open it." He picked up his cell phone again. "John. Colton Blankenship. Riley received another envelope. Large and has something in it." He nodded as John spoke. "Sounds good. See you in a few." He clicked off and stuck his phone back inside his suit coat. "He's about ten minutes away, so he's coming himself."

"So, the creep's mailing them now? You think he knows about the plainclothes officer planted downstairs?"

"I don't know how he could. But I think he probably knows we'd be smart enough to do something like that and isn't taking any chances."

She shook her head. "This is my fault. If I'd told you about them sooner, we might've had someone down there last Monday when the fourth one came."

"This isn't your fault, Ri. None of it." He scanned her desk. "Why don't you go ahead with what you were doing? Concentrate on something else and try not to think about it."

"I can't help it."

He studied her for a long moment. "Okay." He walked around her desk, kneeled in front of her, and took her hand. "Let's pray about it."

Pray about it? Colton wanted to *pray about it?*

He bowed his head. "Heavenly Father, You know Riley's scared right now, so if You could give her a measure of peace, we would sure appreciate it. Please help us find this guy who's targeted her for reasons we don't know so she can get on with her life the way she wants to live it, without constantly being under guard. We thank You for Your presence, even in these difficult circumstances. In Your name we pray. Amen."

When she opened her eyes, he was staring down at their joined hands before he let her go and stood. Still reeling from everything that had happened—the phone call, the new package, Colton *praying* with her—she wasn't sure what to say.

He'd been more focused on the pastor's message the past two weeks at church. A departure from the first service they'd shared, where he'd sat next to her stiff as a board. Had he been making his way back to God after their middle-of-the-night talk?

There hadn't been a day since she hadn't talked to God about him, praying he'd bridge the gap he'd let grow between him and the Savior he used to trust. That he would rediscover the faith he'd left behind.

She started at the light knock on her doorjamb, and her attention snapped to the detective whose gaze traveled from Colton to her and back again.

Colton backed away and moved to the side of the desk. "John. Thanks for coming so quickly."

"Sure thing." John peered down at her. "Your secret admirer decided to reach out again, I hear."

She cleared her throat. "Secret, maybe, but no admirer."

"Let's see what we have."

John gloved up, picked up the envelope by its edges, carefully opened it, and looked inside. "This is interesting."

Turning the envelope over, he held his other hand under it and a lipstick tube fell into his palm.

She gasped. "That's mine. I always carry it in my bag, but I haven't been able to find it. But how—" Her breath caught. "My bag. It spilled onto the concrete during the—in the parking garage. He must've picked it up."

Colton grimaced. "We already determined it was the same guy, but he wasn't aware we'd figured it out. This is his way of telling you it's him, and he knows where to get to you. It's all mind games, Ri."

And he was good at it. It might be time to call her doctor about a sleeping pill. At this point, she had no idea if a good night's rest was anywhere in her near future.

John reached into the envelope and pulled out a folded sheet of paper.

Colton peered over his shoulder as he unfolded the page. "You're kidding me."

"What?" She launched to her feet, her pulse spiking at the vehemence in his voice.

John turned the letter around. A photo had been copied to the sheet. A picture of her standing behind the counter wearing a white apron, smiling and serving a plate to a grateful woman in a tattered coat and floppy hat. Colton stood right beside her. It had been taken from a distance, but there was no way the creep went through the line with her standing there. It had to be while she was on the break Colton insisted she take, and he snapped this picture once they returned.

If they'd only stayed, this could all be over.

Colton's forehead furrowed. "I know of two news agencies who were there. Maybe someone got this guy on film."

"Good thinking," John said. "I'll get the footage."

Riley lowered herself into her chair. "I would have recognized him if he was the same guy who grabbed me, Cole. I would've known his eyes. I should have never left the line."

His mouth pulled into a frown. "Maybe. But we've seen he's a master of disguise. You got a—what? Five-second look at him that day he tried to grab you? He was probably disguised even then."

"I'd know his eyes," she repeated. Her chest filled with heat. If only Colton hadn't pulled her away. "And if he'd spoken to me, I would've recognized his voice. Trust me. I still hear it. Every day."

With his lips pinched into a line, he turned back to John. "She also got another call. We tried to get a trace, but he hung up too soon."

"How did you get the call?" John asked.

"Hallie put him through," she answered.

"Did she put the two previous calls through?"

"Yes." She took a deep breath and willed calmness into her shaking limbs. "But he gave a different name each time."

"Means she's heard him three times now, before he altered his voice to speak with you."

"I didn't think of that. But, yes. I would think she'd be suspicious of the voice I heard, so he has to be disguising it for my benefit."

Colton nodded. "Let's have her listen closely for any other callers who sound like this guy so we can get a head start on the trace next time. And we should put a tap on your phone here, catch him on tape, then we'll have something we can go back to and listen for background noise. See if we can zero in on a location."

"I can't do that. I speak to or about my clients on my line."

His face went slack. "Attorney-client privilege. Right." He turned back to the detective. "Any luck on the phone records?"

John shook his head. "You were right. It's a burner. And fingerprints on the previous cards include the lobby guard, Riley's, her assistant, and a fourth that aren't in the system. Good call getting baseline prints from her staff in case we ever needed to weed them out, and, of course, the guard's are in the system as security personnel."

Riley's heart sank. "So we have nothing. Still. We're no closer than we were before."

"We're going to get him, Riley. Trust me. Every day, we're closer to the day he's ours. We've all got your back on this."

Tears threatened to spill. A weakness she couldn't give in to. "I appreciate that, John. More than you know."

"I'll go make those calls. You both have a good day. Stay safe."

The door closed behind him, and Colton kneeled beside her chair again. "Have you talked with anybody since this all started?"

"I've talked to a lot of people. The police, my family, the girls. You."

"I mean someone professionally."

"Like a shrink?"

"Or a counselor. A victim's advocate. Someone who can help."

The back of her neck tingled, like hackles rising on a wolf protecting its territory. "I'm not a victim, Colton. I don't need help."

He took her hand. "Ri, you're not sleeping. You work like a madwoman. It's like you're frantic. Keep busy. Keep moving. Stay awake. You're going to collapse at this rate. You know that. It's only a matter of time."

Tears welled up again, and she put her head down, pinching the bridge of her nose to keep them at bay.

"It's all right to cry. I wish you would. I was hoping the day I found you in the family room you would have a good cry."

The quiet plea in his voice, the earnestness in his eyes, the warmth of his hand around hers—what she should find strength in, she instead found a weakening to give in to her disintegrating emotions. But if she did, could she climb her way out?

Pulling her shoulders back, she pulled her hand out of his and pushed away the temptation to crumble. "I hate crying. It makes me feel out of control."

"I understand. But you need an outlet. Don't fight the emotions trying to get out. Feel the fear, deal with it, and let it work for you. Not against you."

She stared at him long and hard, wishing like mad he'd pull her close. Let her curl up into him. Hide there until this was all over. Where she'd be safe.

Until he left her. Until his work was done and he let her go and walked out of her life. He was there to do a job. But it was a temp job.

She picked up the rest of her mail. "I'm fine. I'm not going to let this guy do this to me. I'm not his victim. I'm his target, but not his victim."

He sighed and stood. "What can I do to help you?"

"You're doing it." She kept her focus on the letter in her hand without seeing the words. "By doing your job."

The silence stretched, but she didn't dare look up. The temptation to curl into him, and the rejection that would surely follow, would be too much to bear.

"Okay." He moved to the door but turned back. "I know you blame me for pulling you off the line at the Thanksgiving dinner. That it's my fault we missed him. But did you ever consider those fifteen minutes might've saved your life? *That's* my job, Riley. You're my first priority. And something told me you needed to get off the line. Knowing he was right in front of the servers has me believing it was the Spirit nudging me to get you out of harm's way."

He opened the door. "I'm going to go talk to Hallie."

After her door shut behind him, she rounded her shoulders and dropped the letter to the desk. She put her forehead in her hand. If she'd wanted to put him in his place, she'd certainly succeeded.

Except that wasn't what she'd intended, knowing he'd been trying to help her. But after he'd prayed with her ... her hand held snug in his ... those precious few moments with him at the foot of the Throne. It had all felt so intimate ... so personal. Just the three of them—God, Colton, and her—an island of peace amidst the chaos her life had become since this person ... this evil ... had intruded upon it.

But maybe a little distance was warranted. Emotionally. To guard her heart. She relied on him too much. To protect her. To hold her up.

And she couldn't lose herself to a man who wouldn't stay.

Chapter Twenty-Nine

This was going to be a long evening. In an even longer week. And it was only Wednesday.

Colton sat alone at a corner table in the small Italian restaurant, sipping a glass of water, raking his gaze back and forth. Trevor occupied another table across the dining room, both of them trying to be as unobtrusive as possible.

The rich aroma of pasta in tomato and meat sauce blended with a steady hum of conversation punctuated with bouts of laughter. Fat bottles wrapped in twine with dripping white candles sat on each table. The low light made their job that much harder, but it certainly lent itself to an otherwise romantic setting.

After being reminded of his place in Riley's life by the woman herself, the past three days had been more like that first Sunday. His first day on her detail, when she sat rigid and seething in the pew next to him while he'd wanted out of this assignment as soon as possible.

Things had changed over the following days, starting with the fundraising dinner. Then all the conversations in the car, sharing meals with her family, splitting a sandwich in the middle of the night, and telling her about Theresa. The nonprofit that now existed in her name as a result.

He'd begun to consider Riley a friend. His second mistake after not reading her file. But he was determined to see this through. No matter how distant they'd become over the past two days.

"Colton." Paul's voice sounded in his ear.

"Go ahead."

"A dishwasher who wasn't on the schedule just showed up. He checks. Definitely not our guy. Wanted to make you aware."

"Copy."

Riley had received another bone-chilling call this morning, the intent of which appeared to be to inform her he'd seen her leaving the office the day before, complete with a detailed description of her attire. There was also another photo delivered by mail of the line inside the hospital corridor at the donor drive. The creep hadn't come in, obviously, but he'd been too close for comfort. It was irritating how this guy seemed to be everywhere, but they couldn't pinpoint anybody who appeared familiar from place to place.

Even now, he and Trevor constantly perused the restaurant and were instantly on alert every time someone came through the door. He knew what every man in the place was wearing, the color of their hair and how they kept it, their approximate age, and ethnic origin. There were two single guys sitting at the bar, but neither of them had even glanced Riley's direction, instead riveted to the television tuned into a sports channel over the bar.

He'd stationed Paul in the kitchen, securing the back entrance and keeping him close to the SUV if they should need it. They'd vetted the male waitstaff and kitchen crew and checked IDs upon their arrival this evening. Unscheduled dishwashers notwithstanding, nothing so far appeared amiss.

Except for the couple at a table a few yards away. Unlike the other diners laughing and talking over plates of pasta, they weren't smiling. This conversation was one that should've been done in private, as Riley had tried to do when she invited Graham for dinner at the estate last night. The man had insisted on this place, however, and was none too happy they had to put it off a day so Petersen could run their checks.

Riley reached out to touch Graham's hand, but he pulled it back as if scalded. The pain in her expression had Colton clenching his fists before his attention moved to a couple coming in the door. She hadn't wanted to hurt her old friend, but she'd finally decided she needed to be straight with him about her feelings.

Colton's gaze swept back to their table, and the glare Graham sent his way could have stripped paint off a wall. With another glower at Riley, Graham shot to his feet, threw his napkin on the table, and stalked toward the exit. He changed course halfway there, and Colton's eyes narrowed as the man made a beeline his direction.

By the time Harding came to an abrupt stop in front of him, he was on his feet, staring down the man a good four inches shorter than him. "Something I can do for you?"

Rage pinched Graham's face. "Don't go getting any grand ideas about moving in permanently. She may think you're some knight in shining armor now, but when this thing is over, she'll see you for who you really are."

"I'd advise you to back off and get out of this restaurant by the time I count to three, or I'll remove you myself." Although his blood boiled, he kept his voice even. "One ... two ..."

Graham marched out of the restaurant, several of the other diners staring after him in stunned silence. Colton brought his focus back to Riley, who still sat wide-eyed and slack-jawed.

His heart went out to her. That friendship was likely over, the one thing she'd hoped to avoid. But if these were Harding's true colors, she was better off.

She put her napkin next to her still-full plate of lasagna. After pulling a few bills from her pocketbook, she laid them on the table and stood.

"Paul, we're ready."

"Copy. At the front curb in two."

Riley walked toward the exit, where he and Trevor met her and took up their usual positions. She kept her head down, and no words were spoken while they waited inside for the car. The SUV pulled up to the curb, and Trevor preceded them out, holding the car door open for her while Colton walked around to the other side. The twenty-minute drive back to the estate was tense and quiet, Riley never pulling her attention from her window.

At the house, Paul pulled around the flagstone circular drive and stopped at the front steps. She waited until Trevor opened her door, and Colton met them at the side of the SUV.

Watching as Trevor held his hand out for her, he couldn't ignore the twist in his gut, reluctant to admit he missed that one brief opportunity to touch her. Connect with her.

Trevor walked with them to the door, taking point next to her while Colton brought up the rear. "Are you going to be all right, Riley?"

She gave him a sad smile. "I will be. Thank you."

"If it's any consolation, you're much too good for that guy."

"I'm sure Graham's of a different opinion, but I appreciate the sentiment."

Once inside and Riley had retired upstairs, Paul came in the door, pinning Colton with an uncharacteristic frown. "A minute of your time?"

"Sure." The sharp edge in his friend's voice alerted him he was about to get an earful. Paul and Trevor had no doubt noticed the coolness between him and Riley, but they hadn't witnessed the encounter in her office earlier in the week. The day she'd reminded him of his place.

Trevor's gaze moved between them. "You need me for this, or can I call it?"

Colton deferred to Paul, who shook his head. "No, I just need to talk to Colton for a minute."

"See you in the morning, then." With another glance between them, Trevor left through the front door.

Paul gestured for Colton to precede him into Drew's study and closed the door behind him.

Colton faced his friend and co-worker. "What's up?"

"Kinda what I'd like to know."

"Know about what?"

"You and Riley."

Colton released an impatient sigh and stuck his hands on his hips. "I told you before. There's nothing between Riley and me. I don't know why you keep thinking otherwise."

"Because I knew there was the last time I asked. Now you're barely speaking. What happened between you?"

"Nothing happened. She's a principal. I'm treating her no differently than any other."

"Right."

Colton stared at him a moment. "Okay, so maybe I got closer to her than usual, but you know Riley. She makes friends of everybody she meets. She asked me to chair Theresa's board and helped me get started. But that's it. I need to keep my perspective here, for her own good."

"Perspective, I get. But you've gone back to the brooding we thought you'd finally moved past."

"I don't brood."

"Trust me. You brood. But even she's quieter. Makes me wonder what you did."

He'd confided in her. Prayed with her. He'd held her hand. "You know as well as I do if I'd done anything, she wouldn't just pout. She'd definitely let me know. You're making too much of it."

Paul shrugged. "Okay. If you say so. I'm just telling you, Pax and I have picked up on the tension. We were wondering if maybe something had happened. With you staying here and all. That maybe … you know. Something had happened."

"Nothing happened. Nothing will."

Chapter Thirty

Another long week. Waiting. Watching. Wondering when the next call might come. When the next message might arrive in her stack of mail.

Sighing in the dark, Riley rolled onto her back and clasped her hands on her stomach. Wednesday's call still made her skin crawl. The way he'd described what she'd been wearing the day before, down to the cross pendant around her neck, put her on notice that he'd been close. Too close. And they'd had no idea.

This afternoon, another package had arrived, like clockwork, two days after his last with that bone-chilling photo of the line at the donor drive. Today's missive included a pen from her purse.

After John phoned with that bit of unwelcome news, she'd dumped her bag onto her desk and scoured the contents to determine if anything else was missing. Everything appeared to be accounted for, so, hopefully, those were the only two items he'd picked up during his getaway. Along with his gun, unfortunately.

Shaking off the memory, she instead turned her focus to the

progress they'd made on Shane's case. Precious little, to her frustration.

Her meeting early on with his previous defense team hadn't helped much. She disagreed with almost every decision they'd made but didn't argue. Their part was over, but they hadn't made it easy for her with their sloppy investigation.

Shane and his parents had certainly wasted their money on his former representation. But to keep his family from going further into debt, she'd anonymously paid the balance of his bill.

With another sigh, she threw her legs over the side of the bed, grabbed her Bible, and headed for the door. A cup of hot chocolate and some time spent in the Psalms should be the balm she needed to help her relax.

After making her way through the dark and quiet house, she pushed open the swinging door to the kitchen. It banged into something and popped back at her.

"Ugh."

Her hand flew to her mouth at the pain-filled grunt. Tentatively, she reached out again and pushed it forward ever so slowly. The overhead light came on, and she blinked in the sudden brightness.

"Colton!"

Standing a few feet away, he grimaced as he held a hand to his eye.

She hurried to the island and put her Bible down on the counter. "I'm so sorry."

"S'okay." He took his hand away, glanced at it, and put it back.

"Oh, no, you're bleeding. Let's get some ice for that, or you'll have one whopper of a goose egg."

She grabbed a paper towel and took him by the arm to walk him to the table. She nudged his hand away from the cut over his right eyebrow and pressed the towel to it. "Hold this here. I'll get some ice."

"Really, Riley. It's not necessary."

She ignored his protest as she grabbed several cubes out of the freezer and put them in a plastic bag she rolled up in a dish towel.

"Here." She moved his hand again, taking the paper towel with it, and put the make-shift ice pack gently against his forehead. "This should keep the swelling down."

"Thanks."

She stood next to him holding the towel. He'd once again made a middle-of-the-night visit to the kitchen in pajama bottoms and a T-shirt, this one touting the Houston Astros logo.

"I really am sorry, Cole. I didn't notice any light coming from under the door."

"I'd just flipped it off a few seconds before you came in."

"And almost knocked you flat. I feel terrible."

"You shouldn't. It's not a big deal."

"I just can't stand that I hurt you." In more ways than one.

"Riley, chill." He took the towel from her. "I'll hold it. You do whatever it was you came down here to do."

"Well ... all right. I was going to make myself some hot chocolate. Would you like some?"

"Actually, yeah. That sounds good."

"Coming right up."

She busied herself with her task, concentrating on the hum of the refrigerator to give her heart rate a chance to slow to its natural rhythm. They hadn't been alone since that morning in her office. The day she'd been terrified and he'd tried to help, and all she wanted was for him to hold onto her. Wrap her in his arms where nothing could touch her.

Her comment about his doing his job hadn't been meant to hurt him. She'd needed to get her perspective on track, remind *herself* of his place in her life. Because, if truth be told, she'd been considering him less her bodyguard and more like someone … special. Even knowing the futility of such thinking.

"Have you been working all this time?" His question cut into the silence.

"Nope. Just can't get my mind to shut down." She stirred hot milk into two cups with powdered hot chocolate mix. Maybe it wasn't the from-scratch stuff Hilda made, but it always did the trick in the middle of the night.

"Tell me you're not losing sleep over Graham of the Fort Worth Hardings."

Chuckling, she shook her head. "Not Graham. I feel bad he was hurt, but you were right. I should've said something a long time ago."

"He's a big boy. He'll survive."

"No doubt. But our friendship won't, I don't believe." She walked their cups over to the table and put one in front of him before taking a seat. "So, if I may ask, what did he say to you? On his way out that night?"

He shrugged, still holding the towel-wrapped ice pack to his head. "Nothing really. Seems to have the idea I had something to do with you sending him packing."

Her eyes widened. "I didn't even mention you."

"He's insecure. Needs someone to blame. I just happened to come into the picture at the same time you told him you didn't want to move forward with your relationship. Trevor was right. You deserve better. Someone with your same values, work ethic, and integrity. The same confidence. Someone who loves God as much as you do."

Her skin warmed with the compliment. "That's nice of you to say."

"It's just the way it is. Is he even a believer?"

"He is, but I don't think his faith plays a big part in his daily life. I could never be serious with someone who didn't love God more than they did me."

He regarded her for a long moment. "Still having nightmares?"

The blood drained from her face. "What makes you ask?" His room might be next door to her suite, but it shared a wall with her study. Even if she'd cried out in the night, he shouldn't have heard her.

"I've been there. The nightmares are the worst. Had them for weeks after I was shot. After a body comes so close to death, or a violent act, the mind has to compensate somehow. That's what yours is doing."

"When did they stop?"

"After I started talking about what happened."

"You saw a counselor." She lifted her mug to blow across the top of the steaming cocoa.

"While I was in rehab. I had to learn to walk again, run. All those things. They worked on the mind and the body, I guess you could say."

Holding her cup with both hands, she took a small sip and set it back down. "You really think I should talk to a professional?"

"Yes. I do. It's been three weeks since the attempt to abduct you, but only hours since the last note. He's keeping it fresh in your mind. He knows the longer he draws it out, the weaker you'll get. The more off-balance. Emotionally. Mentally."

Nodding, she stared down at her cup. "It sure feels like it sometimes. Like I'm losing my mind."

"I can get some names for you. Of counselors. Victims' advocates. If you don't already have someone in mind."

"I don't know of anyone. I know counselors, sure. We use them all the time for the shelter. And my parents have two good friends who are shrinks. But I don't think I could let down with people I know. Who know me."

"I'll have some names for you tomorrow. I mean, today. Later today."

She chuckled and took another sip. "Thanks."

"You're welcome."

"So, couldn't you sleep?"

He took a swallow of his chocolate. "Got hungry."

"You should eat before you go to bed. Then maybe you'd sleep all night."

"Not a bad idea."

They sat and quietly enjoyed their cocoa in companionable silence for several minutes before he took the towel away from his head.

She examined the small wound above his brow, guilt-ridden she'd caused it. "I think it's stopped."

"Great." He held up the towel. "I don't know what to do with this. I don't want Hilda to freak tomorrow morning at the sight of a bloody towel."

She stood and reached for it. "Here. We can throw it away. She'll never miss it."

After dumping the ice in the sink, she threw the plastic bag and towel in the trash bin and joined him again at the table.

"Colton … I'm sorry if I said anything—wait. Let me start over. I'm sorry for what I said. On Monday, in my office. When you were trying to get me to cry? I think I pushed you away because I was feeling a little vulnerable, but at the same time, I knew you were right. I don't blame you for taking me off the line that day. I appreciate that you were looking after me. That you're always looking after me."

"No apology necessary. I overstepped the parameters of our relationship. You were right to remind me of my place."

"But your place over these last few weeks has been right next to me, and I feel safe knowing you're there. Not only as part of my protection detail, but as my friend. And I don't put parameters on friendships."

"But our relationship is a professional one. I need to keep that in mind, or I'm no good to you."

Her heart squeezed. Of course that's how he viewed their relationship. It made perfect sense. She was the job. *His* job. And like he'd told her that first night, he was good at it. She didn't know how she would've handled the last four weeks without his steadfast presence. His constant protection.

"It meant a lot to me, praying with you. Really, Colton, I won't forget it."

Chapter Thirty-One

"I won't forget it either, Riley." Colton's voice pressed through the tightness in his throat.

Praying with her … her hand clutched tightly to his … the two of them alone with God. It changed him. Like something inside him opened up that morning. Opened up, then filled with something he couldn't describe. Something … spiritual. Something he hadn't experienced in over four years, since the day he'd blocked God out of his life for taking something precious from him.

Tilting her head, she studied him for a few seconds. "It seems you and God are back on speaking terms."

He nodded, but how could he explain? Since the last time they'd bumped into each other here in the middle of the night, when she'd reached out to remind him how much God loved him, he'd felt pulled back toward the faith he'd left behind. A coming home, of sorts.

His Bible still lay in a desk drawer in his study where he'd put it the day after Theresa's funeral. But he found one in the Hudson's library a few days ago, and while Riley worked in her suite, he pored over Scriptures he remembered from times past.

"I've been getting back in touch, I guess you could say."

"I'm so happy to hear that."

He couldn't help but return her smile, this woman he was trying to keep at arm's length but who invaded his dreams. Dreams that teased him with something he could never have.

It sure didn't help running headlong into that dream in the middle of the night.

He gave himself a mental shake. "Yeah, it's time. All that anger wasn't doing anything for me. Just standing in the way of whatever God wants to bring into my life."

She regarded him for a moment with those emerald eyes he couldn't look away from. "So, we're okay? You and me?"

The earnestness of her question shattered his resolve to keep her at a distance.

"Yes." Before he could talk himself out of it, he reached over to take her hand on top of the table. "We're fine, Riley."

Relief flooded her face.

He let her go and glanced over to the island, where her Bible lay unopened. "I messed up your quiet time. I should leave you alone."

"No, it's all right. I had my quiet time this morning, but I can't stop thinking about Shane's case and how things aren't happening as quickly as I'd hoped. Figured some time in the Word would help me clear my head."

He sat back in his chair and studied her for a moment. "Wanna talk through it? Maybe two brains can figure out what's missing. Or at least where to go next."

"You sure you don't want to get back to bed?"

"I'm here. If it'll help quiet whatever's happening in your head, let's do it."

Sitting back in her chair, she folded her arms across her middle. "Okay, here's what we know. According to Judge Mulaney's testimony at trial, he'd given Caitlyn an ultimatum five days before her death. Either drop *the no-good fortune hunter* or lose their financial support."

"Is that the word he used? Ultimatum?"

"I believe he said *choice*, but the meaning was clear. If she didn't dump Shane, she'd be estranged from her family. Shane said he told Cait he didn't want to come between her and her parents, but she'd claimed to be done with her father's overbearing ways, choosing to be with him."

"His word against theirs."

"Which is precisely what his former defense attorney said the day we met. Who would take Shane's word over a sitting district judge?"

He sat up and clasped his hands on top of the table. "Which begs the question, why didn't they file for a change of venue, since her father's a judge in the same county?"

"Right? He said they didn't believe it was a relevant reason to change venues since a jury would be deciding the verdict, not the judge."

"But the judge runs the trial. And if he's tight with Judge Mulaney ..."

"Exactly. One of the first things I'll do if we're granted a new trial is request a change of venue."

"Good plan. Go on."

She stood and walked to the island. "The day before Caitlyn was killed, flowers were ordered online from a nearby florist using a credit card in Shane's name and billed to his address." She started back to the table, her gaze pinned to the window. "The order also indicated what should be put on the card, and the flowers would be picked up the next day. Not delivered."

Back to the island she went. "A few minutes before closing the day of the murder, a man standing over six foot with dark hair, sunglasses, and wearing a business suit came in for the flowers. The florist further described him to the homicide detectives as *slight of face but bulkier in build.*"

Standing at the table again, she looked down at him. "Shane's six-three and topped out around two-twenty at the time. He was muscular and fit, but full-faced, not slight."

She returned to the island. He grinned. Watching her in thinking mode was entertaining.

"The detective showed her a photo line-up the next day, but she couldn't identify him as the customer. They did a composite, and it only resembles Shane in hair color since she couldn't see the man's eyes. Which is exactly why the prosecution didn't introduce it at trial."

"Please tell me the defense at least did that."

"That much they did do." She stopped her pacing. "I tell you, Colton, I'm tempted to use Ineffective Assistance of Counsel as an appeal. These guys really let him down."

"Use whatever's at your disposal. Trust your gut. It's reliable."

She cocked her head and smiled. "Thanks. I appreciate that."

"What next?"

Her pacing resumed. "By the time his case made it to trial, he'd lost some weight and the florist then ID'd him in court as the man who picked up the flowers. The defense never showed her the picture of Shane from the photo line-up at the time of the murder two years before, when she failed to pick him out. And there was no security tape to refute her claim."

"A lost opportunity for reasonable doubt."

"One of many." She took her seat again. "According to the fitness tracker Caitlyn wore on her wrist, she breathed her last at 6:22 p.m. And this is where things get weird."

"Hit me."

"The florist testified the flowers were picked up—allegedly by Shane—at ten to six, but he says he didn't arrive at her house until almost seven. The nine-one-one call came in at 6:58. The drive from the shop to Caitlyn's was no more than ten minutes."

He cocked his head. "Making the question why the lag time. Couldn't they use his cell phone records to track his movements?"

She sighed. "Shane uses a company-owned cell while he's working, turns off his personal phone, and leaves it in his car. On this day, he claimed his phone disappeared from his car parked in the parking garage. He drives a vintage Camaro. No alarm. His company phone was turned off at 5:12 p.m., the time he stopped working for the day. The only personal calls they found on his work phone were to his cell carrier and to Ferdinand's during his lunch break to make dinner reservations for seven-thirty, and then to Cait a little before one. He said she was excited he was able to get a reservation."

"The call to his carrier was to suspend his service?"

"Yes. And order a new phone. Thankfully, he took the time to do that immediately upon discovering it had been taken. If the person who took it had planned to use it to 'place' Shane at the scene of the crime, the GPS wouldn't work with service suspended."

"But it also leaves no phone record to verify he *wasn't* there. Was it the prosecution's assertion he faked the theft of his phone and suspended his service so he couldn't be tracked?"

"It was. And, of course, the defense didn't argue. He said again there was no way to prove the phone had been taken, so they simply didn't address it."

"I would imagine whoever took it would have had to know Shane left his phone in his car every day. Most people take their phones with them."

"I wondered about that, too, and the only thing that makes sense is that whoever did this planned it out thoroughly. They could've been watching him, following him, and somehow noticed he changed phones before going into wherever he was contracted to work that day."

Needing to stretch, he stood and reached over his head, then stuck his hands on his hips. "Okay, let's track. Everett turned off his work phone around 5:15, flowers were picked up a little before six, Cait died at 6:22, and Everett called nine-one-one at 6:58. From Cait's phone?"

"Yes."

"And where does he say he was from the time he turned off his company phone until he arrived at Cait's a little over an hour later?"

"He went home after leaving his client, then over to Cait's."

He moved to the island and leaned back against it, bracing his hands on the counter behind him. "Could he have gone from his client's place of business to the florist between the time he turned off the phone and then allegedly picked up the flowers?"

"Yes, it could be done. However, the defense put the guy Shane had been working with all day on the stand, who testified Shane was wearing brown slacks and a tan shirt with a print tie for work that day. At the time he was found with Cait, he was wearing black slacks, a gray shirt, and a different print tie. And he had a black suit coat in his car. The clothes he wore for work that day were found during a search of his residence, so it tracked that he went home to change."

"How did the prosecution answer for that?"

"Asserted he went home and changed, then picked up the flowers. The timeline is tight, especially during rush hour, although it could be done. My investigator tried it five times and was successful once, when he allotted only ten minutes for the change of clothes. Shane said he shaved again before heading over to Cait's, so there's no way he could do that and change into a suit in ten minutes."

"Did the florist indicate what color suit the man who picked up the flowers was wearing?"

"On the stand, she said dark. Couldn't remember if it was black or blue."

"What does Everett say happened after he drove to Cait's?"

"Upon arriving at her house, he found the front door ajar and was at first confused to find flowers strewn on the floor amidst shards from a broken vase. Then he found her in a pool of blood on the kitchen floor. He called nine-one-one in a panic, and when the uniforms arrived a few minutes after his call, they found him distraught and cradling her body against him."

"No blood spatter evidence on him?"

"None. But they argued he either covered it up by holding her body against him, or he changed. Thing is, there was no spatter in his hair or on the back of his shirt. Nowhere you'd normally find it if you kneeled over somebody and stabbed them over twenty times."

"Hmm. I always assumed she was stabbed standing up, since she was fighting back."

"The first few blows came while she was standing. But one struck her heart early on and she died instantly. Again, though, if Shane had killed her, there would've been spatter on his shoes at that point. They know the other blows came after she fell, based on gouges in the wood floor from the tip of the knife. As if some of the strikes missed or glanced off her body and hit the floor. Prosecution introduced the possibility he changed his clothes, but no way could he have changed, showered—somewhere else since there was no water or blood in either of her bathrooms—discarded the items outside of her residence and returned in time to make the nine-one-one call."

"And no foreign DNA at the scene?"

"Only Shane's, which tracks since he was there almost every day. None of his DNA in blood, though, but also no blood found with anybody else's. I assert they missed it with there being so much of Caitlyn's blood. And there weren't any cuts on Shane's hand, so I believe they just didn't try very hard to find foreign DNA. I'm sure John would argue with that, protecting his brothers in blue, but I've seen this too often to not be cynical. Police making a snap judgment. The body cams from the uniforms at the scene recorded them already referring to Shane as the killer.

"But I've never seen a stabbing with so many blows where the assailant didn't cut himself. Blood is slippery, and once it's covering the knife, it's pretty much impossible to strike that hard and not have your hand slip down onto the blade."

"Agreed. What was the story with the flowers, then? Are you thinking that's how the killer got her to open the door?"

"Yes. The prosecution asserted he brought them with him, along with the card, she spurned him, and it enraged him. But none of the glass fragments had Shane's fingerprints. If he carried a vase of flowers into that house, his fingerprints would be somewhere. But the only prints they found were Cait's and the florist's."

"I sincerely hope the defense hammered on that."

"I wouldn't say *hammered,* but they did a pretty decent job of pinning down the forensic expert into stating it was inconsistent with what they found on-scene. Which was that Shane was bare-handed. But the prosecution then introduced the theory Shane had worn gloves, explaining how he left no fingerprints or cut his hand during the crime. All conjecture since they could never produce the gloves."

She put her fingers to her chin. "I think that's where I actually rolled my eyes, sitting there in court listening to that. I'm stunned the jury didn't give more weight to the fingerprint and blood spatter evidence, but you never know what they're going to give value to."

"What do you think they valued more?"

"Judge Mulaney's influence and providing the motive. And the flowers charged in Shane's name with a card that said, *my dearest Caitlyn, Please give me another chance. I can't live without you. Yours forever, Shane.*"

"Which, on its face, is condemning."

"It is. But Shane told the uniforms, and later repeated many times in his interrogation, he never picked up any flowers. They checked the credit card he carried with him and verified there was no charge. However, after checking the florist's records, they found there was apparently another card in his name."

"A card he didn't have with him at the time he was picked up?"

"Right. And the flower purchase was the only transaction on that card. Which, again, his defense attorney didn't bring to light. Said he didn't feel it was pertinent. The card was new. In his opinion, it made sense there would be only one charge on it. The jury never heard Shane didn't have the card on him at the time of his arrest, and it wasn't found in a search of his home. The only thing tying him to it was his name, and the fact the statement was mailed to his home a couple of weeks later."

He sat back down in his chair. "You know what I find odd? If you order flowers to be picked up, why have the florist fill out the card with such a personal message? *Give me a second chance?* Who tells someone else to put that on a card?"

"Precisely. And it isn't outside the scope of believability someone could have taken out a credit card in Shane's name."

"Happens all the time."

She leaned in and crossed her arms on the table. "My frustration has been that nobody we've talked to, not even Shane, can think of one person who would want to harm Caitlyn. Much less kill her. But it struck me after we realized the creep is the one sending me the messages and calling ..."

"The messages trying to warn you off this case."

"Exactly." She swallowed hard. "What if the creep is the guy? What if he killed Caitlyn?"

A big *what if*, but not without merit.

He folded his arms on the table and leaned toward her. "Then maybe the question shouldn't be who had it in for

Caitlyn, but who had something against Shane. Someone willing to murder the woman he loved and frame him for it. That's a lot of hate to want someone in prison for most of their remaining life. Almost as if they wanted to punish him for something."

She sat up straight. "I never thought to ask him that. I've always wondered who would want to kill Cait, but I've never asked if anybody had anything against *him*."

"Wouldn't hurt to see what he says." His eyes narrowed. "Slight of face but bulky in build. In a suit. The creep could have disguised himself, like he's been doing the past three weeks. If he is the guy, he planned that whole thing down to a *T*, but then got messy in carrying out the actual murder. Makes me wonder what happened to change up his plan. What made him so mad?"

She nodded. "Cait's fingerprints were on the knife. Not where they would be if she were using it for its intended purpose—"

"But where they'd be if she was pointing it at someone."

"Right. What if he had something else in mind? Something hands-off, like a gun. Or cleaner, like strangulation."

"But Caitlyn grabbed the knife."

"That's my theory. The flowers were scattered in the living room. Maybe she threw them at him and made a run for it. Got as far as the kitchen and grabbed the only weapon she could find."

"Then he took it from her."

"And maybe she said something. Something that angered him. Cait was no shrinking violet. I could see her getting in his face, even if she was terrified."

He rubbed his hand over the stubble on his chin. "That all fits."

"Now, if we only had a name to go with all those faces."

True that.

Suppressing a shudder, he said a quick prayer of gratitude

that Drew Hudson had had the presence of mind to order protection on his daughter immediately following that failed grab. Otherwise, Riley may well have suffered the same fate as her friend.

A fate he wouldn't—he couldn't—let happen on his watch.

Chapter Thirty-Two

"Oh, Frannie." Riley put her hand to her chest as her friend emerged from the bridal shop dressing room in the sixth gown she'd tried on over the past forty minutes. "That's the one."

She'd met her girls for a long lunch this Tuesday to dress-hunt for Fran's upcoming wedding. Their bridesmaids' dresses had already been chosen and placed on order. But the wedding gown was a much bigger deal. Every one Fran had tried on had been lovely, but Riley couldn't imagine it getting any better than this one.

Frances smiled at her reflection, her eyes alight. "It's gorgeous."

"No, *you're* gorgeous. That gown simply accentuates what's already you."

Avery swept a tear from her cheek. "You're stunning."

Barbara took Fran's arm and met her reflection in the mirror. "Kade is going to be a puddle by the time you get down the aisle."

Tears welled in Fran's eyes. "As long as he can choke out the 'I do's.'"

Riley laughed, trying to keep her own emotions in check. Fran. The first of their little quartet to get married. It was all so exciting. "That man is so ready to get to the 'I do's, I'm surprised you two haven't eloped."

Frances giggled and swiped at a tear. "I know. He keeps saying June feels like a year away."

Avery released a heavy sigh. "You're so blessed, Fran. You've found your perfect match, a guy we all adore, he's head over heels for you, and now you're getting married. I can hardly stand it, I'm so happy."

More tears fell down Fran's porcelain cheeks, and they all wrapped their arms around her. "I am very blessed. I thank God every day for bringing Kade into my life." She smiled at Avery in the mirror. "But who knows, Ave? Maybe you'll be next. John sure seems like a keeper."

Avery's eyes lit up as they separated so Fran could study the dress that fit as if made for her. "A girl can hope. I can honestly say I've never felt like this before. And so quickly. He's ... he's ... no words. I can't find words."

"That's a first." Barbara winked at her with a grin.

Riley chuckled. "You're great together, so enjoy it. Who knows? This could be the last time you fall in love. Savor every moment."

Giggling, Avery clapped her hands like a little girl as she turned to Frances. "Honey, I'm trying one of those on. Just for kicks."

"Me, too." Barbara grabbed Riley's hand, pulling her up next to her. "Come on, Ri. Let's get our bridal on."

Laughing like teenagers, they rummaged through the racks, each of them picking dresses to try on. Satiny, skin-tight mermaid dresses, strapless gowns, puffy-sleeved gowns, and frilly Southern-belle confections none of them would be caught dead in. They spent half an hour giggling and teasing each other.

Until Riley walked out in a simple white gown with spaghetti straps, beaded bodice, and wispy long skirt. The girls quieted and stared.

Barbara pushed her glasses up on her nose. "Wow, Riley. That has your name all over it."

At the bank of mirrors, she stepped up onto the small platform. It was perfect. Simple yet elegant, comfortable, and easy to maneuver in.

"It is pretty." She turned one way, then the other. "I love this skirt, the way it moves."

Avery nodded. "Perfect for a summer wedding."

"And it would be great on the dance floor," Barbara said, herself standing in front of the mirror in a dress that sparkled with what had to be a million sequins, pearls, and beads festooned on the bodice and down the ballroom-style skirt. The pouf sleeves reached to her ears, but it was the huge bow on the back that took the whole thing over the top—the perfect dress for the bride who couldn't make up her mind because she liked *everything.* Definitely not Barb's style, but they'd dissolved into hysterics when she sashayed out in it as if she were on a Paris runway.

"Excuse me, ladies."

Colton's voice preceded him peering around the partition between the viewing area outside the dressing rooms and the rest of the upscale bridal shop. "Riley, your meet—"

She spun around, and their gazes tangled. Piped instrumental music filled the silence as those azure eyes raked over her from head to toe, leaving a current of fire in their wake.

"Um … Colton?" Avery said, herself dressed in a gorgeous, straight-skirted, ivory gown. "You were saying?"

"Oh … uh …" He cleared his throat. "Yeah. Sorry. Um, Riley, I wasn't sure if you were aware of the time."

She glanced at her watch. "Oh, right. Thank you." Gathering

the skirt of the gown in her hands, she stepped off the raised platform. "This has been fun, girls, but I'm meeting with a blood spatter expert at three." She glanced back at Colton. "I'm so sorry I've kept you guys waiting. I'll be out in a jiffy."

"No worries." He swallowed. "We can be there in twenty."

Back in the dressing room, Riley took a deep breath and let it out. Her skin tingled, and a swarm of butterflies flew around her insides, as if she were still under scrutiny.

Correction. Under *Colton's* scrutiny. When she'd swung around and encountered his thunderstruck gaze, her heart hammered against her ribs. He'd seen her in the formal dress she wore to the fundraiser at the Cantrells', but the look in his eyes as he'd studied her in this stunning wedding dress had been something else. Something ... electric.

Shaking her head, she reached back to unzip the dress. Nonsense. He probably hadn't been thinking of her at all, but of Theresa, the woman who'd faced him in front of an altar in a white dress. The woman who owned his heart and his devotion. The woman who'd pledged her life to him until death had so cruelly parted them.

Dressed again in her royal blue suit and white blouse, she pulled on her pumps and gathered her hair into the long ponytail she'd had it in before playing dress-up. As she left the dressing room, she ran her hand over the skirt of the gown hanging on the hook. It truly was the perfect dress. If she were getting married, her dress hunt would be over.

Speaking of which ...

With the gown draped over her arm to return to the rack, she stepped out of the dressing room and knocked on the door of Fran's. Her friend cracked it open, buttoning up the black blouse she'd worn with a pair of gray slacks for work.

"What about the dress, Frannie? Is it a keeper?"

Fran's face fell. "Riley, I can't afford that dress."

"It's on me. I want you to have it if it's the one you want. It's perfect, sweetie. If you love it, if it's what you want to wear for your day, then you'll have it. But order it instead of buying the one off the rack."

"I can't let you do that."

"Please, Fran? Let me do this for you? As your Maid of Honor, there's nothing I'd like to do more than give you the dress of your dreams. Please?"

"Riley, seriously, it's too—"

"Listen. I'm giving my card to the saleslady and telling her that's the dress. At least put it on hold so your mother can see it. I'll get my card from you or one of the other girls later."

Fran grabbed her in a hug and held on hard. "I love you." She pulled back and swiped at her face. "Okay, I'll have them hold it until Mom can come see it. And my sister. And Kade's mom. But only if you're absolutely sure."

"I couldn't be more sure of anything. Now, I have to run. Those guys are probably ready to shoot me themselves for keeping them cooling their heels. At a bridal shop, of all places."

Fran laughed and wiped her cheek again. "Oh, I don't think shooting you is what Colton had in mind at all. I think the man was considering proposing right then and there when he saw you in that gown."

Riley grinned as she leaned in close. "Between you and me? I probably would have said yes."

Chapter Thirty-Three

"Yes. I understand. Thank you for calling."

The call disconnected, but Riley still held the phone in her hand. Her stunned gaze went to the man outside her office. As if he could sense her eyes on his back, he turned and peered in the window before stepping into the doorway.

"Another call?"

She stared back at him.

"Riley? Did he call you again?"

She shook her head. "Um, no. That was the donor registry."

His forehead furrowed. "The bone marrow registry?"

"I'm a match."

His jaw fell as he dropped into a chair in front of her desk. "So quick? It usually takes a few weeks. What's it been?"

"Twelve days. The preliminary test on my swab came up a potential match for a critical patient, so they fast-tracked the processing. They want me to come in tomorrow for blood work and a physical."

"Tomorrow."

"I'm sorry. I know it makes more work for you guys."

"Are you kidding? This is important. We'll get on it right now."

He clicked his finger against his ear. "Jamison, Paxton, Riley's a donor match, and they want her at the hospital tomorrow for labs and a physical. Let's start gathering intel. Trevor, I'll relay the info from Riley to you so you can call the hospital for the names of staff she'll have to see. Get them over to Tech Ops. Paul, get on the horn with transportation and logistics. How we're getting in and out of the hospital, what floors and departments she'll need to be in."

He waited a beat and smiled. "Yeah, it's cool. Let's get started."

After clicking to disconnect his mic, he grinned back over at her. "I've been waiting for this call for four years. I can't help but be a little jealous right now."

Excitement replaced the shock of a moment ago. "I-I can't believe it. This is what I wanted to happen so badly, for somebody to get the gift of hope for Christmas. But to actually get their transplant by Christmas? That I never imagined."

"By Christmas? From what I recall when they explained the process to us for Theresa, it can take a couple of months."

"It usually does. But apparently, this little boy doesn't have much time. He was diagnosed four months ago, but it's progressing quickly. He's been in the hospital for treatment the past two months. And he's right here in Houston. This has God's hand all over it."

"That it does. So, they can process you that quickly?"

"Seems so. If my labs and physical show me to be a valid donor, they can pull my marrow as soon as they can get it on the schedule."

"You're donating marrow, not stem cells?"

"Stem cells via apheresis is the most common way they handle bone marrow donation, but for children with an adult donor, straight-up bone marrow is a better bet to prevent rejection."

"That's really brave."

She flipped her hand toward him. "I'll be under, so I'll never even feel it." Despite her bravado, her stomach pitched a little at the idea of the needle they would use to extract her marrow.

"Except for the next few days afterward."

"I'm ready. It's a small price to pay compared to what that little boy has already endured."

Hands down, the best day he'd ever spent on a protection detail.

Colton stood inside the playroom at the hospital Thursday afternoon. The children who could ambulate on their own, and a few on crutches or in wheelchairs, surrounded Riley as she passed out dolls and stuffed animals, coloring books and crayons, sketch pads and markers.

They'd been at the hospital for three hours already, but he was in no hurry to leave, not with all the smiles and laughter going on around him. He'd stayed with Riley while she gave several vials of blood for labs and filled out an extensive medical history. During her physical examination, he'd remained outside the door, but she'd invited him in with her during her consultation with the anesthesiologist.

"As Chairman of the Board for the foundation," she'd said, "this might be good information for you."

He'd agreed, since Theresa's course of treatment never progressed that far. Now, more than ever, he hoped he would get the call somebody needed his marrow. He couldn't think of a better way to honor his wife than to give to somebody else what she had so longed for herself.

A little girl with a knit beanie on her head stood from the child-sized table where she'd been earnestly drawing for the last several minutes. To his surprise, she walked straight over to him and held up her picture.

"Here, Mister." Her pixie face turned up to him with the slightest of grins. She couldn't have been more than seven years old. "I drawed this for you."

"For me? How nice." Deciding Riley was safe where she was for the moment, he kneeled to the child's level. "Tell me about your picture."

"That's you." She pointed to a tall man in the photo, standing in front of an open doorway, with yellow hair, blue eyes, a big smile, and wearing a suit. Or he supposed the black square around the body and bulky pants constituted a suit.

Had he been smiling? He didn't usually on a detail, but today had been all kinds of different. "Wow, that's great. You made me look lots better than real life."

Her giggle brought a warm flush to his skin. "You're silly."

He pointed to the other person in the picture, a tiny girl in a frilly dress with long brown hair holding his hand. "Is this you?"

"It's me and you. We're married."

"Oh, I see." He had to swallow to hold back his chuckle and schooled his features to reflect the seriousness of the one peering up at him. "Well, you are beautiful. Thank you for this lovely picture."

"You're welcome." She grabbed him around the neck, and he held her with one arm encircling her tiny waist. *Lord, please let this little girl grow up to be a bride.*

His little artist let him go with a kiss on his cheek. "See you later, Mister."

Oh, how he hoped so.

He stood and grinned down at the drawing. It would definitely go up on his fridge next time he was home.

He scanned the space, and his gaze met Riley's, staring at him from the middle of the room, surrounded by children involved in various activities. Her gentle smile caused his pulse to skitter, and, as it had the day they'd shared Thanksgiving at the estate—and that moment at the bridal shop two days ago—everything melted into the background.

Except her.

Those stunning green eyes, her dark hair spilling around her shoulders, the flowery blouse with blue slacks belted at the waist accentuating her figure.

I think you might be on your way.

Paul's words of two weeks ago came rushing back to him. On his way to falling for Riley? That couldn't happen. She needed him at his most vigilant, which meant no distractions. Not even her.

A male nurse walked in, pulling his attention away from Riley to check his ID. It matched with the intel he'd received from Tech Ops, so he nodded his approval.

The young man gazed around the room and back to Colton. "Nursing desk said you needed a fifteen-minute notice, correct?"

"Yes."

"The kids should go back to their rooms at three-thirty."

Colton consulted his watch. "We'll head out in ten." He clicked his com. "Jamison, we're leaving the peds floor at 3:25."

"Copy," Paul said through his mic.

"Trev, meet us at the elevator."

"On my way."

The younger man scanned the room. "This was an unexpected blessing today. Thank you all for coming and doing this for the kids."

"It was all Miss Hudson."

"As if giving her marrow isn't enough. Do you mind if I thank her?"

"No problem."

The nurse walked over to where Riley knelt in front of a little girl in a wheelchair, listening to something that must have been of great importance, judging by the earnest way Riley focused on her and listened with her whole self. She stood and accepted the nurse's handshake. Smiling, she shook her head and gestured back to Colton with her arm. Humble as always. Never taking any credit.

Watching her now, bringing smiles to these children who were dealing with challenges they shouldn't even know about, he couldn't help but think Theresa and Riley would've been friends. Different in a lot of ways, yet in others, so much the same. The same heart of compassion, the same love for the Lord. The same work ethic and humility when others tried to give them their due.

Theresa would've loved being here today. And, maybe, in a way she was, since the toys and art supplies—ordered from a department store yesterday afternoon for delivery to the hospital today—were given in the name of the Theresa Blankenship Foundation for Bone Marrow Matching. All paid for by the Hudson family.

His chest filled with warmth. While he kept a constant watch for anybody coming and going from the room, his focus always came back to Riley. Kneeling now beside a small boy, wearing a surgical mask and seated in a wagon outfitted with pillows and blankets to keep him comfortable. With his parents on the floor next to him, she watched as he drew something in a sketch pad. The dark circles under his eyes, bald head under a knit cap, the port in his chest for his chemo treatments, and the IV lines for his nutritional needs were only the outward signs of his illness. The evil ravaging his body was silent, invisible. And cared not who it destroyed.

The boy showed her his picture, and at her look of awe, his eyes lit up with delight at his accomplishment. She'd clearly made his day.

Colton's heart jumped. They'd not seen another little boy as ill as this one.

Could he be looking into the face of his miracle?

Chapter Thirty-Four

"You know, Miss Hudson, you're making our job a lot harder."

Colton grinned down at the woman walking next to him, her hand pulled through the crook of his elbow.

Riley's eyes rounded as they entered the luxurious lobby of downtown Houston's Whitmore Hotel. "I am?"

"Yes, ma'am. We're not only going to have to keep a lookout for the creep, but we're going to have to beat off every eligible male who will be clamoring for your attention tonight."

Her smile rivaled the brightness of the crystal chandeliers hanging overhead. "You can be charming, Mr. Blankenship, when you put your mind to it."

He shrugged. "Just telling it like it is. You look stunning."

Her face colored the most endearing shade of pink, and his heart caught. Had she not been told a thousand times how beautiful she was? Yet it always appeared to be news to her.

She'd spent her morning working on details for their family's upcoming New Year's charitable ball, then asked him over lunch if he'd like to help her go through witness depositions for Shane's case. He'd been only too happy to comply and enjoyed employing a little more of his investigator brain.

But three hours after disappearing to her suite to get ready for the evening, she'd descended the stairs at the estate—a vision in her red ball gown—and he couldn't tear his eyes away.

She'd once again put her hair up, this time in an intricate knot at the back of her head. Delicate straps graced her shoulders, with satiny red gloves pulled up to her elbows. A shimmering ruby and diamond necklace lay at her throat, and matching earrings dangled from her ears. The full skirt settled around her like a cloud, and dozens of tiny crystals sparkled from the bodice.

Although indeed lovely in her Christmas-hued dress, it was the sight of her four days ago—radiant in that white wedding gown—that had taken his breath away, rendering him speechless right there in front of her friends.

"You and the boys had something to eat?"

Her question pulled him back before he could go too far down that road he had no business traveling. "Yes, ma'am. Hilda takes good care of us."

"It's her gift. We're blessed to have her."

They entered the door of the elegantly decorated ballroom, where dozens had already gathered amongst the greenery, red and green ribbons, white lights, and at least ten Christmas trees he'd counted so far for the country club's Christmas extravaganza. A pianist situated in a corner played holiday favorites while guests milled around in groups, conversing while enjoying pre-dinner cocktails and *hors d'oeuvres*.

"There's John, Avery, and Barbara. Frances and Kade are probably on their way." She peered up at him. "I wish you could be at our table with us."

Suddenly, he did too. He'd never once had any desire to take part in high society shindigs until Riley had pulled him into her circle of friends. These ladies didn't hold themselves above others but eked out every bit of joy and laughter they could whenever they were together.

He leaned in and caught a hint of her soft jasmine-ginger fragrance. "Don't worry about me. You have fun. I'll stay as close as I can without getting in your way."

"You're never in my way."

Smiling, he nudged the small of her back and followed behind as she made her way to her table. Several people greeted her along the way, and she responded with a bright smile and listening ear.

The week had been a busy one, what with Everett's case, her charity events, and the unexpected trip to the hospital on Thursday. Unfortunately, the creep had also been busy. Riley received two more letters that week, all with photos of her with her detail right next to her.

It was driving him nuts that they hadn't been able to identify this guy when he had apparently been right in front of them. Granted, any of those photos could've been taken with a long-range lens from a car, a window. Anywhere. Yet it still galled him the creep could see them, but they had no idea he was even there.

Riley's nerves had to be frayed, but so far, she hadn't let it stop her, still going about her life as usual. She had to be the bravest person he'd ever met, and he'd worked with men and women who put their lives on the line for others his entire career.

His gaze panned the large room. Trevor and Paul had taken up the posts they'd been designated last night when they went over the detailed information provided by Tech Ops. All entrances into the ballroom, restrooms, doors to the kitchen area, backgrounds and IDs on all male catering staff. Even the musicians.

Paul and Trevor would stay, for the most part, within their assigned areas, leaving their posts only if they saw something suspicious. Colton would stay as close to Riley as he could without, as he'd told her, getting in her way.

Two hours into the evening, after cocktail hour and dinner, Barbara showed up at his side. "I see you're as diligent as always. Can I bring you anything?"

He glanced at her but returned to perusing the area. "No. But thank you. Company policy."

"I see."

His brow furrowed when Riley walked out onto the floor on the arm of a man who appeared altogether too besotted.

"Grant Bellows."

"Pardon?"

"The guy Riley's with. Grant Bellows. Very successful obstetrician. They've known each other forever, and I think he's been in love with her about as long. He's just never had the guts to make it known."

"I'd say he's making it known right now."

"Ah, yes. The look. I'm quite familiar with that look, knowing Riley for as long as I have. But she's completely ignorant of it." She paused. "Kind of like you the day you saw her in that wedding gown."

He whipped his head around. "I'm sorry?"

She chuckled. "She is a stunner, that's a fact. And as beautiful in spirit. We've all noticed there's … something … between the two of you. You should let her know how you feel, Colton. Before somebody else sweeps her off her feet."

He followed her gaze back to the couple gliding around the floor. "He can ballroom dance."

"Say again?"

"Uh, nothing. Listen, Barbara, I can't talk. Need to stay on my toes here. I hope you understand."

"Oh, absolutely. I just wanted to thank you for watching out for her. It means a lot to all of us. I don't know what we'd do if we lost her. You know?"

He nodded. "I know. We'll keep her safe."

"I know you will. Nice talking to you, Colton. I'm looking forward to working with you on your foundation board."

She walked away, and he again started his scan from one point of the room around to the opposite, always keeping a covert eye on Riley and the people surrounding her. But his focus always came back to her, and lingered too long.

Riley and her doctor dance partner walked off the floor, her hand pulled through his arm until they rejoined their group of friends. After another visual pass around the room, his gaze met hers from several yards away. She excused herself and headed his direction, leaving young Dr. Bellows to watch her with a disappointed frown.

She came to a stop beside him. "How are you holding up?"

"Fine. You?"

"Great. I enjoy seeing people around the holidays. Everybody's so jovial and lighthearted." She sighed and crossed her arms over her midsection. "I can't help thinking what a waste this is, though. All these obscenely wealthy people under one roof and not a charitable donation in sight. I spoke with the social committee a couple of years ago about making this a fundraising opportunity by sponsoring a charity every year, but they shot me down."

"Why's that?"

"They want this to be an event for their club members, to say *thanks for your membership, we appreciate you.*"

"Understandable."

He panned the room, stopping at a waiter staring at Riley from several feet away. Squinting, he finally ID'd the young man as one of the staff vetted by their team. Riley being Riley did, indeed, make their job harder, because she caught the attention of men regularly. Yet always seemed utterly oblivious to it.

"At least the club hosts several other events during the year that benefit charities. No, thank you," she said as an aside to another waiter who walked up with a tray of champagne. "Have you had anything to drink or eat?"

"Not why I'm here."

"I know that. But you three should try the buffet. It's fabulous. Take turns. I'm very safe here."

"Did you know that guy?"

"What guy?"

"The waiter who just walked by."

"No."

"And the musicians. You know all of them?"

"No."

"I see." He let his eyes wander over several guests coming in the door from the lobby. "Do you know the caterer? All the servers, photographers, hotel personnel?"

"Okay, you've made your point. You still need to eat. What if I stay with you?"

"Riley, we already had dinner back at the house. We're fine."

"Oh, no."

"Oh, no, what?" His eyes snapped around the room but noticed nothing of concern.

"Cal Gentry. Two o'clock and approaching fast."

Colton glanced to his right. A tall, dark-haired man walked toward them, his smoldering gaze fixed on Riley.

She spun to face him. "Dance with me."

"Riley—"

"Colton, please. You're supposed to protect me, right? Well, protect me."

He sighed. Not exactly standard protocol, but with her looking at him all desperate-like, what could he say? "All right. Come on."

He led her onto the dance floor by the hand and took her in his arms. They swayed together in silence for a moment, and he couldn't miss the glare the man still standing at the tables shot their way.

"Why do you need protecting from Pretty Boy Gentry?"

She chuckled. "He is rather nice-looking, isn't he?"

"Not really my type."

She laughed outright, and he couldn't help smiling. "Nor mine. We went out once. Major bore. Talked nonstop about himself the entire evening. Not that I didn't want to know about all his travels and his hobbies and whatever else. It was rather interesting … for about the first hour. Then I asked him what charitable organizations he was involved with, and he gaped at me as if I'd asked him to cut off his right arm. The only charitable giving he'd probably consider would be a building or something with his name on it."

"Majorly rich, then."

"Old money."

"Like you."

"Well … yeah. But we all work too. He does nothing other than spend his millions. And not on anything worthwhile. He thinks he lives this exciting, thrilling life. But it's hollow. Meaningless."

He stared down at her. "What do you want in your life? For your life?"

Her fingers did that thing with his lapel that made his neck tingle. "I want my life to mean something. I don't want attention. I just want to do something with what I've been blessed with. I like to think I'd feel that way if I had to live from paycheck to paycheck. As long as you're breathing, you can give something to society. A helping hand, a few hours of your time to serve meals to the homeless, or help build a house for someone who doesn't have one. Even blood and bone marrow. There's no limit to what people can do. You don't have to have money. But I do. So I'm able to do more than the average citizen."

"You give a lot more than money. Charity work is like a second full-time job for you."

"Because I love it. It brings me joy."

He smiled. "I can tell. It shows. You're always happier when you're doing something. Even in your career, you're helping people who can't help themselves."

"As are you. I might give of my time and money, but I don't think I could stand in the line of fire for somebody."

He couldn't pull his focus from her eyes. "I bet you would for somebody you truly cared for. Somebody you loved."

Her expression sobered, and they barely moved with the music. When had the lights dimmed? It was as if they were all alone in the world.

He pulled her closer, their faces inches apart. Her lips parted—

The unmistakable pop of a handgun made her flinch in his arms. He pushed her to the floor before the second pop sounded somewhere near the kitchen.

Pandemonium broke out. People tripped over them as they ran. He balanced his weight on his elbows so he didn't crush Riley underneath him.

"Get down!" he yelled at people either running or frozen in panic around him. A woman stood beside them, so he grabbed her arm and pulled her to the ground as another round popped off, followed by a fourth.

Riley sobbed from beneath him. "Make it stop! Please, God, make it stop!"

When he heard no other shots over the din of screams and shouts, glass breaking, and feet running, he looked up and around. A body lay sprawled on the floor several feet from the kitchen door.

Paxton.

His gaze panned the still darkened room. Paul ran toward the kitchen with his gun unholstered. He glanced at Trevor but kept going. Gut-wrenching as it was to leave an injured or dying colleague, they'd been trained to secure the principal first.

Paul must have seen Colton had Riley, so he was going for the SUV.

Riley's sobs tore him open, but her prayer was now a mumbled one. "Please, God. Please, God."

"Riley, you hit?"

"Please, please …"

"Riley."

"I'm okay."

With Paxton down, he was on his own. But he needed to get her somewhere safe, not in the middle of a dance floor being trampled by panicked people.

"Let's go." He grabbed her and pulled her to her feet, keeping his body around her as he directed them to the perimeter. They needed to get out of the building. But until they could find the shooter, it was more important to get her out of sight.

People lying on the floor or running toward the exits impeded their progress. Once across the room, he grabbed a table near a wall and toppled it, scattering tableware, gourmet food, cloth napkins, and flowers across the floor. He pushed a shaking Riley behind it, shielding her between the table and the wall.

Her tear-streaked face peered up at him. "What's happening? Is he still here?"

"I don't know. I haven't heard any more shots since the first few."

"Where are the girls? My family? Are they okay? Is anybody hurt?"

"I don't know, Riley."

She closed her eyes and tears squeezed through to fall down her cheeks. "Please, God, let everybody be okay."

Colton scanned their immediate area. No sign of the girls or her family, but he couldn't see what was happening in front of the overturned tabletop. His ears strained for any hint of gunfire. Women crying and men shouting, people calling out names to locate others in the dark, but no other shots.

Riley's brother Alex ducked around the table and kneeled on her other side. At least one other Hudson accounted for. "It's okay, Riley. We're all fine."

"The girls?"

"All good."

She put her head down on her arms crossed over her bent knees, the skirt of her red dress pooled around her as sobs shook her body. The first time Colton had ever seen her cry, and it almost undid him.

John rushed over, service weapon drawn. "Looks like the shooter's gone. Somehow got out during all the chaos. Your guy must have seen something, otherwise he'd have never left his post. I'm going to go check on him."

Riley's head sprang up. "Check on him? Who? Was someone hit?"

John and Colton exchanged a look.

"No!" Her scream pierced the air as she tried to stand.

Colton pulled her back down.

"Trevor? Is it Trevor?"

"Yes. But we don't know anything yet."

"Oh, no. No, no, no." She put her head back down on her knees, her whole body shaking.

Kevin ran over, and Colton stood. "Kevin, Alex, can you stay with your sister? I need to check on Paxton."

With a nod, Kevin took Colton's place beside Riley. "We've got her."

"This is my fault." Her voice quivered, muffled by her skirt. "My fault."

Kevin pulled her close. "None of this is your fault."

Colton winced as he left to check on his fallen colleague. No, this wasn't Riley's fault.

This was his.

Chapter Thirty-Five

Police burst into the room as Colton reached Trevor, only minutes after the first shot was fired. Yet it seemed much longer. John barked orders to the uniforms, and Colton dropped to his knees beside his friend, on his back but trying to push himself up.

"Stay down, Pax."

"Why?" His breath ragged, he pushed himself up with one arm. "Hit … my vest."

"You're sure? Nothing penetrated?"

"Pretty … sure. Just … knocked the … air—"

"I got it. Don't talk." Colton put his arms under Trevor's and helped him sit up. "Better?"

Trevor nodded, still working to draw air into his lungs.

Colton examined Trevor's shirt, where a clear bullet hole penetrated through to the soft vest they wore when out with a principal. Lightweight, easy to conceal. Most people weren't even aware they wore them.

He put his finger through the hole to the indentation left in the vest. "You may have a broken rib. Pretty good dent here."

Trevor wrapped his arm across his middle and grimaced. "Wow. I just took my first bullet for a principal."

"And it's my fault."

Trevor's brow creased. "How do you figure?"

"I shouldn't have been on the dance floor." Colton searched for the bullet but came up empty.

"You were with Riley. Exactly where you should've been."

Colton disagreed. "Mind if I pat you down? Can't find the bullet."

"Go for it."

As gently as he could, he patted around Trevor's middle. "Nothing."

"Could've bounced. Hopefully, forensics will find it. We've gotta get Riley home."

"You should go to the hospital. Get some X-rays. Make sure nothing's broken."

"After we get Riley home. Get me on my feet, and I can handle it from there."

"You sure?"

"Affirmative. Come on. We're not done here yet." He sucked in a breath and clutched his midsection as Colton helped him to his feet. "Man, that hurts."

"Sorry, buddy."

"Was anybody else injured?"

"Not that I know of. How'd we miss him? How'd he get so close to her?"

"He must be a master of disguise."

Colton gave Trevor a second to catch his breath once standing. "What tipped you off about the threat?"

"They turned down the lights, and a waiter I hadn't seen before came out of the kitchen." He took a deep breath and winced. "Figured a closer look might be warranted, so I started his way. He had his tray balanced on one hand, but the other was inside his jacket. I saw the butt of the gun and made a beeline for him. Got between him and you guys before he got the first shot off. I didn't have time to take aim myself."

"You did the right thing. Riley's our first concern."

"Yes, she is. So, stop worrying about me, and let's get her out of here."

Colton made his way to the overturned table, Trevor a few steps behind. Riley still crouched in a ball behind it, her brothers flanking her with their arms around her. Drew stood next to his wife behind them, Candace holding onto a tearful Avery while Frances sat between Barbara and Kade at the next table, fear etched into all their faces.

Colton's heart broke at the sight of Riley's shaking shoulders. "Riley."

When she didn't acknowledge him, Kevin stood to let Colton kneel beside her. He put his hand on her shoulder. "Riley. We have to go."

"No. He's out there. I'm safe in here."

"We need to get you home."

She finally looked up, and the stark panic on her face clutched at his gut. "Did anybody die?"

"No. Everybody's fine."

"Trevor?"

The injured bodyguard stepped around the table. "Right here, Ri."

Tears spilled from her eyes. "Are you shot?"

"Hit my vest."

"I'm so sorry. I'm so terribly sorry."

"Not your fault. But Colton's right. We need to get you home."

At Alex's nod, she rose to her feet with Colton's help, visibly trembling from head to toe. When she faltered, he wrapped his arm around her and let her lean into him. Paxton pulled his gun and preceded them to the designated exit, his head moving side to side.

She stumbled again. Before she could fall, Colton scooped her up and carried her against his chest, her legs draped over his arm. He could move them both more quickly with her in his arms than trying to keep her on her feet. She grabbed him around the neck and buried her face against his skin, sending tingles down his spine.

"You're all right. I've got you, Riley. You're okay."

They finally made it out the back exit they'd planned to use in the event of an emergency, hoping, as always, they wouldn't have to use it. After putting her in the car, he climbed in right next to her instead of walking around to the other side. He wrapped her in his arms again and held her close, her face pressed to his shoulder, as they pulled quickly away from the building.

The heater ran full blast, but she shook as if left out in the cold for hours. He let her go only long enough to pull off his suit coat and wrap it around her, pulling her close again.

Her shaking gradually eased as they made their way toward the estate, her tears falling silently now. So many tears she'd pent up all these weeks she'd been terrorized by a madman. Culminating in tonight's almost successful plan to end it once and for all.

He put his cheek to the top of her head. "I'm sorry," he whispered. "I shouldn't have let this happen to you."

She turned her face up to his. "You didn't." Her soft voice quivered. "It's not your fault."

He brushed a loose lock of hair off her forehead and placed a light kiss there. She curled into him again and didn't move until they pulled up to the front steps.

Colton reached for the door handle. "Paul. Get Trevor to the hospital. I'll see her inside."

The driver nodded. "You're all right without the two of us for a while?"

"Yes. The Hudsons are right behind us, and we have adequate security here."

"Copy. I'll come back after we find out what the doctor says."

Colton climbed out of the backseat and reached for Riley's hand, helping her out and wrapping his arm around her shoulders. They walked up the steps to the door. Riley jumped when it opened. No doubt her nerves were vibrating at full tilt.

She put her hand to her heart. "Hilda."

"Oh, honey." The tearful cook took Riley's other arm and helped them in. "We heard. Are you all right, sweetie?"

"Um, I'm not sure."

"She wasn't hit," he assured the older woman. "Just a little shaken up. Can you come upstairs with us and help her out of her dress? She's a little unsteady yet, and I don't want to leave her alone."

"You got it, Mr. Blankenship."

Upstairs, he left Riley in her bedroom with Hilda and Irene, the house manager. Down the hall in his own room, he changed out of his rumpled tux into jeans, a sweatshirt, warm socks, and tennis shoes.

Walking back out into the hallway, he met Hilda coming out of Riley's room with Irene. "How is she?"

Fresh tears fell down her face. "Scared to death, poor thing. I'm going to make her some hot chocolate." She brushed a hand across her cheek. "The girls got here a few minutes ago. They're with her now. Kade's in the living room with the family."

"I'm glad she has such good friends."

"Many. The main line hasn't stopped ringing since it hit the news."

"I can imagine." He glanced over at Riley's door and back again. "If she or anyone needs me, I'll be in the study up here. I need to call in."

"I'll bring some cocoa for you, Mr. Blankenship."

"Thank you."

Irene stepped toward him as Hilda walked away. "How is Mr. Paxton?"

"Paul took him to the hospital for X-rays and a work-up. We'll know more after that, but hopefully he'll just be sore for a few days."

"I'm praying he's well. A hero, he is."

His stomach clenched. "That's a fact."

But Trevor shouldn't have been the one to take that bullet. Colton was lead man, assigned to the principal, not to a position in a room full of people. He didn't want to be a hero, but it rankled that one of his men was this minute being checked in an emergency room because his team lead had been distracted.

"I'll take care of your clothes. Are they in your room?"

"Yes, but I can send my tux out for cleaning."

She flipped her hand at him. "Nonsense. I'll take care of it."

"Thank you, Irene. I left it on the bed."

"Thank *you*, young man. For taking such good care of our girl."

His gut twisted as Irene strode down the hall to his room. He didn't deserve gratitude. Not after tonight's fiasco.

In the upstairs study, he sat behind the desk, took a deep breath, and released it for a count of ten. Shaking his head, he reached for the phone. The line picked up after one ring.

"Mack. I guess you've heard."

Chapter Thirty-Six

"And, Father, we give all of this into Your hands," Frances prayed. "Grateful Riley is safe and unhurt but pleading for the quick apprehension of this man who wishes to cause her harm. Please be with Trevor and help him make a quick recovery from his injury. We pray all these things in the name of Your precious Son, Amen."

Riley stood in a circle with these three ladies she loved like sisters, tears running down their faces, wrapped in each other's arms. "We've been through a lot of stuff together over the past twenty years, but never anything quite like this. Have we?"

Barbara sniffled and pulled a tissue from the box on the end table, then passed it to Avery. "This is definitely a new one. But nothing we can't handle, with the Lord's help."

"That's right." Avery took a tissue and passed the box to Fran. "We're here for anything you need. Through thick and thin."

Fresh tears started down Riley's face as Fran handed her a couple of tissues. "Y'all's lives were at risk because of me. Everyone in that room tonight was at risk because of me. If something had happened to any one of them, to *you,* I couldn't live with it. I can hardly stand Trevor being injured, and he's *paid* to protect me."

Frances gave her a squeeze. "It wasn't your fault, Ri. It was that guy. The one who's doing all of this. You did nothing wrong."

Barbara nodded. "That's right."

Avery dabbed at her eyes while Riley swiped at her cheeks in an effort to stem her flow of tears. It seemed as if she was making up for years of not crying in this one night.

"Thanks, you guys. I can't tell you how much I appreciate you being here."

"Of course we would be here." Barbara put her glasses back on. "We can stay all night, if you need us to. It'll be like college all over again."

Riley's friends were still dressed in their evening finery while she now wore warm sweats, had scrubbed her face clean, and brushed through her hair, leaving it loose. "I'll be fine. Really. You've been here over an hour already and should probably get home to get some sleep. Are you all in separate cars?"

Avery shook her head. "We came with Frances and Kade. John had to stay at the … um … I mean … you know—"

"Had to stay at the hotel. For the investigation. Avery, I'm so sorry. I've intruded on your evening out."

"Now, you just stop, Riley Hudson. Like they said, nobody blames you for any of this. I'm proud of my man for doing his job so well and caring enough about my friend to put in all this extra work. Once this is all behind us, we'll have plenty of time together. And you'll be free to live your life without this hanging over you."

A soft knock sounded on the doorframe before Colton made an appearance. "I hate to eavesdrop, but we can help with getting the ladies home. Paul's back and all set to take Barbara and Avery." He turned to Frances. "And Kade said he's not leaving without you. So, if you stay the night, guess we'll have to find him a spot too. Not that it would be a problem in this place."

Frances laughed as she wiped tears from her face. "That's a fact. We could probably put up a dozen folks here. But under the circumstances, I don't think we want to make all that extra work for the staff. Hilda's already been up here three times to check on us, bless her heart."

"Have you heard anything about Trevor?" Riley asked.

He nodded. "No broken ribs. A deep bruise into some muscle. He'll be paid to lie around and recover for the next few days. They'll send someone to cover in the meantime."

"I need to call Gemma."

"Tomorrow. Tonight, you need to get some rest."

Barbara took her hand. "He's right, Ri. Please try to get some sleep."

Riley could only hope. Sleep seemed a long way off, but she was thankful for her friends' concern.

As they said their goodbyes for the night, the girls hugged and thanked Colton for keeping her safe, although he seemed uncomfortable with their gratitude. Embarrassed. As if he didn't deserve it, when he deserved so much more than she could ever convey.

From the moment he'd scooped her up and held her close on their way out of the ballroom, she couldn't remember the last time she'd felt so safe. So secure. Even amid all that chaos. And once inside the SUV, speeding away from the hotel, he'd held her tight to still her trembling. She'd wanted to stay there until this was all behind her. For as long it took.

But that was impossible—a silly romantic dream about a man she couldn't have.

He was doing his job. And she was falling in love. Opposite ends of the spectrum.

"Riley?"

Her eyes focused on the man now standing in front of her. "Are you okay?"

She stared at him, her arms crossed tightly over her stomach as tears rushed to her eyes.

He stepped forward and enveloped her once again in his arms. "I wish I could help you. Wish I could do more for you."

"More than what you've already done?" She buried her forehead against his shoulder. "I don't know how you could do any more for me."

"It doesn't seem near enough at the moment."

She peered up at him but didn't move away. "They didn't catch him, did they?"

"No. He got away."

Her throat constricted. "He got away."

"They'll get him, Riley."

She rested her cheek against his broad chest, his arms once again encircling her as hers went around his waist. "He was going to kill me tonight."

"He should have never been that close to you. Thank goodness Trevor was on his toes. I sure wasn't."

She pulled back, her hands skimming down his arms until they joined his. "What are you talking about? You were right there."

"But I was watching *you*."

"Isn't that your job?"

His hands squeezed hers. "My job is to watch *out* for you. Big difference. And Pax ended up taking the bullet, not me."

"Would you have taken a bullet for me?"

"In a heartbeat."

"Because it's your job."

His eyes filled with moisture as the silence lingered, their gazes locked. "No." The huskiness of his voice sent tingles along her spine. "Because it's you."

Bringing his hand to her cheek, he brushed away a tear with

his thumb before lowering his face to within a breath of hers. A pause, then the softest, tenderest of touches as his mouth found hers. A moment of discovery, of letting go. An excruciating sweetness before he angled his head to take a bit more.

Riley brought her hands to his chest and gathered his sweatshirt in her fists to bring herself closer. The pull, the longing, increased, and their arms found their way around each other.

Riley had never experienced such comfort in a man's embrace. Had never felt more at home.

Could she hope to live there forever?

Chapter Thirty-Seven

Better than he'd ever dreamed.

Colton had imagined this countless times. Imagined holding Riley close, his arms wrapped around her. Their first kiss and all the kisses after that. The images permeated his sleep, popped into his day at times when his mind needed to be on other things. No matter how hard he'd fought it. Tried to keep his growing feelings for her in check.

All his efforts turned to dust the second he pulled her close. He hadn't kissed a woman in years, yet this kiss felt like … home. As if this weren't their first.

But it was. His first with Riley. The woman who claimed more and more of his heart, his soul, every day, every hour he spent with her.

She rose up on her toes, pressing closer, and he thought he'd combust with a yearning for more. But before things could go somewhere they shouldn't, somewhere they couldn't, he let the kiss soften until he pulled away and put his forehead to hers.

"Riley …" He hardly recognized his voice, thick as it was with the release of everything he'd kept locked inside.

"Don't say you're sorry, Cole." Her hands framed his neck. "Please, please don't say you're sorry."

"I'm not sorry, sweetheart. But, Riley, we need to get some control here." He took a breath, their foreheads still pressed together. "It's been a long time since I've been with anybody this way." He pulled back, her hands slipping to his chest as his came to her face. "And this probably isn't the best time. Emotions are … high tonight."

"Maybe." She peered deep into his eyes, her own shining with tears and something more. Something he'd never expected to see in another's ever again. "But I don't regret it. Not for a second. It's not as if I haven't dreamed about it a hundred times."

He chuckled before giving her another soft kiss. "You're not alone there."

Taking her by the hand, he led her to the sofa and pulled her close to his side, her knees drawn up as she snuggled into him. How could this feel so natural, so familiar, considering they'd never had an intimate moment?

"Stay with me a while?"

"For as long as you need me."

"And I'll be here for you." Her head burrowed into the crook of his neck, and he laid his cheek against her silky hair.

"You already have been. You brought me back to the Lord, Ri. I'd walked so far away, I couldn't even hear Him anymore. Until you showed me the way."

"Oh, I don't know." She brushed her hand over her face. "It seemed to me you were searching for a way back. I prayed for you every day and left you in His hands."

"But you reminded me how much He loves me. And that He loved Theresa enough … enough to heal her. Even if it wasn't on this side of heaven, she is healed. And until you painted the picture for me of her living happy and whole with the Lord, I hadn't realized how selfish I'd been, wishing she were here on this broken planet with me rather than in heaven with God."

"You weren't being selfish. You were being human. This is all we know, and, of course, we want our loved ones with us. What I wouldn't do to have more time with my grandparents who have already gone ahead. But I know they're in a better place, and that gives me peace."

"Well, I'm ready to move into the future and stop holding onto the past."

Silence stretched for a moment. "Maybe with me?" The uncertainty in her quiet voice yanked at his heart.

He tightened his arm around her and closed his eyes. A deep breath in brought her subtle jasmine and ginger fragrance with it. "I can't imagine anybody else."

"I can't imagine being with anybody but you, either."

He tipped her chin up to lay a gentle kiss on her mouth. "You are so beautiful."

"I'm kind of a wreck right now, but that was sweet."

"I love it when you're natural. You're a knock-out all dolled up, that's for sure. But when you're like this—all Riley—that's my favorite."

"You're my favorite too." She yawned and snuggled back into him. "I was under the impression you were completely unaffected. By me, I mean."

"Not since that first night in your dad's study. When you so graciously called me *tactical gear*."

"A name you wear proudly, so you told me."

"I do. I was hooked from that moment, although I didn't want to admit it. Now I'm honored to be your tactical gear, Riley Hudson."

"Hmm. And I love being your principal." A minute later, her even breathing told him she'd drifted off to sleep. Sleep she desperately needed.

After clicking off the lamp beside the sofa, he crossed his

feet on the coffee table, closed his eyes, and held her close. She fit him perfectly. So small and so soft, and she smelled so good.

A small niggling of doubt tickled the back of his mind, but he ignored it. He didn't want to think logically for once. He wanted to live what he'd only experienced in his dreams. Curled up with this woman who'd been nothing but one surprise after another from the first day.

How could she wonder if she affected him? Couldn't she tell? He'd let go with her as he rarely did, having always prided himself on his ability to hold himself in check. Not let anybody see inside. What he felt. But the moment she'd looked at him with those emerald eyes filled with question, he'd lost that resolve. She'd destroyed it with her utter transparency.

In her sleep, she nestled closer and draped her arm across him, her forehead pressed to the side of his neck. He tightened his hold. So comfortable. So natural. Holding her like this. As if he had a million times before tonight.

"I love you, Colton."

Her whisper in the dark lifted the veil of sleep that had begun to lower. His eyes slowly opened as the cloud he'd been trying to push away crashed down on him. Now he understood what that doubt had been trying to tell him. What he'd known all along.

And his heart splintered in his chest.

Chapter Thirty-Eight

Riley woke to the sun peeking through the drapes in her bedroom. Smiling, she stretched before burrowing deeper under the covers. Her head and heart warred, the joy inside an odd juxtaposition to the memory of all that had happened the night before.

The guilt that she'd put all those people in danger by her mere presence. That she'd ruined the club's much-anticipated Christmas ball.

That Trevor had taken a bullet meant for her.

Pressing her eyelids tight, she instead forced her heart's memory over her head's. Colton pulling her tight against him. The gentleness of his kiss before desire swept them up into a sea of sensation. His strength of character to pull back before things went too far.

She'd fallen asleep in his arms, awakening sometime in the wee hours to find herself being carried into her bedroom and placed gently on her bed. He'd pulled the covers up to her chin and kissed her softly before she drifted back to sleep.

Rolling over onto her back, she smiled up at the ceiling. The next days and weeks promised to be new and exciting. Learning more about Colton, hopefully being drawn into his family as he'd already been with hers. Growing into whatever God would have them become.

She sat up and swung her legs over the side, catching her first glimpse of the bedside clock. "Eleven!"

She couldn't remember the last time she'd slept so late, if ever. Apparently, her parents had decided to stay in and watch the church service on live stream. Not a bad decision, since she didn't wish to endanger more lives. Perhaps Colton would like to watch it together.

After showering, drying her hair, and dabbing on a bit of makeup, she pulled on a pair of 501 jeans and an oversized red-and-white-striped sweater. Deciding against shoes, she wore only a pair of fuzzy red socks.

Her stomach growled, and she checked the clock again. 11:40. Time for lunch. And where was Colton?

She opted to leave her hair down and walked out into the hall. As she neared the foot of the stairs, men's voices filtered out of her father's study. Her pulse hitched, and she smiled as she walked up to the door and tentatively poked her head inside.

There he was. Even more handsome this morning than she'd considered him every morning before, even in jeans and a button-down shirt instead of one of his suits. But today he was hers. And that made all the difference.

Her father gestured with his hand. "Riley, come on in."

"Good morning. I can't believe I slept so late."

"Not a problem, honey. I'm sure you needed it."

Colton nodded in her direction before averting his gaze.

Her smile faded as she walked into the room, glancing from her father to Colton and back, the tightening in her stomach now having nothing to do with hunger. Something wasn't right.

To the side, standing where she'd first met her then-unwelcome detail, were two men and one woman. "Mack. Hello."

Mack inclined his head toward her. "Riley. I'm so sorry about what happened last night."

She glanced at the floor and folded her hands in front of her before meeting his eyes again. "It was … awful. But your guys handled themselves perfectly."

"Yes, well, that's kind of why I'm here."

"Oh?"

He gestured to the two at his side. "Riley, I'd like for you to meet Piper Bentley and Nowell Cooper. Piper, Nowell, this is Riley Hudson."

She shook their hands. "Hello, Ms. Bentley, Mr. Cooper."

"Please," the tall, red-haired man responded. "Call me Nowell."

The statuesque, blonde woman next to him gave her a small smile. "And you can call me Piper."

"Piper will be taking over for Trevor for the next week, more than likely," Mack said. "He put up a fight about having to stay home for a few days, but I finally threatened him with time off without pay if he didn't comply with doctor's orders."

Riley tried to smile around the dread moving through her chest. *Something wasn't right.* "Sounds like Trevor. I'm so relieved he's okay. I was praying so hard."

"We all were." He gestured to the man next to Piper. "Nowell here will be replacing Colton. He'll stay here at the house and will be your point man."

The floor dropped out from under her, like that momentary weightlessness when a roller coaster crests the highest peak and starts its descent. "What? Why?"

"Not my call. Colton decided it would be best to turn the reins over to someone else."

She spun back to the man she'd declared herself to, her heart knocking hard against her ribs. "You're leaving?"

"I thought it best."

"Because of what happened … last night."

"Yes."

Regret clouded his eyes and lined his face. Last night he'd said he wasn't sorry. Yet he clearly was. And now he was just … leaving. Leaving her. After all they'd shared mere hours ago.

"I see." She swallowed the lump swelling in her throat. "Then I'll leave you all to brief my new detail on my schedule and such." She turned back to Colton. "Thank you for all you did for me. I always felt safe with you."

Until now.

He reached out and shook her hand. "It was an honor."

Holding on tight, she held his gaze with hers, the air thick between them with the unspoken. She reluctantly let go of him, letting her fingertips linger at his for a brief moment, knowing it would be the last time she'd ever touch him.

Tears fell freely as she made her way back up the stairs, suddenly not hungry as her heart fell into pieces. In her suite, she curled up in a corner of the sofa where she'd fallen asleep in the arms of the man she loved the night before. The same man now walking out of her life.

Wrapping her arms around her knees, she stared at the window. Silent tears spilled down her cheeks as her mind fought to make sense of what had just happened. How could she have been so wrong? She'd believed him when he'd told her he'd be there as long as she needed him. That he cared about her. That he wanted to be with her.

But it had all been a lie.

She threw her head back, willing control over her emotional state. She hated crying. Hated being out of control.

Yet that's exactly what she was. Out of control. Loving a man who didn't—who wouldn't—love her back. She grabbed half a dozen tissues out of the box on the end table and pressed them against her eyelids.

Breathe. Just breathe. She could handle this. She had to. Colton had left her no choice.

"Riley?"

She pulled the tissues away and stared up at the man who'd pulled her together last night ... and shattered her this morning.

Colton walked in and stood inside the door. "I'm so sorry."

"Sorry about leaving? Sorry about last night? What exactly are you sorry about?"

He gave his head a small shake. "I ... I guess about all of it. Mostly about hurting you. I never intended to, Riley. I never wanted to hurt you."

"Then why? Why did you kiss me? Why did you hold me and say the things you did if it was all nothing?"

He held his hands out as he stepped closer. "Things got out of hand last night. Emotions were high. And we went somewhere we shouldn't have."

Against her will, another tear slipped down her cheek. "I'm in love with you, Colton. It doesn't have anything to do with emotions or fear. It's simple fact. I know my heart."

"Riley, you only think you're in love with me. I'm here in the form of your protector. Someone to keep you safe. I've seen it happen before."

"Oh, you've had other women fall in love with you on the job before. Is that it? Did you kiss them and tell them you'd be there as long as they needed you? No wonder they think they're in love with you."

"No. I've never crossed that line. Just with you."

She stood to face him. "If I'm only in love with you because you're my big knight in shining armor, how come I don't have feelings for Paul? Or Trevor? Trevor took a bullet for me, after all. Why aren't I fawning all over him?"

"Because Paul and Trevor aren't available. You'll see, Riley. Once I'm out of your life for a while, you'll see it wasn't me. It was just the idea of me."

Pain filled every crevice inside of her. "You think you know so much. But you don't, Colton Blankenship. You don't know what's right in front of you."

"Riley, it would never work with us. Think about it."

"Think about *what?*"

"You and me, we're from different worlds. Polar opposites of one another."

"This is about my *money?*"

His sigh came from a deep place. "It's not the money. It's the life. Look at all this. This house where you grew up. Look at the events and activities you take part in. Even the clothes you wear. I never owned a tux in my life until I started this job. And if I didn't have to wear suits for work, I'd live in jeans."

She glanced down at her denim-covered legs and bulky sweater before looking back up at him. "This has nothing to do with social status." Her voice trembled. "Or a damsel in distress falling for her rescuer. Admit you're scared. Isn't that what you kept telling me to do? Face the fear head-on. Deal with it and let it work for you. Isn't that what you said?"

His eyes narrowed. "And what is it I'm supposed to be afraid of?"

"You're afraid you're going to let someone else into your heart, and they'll leave you. You're afraid you're going to love someone again and lose them. You're scared, Cole. You know we could have a really great thing. A lasting, maybe forever thing, but you're afraid. And you can't move forward until you face it. With me or anybody else."

"Riley … I don't know what to say. What to tell you to make this better for you."

"Then I guess goodbye is all that's left."

He stood there and stared at her. His jaw flexed, his eyes traced her face. Would he change his mind? Jump in and trust God to grow them together?

She held her breath. But he shook his head and turned away. "Goodbye, Riley."

Chapter Thirty-Nine

Colton picked up his guest badge at the HPD Central Patrol Division and stood to the side instead of taking a seat, waiting for his escort to the Detectives Unit.

He hid a yawn behind his hand. Sleeping in his own bed under his own roof last night for the first time in months hadn't gone as expected. Every time he closed his eyes, all he saw was the devastation on Riley's face yesterday morning.

When he left her.

Shaking off the memory and self-recrimination, he stepped up as John Stapleton emerged from the restricted hall into the lobby.

He offered his hand. "John. Thanks for seeing me on such short notice."

The detective accepted his handshake with narrowed eyes. "Blankenship. Something I can do for you?"

"I'm hoping it's more what we can do together. Two heads and all that."

John crossed his arms. "Go on."

"Say hello to your new partner."

One eyebrow rose. "You got a badge over the weekend I'm not aware of?"

"Look." Colton sighed and splayed his hands on his hips. "I may no longer be on Riley's detail, but I'm not walking away from this. Petersen Security works alongside law enforcement all the time. I could get my boss to call your boss and blah, blah, blah, but you and I have already established a good working relationship. Let's put our heads together and solve this thing. For Riley."

"Riley. Speaking of—"

"Don't start. I've already had a barrage of texts from the girls. Including your beloved." His fault for letting Riley give them his number a few weeks ago in case they needed him or had information for him. "Let's just say I made a decision that was best for Riley."

"Best for Riley. To leave her detail."

"Trust me. Nowell's a top-notch lead man. He'll do right by her."

"Better than you, I hope."

A gut punch would've been preferred. He'd recover more quickly. It wasn't news to him he'd let Riley down. That he said things, did things, had her believing things, he couldn't follow through on.

"I deserve that. Nobody knows better than I how I blew it."

With a sigh, John stuck his hands in his pockets. "That was out of line. I apologize. Your reasons are your reasons, and I trust they were truly in her best interest."

Colton answered with a nod. "Now, do you think we can work together to get this thing done?"

"You think I haven't been trying?"

"I have no doubt. There's simply not a lot to go on so far. But, like I said, maybe two heads can bring this thing into the light."

John stared at him, then, apparently giving in, gestured for

Colton to follow him. Without a word, they took the stairs to the third floor and entered a large room where a dozen or more officers sat at their desks, either on the phone, staring at their laptop screens, or studying case files. Ringing phones punctuated the steady hum of conversation, and the aroma of strong black coffee wafted from a counter sitting inside the door.

John motioned to the pots lining the wall. "Help yourself."

"Think I will. Thanks." Colton poured himself a cup of the steaming brew, then joined John at his desk, planting himself in the chair next to it.

John tapped some keys on his laptop and studied his screen. "Okay, this all started with the attempted grab Saturday, November ninth. No video. Composite drew only a few dead-end tips."

"But we now know the guy disguises himself, so that tracks."

"Affirmative. Suspect left a card for Riley at the front desk of her building on Monday, November eleventh, another Wednesday, November thirteenth, and one on Friday, November fifteenth. Video footage shows what appears to be a different person each time, but we've pretty much verified it's the same guy. He also called her on that Friday, clearly altering his voice.

"Our cyber team—working in conjunction with Petersen—discovered a cloned social media page had been created on Wednesday, November thirteenth, five posts altogether, including the three with doctored images. Petersen had it taken down by Saturday morning, November sixteenth. We also know sometime that week—we suspect between Tuesday and Friday afternoon—he broke into her home and trashed the place."

"That window is based on …?"

"No muddy footprints or anything else he might've tracked in. It was a downpour on Friday, with the storm parked over us well into Saturday evening."

"Makes sense."

"We have nothing to tie the break-in to the messages she's received, so that's conjecture at this point."

"I don't believe in coincidences."

"I don't either, so that's why we're assuming it's connected. Riley received another card Monday, November eighteenth."

"That's when we tied him to the grab."

"Affirmative. We do have fingerprints from the envelopes, but nothing in the system. He used water to close the envelopes, so no DNA. Still, I'm shocked he delivered them without wearing gloves. It's winter. It wouldn't have been out of the ordinary."

"Maybe he isn't aware we can get prints from paper. Or maybe he expected Riley would open them and throw them out."

"All decent possibilities. Moving on. We didn't think anything else had happened that week until he made us aware he'd been at the shelter Thanksgiving dinner."

Colton rubbed his brow. "That kept me awake that night after seeing that photo, wondering how we missed scratch marks on the guy's hand. I talked to Paul and Trevor about it the next day, and Trev mentioned there were three that day who were amputees. One missing his left arm, but two missing their right. We know this guy can disguise himself. What if he somehow concealed his arm under baggy clothing and presented himself as an amputee?"

"Hmm." John rubbed his chin. "We have video from the two television stations that were there. We can run through it to see if anyone sitting in the photo's vantage point area has only one arm."

"Okay, next."

"Next came the call on Monday, November twenty-fifth, followed by the package with the photo from the Thanksgiving dinner and a tube of lipstick from her purse the day of the abduction attempt. Tuesday, he saw her leaving the office with her detail, then called her on Wednesday to tell her about it. She also received a photo in the mail of the donor drive. At least she wasn't in this one, so he didn't get that close."

"Close enough. How can we not spot this guy when he appears to be everywhere? He must not be a great shot, or doesn't have the firepower, because if he wanted to take her out long-range, he could've done it by now. That and taking the chance on Saturday tells me he needs to be close to get a shot off."

"I tell you, when I heard those shots Saturday night, I couldn't get Avery on the ground fast enough. It wasn't about anybody but her at that moment."

"Yeah. I hear ya." He knew exactly how that felt. The second he'd heard that first pop, his training had him pushing Riley to the floor in the split second before the second. But if that first round hadn't hit Trevor center mass, would it have found its mark? Or would he have been the one to take her bullet?

As it was, they were fortunate that only one of the other shots grazed a gentleman who was treated and released at the scene. It could've been a hundred times worse if anybody had been seriously wounded or killed.

John gave his head a shake. "Anyway, no cards last week but two phone calls, then the shooting Saturday, December seventh."

"We did catch video footage of him coming in with other kitchen staff. And the guy looks nothing like the composite or the videos of the card deliveries. He must have ditched the disguise on his way out, though, because there's nothing showing him leaving. Unless he waited it out somewhere and simply walked out later like any other guest of the hotel."

"Sure would help if we had a motive for all of this."

Colton scratched his chin. He probably should've shaved that morning, but after a restless night and no assignment to report to, he didn't want to waste the time he could be meeting with John. "We might."

John sat up straight. "I'm all ears."

"What if this all ties into the Shane Everett case?"

With a nod, the detective glanced around the bustling room before leaning closer with his arms crossed on the desktop. "That one's on my list, too, since the messages she received appear to be warning her off."

Colton kept his voice low, considering their location. "The abduction attempt occurred five days after her press conference announcing she was taking over Shane's appeals. I was out of the country at the time, but I watched a tape of it later, and she says right out Everett's innocent, and she's putting all the resources at her disposal into finding the truth."

"Interesting timing. Nothing like a little threat of exposure to put the fear in you." John glanced down and back up again. "But anything about getting a convicted murderer off doesn't sit well around here."

"I get it. I do. But if this all ties into Everett's case, are you willing to do whatever needs to be done to find the truth, even if it means your brothers got it wrong?"

John sat back in his chair and folded his arms. "Riley's pretty sure of this guy?"

"Extremely. She ran the case by me one night, and I have to say, John, I'm not convinced it was as open-and-shut as first assumed."

John sat forward and laid his crossed arms on the desk again, his face mere inches from Colton's. "I don't relish going up against any of my fellow officers. That case was investigated from this very room. But as a man of God, I do care about the truth. If finding out the who and why of Riley's case means Everett is exonerated, I'll bear the consequences."

Colton grinned at his new partner. "Exactly what I hoped you'd say."

Chapter Forty

Riley nodded to the prison guard upon entering the stark room, followed by Detective Stapleton. And Colton.

Knowing ahead of time he'd be present today hadn't lessened the impact of seeing him for the first time since he left four days before. She hadn't even heard his voice until his quiet *good morning* when she met them at the gate with Nowell and Piper flanking her. It had been John, not Colton, who called her Monday, asking if they could join her for her meeting with Shane.

After checking with her client, since he would have to waive attorney-client privilege, she'd confirmed they could take some of the time allotted to her to ask whatever questions they may have. And only those questions that wouldn't compromise his case.

With her arms crossed over her white blouse under a black suit coat, she stood by the table, not allowing herself to look at Colton standing adjacent to her. A tense silence permeated the small space until another guard brought Shane into the room.

It appeared he'd taken advantage of the weight room for some workouts. But more than the healthier physical condition, hope shone in the eyes that held such despair during their last meeting here.

"Shane." She smiled and shook his hand. "Good to see you."

"Good to see you, too, Riley. I'm anxious to hear how things are going."

She wished she had better news for him, but they'd get to that. She gestured to the men with her. "This is Detective John Stapleton, Houston PD, and Colton Blankenship, a consultant with Petersen Security International."

"Gentlemen." Shane shook their hands, and they settled around the table. "A police detective? I assumed you used your own investigators."

She understood Shane's hesitation. It had been Houston PD who'd done all they could to put him here.

"I do have an investigator. Detective Stapleton's here in another capacity. I've had some … trouble, I guess you could say. With a stalker. Started right after I took this case, so they're here to determine if it might be tied together somehow."

His brow furrowed. "Like somebody doesn't want you to help me?"

"Could be. We're just considering the possibility."

"I hope not." Alarm filled his eyes. "If you were to get hurt because of me—"

"We don't know anything yet." She gestured to John. "Detective, why don't you start."

John turned his attention to Shane. "Ms. Hudson has been receiving some messages that lead us to believe the suspect is warning her away from this case. Do you have any ideas as to who or why that might be?"

Shane scoffed. "Whoever killed Cait. That would make sense, right? They figure they got away with it, I'm doing the time, so they don't want her rocking the boat."

Colton nodded. "That was our thinking."

Riley twisted her hands together on top of the table. His

voice still caused her pulse to race. Not to mention the sight of him standing at the prison gate when she pulled up today with her detail. Nowell so far had proven to be an excellent point man, but whenever she glanced up from her desk at the office, it took her a moment to realize it wasn't Colton at her door or pacing the hall. And her midnight trips to the kitchen had her sitting alone, usually with her Bible.

Piper, every bit as diligent and competent as the men, also had a soft spot for fashion and all things girly. They'd enjoyed a few fun conversations that had the guys sitting stupefied. Still, she missed Trevor and would be glad to have him back.

If sleep had been in short supply before Saturday night's events, it was worse now. The sound of the gun ... the screams ... Colton's body over hers ... protecting her. All running through her head every time she closed her eyes.

John pulled four eight-by-ten still photos from a file folder, pulling her attention back to the matter at hand. He placed them side-by-side in front of Shane. "Are any of these guys familiar to you?"

Leaning in, Shane studied each photo. "This the best you have? Kind of grainy."

"Unfortunately, these were taken from a security camera in the lobby of Ms. Hudson's building. Camera's mounted above the front desk, so the angle is wonky, and they've been enlarged."

Shane studied them again. "No. I'm sorry. I don't know any of these guys."

John left the photos where they were and produced the composite drawn from hers, Logan Devers', and Avery's descriptions. "What about this guy?"

Shane studied the drawing for several seconds, then shook his head. "No. Nothing."

Her spirits fell another notch. She'd so hoped something about the man would ring a bell.

"Do you know of anybody who had it out for you?" John asked. "Somebody who might want to hurt you badly enough to kill Caitlyn and frame you?"

Shane's face blanched, and his wide-eyed gaze bounced between Riley and the detective. "You think Caitlyn was killed because of *me*? Because somebody had it out for *me*?" He put his head in his hands and buried his fingers in his hair. "Then I do belong here. If this is my fault, I do belong here."

"That's not true." Riley placed her hand on his arm. "Shane."

He dropped his hands and brought his tear-filled eyes up to meet hers.

"The *only* person at fault here is the one who yielded the knife that day. Whatever his motive, he chose to carry out that horrible deed. This is not on you. But you can help us find him, if you can think of anybody you might've been crosswise with."

Colton cleared his throat. "She's right. I lost my wife to cancer and blamed myself for not being able to help her. I knew I wasn't the cause, but she was mine to take care of. It took a long time …" He glanced at Riley. "And somebody God put in my path to come alongside and tell me it was out of my hands. That I wasn't to blame, and to continue to carry the guilt squelched the Spirit from working in my life. Don't let the enemy defeat you. Keep the faith."

Riley pulled her hand back and clasped it with the other on the table, twisting her ring. Her heart squeezed in her chest. Even with the pain of missing Colton permeating every inch of her, she couldn't regret the time she'd had with him. Not with seeing him walking again with His Lord.

Shane swallowed and scraped a hand across his eyes. "I'm sorry about your wife."

"And I'm sorry you lost Cait. From all I've heard, she was a spectacular person."

"Very much so." Shane took a deep breath and let it out. "Okay. Ask me whatever you need. I want to get the guy who murdered Cait, but I'd also like to help you find whoever's after you. Especially if they're one and the same."

She reached out again and gave his hand a quick squeeze. "Thank you. And if you have any other thoughts like that, get with Tommy. He'll help you with it. He carried a lot of guilt for not taking their neighbor more seriously before his wife was killed. He understands it."

He nodded. "Tommy's been a great comfort since I got here. Helped me tap back into my faith. And Barbara ... she's been a blessing."

"I'm so glad to hear that."

After Tommy suggested having his sister write to Shane as a voice of encouragement, Riley had been delighted to give her the go-ahead. Nobody was more positive and encouraging than Barbara.

John pointed to the photos. "The thing is, these are all the same guy. Even the composite."

Shane peered at the images. "All these guys are the same person?"

"Verified. So, taking another look, is there anything at all familiar, anything you might recognize, between all five—the photos and the composite?"

Shane started with the first again, picking up and studying each photo. He then picked up the composite and placed it in front of him. After several silent moments, he covered the beard with one hand and the baseball cap with the other, leaving only the eyes, nose, and mouth.

"Huh."

Riley exchanged glances with the two men before looking back at Shane. "See something?"

The clock behind her ticked for several seconds before he tilted his head, still focused on the drawing with a furrow in his brow. "I can't be sure, but he reminds me of Warren. I'm just not sure how that can be."

"And Warren would be …?"

His gaze snapped up to her. "Oh. My stepbrother."

Her head jerked back. "Stepbrother? I didn't know you had a stepbrother."

"Estranged, I guess you could say."

Colton leaned forward. "Estranged? As in, not on good terms with?"

"More like no terms at all."

"Explain."

"I haven't seen him in over ten years. I was home for Thanksgiving my first year of college. So, I was eighteen, I guess. Thirteen years ago. He came to my dad looking for money."

"And you haven't seen him since?" John asked.

"I haven't. I know my dad's seen him a time or two." He sighed. "Warren hasn't had it easy. My dad divorced his mother, and Warren went with her. I was almost two when my mom married his dad. My dad. He adopted me. My biological father was killed in a car accident a month after I was born."

"And Warren's how much older than you?"

"Five years. He was about seven, I guess, when we came into the picture. Apparently, the divorce was big-time ugly, with Warren's mom using him as a pawn to get more money or flat-out revenge. I didn't know all of this as a kid. My dad explained it to me a few years ago when I got curious about his first family. I think it hurt him that Warren's mom kept him away so much. But every time he tried to get custody, the court sided with her."

Colton sat back in his chair. "So, you weren't raised together. As brothers."

He shook his head. "The few times Warren was there, things were tense. He didn't like me at all, and I never understood it. Not as a kid. I always hoped we could be more like brothers, but Warren wasn't having it.

"His last visit—I was ten—he beat me to a pulp. Dad had to pull him off me and never had him back over again. If he met with Warren at all, it was away from the house. And me. But those visits were few and far between, especially once Warren was out of high school."

"He was fifteen when that incident took place?"

"Yes. I had no idea what set him off."

John glanced at Colton and back at Shane. "And no contact with him after he showed up thirteen years ago?"

"None. I didn't even talk to him that day. He came to the door, and Dad went outside. All I could hear was the shouting. Something about how Dad owed him for not being there. For choosing another son who wasn't his over the one who was. A bunch of stuff. It really hurt my dad, because he wanted Warren after the divorce. I can't help but think Warren's life would've been much different had he been able to stay with Dad."

He gave his head a shake. "Boy, his mom was some kind of scary. I hated it when she'd pick up Warren the few times she let him come for a visit. I was little, but that woman—I could tell even then there was something off about her. Called me … illegitimate, to put it nicely, to my face when I was about six. I didn't even know what the word meant until much later. But who says that to a little kid? Evil, I tell you."

Riley's head spun. A man bitter about his father raising a son of his choosing rather than the son of his own blood. Could that bitterness have grown so deep, he would commit such a heinous act to put the favored son in his place? A place where he lost his freedom? His identity?

"If you haven't seen Warren since you were eighteen," she said, "then there's no way he would've met Caitlyn, right? Assuming she was ever at your parents' home?"

"Oh, she was there. Several times over those four months. Had dinner with us, went to church with us. My mother adored her. But, no. Warren never met her."

"Hmm."

"Unless …"

She cocked her head, waiting for him to finish.

His brow furrowed again. "I guess it's possible they could've met at the club."

Riley sat up. "The country club?"

"Yeah. I guess about a year before I met Cait, he had a job there. I remember my dad saying he hoped Warren finally found a decent one. I guess it didn't stick, though."

"He was fired?" John asked.

"Not sure. Dad never said."

Colton leaned forward in his chair. "Do you know what other jobs he might've had? Or where?"

"I don't. Dad might, though." Shane paused before regarding Riley again. "But I can't see how my relationship with Warren would have anything to do with either of our situations. He's been out of my life for years."

Riley's gaze met Colton's, and she saw the same question there that swirled in her own mind. Maybe Warren was out of Shane's life.

But was Shane out of Warren's?

Chapter Forty-One

Colton checked his watch. Again. Had to be the longest Monday on record.

John glanced at him from the driver's seat of his unmarked car. "Got somewhere you need to be, Blankenship?"

"Just to the Everetts' with you."

"Am I driving too slow for you? Afraid we won't make it there on time?"

Colton chuckled. "No. Sorry. A lot going on today. Hoping I might have time to go by the hospital later."

John's expression sobered. "Oh, right. Today's the day. What time was the procedure?"

"Now, if they're on time."

"You talked to her, then. To know what time she was going in."

He shook his head. "Nowell."

In all honesty, he'd texted Riley's new lead man several times since leaving the detail. Some things were harder to let go of than others. Said a lot about Nowell that he hadn't yet put him in his place but kept him informed of anything new or noteworthy.

He was aware the moment Riley opened another package last Wednesday, when the creep called her on Friday. About the macabre box of long-stemmed white roses she received Saturday with theatrical blood spilled over them. Delivered right to the main gate of the estate by the creep himself, disguised yet again.

John had raced out to the house that afternoon to pick up the flowers as evidence, but Colton believed it best to stay behind and continue sifting through the case file. Last thing Riley needed was him there causing more drama for her.

"So, you haven't spoken at all? Since Thursday's visit with Everett? When, really, you hardly said two words to each other."

Colton stared out his window. "No."

John pulled off the freeway onto an exit in a well-established Houston suburb. "Avery and I saw her last night. Went over there for dinner to celebrate her procedure today. That's what Riley called it. A celebration."

"Sounds like Riley."

"Yeah, but for a celebration, she didn't say much. Ate even less. Seemed … sad almost. Not like the Riley I've come to know. Avery cried all the way home after we left. She's really worried about her."

Colton regarded him from the passenger seat. Nowell hadn't said anything about Riley's state of mind, only that she was glad they'd been able to expedite her tests so she could donate before the holiday to, hopefully, give the boy's family renewed hope. "Is she all right? Riley, I mean?"

John shrugged as he drove through an intersection. "For someone scared out of her mind, I'd say she's holding up fine. Still goes to the office, works with her charities. At this point, she's only forgoing church, all the Christmas parties she's been invited to, and shopping. Apparently, that's a big thing the girls do together at Christmas, but they're doing it without her this year."

"She's not getting out except to work?"

"Nope. She gave Frances the last of her Christmas shopping list last night. And you know Riley. Has it all typed out with exactly what gift, where to get it, how to have it monogrammed, if it should be. All that stuff." He glanced over at Colton again. "You should call her. See how she's doing."

"I'm sure she's fine. I gave her some names of psychologists. I just wish she'd call one."

"Oh, she did. Met with her last week. Hopefully, it'll help her deal with things."

"Hmm." Clearly, Nowell hadn't told him everything. "I hope so. The girl needs to sleep."

"She should get plenty today."

"Yeah, but it would be nice if she didn't need anesthesia to do it."

"Good point. I guess we'll all have to pray her through this. And pray we're not chasing a dead end here."

Colton had been praying. For Riley. For her safety, her state of mind … her heart. If he could fix it, he would. But time travel hadn't been invented yet, so he'd have to leave it to the Lord to mend what he broke in a moment of weakness.

He swallowed the bitter taste of guilt. "Too bad the Everetts were out of town last Friday. I know Riley wanted to be here."

"I was surprised she gave us the go-ahead to do this without her."

"Probably didn't want to put off finding whatever we could to determine if this is a viable lead. Jealous stepbrother could be nothing more than sour grapes, or it could have festered into a bone-deep hatred. And that's even if we can get any good intel from the dad and stepmother."

John parked in front of a well-cared-for, single-level home and killed the engine. "Call her."

He'd love to do that, to hear her voice if nothing else. But he couldn't keep her on the hook. Have her hoping there was a chance for them. A clean break was better.

He reached for the handle and pushed open his door. "I'm sure I'm the last person she wants to talk to."

Even if he were the last man on earth.

———

"Warren?" Mr. Everett's brow creased as his eyes moved from John to Colton and back again. "I thought you were here about Shane."

Colton nodded. "Yes, sir. Just info gathering, at this point."

John placed his cup of coffee on the saucer. "We're following a lead on what might be a completely separate matter. It may mean nothing, but we hoped you could tell us about your older son. Shane said he hadn't had any contact with him in years but that you might be able to answer some questions."

Mrs. Everett put her arm through her husband's, seated next to her on the sofa in their tidy living room. Photos of a happy family of three lined the walls, with pictures of Shane at various ages. Shane in his Little League uniform. Shane in full football regalia, teenage Shane in a suit, accepting a trophy with *MVP* engraved across the bottom. Shane's graduation with several cords hanging around his neck signifying his leadership and intelligence. His college graduation photo. *Sigma cum laude.*

Shane had definitely been the center of his parents' world. Their golden child.

Who now sat in prison for the most heinous of crimes.

"We'll do everything we can to help," she said. "What do you need to know?"

John pulled out his notebook and a pen. "Do you know when Warren was employed at the country club?"

Mr. Everett sighed. "Uh, well, let's see. Would've been three, maybe four years ago."

"What did he do there?"

"Not entirely sure. I know some landscaping. Maybe the pro shop? I think he mentioned something about working with the golfers. That they were high-maintenance or something along those lines. Warren had a bit of a chip on his shoulder. Always felt he deserved more than he was willing to work for. Got that from his mother."

Golfers. Caitlyn had been an avid golfer. Could they have crossed paths in the pro shop? On the course?

"Dear." Mrs. Everett gave her husband's arm a squeeze. "We don't want to speak ill of the dead."

Colton peered at Shane's mom. "Warren's mother passed away?"

"Little over two years ago. Overdosed on some sleeping pills. Poor thing. She was … fragile."

"Fragile." Mr. Everett *tsked*. "Fragile like an iron poker. And as lethal."

Interesting. Colton sat up in the armchair he'd taken upon being invited in and clasped his hands between his knees. "Can you elaborate?"

Mr. Everett turned to his wife. "I'm sorry. I know you always try to find the good in everybody, but Marta was not fragile. I still find it difficult to believe she took her own life."

Colton's gut coiled. "Suicide?"

"According to the authorities."

His brain quickly did the math. Warren's mother had died, allegedly by her own hand, around the same time as Cait's murder? What had he told John about coincidence?

Mr. Everett took a sip of his coffee and placed the cup on its saucer. "I met Marta right after college. Whirlwind romance. Got married too quickly. By the time I saw her true colors, she was pregnant. Warren was three when we split. I fought for him, but the court sided with his mother and forced me to pay exorbitant child support."

"Shane mentioned Warren always seemed angry. Is that your take?"

"Absolutely. Marta had put such poison into his head—that Shane had stolen me away, that I favored Shane over him, that my wife controlled me and didn't like him. All nonsense, but he was just a kid. Of course he was angry. Couldn't stand Shane. Things finally came to a head when Warren almost killed him. If I hadn't walked in—" He dipped his head.

Mrs. Everett put her arm around him, her eyes filled with tears. "Only ten years old and beaten by his own stepbrother. Can you imagine? We couldn't have that boy here again. We just couldn't. We were aware Warren wasn't fond of him, but to do something like that? We were broken over it. It took a long time to heal from that."

"We should've pressed charges," Mr. Everett said. "I know we should've. But I felt so guilty. Like I was somehow the cause of his behavior. Family counseling—my wife, Shane, and myself— helped us see Warren's choices weren't our fault. I had tried everything to get custody of him when we divorced, but Marta always threatened to disappear with him. He was my son. I couldn't stand the thought of never seeing him again. Turned out that's pretty much what happened, anyway."

Mrs. Everett nodded. "Marta wouldn't let him visit regularly. Always had an excuse as to why he couldn't come. Once he was an adult, he only came around if he needed something. But we haven't had any contact with him in about three years."

"Did he attend the trial at all?" Colton asked.

Shane's dad shook his head. "Not that we saw."

John looked up from his notebook. "Do you know if Warren was fired from the country club or left on his own?"

"No. I only know he was suddenly without a job. Again."

"Do you know where he worked after that?"

"Some fancy hotel downtown. In the kitchen. Warren was actually a pretty good cook. Had a few kitchen jobs."

Colton exchanged a glance with John. "The Whitmore, by chance?"

"Yes. I believe that's right."

John scribbled in his notebook. "Is there anything else you can tell us about Warren? Any specific hobbies, habits, what he drives, where he spends his time?"

"The theater. He always loved working at the theater. The one thing he kept at for years. And by working, I mean volunteering. A community thing. Over in the Arts District."

Colton sat up. "The theater? Doing what, do you know? Performing, directing …"

"Behind the scenes stuff. Building sets, graphic design for their posters and programs, costumes. Even makeup. He used to have a social media page where he posted photos of himself dressed up for Halloween in spectacular costumes. Completely unrecognizable. I told him he should find out how to make a living in that, but he never pursued it outside of that little theater."

Colton's stomach lurched. *Completely unrecognizable.*

"Do you have a current address?"

Mrs. Everett clasped her hands in her lap. "The last birthday card we sent him over a year ago came back as not deliverable. We have no idea where he is now."

John shut his notebook. "You wouldn't happen to have a photo, would you? From the past few years?"

She scrunched her mouth to one side. "Nothing over the age of thirteen or fourteen, when he was still coming for visits."

"No problem. Thank you for your time today. If you think of anything else, please give me a call." He placed a business card on the coffee table and stood.

The couple walked them to the door, where Mr. Everett regarded the detective. "This separate matter you mentioned. It doesn't have anything to do with Shane's case?"

"We don't know enough yet to determine if they're linked."

The man's eyes clouded as he swallowed. "You don't think … that Warren … How would he have even known Caitlyn?"

"We don't have any evidence of the kind right now. We're following up on several leads. The strained relationship between the stepbrothers came up, so we said we'd look into it."

There were no other leads, nothing of substance, but Colton understood why John would downplay the significance of this visit. No reason to concern the family at this point. Not until there was more to go on.

John tucked his notebook into his jacket pocket. "Unfortunately, that's all I can tell you at this time. Once we know more, we'll give you whatever information we can. In the meantime, if Warren should get in touch, please let me know."

They walked out the door onto the front porch.

"Oh, I guess there is one other thing. I don't know if it has any significance or not."

Turning back, they waited for Shane's dad to continue.

"Warren is his middle name. First name is Jacob. In case that might help you locate him."

John nodded. "We'll make a note of it. Thank you again."

At the car, Colton met his friend's gaze over the roof of the vehicle. "He's our guy."

"Best thing we have going at the moment."

"Now we just have to prove it."

And find a man who could make himself unrecognizable.

Chapter Forty-Two

Riley groaned through a stretch before she'd even opened her eyes, wincing at the persistent ache in her hip. Two days since Monday's procedure, but hopefully today would be better, and she could get some work done.

With a grunt, she raised herself on her elbows and gradually upright to sit with her legs dangling over the side of the bed. Yes, definitely better today. Yesterday, it had taken her another five minutes to get to this point.

Her phone notified her of an incoming text, and she picked it up from the nightstand.

John:

Morning, Riley. hope ur feeling better. good time for a call?

Sure thing.

Instead of trying to get out of bed and talk at the same time, she stacked her pillows against the headboard and scooted back against them, grimacing as pain shot through her hip and lower back. She pulled her covers up to her lap before her cell phone rang.

"Good morn—" She cleared her throat of the morning raspiness. "Sorry. Good morning, Detective."

"Uh oh. Did I wake you up?"

A glance at her clock told her it was nearly half past ten. "No, I was awake. Lying here thinking about everything I'm getting behind on, especially with Christmas a week away."

"Take the time to rest. Don't push too hard."

"I'll try. So, what's up?"

"I didn't want to bother you yesterday, but I thought you'd like to know where we are with the case."

"I absolutely would."

"We met with Shane's parents on Monday. Very interesting visit."

She listened to the highlights of their conversation with Mr. and Mrs. Everett, her pulse rate increasing by the minute. "Warren has to be the guy. Way too many coincidences."

"Exactly what we thought. Worked at the country club at the time Cait had been a regular there. Serious issues with his biological father raising, and favoring, a son who wasn't his by birth. A son who apparently excelled at everything he did. Warren's also a long-time volunteer with a community theater where he does everything from graphic art to makeup and costumes. And previously employed at the hotel where the country club Christmas ball was held."

"And he was fired from the country club?"

"The dad didn't know if he was fired or left, but said it was about four years ago. Had a problem sticking with a job. Always felt he was entitled to more than he got."

"But no idea right now where he is?"

"None. Ran him in the system, but he's no longer at the address on his current driver's license, and there's no forwarding. We went by the theater yesterday and talked to the manager. He knows Everett but said he's not working on their current production. Last he knew, Warren was employed at an assisted living center somewhere but couldn't tell us where."

"Wait." She stared at the painting on the wall in front of her, shuffling through the information in her head. Something about … assisted living center … "The car."

"The car?"

"The burned-up one. Wasn't it—"

"—stolen from an assisted living facility. I'd forgotten that. I've been so focused on Shane's case file, trying to connect the dots, I wasn't thinking about the attempted abduction. My apologies, Riley."

"No worries. The brain can only process so much at one time. That's why we're a team. You, me, and … Colton." She swallowed. Just saying his name made her chest hurt. "And the Houston PD, of course."

"Of course." He chuckled. "Let me get with the facility to see if he's working there. Could be he took advantage of the situation and boosted the resident's car. Probably planned to return it, but then you and Devers got too good a look at it. Had to burn it."

"If he does work there, or did, maybe they have a better address for him."

His voice went distant, as if he were speaking to someone else. Her stomach dropped at the sound of Colton's muffled voice. They were there together. But it had been John who called to update her. Was Colton that eager to keep his distance?

Or was he still protecting her? This time from himself?

"Okay, we're going to head to the facility now. We went through the responding officers' body cam footage from the original crime scene—Caitlyn's—and Colton's now reading through all the old notes from the investigative team. Nothing stands out yet, but there's a lot more we need to weed through."

Riley's skin crawled. She'd been through the body cam

footage herself. Not for the faint of heart. Scenes like that were hard enough to see when the victim was a stranger, but now that was the last image she had of her friend.

She shook off the picture in her mind. "My investigator has been re-interviewing the trial witnesses. I'll send you his contact info. You can loop each other into what you're covering so there's no duplication of effort."

"Another member of the team would be welcome. You're not going into the office, are you?"

"No, we digitized whatever we could, including all the investigative notes. I can see it from my laptop. And I'm going to start on my brief for the appeal."

"I'll text you the driver's license photo to give you an idea of what this guy actually looks like. Or did four years ago."

"I appreciate it." Not that she relished looking into those eyes again—if indeed Warren was their man—but she needed to know.

"I'll let you go. We've been praying your recovery is quick."

"Thanks for the prayers. I only wish I knew if everything went well with the transplant. I understand they won't know if it took for a while yet, but it's hard having to wait a year to know who he is."

Although she'd wondered about the boy in the wagon. She'd visited the rooms of the children who hadn't been in the play area, but he seemed the most ill of the leukemia patients she'd met. Either way, they'd all been in her prayers every day since, including the tiny girl who had wanted to marry Colton.

The memory of him embracing the little one brought a warmth to her chest missing since he'd walked out of her life. If she could keep the good memories alive, maybe she'd recover more quickly. As it was, the pain in her hip would dissipate long before the ache in her heart.

"Hold on." John's voice said something in the background, then silence for a second.

"Riley."

Her pulse jumped. "Co-Colton. How are you?"

"I'm fine. John passed your question to me. I know the recipient. Met the family. The registry looped me in since the match was found through the foundation. I can't tell you who he is since, as you already mentioned, recipients and donors can't know the other's identity for a year post-transplant. But I can tell you it all went well, and the family was grateful. That's all I know right now, but I'll keep you posted."

"You were there? When they did the transplant?"

"They brought your marrow up after your procedure, and I got there right after they started the boy's IV. It was that quick."

"Wow. Thank you." A relief to know at least Colton had the information. While it could be a month or so before they could confirm it as a success, improvement in his blood work should show signs of healthy cells and platelets within the next two to four weeks. "I appreciate it."

"No problem. John'll shoot you the DL pic. Let us know if you see anything. But get your rest. Don't work too hard. We're on it."

"I know you are. It's been a lot less stressful knowing you two are working together. But I want to help where I can. Hopefully, that little boy will get a second chance at life. It would be nice if the same could be said for Shane."

"Agreed. Take care of yourself. We'll be in touch."

Before she could respond, the call disconnected.

She stared at her phone. His voice still sent tingles along the back of her neck. How she would miss it after this was all over and they had no reason to stay in contact.

Her phone dinged again, and she brought up the photo of the driver's license. Too small to see the actual photo clearly, so she emailed it to herself to check on her laptop.

It took her a couple of minutes, but she finally made it to the bathroom to brush her teeth and do something with her mop of hair. A messy bun was the perfect solution. After washing her face, she ambled into her study.

She stopped short at the sight of a huge bouquet of roses sitting on the dresser. When had those arrived? She'd spent Monday night and most of yesterday in bed, but they hadn't been there last night.

She must have been in a deep sleep this morning since she never heard anyone come in, much less leave the gorgeous arrangement of yellow flowers. As she walked over to her desk, the pain gradually diminished. She found the card in the arrangement and pulled it out.

Thank you for your generous and life-giving gift. We so appreciate your loving spirit and open heart.
Your friends at the Theresa Blankenship Foundation

"Colton."

Two dozen roses. The foundation would probably do something like this for all their donors, but for now, she'd savor the idea they came from Colton.

Fingering the delicate petals, she closed her eyes. Eleven days. It had been eleven days since he'd walked away. He said a little while out of her life and she'd see what she believed to be love was actually infatuation with an image.

How was it, then, every day the ache grew more intense? He might be gone bodily, but he remained in her thoughts, her dreams, and her heart.

It wasn't a crush, an infatuation. It wasn't gratitude or a need to feel safe. It was *him*. Who he was as a person. A good man. A godly man. A man who'd suffered and questioned and still come back to the Lord.

A man she could build something with if he'd give them a chance.

Her eyes opened as her mother walked into the study. "Hey, Mom."

"You're up." Mom's smile lit her face. Her mother always had an inner glow, a peace about her only God could provide. "Feeling better?"

"Yes, better. Only took me three minutes to get out of bed. Much improved over yesterday."

"Glad to hear it. I was coming up to see if you wanted me to bring you some breakfast."

Riley cocked her head to the side. "I think I'll come down. I'm getting tired of this room."

"Sounds great. Do you want to take the elevator?"

"No, let's try the stairs. I think I'll be all right."

After breakfast—or brunch, since it was nearly eleven before she ate—she and Mom took advantage of a sunny early afternoon to walk through the garden and greenhouse, admiring Grandpa Kevin's roses and orchids. He'd outdone himself this year. Maybe he'd let them use some for the head table arrangements at the New Year's Charitable Dinner and Ball.

"I sure hope I can dance at the ball," she said.

Mom nodded, walking arm-in-arm with her on their way back to the house. "I'm sure the soreness will be gone by then. You have two more weeks to recover."

"Hopefully." She yawned. "Speaking of recovering, I think I'm going to go lie down."

"Good idea. I'll walk you upstairs."

They entered the house, and Riley stopped at the bottom of the stairs, looking at the upper floor. "I think I'll take the elevator."

Upon returning to her room, she spotted her laptop. "The DL pic. I forgot all about that."

She lowered herself gently into her office chair, thankful it was well-padded. After booting up her PC, she waited for her email to come up and clicked on the one she sent from her phone almost three hours earlier. She opened the attachment, then zoomed in on the face.

"Four years ago."

Thick, shoulder-length hair, facial stubble above his lips and trailing down onto his chin. Thin face. *Slight.*

Taking her cue from Shane, she covered the bottom part of the face with her hand.

Her stomach somersaulted.

The eyes. The same ones she'd encountered after she'd twisted out of his grip that day in the parking garage. The same ones from the composite.

Dark, penetrating, yet void of any life. Soulless.

Removing her hand, she leaned in to get a closer look. Something about him … familiar besides the eyes. But that's all she'd seen that was *him.* Beyond the longer beard, the baseball cap.

"Do I know you?" She spoke aloud, her voice quiet, pondering. "Jacob Warren Everett." The name rang no bells, brought nothing forth from the recesses of her brain.

"Four years ago."

I guess it's possible they could've met at the club.

The dad didn't know if he was fired or left, but said it was about four years ago.

Jacob.

Cait … Jacob … country club.

A memory flashed, and she sat back so fast, her rolling chair banged into the credenza behind her. Pain shot through her hip, but she couldn't pull her attention from the screen as a scene played out in her mind.

Caitlyn … at the country club … they were meeting for a game of tennis. Riley walked out of the women's dressing room. On her way to the courts, she saw Caitlyn—yellow pleated short skirt, white tank top, her long legs bare down to the tennis shoes from a sponsor paying for some time in her wide circle of online influence. Duffel slung over her shoulder with the racquet grip sticking out.

A man Riley hadn't recognized, dressed in long black pants and light green polo shirt with the country club logo on the shoulder, stood in front of her. He reached for the bag, but Caitlyn swung out of his reach.

No.

Riley couldn't hear the words, but her friend's lips were easy to read.

I told you. Leave me alone.

The man's face flipped like a switch. From cordial and smiling to dark and angry.

Riley walked in their direction.

"You snobby rich girls." He spat the words. "Don't know a good thing when you see it. You'll regret it someday. Just wait."

Caitlyn, being Caitlyn, leaned in and stared him down. "Leave. Me. Alone. One word from me and you're history here."

Caitlyn stepped away and headed toward Riley, putting on a bright smile. "Hey, girl, ready to be humiliated on the court?"

"Uh, sure." Riley studied the man now standing several feet away, glowering at Cait's back, his hands fisted at his sides, face and neck red. "Who is that guy?"

Her friend flipped her hand as if shooing away a pesky fly. "Jacob. Works at the bar and grill."

Jacob Everett. She was as sure of it as she was of the sun filtering through the blinds.

Dark hair worn to the collar and pushed behind his ears. Stubble from his mouth down to his chin. Thin but fit, *slight of face.*

And seething.

Caitlyn pulled her arm through Riley's to steer her toward the courts. "Keeps asking me out, always after me to carry my bag or be my caddy. Can't seem to get the message I'm not interested."

"You should report him."

Cait shrugged. "I might. It's getting a little old."

Riley's skin tingled as she stared back at the man on her screen. She slammed the laptop closed.

And everything clicked into place, like a key finally turning in a stubborn lock.

"You mean that Jacob guy?" Cait had said at lunch only four months before her death. *"He was harmless. I never saw or heard from him after that day …"*

Warren Everett wasn't after her simply to dissuade her from defending Shane. He was after her in case she remembered.

After her to keep her silent.

Chapter Forty-Three

Colton scrubbed his fists into his eyes.

Police detectives' handwriting was as bad as doctors'. He'd already downed three cups of coffee and four ibuprofen in the hours he'd spent poring over printed copies of the notes from the Mulaney case investigators. Their only break had been to grab lunch on their way to the assisted living facility where the car had been stolen.

He and John had moved from the precinct and commandeered a conference room at Petersen headquarters. Much easier to spread out and go through the original case file without the curious stares of John's co-workers. The badge created a tight-knit band of brothers and sisters. John didn't want to burn bridges, but even he'd seen over the past two days that conclusions may have been formed much too quickly.

Watching all the body cam footage from the crime scene had been brutal. So much blood. Caitlyn's butchered body. All the fight gone as she lay crumpled at her killer's feet.

Lifeless eyes … staring but unseeing.

Scenes like that angered cops. No matter how neutral they tried to be, they were human. And finding her blood-covered boyfriend hovering over her added fuel to the volatile emotions of the moment. Add in the flowers and the card, her father's ultimatum, the conveniently stolen cell phone.

For them, it all fit. Case closed.

Planting his elbows on the table, Colton rubbed his temples with his fingers.

John looked up from the trial transcript in his hand. "Hangin' in there?"

"Barely. Y'all really need to work on your penmanship."

"That's a fact. I can hardly read my own notes sometimes. That's why it took me so long to find the ones about the burned car." He pursed his lips and shook his head. "The fact a victim had to remind me about my own lead makes me nuts."

Colton chuckled. "Riley's nothing if not gracious. She told you not to worry about it. So, don't worry about it." He gestured over the avalanche of paperwork, files, notebooks, and photos strewn across the table. "This is a lot of stuff to keep track of. The fact you forgot one thing isn't a big deal."

"I should've remembered," John muttered.

"Regardless, I wish the HR manager at the assisted living facility could've told us more about Everett."

"Other than how great he was with the residents and how much they missed him."

"Right? Most bosses would be angry about an employee who simply quit coming to work, and she was just hoping he was okay."

"But we also got information that adds more bricks to the case we're building against him."

Colton stood and stretched his arms over his head before leaning against the whiteboard on the wall where they'd scrawled their notes outlining the case. "We know he worked there at the time the car was boosted, and he knew the owner. It was common knowledge the elderly man rarely left the facility, and his car sat there mostly unused. Would've been easy for Everett to lift the car keys while the guy was out of his room."

John dropped his pen on the table and sat back with his hands clasped behind his head. "And he stopped coming into work a month ago. The same time as Riley's attempted kidnapping."

"And the car was incinerated. He must've seen a clip on the news that it had been identified as stolen. Was aware y'all had traced the VIN."

With a heavy sigh, John lowered his arms. "Too bad the address they had for him didn't pan out. We have all these *things* pointing right to him, but he's a ghost. Where is this guy?"

"Good question."

Colton took his seat again and picked up the next batch of notes. The investigator who interviewed the florist the day following the killing. The detective had jotted down the florist's name, the name of the shop, the time the order came in the day before, the card number it was charged to, name on the order, and time the customer walked into the shop to pick up the arrangement.

"Five-fifty-two," he mumbled, reading through the chicken scratch on the page. "Card had already been written out. Slight of face but bulkier in build, tall, probably six-foot two or thereabouts, blue suit, sunglasses, dark hair."

Wait a second. He read back through the description of the customer. "Blue suit."

"What's that?" John asked from the other end of the table, several photos spread out in front of him.

Colton's head snapped up. "I distinctly remember Riley telling me the florist testified in court she couldn't remember the color of the suit the customer wore. Only that it was *dark*. Shane was found with Caitlyn wearing a black suit."

He popped out of his chair and carried the page over to John. "What do you see here?"

John took the sheet and read over the notes, bringing the page closer to his face. "Blue suit. She says specifically it was a blue suit."

"She was interviewed the day after the murder. Said it was blue. Then at trial two years later, she can't remember. I'd give more weight to the interview than the testimony."

"A hundred percent."

"And it's all right here in the case file. We need to have Riley check the file she obtained from the former defense team to see if this was in there. If not—"

"That's bad. For the prosecution, that is."

"Exactly. Looks like Riley could get twisted up with another DA if she files for prosecutorial misconduct."

John dropped the sheet and put his head in his hands. "This keeps getting worse. I may have to transfer to another department. In another city. Maybe another state."

Colton grinned. "A bit dramatic, don't you think?"

John dropped his hands and lifted his head. "I'm pretty much playing for the other team right now. Cops don't work for the defense. We answer to the prosecution. When this all comes to light, I could be shut out by my own team on any future cases. Nobody will want to work with me. It doesn't matter what the truth might be. I'll be the traitor."

His grin disappearing at his friend's obvious apprehension, Colton took the chair adjacent to him. "I understand. But what's your gut telling you to do? If you want to leave this to Riley and her investigator, then we'll do it. We'll leave Shane out of it and focus on how we link Warren to Riley's abduction attempt. We already have a lot to go on. She can tie it back to Shane as a motive, if we can provide her with one. She would never want to compromise your career. I can guarantee you that."

John stared at him, then shook his head. "My gut is telling me we need to get to the truth. If that makes me a pariah, so be it. I don't believe God puts us in places if He doesn't intend good to come of it. Doesn't mean that good is mine. Could be it's for Shane." He waved his hand over the mess across the table. "I couldn't, in good conscience, leave this now. No, I'm in. Regardless of the stakes."

Colton patted his arm on the table. "You're a good guy, Stapleton. I'm sure Riley's grateful for all your work on this, knowing what it could cost you. She'll do her best to protect you if you stay with it, but I know she'd understand if you needed to walk away."

John narrowed his eyes at him. "You sure seem to know a lot about her, the woman whose detail you left because you, how did you say? *Blew it?*"

Acid churned in Colton's stomach. "I almost got her killed, John. So, yeah, I blew it."

"What happened at the ball wasn't because you were out on the dance floor with her. In fact, if she *hadn't* been on the floor, he could've walked right up to her and had a shot off before you knew what was going on. She wasn't right next to you the entire evening. I was there, remember? You guys gave her the room to mingle, be with her friends, have a nice night out.

"It was this monster out there hunting her who blew it. Blew it by underestimating her detail. If you hadn't been on the floor with her, could you imagine if you'd had to try to get to her in all that chaos? Paxton followed his instincts and already had the perp in his sights before he ever got a shot off. Working exactly as a team should. *Your* team. The team you should be with right now, working with her, not me."

Colton stood and shook his head. "You don't get it."

"Oh, but I think I do. You didn't blow it as lead man on her detail. You think you blew it because you fell for her. So, what happened? You couldn't follow through? Because of your past experience?" He leaned forward with his arms crossed on the table. "I can't imagine how tough that would be, losing someone like you did your wife. But would she want you to be alone the rest of your life? Or would she be the first to bop you upside the head for not moving on? Maybe with someone as great as Riley."

Colton's heart pounded. He could hear Theresa in his ear, telling him what an idiot he was to close himself off. To not find a wonderful woman to settle down with. Settle in and have babies and make a life and grow old with.

He took the chair again and matched John's posture, arms crossed on the table. "How do you guys do it? You and Avery?"

"How do we do what?"

"Make it work. You two are on opposite ends of the social spectrum. The girl comes from money. You're a working-class Joe."

"Ah, I see." John grinned. "Something happened between you and Riley, but it threw you. And now you're using her social position as a reason not to pursue it."

"I honestly don't think it could work."

"So, what happened? Between the two of you?"

Colton released a sigh and pushed his hand through his hair, wishing for three more ibuprofen. "That night, things got … intense. Some things were said … professed … however you want to put it." He gave his head another shake. "She thinks she's in love with me."

"She thinks? Or she told you outright she loved you?"

"She told me. But I don't believe she could be in love with me. More like the idea of me. The guy standing between her and the big, bad wolf."

John laughed, taking him by surprise. "Colton, think about who we're talking about here. Riley Hudson is mature, generous, compassionate. Stubborn, yes, but off-the-charts intelligent. She's not some wishy-washy, club-hopping, self-involved girl who goes weak in the knees at the sight of a good-looking guy who makes her feel safe. She's secure in who she is. Confident in her faith. If she opened her heart and told you she was in love with you, you can take that to the bank, my friend."

Colton stared hard at the detective. What he said held a ring of truth. Riley was all those things. And more.

"Even if that's true, how could I stay? It would have been tough to do my job."

"Because you would have been distracted by your own feelings?"

"Maybe. I don't know. I'm not even sure what I feel. Am I attracted to her? Of course. Her inner spirit is as beautiful as the outside. Am I in love with her? How could I be? It hasn't even been six weeks since we met."

"Same day I met Avery, if memory serves. And, pal, let me tell you, I am crazy about that girl."

"And you think you can make it work?"

"Why wouldn't we? We care about each other. She's spent time with my family, they love her, and she loves them. I've been with hers and was just as comfortable. We're even splitting Christmas Day next week between her family and mine. Her mother can be a little uppity, but we have a mutual respect for each other. She knows how much I care about her daughter, and I know I have her blessing.

"The Hudsons are some of the least pretentious people I know. You don't think her family would accept you with open arms? Do you think Riley would look down her nose at yours? If you do, then you don't know her well enough to be in love with her."

Colton nodded, studying his hands folded in front of him. "You're right. I just don't want to hurt her."

"Then don't. Pray about it. And if you believe God brought you two together for a reason, you need to act on it. You'll be missing out if you don't."

"Yeah, I appreciate your—"

John's phone buzzed, and he peered down at the screen

before picking it up. "Her ears must've been burning." He pressed the green icon. "Riley, what's—" He sat up straight. "Seriously? Wait." His eyes snapped to Colton. "Let me put you on speaker. I think Blankenship needs to hear this."

He pressed the speaker button and laid the phone on the table.

Colton cleared his throat. "Hey, Riley."

"Colton, it's him." The pitch of her voice, the urgency in it, had his skin erupting in gooseflesh. "He was with Caitlyn. I saw him."

"Hold up. Who? Warren Everett?"

"Yes. At the country club. Except he was going by Jacob then." She took a breath and released it slowly. "Okay. Sorry. My heart's racing."

Colton exchanged a look with John. *Jacob*, he mouthed. They hadn't thought much of the fact Warren Everett's first name was Jacob when his father mentioned it. Another brick in the wall of evidence piling up against *Jacob* Warren Everett.

"Remember Shane said Warren had never met Cait," she continued, "unless they met at the country club before Shane and Cait got together?"

"Yes."

"I saw them. He was coming on to her. I guess it had happened before. But this time, she put him in his place, and he was livid. I told her she should report him, but a few months before she died, I asked her about that, and she said she didn't because she never saw him again."

He sat up and grabbed the phone. "Riley, think back. Did he see you?"

"Yes. I started toward them when I saw they were arguing. He glared at me. It's those eyes, Cole. Those same eyes. I can't believe I'm only now remembering that."

John leaned in. "It was a long time ago, Ri. Don't beat yourself up."

"Yes, but what if I'd remembered Cait had been harassed by this guy at the club? If they'd investigated and found the record of his employment, they would've seen he had the same last name as Shane, and probably asked the questions we're asking now, only face-to-face. What if—"

Colton glanced at the phone as the silence lingered, wondering if they'd lost the connection. "Riley? What if what?"

"What if Shane's in prison because of me?"

Chapter Forty-Four

Another week. And nothing.

Colton's mind kept drifting back to the case when he should be taking part in all the Christmas morning festivities. It wasn't as if they didn't have the evidence. It seemed to mount by the day, making them more and more confident Warren Everett was the guy.

If only they had an inkling where he might be.

"Uncle Colton, look!"

Quinn's voice pulled his attention to her, holding up a brand-new dress from Grandma.

He blew her a kiss. "You're going to look like a princess in that dress, sweet pea."

Her giggle warmed his chest. Time to put work aside. This was family time.

The holidays had been difficult the past few years, since Theresa left. And his faith seemingly went with her. He couldn't wait to get through the days from Thanksgiving to New Year's, when the world would finally get back to normal.

But this year … this year had been different. Redeeming. Soul-filling. Thanksgiving at the shelter, followed by the evening with a blending of families from all walks of life at the Hudson estate. The bone marrow donor drive that exceeded all expectations. Spending a good chunk of yesterday cooking at the shelter. Giving folks at least one day they didn't have to worry about where their next meal would come from. Or if they'd have gifts for their children.

Now, Colton sat on the floor of his parents' living room amidst the remnants of wrapping paper and bows, boxes and packing material, as Lisa's kids tore into their gifts. He'd already unwrapped his, including a hefty monetary donation from his entire family for Theresa's foundation.

These were his favorite people. The ones who'd kept him together after Theresa died. Loving him through the darkest time of his life. By last Christmas, he'd finally found contentment in his singleness, choosing that over the idea of ever finding another. Even watching his sister's children squeal with glee over their gifts, having finally accepted he would never have his own.

Why, then, was he at such a loss *today*? When he'd come back to God and found joy in serving others? Where had that contentment gone?

After the last gift had been opened, he stood and walked over to peer out the big bay window in his parents' living room. Gray clouds hung low, and a light rain fell on the front lawn. A great backdrop for his mood. Not at all Christmas-like.

He sipped from a mug of hot chocolate and turned when a hand clapped on his shoulder. "Dad."

"Son. You seem a little distracted today. Anything I can help with?"

"No, sir. A lot on my mind, I guess."

"Riley?"

"Riley?"

"Her case. I know you've been putting in a lot of hours on it."

"Right. Her case. Yes, we've been working day and night on

it. And we know we have the guy. We just can't find him. I hate that we have to wait for him to do something and hope we catch him before he can …" Looking down into his cup, he shook his head.

"She must be frightened. Poor girl."

"She is. But she's a trouper. Won't let him keep her down. I know she's canceled some of her non-essential outings, which for Riley are few. Everything she does is essential to somebody."

"She's a jewel, that's certain. The whole family is rather special. In fact, her parents sent us an invitation to their New Year's Ball, with a handwritten note. They're nice folks. Very down-to-earth for people who have so much."

"You're going to the ball?"

"Planning to. Could be rather fun, your ma and me hobnobbing with the cream of Houston society, getting all decked out for the evening, eating gourmet food. Sent back our response last week. We're going shopping tomorrow for a gown for your mother. I've never bought your mom an evening gown. I'm quite looking forward to it."

"You need a tux?"

"Renting one. Figured you'd be wearing your own."

"I have two. I'll go grab it later, and you can try it on."

"All righty. Thanks." They stared out the window, listening to the rain splatter against the glass. "So, the last time you talked to Riley, she was doing well?"

"Appeared to be, as of last week."

Dad's forehead creased. "You haven't spoken to her since last week?"

"Hasn't been any need to." Other than his desire to hear her voice. To bridge the distance between them. Completely selfish and not at all what Riley needed. "I check in with Cooper from time to time." Or every day, if truth be told.

No, better to keep his distance. At least until the New Year's Ball, where he was running point on event security. He'd have to see her then. Dancing the night away with the likes of young Dr. Bellows. Maybe even Pretty Boy Gentry.

"I see." Dad stuck his hands in his pockets and stared out the window. "You know, we never did quite understand why you left her detail. You don't have to explain to me. It was just unlike you. You always see things through. We figured something happened that made it impossible for you to continue."

"You could say that." He sighed and peered down into his cup, even the sight of the rich cocoa bringing her to mind. How many cups of hot chocolate had they had together? "We got too close. Nothing inappropriate, don't get me wrong. But she thinks she's in love with me."

"She thinks? Or she knows?"

"How could she *know*, Dad? How could we fall in love in four weeks? It doesn't happen that way."

"We?"

"Excuse me?"

"You said *we*. 'How could *we* fall in love in four weeks.'"

"I mean her. How could she know she was in love with me in only four weeks?"

"But you said *we*. I think you need to quit worrying about Riley and start trying to make sense of what it is *you* feel. Can people fall in love in four weeks? I believe they can fall in love in four hours, if it's meant to be. I was with you two for an entire evening at Thanksgiving. And what I saw, even after you'd been together less than two weeks, was more than two people with a professional relationship."

Colton couldn't argue. "I respect her. A lot. She's an incredible lady, and, in all honesty, that came as a surprise to me. She's not living off her name and social status. That woman would give her right arm to somebody if she believed they needed it more than she did. We'd developed a friendship, which was fine. I just let things get out of control in a weak moment. She's a beautiful woman, and I'd have to be dead not to notice. But that's as far as it goes."

Dad nodded, but his gaze remained fixed. "If you say so. We'd just like to see you with a good woman, Colton, my boy. And Riley's as good as they come."

Colton stared after his father as he walked back over to the children still playing in the remnants of their gift-opening. *Riley's as good as they come.* He didn't disagree. She was everything a guy could want in a woman. Everything he needed.

But could he be everything *she* needed?

Riley laughed as she blew bubbles into the air for her nieces and nephews. Every member of the family had received a bottle of bubbles in their stocking, and they now sat around the fire and the Christmas tree in the cozy family room. Colorful paper, bows, and boxes of every size lay strewn on the rug as the kids chased bubbles they would never catch. Still, they never gave up.

Yesterday afternoon and evening had been spent at the shelter, as they always did on Christmas Eve, serving dinner, handing out gifts and clothes, and singing carols into the night. Knowing the creep—no, *Warren*—had made an appearance at the Thanksgiving dinner, Mack had supplied two additional teams besides hers for the Christmas event. She'd been hyper-vigilant herself, but nobody spotted anyone they believed could be her nightmare in skin.

But today was all about family. While the kids chased bubbles, Grandpa Kevin sat in the middle of the mess, putting together all the toys as he'd done for Riley, Alex, and "Little" Kevin in years past.

From as far back as she could remember, the Hudson family tradition had been to come down to a hearty Christmas Day breakfast in their matching pajamas before opening gifts. That's probably where she'd learned to stuff her food down as quickly as possible, so they could get to the fun part faster.

Yes, today was all about family. Except for the usual rotation of guards in the security room, watching the gate and the grounds. Riley had promised her guys she wouldn't even peek out a window so they could spend the day with their families. Even Nowell had been with his family since leaving her back at the estate last night.

She closed the bottle, put it aside, and joined her grandfather on the floor. "Thank you again for my beautiful locket. That it was Grandma's makes it even more special."

The wistfulness in his eyes made her heart catch. "She was thirty when I gave it to her for Christmas, with each of our pictures from our wedding day. I know she'd love for you to have it, to put your own pictures in there when the time comes."

"*If* the time comes." If she could ever lay aside the conviction that she'd already met the love of her life. A man who chose to walk away instead of staying to discover what they could become. Together.

"It'll come. And if God has something else for you, He'll fill your heart so much, there's no room for anybody else."

A tear escaped, and she swiped it away. "I love you, Gramps."

"I love you, too, Riley-girl. Now, help this old man with this dollhouse."

"You got it."

Twenty minutes later, the dollhouse built and put aside, Riley returned to the loveseat. Hilda, who was more family than employee and always opted to stay on holidays, brought in a tray full of cups of hot cocoa and coffee.

Mom thanked her and brought her cup of coffee over to join Riley. "You look like you're doing so much better today, sweetie. I was a little concerned yesterday."

"Yesterday?"

"At the shelter. You've always loved the time spent there on Christmas Eve as much as the time spent here on Christmas morning. But you seemed a little distracted."

"I hope nobody else noticed. I would hate it if anyone thought I didn't want to be there."

"I'm your mom. I notice things about you others don't."

"I guess I was a bit distracted. I kept looking around at everybody, wondering if they were ... you know." Saying his name always put an acid taste of fear in her throat. "I hated being suspicious of every man I saw. And I was worried about my family, and my friends, and the people at the shelter. I know everybody at the Christmas Ball was okay, but I kept thinking maybe I should stay in until this is over, to make sure nobody else gets hurt. I was so stressed by the time we got home, I did a half hour of laps in the pool, then sat in the spa with Delia and Sadie for some girl time."

"You shouldn't worry about us or anybody else. The Petersen guys are on top of things, and John had half a dozen officers there yesterday." She paused for a moment. "I thought maybe you were searching for someone else. Someone you hoped might be there."

Riley bowed her head and took a sip of her hot chocolate. The warmth cascaded down her throat but did nothing for the ache in her chest. "Colton. He loved being at the shelter on Thanksgiving, so I wondered if he would show."

Mom pulled her close. "Oh, honey. I'm sorry this is so difficult for you. Not only with this guy making your life miserable but the way your heart hurts. I understand it. I loved your father for months before he finally came around."

"You didn't give up hope?"

"I couldn't. I was in love. Nothing changes that except time. And the more time that passed, the more I loved him. I simply had no choice but to wait."

Riley shrugged. "Then I guess I have no choice."

Chapter Forty-Five

"I think we have a good plan of action here." Colton skimmed the final page in the notebook in front of him, then took a bite of syrup-drenched pancakes he hardly tasted.

"*We?*" John chuckled. "This is your show. All the way."

Colton glanced out the window of the restaurant where they'd met for breakfast this cold, gray day after Christmas. "I might be point, but it wouldn't have come together without your input and resources. I'll send it over to Petersen so they can start staffing personnel."

"Still, I like to give credit where it's due." John consulted the time before downing the last of his orange juice. "We should probably hit it."

"Nice watch." Colton closed the notebook and took the last swallow from his now lukewarm coffee. "New?"

"Christmas gift from Avery. I'm afraid to think what she paid for it."

"What'd you give her?"

"A tennis bracelet. Probably more modest than she's used to, but she squealed as if I'd given her the Hope Diamond."

"Really?"

"No. She went on a tirade about how cheap I am. Of course, really. I guess the girl loves me. Doesn't care that I'm a poor civil servant." John swiped a napkin across his mouth and set it on his empty plate. "You ready? We're slated to be there by ten, and I don't want to leave my men cooling their heels outside."

Colton grimaced and pulled his wallet from his back pocket. "Yeah, I guess we should go."

John's brow furrowed. "Nervous?"

Frowning, Colton dropped some bills on the table to cover their meal plus a generous tip for their attentive waitress. "Why would I be nervous?"

John's gaze went from the money on the table back to Colton. "I can pay for mine."

"Nah. I got it. Merry belated Christmas."

"Thanks. I'll cover lunch next time."

"Deal."

John shrugged into his jacket. "I have to meet with my captain this afternoon about this op, so I'll ride back to the precinct with one of my guys after we brief Riley and your crew."

"No problem. I'll wade back into the file at Petersen until you get back."

"Sounds good." John regarded him for a moment. "You didn't answer my question, except with another question."

"And that was …?" He'd hoped Stapleton would drop it, but what was that saying about a dog and a bone?

"You nervous about going back out to the estate?"

He turned and started toward the door. "No."

"When was the last time you spoke to Riley?"

Yep. John got hold of that bone and wouldn't be satisfied until all the meat had been picked off.

Colton frowned at his friend as he held the door open. "You know the answer to that."

The detective's jaw fell slack. "Last week, when she called to let us know about Warren and Caitlyn's dust-up?"

"Correct." He followed John out the door, the biting wind prompting him to pull up the collar of his coat.

"Didn't you go to the shelter on Christmas Eve?"

"I did."

"So, you saw her but didn't talk to her?"

With a sigh, Colton came to a stop at the door of his Jeep. "Why all the questions?"

John peered at him across the top of the vehicle. "It seems odd to me you haven't spoken. You're friends. Her feelings notwithstanding, that shouldn't change."

Shaking his head, Colton unlocked the doors with his fob and slid behind the wheel. He started the Cherokee and ramped up the heat before addressing his friend's question. "I worked in the kitchen for the shelter dinner. Cooking in back, not serving up front. Riley stayed in the common area with the families. Petersen had six other security specialists there besides her usual detail." He swallowed as he put the car in gear and backed out of the parking spot. "She didn't need me."

"I don't know about that. I think she likes knowing you're still on the job for her, even if you aren't with her every day. She's a good friend. Don't throw that away."

Sitting at a red light, Colton propped his elbow on the window and rubbed his brow with his fingers. He wasn't sure how many more sleepless nights he could endure and still keep his head in the game. The Bible said he shouldn't worry, to leave it all in God's hands and trust.

And he was trying. Trying so hard to believe this would all work out the way everybody hoped it would, with Riley safe and able to move on with the life she lived so well.

John cleared his throat. "Look, Blankenship, I haven't known you long. But we've been working a lot of hours together the past couple of weeks, and something tells me you don't turn yourself inside out like this for every assignment you get. If you did, you'd have burned out long before now."

Colton shook his head. "I don't know. I can usually walk away once a detail ends or I'm pulled off. But this one's … special."

"The assignment? Or the girl?"

"They're one and the same, aren't they?"

"You tell me."

Colton didn't know what to say. Yes, Riley was special. More special than anyone had been to him in a long time. The two-and-a-half weeks away from her hadn't eased his feelings for her like he'd hoped they would. Maybe immersing himself in her case was the reason, keeping her at the forefront of his thoughts, the focus of all his energies. Maybe once this was over, it would be easier to walk away. And let his life get back to normal.

Whatever that might look like without the woman who'd forever changed him.

Chapter Forty-Six

"Hi, John." Riley greeted the detective with a smile as he and three other officers walked into the family room. "Please, have a seat."

"Thanks for seeing us today." John lowered himself into a leather chair.

"Of course." She took a seat in the matching chair while the others took the couch and loveseat. "So, you're here to talk about the New Year's Ball next week?"

He nodded. "We believe that, as director of the event, you should know what the security plan is."

"We?"

"Blankenship's running point on event security. This plan is his, but we're using both Petersen and HPD assets and personnel."

Her pulse skittered. "I see." The plan was Colton's, but he'd sent John to talk to her about it. Apparently, his work ethic compelled him to see her case through to the end while he also appeared bent on keeping his distance. She cleared her throat. "Let's see this plan."

John handed her a notebook, and she opened it to a floor

plan of the entrance, lobby, and ballroom. "Since the ball's at another hotel, it's a little more difficult for your security detail. There are a lot of other people around he can blend in with."

"How can we make sure we see him, if he's always changing his appearance?"

"We blanket the place. We already have a couple of guys training with your caterer to be servers, much to his chagrin. He wasn't at all easy to convince these guys could handle trays of champagne and *hors d'oeuvres* without dumping them all over the guests."

She put her hand to her mouth and chuckled. "Yes, Henri is quite particular about his events. I'm sure he's putting your guys through waiter boot camp."

"Something like that." He glanced at a dark-skinned man sitting on the loveseat. "Anyway, Detective Cyrus here will be there as a photographer. And don't worry. He's excellent. Has done several weddings and bar mitzvahs and such for guys at the precinct. The pictures will be legit."

She exchanged a grin with the other man. "Thank you for your help."

"A pleasure."

John pointed at the two men in uniforms on the sofa. "Officers Baldwin and Macias will be working as valets, and some Petersen Security operatives will be there as guests."

"Thank you all. Really. I appreciate it."

The men nodded at her, and she turned back to John. "Nothing new on the whereabouts of Warren Everett?"

His lips pursed as he shook his head. "No, unfortunately. We had a unit on his parents' house, hoping maybe he'd show for the holiday. But no go. We're checking into a lead on a supposed girlfriend. She also works with the theater. We've had a unit on her place the last two days, but no sign of our guy."

"He's getting all of this stuff from somewhere. For his disguises and the theatrical blood on the roses."

"Agreed. We asked the theater manager if they were missing any costumes, beards, wigs, and he said they weren't. We've checked local novelty shops, showing his picture. So far, nobody recognizes him. Your gate guard took a look at the DL and said Warren could be the guy who dropped off the flowers, but he was wearing a hat, bulky jacket with the collar pulled up around his face, and glasses, so it was hard to get a good look."

"He has to know you're on to him by now. Somebody from the theater or a former place of employment could have reached out to let him know the authorities were coming around asking questions."

"It's very likely. Which could make him run or make him desperate."

Neither a good option. She shivered despite the warmth from the fireplace and wrapped her arms around her middle.

"Nowell will be given all of the stills we have, and the composite, along with some computer-generated images of how he might present with various hair colors, different types of facial hair, padding. I want you to take a look at them yourself and memorize them."

"I will. Thanks." She scanned the room, her brow furrowing. "Speaking of Nowell, where are my three musketeers?"

"Being briefed with the rest of your family's security detail and other Petersen personnel in your father's study. There's an army of bodyguards in there."

She chuckled. "So, Mack's here? Briefing them?"

"Colton, actually."

"Colton's here?"

"Yeah. I was to brief you, and he was going to meet with his guys."

"I see. Well, it appears you all have this well in hand. Now, if we can just get the creep and get it over with."

"I'm with you. And we will get him."

She escorted the men to the front door, where several

security personnel were already filing outside to a caravan of black SUVs she hadn't even known had shown up. No sign of Colton, which meant he'd probably already left.

She took a deep breath to squelch the pain in her chest. He certainly appeared to be going out of his way to avoid her.

With another smile she hoped didn't look as forced as it felt, she shook the officers' hands on their way out the door.

John stopped in front of her. "I mean it, Ri. We'll get him. Even if he doesn't show at the ball, we'll find him."

"I have faith you will. Say hi to Avery tonight when you go to dinner."

"Will do. I know the girls miss having you with them."

"I miss it too. But with everything going on, my friends are safer not being around me so much in public."

"Those three would walk through fire with you."

"And I for them. Oh, before I forget. I found that page Colton referred to from the initial interview with the florist. It was in the file. The defense just missed it. Another stellar job they did."

John shook his head. "Shane should ask for his money back."

"Right? If we can't prove Warren killed Cait, I'm falling back on ineffective counsel in our appeal."

"Whatever you need to do. We'll see you later, Ri."

"Bye, Detective."

He walked out to one of the three unmarked police cars the officers had arrived in, and she waved from the doorway as they pulled around the large fountain in the center of the circular, flagstone drive.

"What do you think you're doing?"

She started at the sound of Colton's voice behind her, a split second before the door was slammed closed.

"Uh ... I was just—"

"Don't stand in an open doorway, Riley." Those icy blue eyes glared down at her. "Haven't you learned anything from all this?"

She finally recovered from her shock at seeing him for the first time since their visit with Shane and tilted her chin. "I doubt seriously the creep is standing somewhere with a high-powered rifle pointed over the brick wall on the off-chance I might come to the door. Besides, I didn't think watching out for me was your job any longer."

Emotions she couldn't define swirled in those eyes that could pierce right through her. "You're still my responsibility. I haven't lost anybody yet, and I won't start with you."

"How special I feel." She hoped her saccharine smile would mask her heart crumbling in her chest. "Now, if you'll excuse me, I have some work to do."

She started to walk away, but he pulled her around by the hand. "I'm sorry I scared you. I don't like you being where there's nobody around you."

Gooseflesh erupted all the way up her arm. "Because you had my guys tied up." Although she wanted with everything she was to hold onto him for as long as she could, she pulled her hand free. "If there's nothing more …"

He shook his head, and she walked up the stairs, willing back the despised tears she'd given in to much too often lately. She'd wanted to see him so many times the past week, but none of the pictures in her mind had included cold blue eyes and harsh words. It was as if they were back to Day One of their relationship, when he could stare daggers into her with that penetrating, icy gaze and raise her hackles with a simple look.

Once in her study, she closed the door and sagged against it, her pulse racing and stomach roiling. Had they lost everything?

Chapter Forty-Seven

Colton stood in his darkened kitchen and swallowed two over-the-counter sleep aids. He'd used them before to combat jet lag. Hopefully, they could drown out the sound of Riley's voice when she'd stared up at him that afternoon, the shock in her eyes turning to pleasure for a split second before the hurt pushed it away.

Then the ire. *How special I feel.*

She *was* special. But his gut-level reaction to her standing in an open doorway had made her feel anything but. Again, something else he'd broken he had no idea how to fix, especially from the distance he needed to keep. For her own good.

The clock on the microwave told him it was well past eleven. These days, it seemed he left in the dark and came home in the dark. But even as the case against Everett strengthened, his whereabouts remained unknown.

Upstairs in his bedroom, Colton plugged his cell phone charger into the wall. The device had run out of juice a couple of hours earlier, so he flipped through his mail, waiting for it to charge enough to check texts and voicemail. When the phone lit up, he had no missed texts, but he did have three voicemails.

He punched in the number to retrieve the messages and hit Speaker. He deleted two hang-ups, and when he heard nothing but silence on the third, moved his thumb to delete it too.

"Um, hey, Colton." His heart lurched, thumb jerking away from the delete button. "It's Riley. I'm sorry for calling so late. It's almost eleven, and I've called twice before but didn't leave a message. But then, this isn't something I wanted to leave on voicemail. Can you please call me? I don't care how late it is. And don't worry. I'm not going to propose to you." Her chuckle sounded a bit forced. "Please, Colton? Please call me? Thanks."

He stared at the phone, willing it to ring again, not at all sure he had the courage to make the call himself. He checked the time. Ten minutes till midnight. It really was too late to call anybody at this hour.

I don't care how late it is.

His pulse raced as his thumb hovered over her number. Then with a shake of the head, he set the device down on the bedside table. In the master bathroom, he brushed his teeth and crawled into bed, realizing his almost slow-motion movements were his way of waiting to see if she'd call again. By the time he flipped off the bedside lamp, he'd accepted the fact she wasn't going to.

He stared up at the dark ceiling. Maybe two more sleep tablets were in order.

Riley rolled over and checked the time on her phone. Twelve-twenty. Her heart fell. He wasn't going to call. But then, how could she blame him? He'd only been trying to protect her, as he'd always done, and she'd returned it with cold sarcasm, allowing all the hurt she'd endured since he left dictate her words and actions.

The ringing of her cell phone shattered the stillness, and she snatched it up. "Colton?"

"Riley." The familiar deep rumble of his voice brought tingles up the back of her neck. "I'm sorry it's so late."

"No. No, please." She scrambled to sit up, only a twinge in her hip left from her procedure. "I'm glad you called." Closing her eyes, she took a silent deep breath. "How are you?"

"Fine. I hope I didn't wake you."

"No. I'm … uh … still having a little difficulty in that area. My therapist prescribed me a sleeping pill, but I … I didn't take it tonight."

"Listen, I want to apologize for what happened earlier today."

Her brow crinkled in question. "What do you have to apologize for? That's actually why I was calling you. To apologize."

"No, it was me. I was harsh, and I scared you. That's not what I intended. I guess knowing the guy was standing at the gate less than two weeks ago unnerved me a little to see you there with no one around you."

"It probably wasn't the brightest move on my part. And I certainly don't believe you need to apologize. I was rude to you. I try to never go to bed with unfinished business, and the way we left things today didn't sit right with me. So, please accept my apology. I know you had my best interests in mind, as usual."

"Let's call it even and forget about it."

"Sounds good." The line sat silent between them for several seconds. "Well … I should let you go. So you can get some sleep."

"No, it's all right. I'm a little too wound up to sleep, anyway."

"I know the feeling."

"I'm glad you decided to see a therapist."

She snuggled back down into the covers. "She's helped me a lot. That was great advice, to talk to somebody. Somebody not involved with me or this mess. The day I got those awful flowers, Mom called her, and she came right over. I felt guilty since it was a weekend, but until she got here, I hadn't realized how affected I'd been. I completely went to pieces once we were alone."

"We hold back with our family and friends. We don't want them to worry about us. I didn't talk to Theresa or my parents about how I felt after I got shot. Kept telling them I was fine. But with my counselor, I unloaded. It made it easier to talk to the people close to me about it, but I think you have to get rid of all the garbage first."

"It's definitely helped me navigate all of this a little better."

"Glad to hear it."

"So, what's got you wound up?"

"Pardon me?"

"You said you were too wound up to sleep."

"Oh, right. The case, I guess. The fact we can't locate this guy is driving me crazy. And going back through Shane's case file makes me cross-eyed by about nine o'clock."

Her jaw fell slack. "At night? You're putting too much time into this, Colton. You need to take some time for yourself."

"I will after he's caught. I'll take a month or so off. Go to Arizona to play some golf."

Her heart clutched. He might not be working her detail, but he was putting even more time into working her case—Shane's case—instead of starting his golf holiday the day after he'd left her sitting in her study. Such a man of integrity.

She cleared her throat. "I wish John could take some time away too. I know Avery would love to see more of him but doesn't want me to feel guilty about him putting in so much time on this."

"And we all know it's not your fault. You know that, don't you? You know it's not your fault?"

"In my head I do. But it's hard knowing how stressed everybody is. It scares me to have people I love around me when

I'm out. I couldn't handle it if anybody got hurt. I'm always wondering if I should go away for a while or if it's better to stay put so we can get him that much sooner. How long will I need protection? How long before I can look for a new home of my own? It all just spins around in my head."

"You're doing terrific, Riley. I'm glad you haven't left and are still getting out some. The shelter event went well, record number, they told me. I'm happy you got to be there."

Her brow crinkled. The shelter event? "Who'd you talk to?"

"I was there. Working in the kitchen. You know I love to cook."

So, he had been there but kept himself in the back and not out front with everybody else. Even walking through the buffet line, she'd had no idea he was in the back helping to prepare their roasted chicken dinner.

She swallowed her disappointment that she'd missed him. "I'm glad you could come out for it. And the food was amazing."

"Thanks." He yawned. "So, how was your Christmas?"

She should let him go, but wasn't ready quite yet to break this tenuous connection. "Very nice. Did our usual gather-around-the-tree-in-our-PJs-and-tear-into-our-gifts thing. It's utter chaos and as much fun as Christmas Eve at the shelter. We drink hot chocolate and make a huge mess and watch the kids play with their toys. It's a great time."

"Sounds a lot like what we do. Only we get dressed first. Then we always do Mexican food—enchiladas, tamales, the whole nine yards."

She closed her eyes, imagining Christmas morning with Colton and his family. Exchanging gifts and enjoying an enchilada dinner around the table. A dream.

Her eyes popped open. And a dream it would stay.

"I'm just glad you didn't spend the day worrying about me. Or I guess I should say my case."

"Hmm. So, what did Santa bring you?"

"A book I've been wanting to read, a beautiful locket from Grandpa Kevin that was my grandmother's. Very special. And they always make a charitable donation to the Lend a Hand shelter and Save the Children. Oh, and I got a new set of golf clubs."

"You play golf?"

"Have since high school."

"Why didn't you ever say anything?"

"Why? You wanna take me to Arizona to golf with you?" When no response came, she wanted to bite her tongue. "That was a joke, Colton. I told you I wouldn't propose."

He laughed, and she relaxed. "I know. I just didn't know you golfed. And your family also made a donation to the Foundation. Very generous."

"Mom said she got your thank-you note. She thinks you're quite eloquent."

"Boy, she's easy."

She picked up a lock of hair and twisted it around her finger. "You underestimate yourself. Isn't that a little unusual for you?"

"You're never going to let up on me about that, are you?"

"Are you kidding? One of the first things you ever said to me was that nobody would have come near me if you'd been with me. You weren't wrong. Just a little cocky."

"Like I said, I'm confident in my work. It's some of these other things I'm not so sure of."

Her smile diminished as his words hung in the air. She knew some of the things he wasn't so certain about. Like his dancing abilities, which she felt were just fine. Or his ability to chair the board of a major charity, of which she'd had no question.

And his ability to give her what she needed to be happy. Yet not once did she doubt.

"Riley?"

"Oh … sorry. I was just thinking."

"You should get to sleep. Knowing you, you have a million things to do tomorrow."

"I guess. Mom and I are working on some last-minute details for the ball on Tuesday. What are you doing?"

"Trying to find Warren Everett."

"Really, Cole. Take a day off."

"After it's over."

She sighed. "All right. Sleep well. Thank you for calling me back."

"You're welcome. Thank you for leaving your message. I'm glad we could talk."

"Me, too." She gripped her phone, not wanting to hang up.

"See you Monday," he said after a silent moment, as if perhaps he, too, was reluctant to sever the connection.

Or maybe that was her wishful thinking.

Chapter Forty-Eight

The pizza Colton had wolfed down in the mobile Tech Ops center twenty minutes ago roiled in his stomach as he stood at the back of the ballroom in yet another high-end hotel.

Everything was set for Riley's big night. The night of her family's charitable ball, the one she'd put so much time and effort into planning over the past year.

Another visual scan of the room verified all law enforcement and Petersen personnel were at their assigned positions. Male and female operatives stood around the room, no one the wiser to the firepower hidden beneath their tuxes and formal gowns. He nodded at John, also in a tux and posing as a "guest."

"The Hudsons are en route to Tech Ops," one of the officers assigned to valet duty said in his earpiece.

"All of them?"

"Three cars so far. Cooper and Paxton are bringing the principal in now."

"Copy."

He made his way out of the ballroom and across the wide hall to the conference room where they'd set up their base of operations. Two Petersen cyber techs manned the room, watching various monitors covering the entrance, the lobby, the ballroom, and the kitchen. The entire Hudson family had been told they were to go there first for briefing.

As he moved across the wide hall, he caught sight of Riley walking between Nowell in front of her to her left, Trevor behind her to her right. Standard protocol he should've followed himself instead of getting too close.

They disappeared into the conference room, and he followed.

"Good evening, everybody."

When she turned and sent him a tentative smile, his chest tightened. Breathtaking in her bright pink, strapless ball gown, with a wrap slung over her arms, she'd left her hair down to cascade over her shoulders. Just the way he preferred it.

Drew stepped forward and offered his hand. "Colton. This is quite the operation you have here."

He pulled his attention from the vision she made to shake her father's hand. "Yes, sir. We just incorporated a few more things into your usual security for this event. Piper and another female operative are here tonight, so Riley will be accompanied even in the lounge. She won't be alone for a second."

Her smile widened. "I hope you supplied some dance partners for me, then, because I plan on dancing till dawn."

He couldn't help it when the corner of his mouth twitched a little. "I'm sure that won't be a problem. The gentlemen will be standing in line to dance with the belle of the ball. As long as we know who they all are."

She laughed, lighting up those emerald eyes.

It took a concerted effort to pull his attention from her to address them all. "We have no idea if he'll show or not. But if he should, we're ready." He pointed to several composites on the wall. "If Everett is our man, he may look like any of these or none of them. So just be vigilant. If anyone appears to be acting suspiciously, we want to know about it. You'll know who we are because we're all wearing yellow roses on our lapels. Any questions?"

The Hudsons looked at each other before shaking their heads.

"Okay, then. Have a wonderful evening."

The family and their security detail made their way out of the room, Riley's guys hanging back as she walked up to Colton.

"You look very nice tonight, Mr. Blankenship."

"As do you. Beautiful as always."

Her smile did that funny thing in his chest, as it had from that first day. "Thank you."

He looked around for a moment before addressing Nowell. "Why don't you guys go on into the ballroom? I need to speak with Riley for a minute. I'll walk her over myself."

"Yes, sir," Nowell answered before leaving with Paul and Trevor.

Uncertainty clouded the previous light in her eyes. "Something wrong?"

Smiling, he scratched his temple. "I … well, I was hoping to see you before everything got started tonight."

"Why's that?"

"Oh, wait." He reached back and under his jacket to the small box attached to his belt. "I forgot this was on."

"What's on?"

"My mic. Okay, now we're alone."

Her forehead furrowed. "So, why did you need to see me?"

"I have something for you. A belated Christmas gift, I guess you could say."

Her jaw dropped. "Really?"

"I hope you don't mind. I saw this and it just seemed like you. It's nothing big."

"Maybe I should be the judge of that."

He pulled a small box out of his inside pocket and held it out to her. "Merry Christmas. A week late."

At the time, he hadn't been sure of the wisdom in buying her a gift. But during their midnight phone call a few days before, they'd built a bridge, of sorts. As if they could possibly reclaim the friendship he'd left in tatters with his clumsy exit.

After tearing the paper from the box, she opened it, and her eyes widened at the diamond heart-shaped pendant on a delicate gold chain sitting inside. "This is stunning."

"It's pretty modest compared to some of your other pieces, but I thought it looked like you. Elegant but not flashy. And you're full of heart, so it seemed appropriate."

"I love it. Thank you. May I wear it tonight?"

He was taken aback. His small gift with her spectacular ball gown? "Sure. If you'd like to."

She removed it from the box and held it out for him to clasp around her neck. His skin tingled as his hands moved under her hair. This was the closest they'd been in weeks, and the power of it hadn't diminished since that night.

"There you go."

She turned back, taking the pendant in her fingers and staring down at it. "I do love it, Cole. Thank you so much."

"You're welcome. Now, I guess we should go so you can start greeting your guests."

"In a minute. I … uh … have something for you too. I brought it tonight, but I wasn't sure I'd have a chance to give it to you."

She opened her tiny, hot pink, beaded handbag and took out a small package, much like the one he'd given her. He removed the paper and opened the box to reveal two square gold cuff links with *CB* engraved in cursive on each.

"Wow. These are great. Thank you."

While he replaced the cuff links he'd donned earlier, she told him Paul had received cuff links in the likeness of steering wheels, Nowell sported a tiepin in the shape of a bicycle—his favorite hobby—and Trevor wore a lapel pin resembling a miniature purple heart.

"For taking a bullet for me and all," she said with a shrug.

Her smile disappeared as panic filled her eyes. "I don't want anybody taking a bullet for me tonight, Cole. Not my guys, not any of John's guys. Not you."

The urge to pull her into his arms was strong, but he settled for taking her hand. "This place is locked down tight. We won't let him anywhere near you if he should show. I promise you that."

The trust that replaced the fear almost undid him, and he would do everything in his power to prove himself worthy of it.

Chapter Forty-Nine

So far, so good.

Standing in the back of the ballroom, Colton applauded with the rest of the attendees as Riley took her seat at her family's table. The elegant three-course dinner had been served three hours ago, and after her guests had enjoyed dancing to the string ensemble or visiting at their tables, she treated them to a video presentation highlighting her Lend a Hand and Save the Children charities. What he hadn't expected was the plug for Theresa's foundation, and judging by the response, he had no doubt the evening's pledges would exceed their goal.

Then again, Riley represented her causes with such grace and eloquence a miser would gladly relinquish his last dime.

While several people again took to the dance floor—with more modern, faster-tempo music now supplied by a deejay— he strolled the perimeter of the ballroom, as he'd done several times throughout the evening. Perusing the crowd, he confirmed no new faces had appeared.

Completing his circuit, he joined Trevor at the ballroom entrance. "How are you doing? Since the shooting."

"Back to normal." Trevor glanced around the room and back again. "Just a bit of a bruise left."

"Glad to hear it. And the other?"

Trevor's brow wrinkled. "Other?"

"The mental healing can be a longer road."

With a shrug, Trevor took another scan of the room. "All good." His gaze came back to Colton. "I appreciated everybody's cards and notes. The prayers."

"Prayer's the key."

"Amen, brother."

Colton clapped him on the shoulder. "Happy New Year, Trev."

"Yes, sir. You too."

Again taking his place in the back of the room, Colton panned the crowd milling around in groups. It had been easier with everybody at their tables, but this was a party, after all, so constant movement was to be expected.

The New Year would dawn in less than thirty minutes, but their job was far from over. From what he'd been told, any partygoers with enough stamina would dance until the sun came up.

"Colton," Dillon said in his ear.

"Go ahead."

"We have a situation."

"On my way."

His gut tightened as he exited the beautifully dressed ballroom. Would this be the first hitch in an otherwise flawless op? Whatever this *situation* was, he prayed they could resolve it without anybody in the ballroom being the wiser.

"What's up?"

Dillon, one of two agents monitoring live-stream footage from various vantage points around the ballroom, ran his finger across his neck. Colton muted his mic.

"Just got off the phone with Houston PD. Med called them

about fifteen minutes ago. A girl was brought in. Beaten. Found by a friend who happened to stop by. Barely coherent. Kept repeating something about the Hudson Ball and mentioned a couple of names. One was Terence. The other sounded like Warren. Decided they should call it in since she appeared agitated, like she was trying to get a warning out."

Colton's blood ran cold. "Who is she?"

"One of the members of the theater where Everett volunteers. Units are at the hospital and at her place now. Looks like we found where he's been holing up."

"Not the woman we were sitting on?"

"No. Someone new to the group. Could be the theater manager didn't know they'd hooked up."

Fifteen minutes. And no telling how long she'd been lying there, beaten, and for what reason? Because she'd pushed the wrong button and set Everett off? Or did she know something she shouldn't?

"Do we have a Terence on our hotel personnel list that we've vetted?"

Dillon brought up a screen with a list of names the hotel had provided of all male staff assigned to the event. "Terence Drummond. Waitstaff. Contracted through an agency. This is his first event here at The Cheshire Hotel."

"Picture."

Dillon hit more keys. A photo popped up. A man, long face, blue eyes, brown hair, six foot one, slight build. Same description could be made for Warren Everett.

"What do we know about this guy?"

"Waiter at the Derby Ranch Steakhouse. Works contract catering jobs on the side. Before that, he was with ..." Dillon scrolled down the page. "The Whitmore. Kitchen staff. Three years."

Colton's inner radar sounded off. "Same time as Everett, so

we can assume they knew each other. Can we locate him in the building?"

Dillon brought up the footage from the kitchen and bar, and they studied the monitors for any sign of him. Nothing. If Everett had shown up in place of Drummond, doubtful anybody on the wait crew would be the wiser, since this was Drummond's first gig at this location.

"Get units to his home address now. Could be he either allowed Everett to work in his place, or we have another victim."

"On it."

Colton activated his transmitter on his way back to the ballroom. "Listen up, everybody. We got a viable tip Everett could be impersonating somebody we vetted on the waitstaff. Name Terence Drummond. Lanky build, brown hair worn to the collar are distinctive markers."

Back in the ballroom, he spotted Riley dancing in a circle and laughing with her three best friends. "Cooper, get Riley off the dance floor. I need her with you."

Nowell put his hand to his ear. "Copy that."

"Paxton, I need you with Nowell and Riley right now."

"On it."

"Jamison, have the SUV running at the emergency exit."

"Already headed that way."

"Good work. Anderson and Wiley, check the kitchen and bar for anybody matching the description."

The two agents responded in the affirmative as Colton moved quickly through the room. As Nowell escorted Riley to the side where Trevor met them, Colton spotted John walking up to Avery still on the dance floor. He said something to her, she nodded and grabbed Frances and Barbara by the arms, pulling them off the floor to a far corner. John then joined two of his men heading toward the bar. Several others in the room, both Petersen personnel and cops in plain clothes, were suddenly in motion.

"Blankenship."

"Go, Wiley."

"Nobody in the kitchen matching that description. Everybody checks."

"Same at the bar," John reported back.

"Okay, stay alert. Check every waiter you see. There could possibly be scars from scratch marks on his right hand."

Adrenaline pumped through his system as he circled the room, his gaze pinning on every red-coated server he passed. He caught John's concerned glance from several feet away. The music continued, the heavy bass line adding to the tension of the moment. The hundred-plus guests talked, laughed, and danced, unaware of any lurking danger. Caterer's assistants kept food in plentiful supply, and waiters lined up at the bar, picking up trays of champagne to pass out for the New Year countdown.

He consulted his watch. Eleven minutes to midnight.

Several servers had already received their trays and were making their way around the room.

Riley stood behind a table flanked by Nowell and Trevor.

"Cooper, you and Paxton walk Riley out as unobtrusively as possible. I want her in the SUV and off the premises in the next two minutes."

"Copy that."

Nowell bent to speak in Riley's ear, and her face fell. Colton winced. She'd been so looking forward to this evening, had put hours of work into preparing for it, and he was making her go home. She nodded, apparently accepting it was for the best, and the trio started around the perimeter.

Letting his gaze do another pass around the room, he spotted a waiter coming through the main doors, holding a tray against the front of his jacket. Odd that a member of the waitstaff would enter from the lobby and not the kitchen. Colton's eyes narrowed on the man. Tall, lanky. Brown hair worn a bit shaggy. Right hand hidden behind the tray. Focus pinned on Riley as she made her way with her detail to a side exit.

Colton's pulse beat in time with the thumping bass as he broke into a run from across the room. "I have visual." He weaved around startled partygoers. "North side, brown hair, six-two, trailing the principal. All hands out here now."

Nowell pulled Riley in front of him, shielding her with his body.

Trevor spun, weapon drawn, walking backward to stay with his principal while taking aim at the alleged threat. "Can't take the shot. Too many innocents."

Before Colton reached the mark, the man spotted him. Their eyes met.

Warren Everett. He'd know that soulless gaze anywhere.

Everett threw the tray, exposing the firearm he held in his other hand. Colton raised his arm as the tray hit.

Everett took aim at him, but Colton didn't have any cleaner shot than Trevor. A woman screamed. Alarmed guests moved in every direction. Everett whirled and ran back the way he'd come.

Finally clear of the panicked crowd, Colton sprinted after Everett into the lobby. "Cooper, keep Riley inside until we secure the area. Behind the bar."

Everett reached behind him and took aim. Colton flinched at the *phfft* of the bullet as it left the silencer. He took his own shot. With a loud grunt, Everett grabbed his right shoulder but didn't drop his weapon. Instead of falling, he regained his balance and hurtled toward the sliding glass doors.

Colton picked up his pace. This was the guy, the monster, who had invaded Riley's life for the past two months. He was putting a stop to it now. Tonight.

No matter what it might cost him.

Chapter Fifty

Riley recoiled at the sound of the gunshot. Heart hammering against her sternum, her head swiveled to the ballroom doors. Where was Colton? A shout from the lobby brought her to a stop, and she yanked her arm free from Nowell's grasp.

Not again. This couldn't be happening again.

John and three other men made a beeline toward the doors, weapons drawn. Others stayed with the crowd, instructing them to hunker in place.

Nowell grabbed her arm again and steered her toward the bar instead of continuing to the exit they'd designated as her emergency egress. Trevor kept pace on her other side.

"What's happening?" Her voice quivered with a surge of adrenaline. "Is Colton okay?"

Nowell nodded. "He ordered us to keep you inside until Everett's apprehended."

More shouting from the lobby drew her protectors' attention. Under her dress, she slipped out of her shoes and made a break for the lobby.

"Riley!" Trevor called after her. "Stop!"

If she could just see for herself …

"Riley!" Nowell's voice came from too close behind.

She gathered up the full skirt of her dress, tapping into her high school regional champion sprinter days to stay out of his reach. If she could just get outside to make sure Colton was okay. That nobody else had been hurt on her account.

The glass doors opened with a *shwoosh*. Outside, Colton ran after a red-jacketed waiter. The man turned, aimed—

A shot rang out.

"Cole!"

Someone grabbed her from behind and pushed her to the ground. Her breath left her as she hit the pavement.

"Sorry, Riley," Nowell said from on top of her.

"He's down! He's down!" a voice yelled from a distance.

Trevor positioned himself, weapon drawn, between them and the scene several yards away. Too many people. She couldn't see.

Panic tightened her throat. "Who's down? Who is it?"

"Everett," Trevor threw over his shoulder.

"Colton—"

"He's fine." Trevor holstered his gun, still watching the scene in the parking lot. "Looks like Everett took one in the leg. Squealin' like a stuck pig, as we used to say on the ranch." He grinned down at them. "He'll live, but he'll be gimped up for a while."

Closing her eyes, she put her forehead down on her crossed arms, her shoulders shaking as the torment of the last several months left in a torrent of tears.

Nowell lifted his weight from her and put his hand on her back. "You're okay, Riley. It's all over. You're okay."

When she could speak, she lifted her head and swiped at her cheeks. It didn't matter if she had tracks in her makeup or stains from the pavement on her dress.

Colton was safe. And she was free.

"Thank you." She swallowed the thickness in her throat. "All of you."

Trevor glanced over his shoulder to his team lead. "Blankenship's on his way."

Nowell sighed as he stood. "I'm so fired."

"We both should probably update our resumes."

Nowell offered his hand to help her up.

"I got her." Colton took her by the hands to draw her onto her feet, then lifted her into his arms, like he had at the Christmas ball. Holding him tight around the neck, she gave in to a fresh spate of tears.

"It's okay, Ri. You're all right."

Once somewhat composed, she pulled back and wiped her face with her hand. "I thought he shot you." Her breath hitched. "I saw him turn … and the gun—"

"I got him first."

She nodded, unable to do anything but stare into those crystal blue eyes.

"What are you doing out here?" He still held her clutched to his chest, despite all the activity taking place around them.

"I had to see. Had to know you were okay. It wasn't Nowell's fault."

Nowell cleared his throat. "One hundred percent my fault. Caught me off guard. Never had a principal run from me before. And she can sprint like a jaguar."

"No. He trusted me to do as instructed, but I couldn't leave with you out here facing what I didn't know."

Colton lowered her to the concrete, chilling her bare feet. His hands held tight to hers. "Scared me to death when I heard you."

"I'm sorry. Please don't be mad at these guys. They've done everything for me."

"I'm not mad. Just relieved to know you're okay. Oh. Almost forgot. Jamison, you can leave the SUV. Everett's in custody."

After Paul's response, he reached behind him and turned off the mic before taking her hand again.

Trevor pulled Nowell away by the arm, grinning back at them. "Our work here is done. You two take your time."

Colton's brows drew together. "Did you shrink?"

She lifted the skirt of her soiled dress, wiggling her toes with their magenta-painted nails. "Couldn't run in those heels. The guys didn't notice I took them off. That's how I gave them the slip. They tried, Cole. But there was no way they were making me leave with you still here."

She peered up at the face she loved with her whole heart, a wayward tear slipping down her cheek. "I didn't want to lose you. I had to know you were all right."

He studied her, his blue gaze penetrating. "Do you really believe you're in love with me? With *me* and not"—he waved his arm around at the controlled chaos, red and blue lights flashing, cops and Petersen personnel swarming around the parking lot —"all this?"

"Yes. I know I'm in love with you, Colton Blankenship. I'm yours whether you want me or not."

"I do want you. I always wanted you. I just couldn't imagine that you could want me."

"Heart and soul."

Placing a hand along her face, his eyes lingered on hers before he bent to kiss her. Gently at first, then with more fervor as he wrapped her in his arms.

Finally. Back where she felt the safest. The most at home. With this man. She wanted nothing more than to stay here for a while.

But he instead pulled back and chuckled. "We're not exactly alone."

She glanced over her shoulder at the crowd gathered inside the glass doors, where the cop-valets had stopped them.

Including her girls, her parents, and the Blankenships. Even in the cold, her cheeks heated as she turned back to him.

He ran the backs of his fingers down her face. "I'm in love with you, too, Riley Hudson."

Her heart grew with her smile. "I knew you were."

"I don't know what I have to offer you, but I'll give you all I can."

She grabbed the lapels of his jacket in her fists. "I just want you."

"That much I can give you. All of me, Riley. Everything I am is yours." When she shivered, he shrugged out of his jacket and laid it around her shoulders. "Let's get you inside. Your feet must be ice by now."

Fireworks burst in the sky overhead from a nearby park.

"It's midnight," she whispered.

"So it is." He leaned down and kissed her again, the past giving way to the future. A future she couldn't wait to live. With this man who'd put himself in the line of fire to ensure she would have one.

She drew back and smiled up at him. "Best. New Year. Ever."

Chapter Fifty-One

If there were ever any question that evil existed in the world, Jacob Warren Everett would put those doubts to rest.

Colton took another sip from his cup of black coffee, the strong brew scalding a path down his throat. Hopefully, it would be the jolt he needed to keep him on his feet.

Instead of being with the one he most wanted to be, this first day of the New Year had been spent at HPD Central Patrol Division. First with John putting together their case for the DA, and now watching the bedside interrogation of Warren Everett unfold from a monitor in their version of Tech Ops.

The vermin would heal from the bullets Colton had put through his shoulder and leg, since they had missed any major arteries. The off-center-mass shots had been to incapacitate him, not take him out before he could answer for his crimes.

Starting with the murder of Terence Drummond, found with a gunshot wound to the back. Questioning of the kitchen manager revealed he'd never met Terence and had no idea someone else had shown up in his place.

"What precipitated the beating of Miss Jansen?" John,

standing at the head of the bed, continued the questioning that had begun nearly an hour ago.

Warren dipped his head and stared at his hands. "I don't know what you're talkin' about."

"Doesn't matter. We have her statement. Said she got curious when the theater manager told them the police were looking for you. Went through your things when you weren't home, found a waiter's uniform with Terence's name badge, a brown wig, and a gun. When she asked about the uniform and name tag, you shrugged it off as a friend letting you work the Hudson ball at The Cheshire in his place to make some extra money. Last thing she remembers is asking you why the cops wanted to talk to you. Sound about right?"

"Like I said. I don't know nothin' about that."

The Assistant DA assigned to the case crossed his arms. "Terms of the deal you accepted require full disclosure."

Everett scowled at the man standing next to John. "I plead the Fifth."

"Full. Disclosure. Do I need to spell that for you?"

Warren pinned his gaze on someone sitting off-camera. "Can't you object or somethin'?"

Court-appointed defense attorney, apparently. "I told you the terms. No death penalty for a full confession."

With a sigh, Everett focused on his hands again. "I didn't mean to hurt her that bad. Just teach her a lesson about stayin' in her lane."

John consulted his notes. "Concussion, dislocated shoulder, fractured ribs, multiple contusions." He looked back at Everett. "Pretty harsh lesson."

When Warren said nothing, John flipped the page in his notebook. "So, why Caitlyn Mulaney? More than a year after you last saw her?"

"Caitlyn." The man all but spat her name. "That uppity rich

girl didn't know a good thing when it was right in front her. Still, I waited for her. Thought she'd come around."

"Waited? Or stalked?"

"Waited," he repeated with a glare.

"Here's the thing. Our cyber guys have your laptop and cell phone. They notified me fifteen minutes ago that they got in. Guess you know what they found."

"So, I like to take pictures."

"Over three hundred photos of Caitlyn over the last year. Walking into the country club, shopping, pulling in and out of her garage, out with Shane, among others. They also found the online aliases you used to comment on her social media posts and the messages you sent sliding into her DMs. If you were *waiting* for her to come around, why kill her?"

Everett's face reddened and fists clenched in his lap. "Shane took everything from me. I made sure Caitlyn was the last."

Heat traveled up Colton's spine. Killed an innocent girl out of spite. How sick was this guy?

"How'd you know about Shane and Cait?" John asked.

"You kidding? Her life played out on social media. Then Shane started appearing all over her posts. Pretty clear they had a thing going." He shook his head. "Last straw."

"Is that how you knew their routine? By tailing them?"

"Watched them for a couple of weeks. Creatures of habit. He came over to her house every night. Always between 6:45 and seven. Sometimes they went out. Sometimes they stayed in, but he never spent the night. Idiot."

Colton's jaw flexed. Made sense a man like Warren Everett would have no regard for a woman's virtue. Would never understand how Shane doing so was a deeper expression of his love and respect for Caitlyn than a man only interested in something physical.

"You took a credit card out in Shane's name?"

Everett shrugged. "Wasn't that hard."

"Then what?"

The man released another deep sigh. "Ordered the flowers, gave them the message for the card. I followed him around for a few days, to his different job sites. Noticed he always changed phones before going in. It was easy to simply pop the lock on that vintage car of his and lift the phone. No alarm. Bummer that he realized it so early in the day and suspended his service."

"What did you wear to pick up the arrangement?"

"Blue suit. Cost me a bundle. Should've put it on that credit card."

"Is that what you wore to Caitlyn's?"

He shook his head. "Changed into clothes like a delivery guy. Wore a ball cap. Cait opened the door, smiled when she saw the flowers. Probably thought Shane had sent them. Pathetic."

"Did she recognize you?"

"She barely looked at me. Like an entitled princess dismissing a servant. I handed her the flowers, and while she was staring at them all starry-eyed, I pushed her back and walked in." Grinning, he shook his head. "Man, the look on her face changed so fast. From happy one second, to shocked. Then fear when she finally realized it was me."

Watching his expression on the screen, it seemed to Colton the guy reveled in the memory.

"The knife was Caitlyn's, so we know you didn't bring it. What was the original plan?"

"I wanted to choke the life out of her. No noise. No mess. My face the last thing she ever saw, so she'd know she shouldn't have discounted me. But then she threw those blasted flowers at me and ran for the kitchen. Picked up the knife, which I took from her in about two seconds."

He pointed his finger at John. "It's her fault what happened. If she hadn't screamed at me that her *boyfriend* was on his way over and could snap me in half, I wouldn't have lost it. But how's a guy supposed to take that? Throwing Shane in my face. I honestly lost my mind. Didn't even remember doing it until it was over." Everett turned his attention to his attorney again. "There should be a defense for that, right?"

All Colton heard was an impatient sigh. "You've already agreed to this deal."

Everett scowled. "Guess I should've thought that through. I was insane. I know I was. It was like comin' out of a blackout. I don't remember none of it."

A convenient excuse that held no merit. Even without the deal, it was doubtful a judge would grant a motion to plead insanity. Everett was too clever. Too thorough. All he'd done prior to the offense, and everything he'd done to Riley over the past several weeks, was proof of his state of mind.

Twisted, yes. Insane, no.

"Have to admit, it threw me off my game for a minute. I just sat there, catching my breath. But with Shane coming, I had to get out of there. Grabbed a man's jacket from her closet— probably Shane's—because ... well ... she made a mess of me. Stuck the hat inside, and left the way I came in, right through the front door."

Typical sociopath. It wasn't his fault he stabbed Cait to death. It was hers for grabbing the knife. It wasn't his doing that had blood splattered all over him. It was Caitlyn's for bleeding.

It was probably a good thing Colton had stayed back at the precinct. He wasn't sure he'd have the self-control John possessed.

The detective consulted his notes again. "You wore gloves?"

"I'm not stupid. Didn't wanna leave fingerprints behind, now, did I? Once I was in the car, though, I realized I'd sliced my hand along the base of my thumb." He glanced at his hand. "Still have that stupid scar."

Just as Riley had suspected. But with all the blood and no cuts on Shane's hands, the police simply hadn't looked hard enough for foreign DNA.

Chuckling, Warren shook his head again. "The day Shane's arrest hit the news, I bought a bottle of champagne. Never had it before and wished I'd opted for a good bourbon instead. But it was a celebration. Champagne seemed appropriate."

John exchanged a tight-lipped look with the prosecutor, but Warren went on without missing a beat. No emotion. Only arrogance.

"The trial was a blast. Sat through every second of it, disguised, of course, so Dad and that witch he married wouldn't see me. Watching them sitting there every day, devastated, was an extra bonus. It's what they get for tossing me out of their lives. I was every bit as good as Shane. They just didn't care.

"And that Riley Hudson. Sitting there so self-righteous. Every day, she looked right past me. I was worried early on that she might say something to the cops about seeing me arguing with Cait at the club, but apparently, she hadn't remembered."

John shifted his weight to one hip. He had to be as exhausted as Colton, having been up all night putting together the arrest warrant, obtaining search warrants from a judge willing to sign off on New Year's. Still wearing the tux from the party, sans tie and suit coat.

"Why go after her now? Even if you'd succeeded, it wouldn't have changed the outcome. Her office would've still worked Shane's case."

"I saw that press conference on TV. Thought she'd taken Shane's case because she remembered seein' us that day. But when nobody showed up to question me, I knew she hadn't put it together. Didn't want to take the chance that she might at some point. She was the only loose end. Cut that off, and Shane's gone for good." He shrugged as if talking about squashing a bug. "Can't blame a guy for trying."

Colton's body heated from the inside out, his blood boiling as it raced through his veins. Yes, definitely a good thing he wasn't standing in that room.

Can't blame a guy for trying? Oh, yes, he could. He most certainly could.

Chapter Fifty-Two

Colton handed Riley a cup of hot chocolate and sat next to her on the couch in front of his fireplace. Stretching his arm around her, he pulled her close to his side. "Get enough sleep today?"

"The most sound sleep I've had since November ninth. Except for the anesthesia."

"Glad to hear it."

"What about you? A couple of hours before I got here couldn't have been enough. Not when you went straight to the station after the party."

"It'll get me through for another few hours. There was no way I was wasting your first night of freedom sleeping."

She giggled. "Driving my car over here was weird. Feels so teeny after the SUV. I'm considering trading it for something bigger."

"I wish you would. The thought of you in that minuscule car in Houston traffic doesn't thrill me."

"Let's go car shopping this weekend, then."

"It's a date." He tipped his head and kissed her, regretting he hadn't put his mug down first to wrap her in his arms. Then again, it was probably good to have a barrier. Kissing her ignited a fire in him he had to work to control.

But he would. Until the day she wore his name, if he should be so blessed.

He pulled back and grinned at her. "The first of many."

"Oh, I certainly hope so." Leaning in, she pressed her mouth to his again, letting the kiss linger while flames crackled in the fireplace.

She pulled away and laid her head against his shoulder. "Did Warren say anything about how he got photos of us when we had no idea he was there? Or how he got into the Thanksgiving dinner?"

He nodded. "Turns out he's a pretty good amateur photographer. Has a long-range lens. Said he took them either from down the block or from his vehicle. And he did pose as an amputee for the homeless shelter dinner. Trevor was livid when I told him that. Couldn't believe he had Everett right in front of him and missed it."

"Not his fault. The guy's a master of disguise."

"Exactly what I told him. Still, he didn't take it well."

"And what about the girl?"

"Everett's girlfriend? She'll be fine. Physically. No telling what the psychological scars might be, though."

"What set him off? Was she able to say?"

He set his cup down on the coffee table. "Asked the wrong questions at the wrong time and paid the price."

"She's the real hero of all of this." She raised her head from his shoulder to take a sip of her cocoa. "I should go see her. To thank her. We might not have known he was there if she hadn't tried so hard to get the message to the hospital staff."

"Makes me crazy. Even with all our safeguards, he got through."

"Weren't they checking the staff for weapons?"

"Checked bags and coats, light pat-downs. He planted it in a ceiling tile in the men's restroom before reporting for work. We couldn't locate him anywhere right after we got the tip, then he was suddenly on the floor heading toward you. He went to retrieve the gun and planned to take you out during all the hoopla at midnight. Had somehow obtained a silencer. Probably because of the mess he made at the Christmas ball *not* using one. Figured he could get a shot off without anybody being the wiser until after the deed, and he would already be lost in the crowd."

She shuddered and pressed in closer. "That whole thing had to be God. Her friend dropping by and finding her, being coherent enough to get some information out, and the ER staff taking it seriously enough to call the police. All within minutes of him carrying out his plan."

"Most definitely a divine hand in all of that. We're re-evaluating how we handle IDs on ops like this one. The cop monitoring the waitstaff glanced right over him when he checked the DL. And why wouldn't he? Everett came in looking like Drummond, and there was no visible weapon on him. Even covered the scars left by your fingernails with liquid latex, like they use in the theater. Nobody would know without touching it. Another well-thought-out plan. He's not a stupid guy. Thorough. Analytical. It's too bad he didn't use his smarts like Shane did and make something of himself."

She lifted her head. "His mom's influence, you think? Shane said she was a piece of work."

"Mr. Everett thinks so. Quite the roller coaster for him. Relieved to know Shane will be getting out as soon as all the paperwork goes through—since the DA's filing it himself—but grief-stricken his other son killed an innocent girl out of revenge. Told John he feels responsible."

"That's not true."

"Not a bit. After our interview with them, John checked the court records from twenty, thirty years ago. Mr. Everett filed several times to get Warren, but the judge never awarded him full custody."

"So sad."

"Speaking of the mother, they're reopening her death investigation. To see if it truly was a suicide or if Warren might have had a hand in it. Apparently, several people reported doubts about the suicide ruling at the time, but the police didn't agree."

Riley shook her head. "His mother, Cait, Shane, his girlfriend, Terence. And me. He considers anybody expendable if they get in the way of his agenda. That's some kind of evil."

A true statement. They'd all breathed a sigh of relief when he agreed to the plea deal. His confession in exchange for life without parole. No death penalty, but at least he'd never be free to harm another person.

Riley sighed. "I hope John's getting some sleep after working all night and today."

"I'm sure he is. He left when I did, and we were both going straight home."

After all the drama, the Petersen folks packed up the control center while the police worked the crime scene in the lobby and outside, where it all ended. Once Tech Ops shut down, he joined Riley in the ballroom, as did Nowell, Trevor, Paul, and several other Petersen personnel, ready to celebrate the successful end of the operation. The law enforcement guys acting as waiters, valets, and the photographer stuck around too. Said a lot about them that they finished out the party in their designated roles instead of leaving the staff shorthanded.

After leaving Avery with a New Year's kiss, John had to report to the precinct to process Everett, who was under arrest even while being treated for his wounds. Colton joined him after seeing Riley home just before dawn, bringing breakfast he'd picked up on the way. By the time John had completed his interrogation that afternoon, they'd both been about to drop and left each other with a congratulatory handshake before heading home.

Riley laid her head on his shoulder again and snuggled in. "My girls were amazing last night. This morning. Whenever it was. God really blessed me with them."

"Four peas in a pod."

"Not the first time I've heard that."

He put his cheek against her head and watched the flames lick the logs. He should probably put more on, but he didn't want to get up, content right where he was.

"So, tell me. If you're not going to have to work on the Everett appeals case, can you take some time off in the near future? Like, maybe a month?"

She pulled back and grinned at him. "To go golfing in Arizona?"

"Actually, I was thinking Hawaii."

"Hawaii? I'd love that."

"I can get a place there for a few weeks, say, around April? May? A friend of mine has a bungalow on Kauai, and I've used it several times to get away. Very secluded. Right on the beach. Very romantic."

"Sounds wonderful. Two bedrooms?"

"No, but I think I have it covered. I figured we'd need at least a couple of months to plan a proper wedding, after all."

Her eyes widened. "Is that a proposal?"

"Maybe not the most romantic one, but yes. If you'll have me."

"You want to marry me?"

He chuckled. "I thought that much was pretty clear."

"Boy, when you make up your mind, you really make up your mind."

"Having second thoughts?" His teasing grin belied the knot in his stomach. She'd said she was in love with him, but marriage was a whole different game.

"No. I want to be with you. I just need to know you're absolutely sure. There's a lot we need to talk about."

"I'll sign anything you want me to or your family asks me to. This has nothing to do with your money."

"Sign? The only thing I want you to sign is the Marriage Certificate."

That knot uncoiled with her answer. "I insist on a prenup, Ri."

"Why?"

"I don't want there to be any question."

"There is no question. Not for me, anyway. It was our socio-economic status that almost kept us apart. I certainly don't believe you've suddenly decided what a great way to live a life of leisure. My mother didn't sign any agreement. Neither did Delia, and she was a secretary at the company when she met Alex. Sadie's the only one who brought as much financially into the marriage as Kevin."

"I may need a little help in knowing how to handle this. Like providing for you. I obviously don't need to. But I want to keep my job. I want to feel like I'm contributing."

"You absolutely can. And money isn't the only contribution people bring to marriage. You know that from experience. We have our faith, our families, our goals and dreams. All things we can experience together."

She heaved a sigh. "Although I'm going to miss you something awful while you're working an assignment."

He tipped his head. "There might be a way around that."

Her eyebrows rose above those green eyes he could stare into all night. "Do tell."

"Mack made me an offer a couple of months back, but I told him I'd have to think about it. It wouldn't take place until March, anyway, so I had time to consider it."

"What offer?"

"The business has grown considerably, and we're getting

more and more high-profile clients from all over the world. Mack needs help at the administrative level and asked me to take a VP position. Vice President of Security Operations."

"Oh, wow, that sounds impressive. But that would mean office work, right? Could you stand that?"

"Sure. If it meant being with you evenings and weekends. And that sounds pretty fantastic to me."

Her smile lit her face. "To me too. But you need to be happy with how you spend your days. In your career. I know you like to be in the thick of things."

"I'd still be involved in training new agents, planning ops, and I'd probably do field work from time to time, like Mack did with your case. I'd be very happy, Riley. Working at what I love during the day, coming home to the one I love at night."

She reached up and put her hand along his face. "And the one who loves you."

"Forever?"

"Forever."

He grinned at her before kissing her again. This time, with nothing in his hands to keep him from wrapping her up in his arms.

Pulling back sometime later, he gazed down at her. "This is going to be some wild ride."

"Guess you'd better hang on."

Epilogue

Riley couldn't have imagined a more perfect day.

Laying her forehead against Colton's jaw, she let him lead her on their first turn around the dance floor as Mr. and Mrs. Blankenship. Could a heart burst with too much happiness? If so, hers must be made of some tough stuff, because she'd never known such an overflowing of joy.

The past five months leading up to their May wedding on the estate grounds had been busy and full.

Full of life. Full of fun. Full of love and laughter and new hopes and dreams. Most of which had been launched the second Colton's father pronounced them husband and wife, little more than an hour before.

And she couldn't wait. Couldn't wait to live in the new house they bought after selling her townhome in January and his house last month. Much more modest than the estate, where she'd stayed during their engagement, but a bit more substantial than his previous home, complete with a gate. The new neighborhood was in a good area, and the house much closer to other homes than the estate was to its neighbors. But her new husband—Petersen's Vice President of Security Operations—insisted on safety first when it came to being married to a Hudson, with little heirs and heiresses running around in the future.

Little heirs and heiresses she couldn't wait to get started on.

After a gourmet dinner of prime rib, lobster, and all the side dishes a body could desire, they'd taken to the dance floor.

She gazed up at the man who owned her heart. "What a beautiful day."

Leaning in, he kissed her, to the delight of their guests. "My gorgeous bride. That first wedding dress I saw you in was spectacular, but this …" He shook his head. "You take my breath away, Mrs. Blankenship."

"Oh, how I love the way that sounds. I couldn't wait to be Riley Christine Blankenship. Has a great ring to it, don't you think?"

"Absolutely. But you still don't regret not hyphenating your last name?"

"I don't. I always knew when I found my soulmate and married him, I'd take his name. I'm still a Hudson. But I'll forever be yours."

He kissed her again as their chosen song ended, after which they cut their cake, then posed for some nighttime photos outside. Upon returning to the tent, they were pulled into a line dance, and the party was on. Best Man Paul handed Colton a black Stetson while Fran plopped a white cowboy hat on Riley's head, matching the sage green hats of her bridal party.

The next jaunty country tune kicked in, and Colton grabbed her in the classic hold for the two-step. Passing another couple as they meandered around the floor, she couldn't help but join in their laughter. It was good to see Shane happy, back to his healthy physique … and with a great girl.

After exchanging a barrage of emails for a couple of weeks, Barbara had visited him at the prison. That visit led to two others. It wasn't until Riley witnessed their embrace the morning Shane walked out the prison gate that she understood a romance was brewing.

And had been going strong ever since. A romance she couldn't help but be behind one hundred percent.

The Mulaneys had held a press conference following Shane's release in January, not only issuing their regret for the time he'd spent behind bars but thanking him for blessing the life of their daughter in the weeks before she was taken. The judge, his wife, older daughter, and her husband were there somewhere, enjoying the evening with their old friends. How like the Lord to restore what once was broken. In so many ways.

Riley grinned as they passed John and Avery, the newly engaged couple ignoring the two-step and instead swaying in a tight embrace. Their wedding was slated to take place in six months. A year to the day they met, the day Warren Everett first appeared in Riley's life. Another picture of God taking something ugly and redeeming it for something beautiful.

All of the evil wrought by Warren's hand had caught up to him. Not only had they proved beyond a doubt he killed Cait, but he would also pay for the assault of his girlfriend and the shooting of Terence Drummond. Unfortunately, the authorities were unable to ascertain whether he'd had a hand in his mother's death, but it was enough that Jacob Warren Everett would never experience a day of freedom again. Not unless he came to the Lord and received it on the other side of this life.

After a couple of hours of dancing and celebrating, she once again found herself in her husband's arms, swaying to a ballad in the middle of the floor, surrounded by the people they loved most in the world.

Colton swept the backs of his fingers down her cheek. "As amazing as this has been, I'm ready to ditch this place. You with me?"

Her skin tingled along the track of his fingers. "You know I am. Ready for anything. As long as I have my tactical gear by my side."

"And you, my lovely wife, will always be the one I'd give my life for."

Acknowledgments

Thank you for spending your valuable time with the characters in my first romantic suspense novel, *Mistletoe and Malice*! Venturing into something new can be intimidating and a little scary. Romantic suspense is a bit of a departure from my previous novels in the True Calling Series, but when this story came to me, I couldn't get it to leave me alone. So, I took a deep breath, prayed a lot, and kept those fingers typing until this story was complete. This one posed a few more challenges for me, but I loved getting to know Riley and Colton and writing their story. And I hope you liked Trevor, because Book Two, *The Quiet Watch*, is his story. Watch for that in September 2026!

As always, I couldn't do—and wouldn't do—any of this without the blessing and constant presence of Jesus, my Lord and Savior. He's there when I'm searching, there when I'm confused, there when I'm excited, and there when I type "The End." How wonderful that our life stories will never see those words, but that we'll simply move on to the next chapter in eternity with our Father.

My heartfelt appreciation goes to Linda Fulkerson of Scrivenings Press, Elena Hill, my content editor, and Kaci Banks, my line editor. It's been an honor and blessing being a part of the Scrivenings Press family.

This book would not have happened without my wonderful critique partners, Kristi Woods and Wendy Klopfenstein, who went over and beyond to help me get this manuscript turned in. Also to my "huddle-mates" Teresa Wells and Liana George, for all their wonderful advice and support. These four ladies bless me every day with their friendship, encouragement, and excellent feedback.

A huge thanks to Bruce Hammack for all of the brainstorming help and information on the legal and prison system.

I'm so thankful for the unwavering support of my husband, Eric, and my daughter, Michaela, who cheer me on and keep me going when I sometimes wonder if I really should be writing at all. That imposter syndrome is real, y'all, and it takes an army of people to come alongside and keep me going some days. I'm grateful for the writing groups and the many writer kindred spirits I've met along the way who keep the fire burning and my fingers typing. Words cannot convey how much I appreciate them.

And to you, dear reader, I offer my sincerest gratitude and appreciation for the time you spent with Colton and Riley and the others who contributed to their story. If you enjoyed this book, please consider taking a couple of minutes and leaving a review on Amazon, GoodReads and/or BookBub. As Christian authors, reviews are how we get the word out about these books with messages of hope, peace, joy, and redemption. Thank you from the bottom of my heart.

If you'd like to follow along on my writing journey, you can subscribe to my newsletter at https://loridejongwrites.com. It would be an honor to have you on board!

Much love,
Lori

About the Author

Lori DeJong (pronounced DeeYUNG) is a contemporary Christian romance author who enjoys penning stories full of grace and the redemptive power of God's love that inspire others to hope regardless of circumstance, find joy in the moment, and grow in their faith.

Born and raised in Phoenix, Arizona, Lori arrived in Texas in 2005 and dug those roots right in. She currently resides in beautiful Georgetown, north of Austin, with her husband of thirty-two years. Other than their two fur-babies, their nest is empty. Her daughter and son-in-love live in the DFW area with Ranger, the sweetest grand-dog ever.

Lori loves to write about love and romance and all that fun stuff, with a firm foundation of faith. Clean but sassy, sparkly, and even goose-bumpy romance, with God in the middle and characters seeking and learning and changing, couldn't be more heartwarming or spine-tingly, in her opinion.

Lori's debut novel, *Love's True Calling*, released in 2023, was the 2022 winner of the ACFW Genesis Award for Romance, a double finalist in the 2024 Selah Awards, and tied for the 2023 Scrivenings Press Contemporary Book of the Year. *Love's True Home*, released in June 2024, was also a Selah finalist. *Love's True Measure*, the final book in the series, released in June 2025. Lori's Christmas novella, *Jingle Bell Matchmakers*, a part of *A Match Made at Christmas* novella collection, is also available and was named a 2025 ACFW Carol Award finalist.

Also by Lori DeJong

Love's True Calling

True Calling Series—Book One

After years of jumping through other people's hoops to be all they thought she should be, and enduring a tragedy no mother should, self-described "newbie" Christian, Harper Townsend, has finally found her true calling … and her true love. Until it appears that to follow one may mean leaving the other behind.

Adolescent Psychologist, Wyatt McCowan, is beyond delighted to have *the-girl-who-got-away* back in his life—and his heart. But even as they fall more in love, he realizes that being obedient to God's calling on each of their lives may pull them apart. She rejected him once in favor of another, which left him hurt and angry. But this time, he can't fault her for following hard after the God she loves with all her heart, even if it means leaving him once again.

Get your copy here:

https://scrivenings.link/lovestruecalling

Love's True Home

True Calling Series—Book Two

Allyson Kincaid needs roots. Born and raised on the foreign mission field, all she wants is home and hearth on American soil. Finally past the break-up with the man she'd thought was the love of her life, she's ready to put herself back out there. Too bad the first guy who's made her pulse skip in nearly two years dreams of a life spent in foreign missions. She's been there, done that, and, although she supports him in his calling, knows his choice means she'll be laying even more broken dreams, and a newly shattered heart, at the feet of Jesus.

When Zane Carpenter relocates to Arlington, Texas, his seventh move in thirteen years, his only thought is to meet his obligation with Becker Ministries in a few months, then take a foreign mission assignment, his dream for the past several years. But working so closely with Ally in student ministry has him feeling things he's never experienced. He's ready for a future with her, until he accepts an opportunity to work on foreign soil and Ally stays behind. He knows God put him there for a reason, although his heart still longs for the girl back home.

Get your copy here:

https://scrivenings.link/lovestruehome

Love's True Measure

True Calling Series—Book Three

A guilt-ridden woman with everything to gain, a self-made man with everything to lose, and a Father who desires to show them their true measure is more than they could ever imagine.

Shannon Trent has dedicated her life to ministering to teens, even as she hides secrets that haunt her past. Born into privilege but starved of unconditional love and acceptance, she's built a simpler life away from the expectations of her influential family. Shannon is content on her own, believing that to open her heart would mean unearthing her deepest shame. But when her charming neighbor stirs feelings she's never allowed herself to entertain, his lack of faith provides the perfect excuse to keep her distance.

Hunter Kavanaugh has spent years chasing his dream of becoming the youngest partner at his prestigious Fort Worth law firm. But when his mother's sudden death leaves him the sole guardian of his teenage sister, his carefully curated world begins to crumble. Struggling with grief, anger at God, and the demands of his career, Hunter is surprised when Shannon's unwavering faith begins to resonate with him—and her ability to connect with his sister draws him closer.

As Hunter and Shannon navigate their growing bond, unexpected challenges force them to confront their fears and priorities. Both must either choose to trust God's plan is far greater than their own, or risk losing the love of a lifetime.

Get your copy here:

https://scrivenings.link/lovestruemeasure

A Match Made at Christmas: A Novella Collection

"Jingle Bell Matchmakers" by Lori DeJong—When country music star Aubrey Mayfield is lured home after years away, she's bewildered when she and ex-fiance-now-widowed-dad Cody Lansdale keep finding themselves in the same place at the same time. As they become reacquainted, however, old feelings stir. Aubrey's at a crossroads in her career and is contemplating a change. But when a chance at headlining her own tour takes her back to Nashville, Cody realizes her dreams may once again come between them. Unless God, with a little help from the Jingle Bell Committee, has a better plan.

Get your copy here:

https://scrivenings.link/amatchmadeatchristmas

Stay up-to-date on your favorite books and authors with our free e-newsletters.

ScriveningsPress.com

www.ingramcontent.com/pod-product-compliance
Lightning Source LLC
Chambersburg PA
CBHW071737110726
47908CB00006B/1620